FREE RIDE

Ronald K. Myers

FREE RIDE

DOUBLE DRAGON

Dedication

FREE RIDE is dedicated to the inspiration for
the character called Hog:
My Brother, Larry

CHAPTER 1

With a grime-coated light bulb bathing him in an unearthly glow, Breed leaned through the open door of the Horseshoe Lounge and watched in hushed astonishment. The loud ringing of a filthy phone interrupted the partying atmosphere of the dimly lit bar. The bartender lifted the phone. Before he could speak, mill workers with the suffering look of people condemned to a mental institution stopped guzzling Pabst out of ice-frosted bottles and stared straight ahead. As if it were a ritual, they inclined their heads toward the bartender, and yelled, "I'm not here!"

Breed laughed and the men at the bar laughed, too.

After the bartender slammed the phone down, laughter subsided, and a man with an unshaven face and slobber running from the side of his contorted mouth turned toward Breed. "Hey! Creep!" the man shrieked in a voice that was surprisingly high-pitched. "What you laughin' at?"

Wincing at the degradation of being called a creep by a man who didn't have enough brains to be unhappy, Breed quit laughing but managed a wisp of a smile. Just to be defiant, he replied, "The circus is in town. Are you having a family reunion at the sideshow?"

As the man stared at him in total incomprehension, Breed realized that the comparison of the man's family to freaks of a sideshow hadn't registered in the man's beer-brained mind.

When the comparison finally entered the man's mind, he jerked back from the bar so fast, the bar stool tipped over and banged on the floor. With his mouth curled into a vehement sneer, he came charging after Breed. "You makin' fun of my family?" he screeched. "I'll kick your creep ass all the way back to Shitsplat."

In a panicked gasp, Breed reached for the door knob, grabbed it, and slammed the door right in the advancing man's face. Before the man could recover from the unexpected door in the face, as a final gesture, Breed mimicked the man's high-pitched voice and yelled though the door, "I'll kick your creep ass!"

Being reminded that he lived in a grimy neighborhood, caused Breed to feel ashamed, but he didn't have time to be ashamed. When the man opened the door, he would be on Breed and in a flash.

But Breed was in luck.

The man was too angry or too drunk to turn the doorknob. While he kicked at the door, Breed dashed away. Under a smoked smeared sky, he sprinted toward a place sure to be teeming with more degradation.

With ear-piercing steel mill whistles screaming above the cacophony of rumbling trucks, metallic clanging, and a deep base pounding of diesel locomotives, the battered and villainous hard cases of the bar who had had enough of an enjoyable evening that would provide them with material to brightened their uneventful lives staggered home to the cries of unhappy wives and resentful children. Then air-blown molten iron, in open-hearth furnaces, blazed orange and belched heavy crimson smoke out tops of towering masses of steel stacks, where it jutted into a gloomy sky and created smoky shadows that resembled limbs of death slithering out from under dilapidated shacks, creeping over rubble that was scarcely shaded with black limbs of defoliated trees.

But the spatter of land hadn't always been like that.

In better times, dazzling sunlight had glanced off crystal-clear streams, bordered with lush hillsides, rich with green vegetation, and tops of tall trees had reached into a bluebird sky and immersed their thirsty roots into pure water. Then pie-faced people with dreams of a better life toppled the trees, slapped together a hodgepodge of wood, tin, stone, and junk, and built shacks to live in. Years of various repairs and additions transformed most of those shacks into fairly decent homes.

On the hillside, west of the Shenango River, little could be called refinement. Dirt-filled smoke constantly wafted from the steel mills and smothered shacks that had sprung up on debris that retained an irreducible grime. Open sewers, running into the once willow-shaded banks of once pristine streams that ran cool and clear over pebbly beds, contributed to the decay of those shacks. The rotting window frames, and tar patches on tin roofs, not only caused the shacks to become a hopeless blotch on the dark land that broadcasted the stench of poverty, but also had earned the west side of town the moniker "Shitsplat".

It was here that a lone ray of morning sun poked through a ragged cloud of purple smoke and beamed on the unpainted shack with the dirty-white picket fence where Breed lay on his raggedy bed, hoping he wouldn't have to fight off more degradation.

Downstairs, staggering to keep her drunken balance, Breed's mother flung an empty beer bottle into the rust-stained sink. The sound of it breaking, crashed through the morning's silence.

Breed's eyes flew wide open. He jerked awake, sat up, faced the window, and stared into the purple distance. Even though he told himself he was long past caring about his parent's psychotic behaviors, every night he had gone through a series of appalling nightmares, and every morning brought some kind of threat. This lingering atmosphere of despair should have made him want to cry with weakness and frustration, but he gritted his teeth and wondered what kind of pain would be inflicted on him today. Using it as protection, he pulled his thin blanket up around his chest and listened.

There was a great scraping of his stepfather's heavy work shoes coming up the worn stairs. "You might as well break all the bottles," he roared. "They're all empty." The scraping trailed off into the other room. After another night of drinking, he was finally going to bed.

Relieved, Breed lay back on his raggedy blanket, closed his eyes, and returned to the sublime narcosis of sleep.

10

Wham! Like the surprising bang of a firecracker, the sound smacked into Breed's chest. His eyes flew open. At the bottom of the stairs, his mother had slammed the door. With his body begging for sleep, he hoped the slam was the final epilogue of the night. In an attempt to insulate himself from the anguish, he plowed his head under his pillow and held it tight to his ears. But the deliberate pock-pock of high heels striking the wood stairs told him it was not over.

To agitate his stepfather, his mother stood halfway up the stairs, leaned drunkenly against the wall, and bellowed, "If you think you're going to drink all night and sleep all day. . ." She stomped down the stairs and stopped at the bottom. Bang! She slammed the door. "You got another thing coming."

Feeling like a trapped animal fighting to make the last moments of its life bearable, Breed jammed the pillow tighter against his ears. But the noise came through. His mother and stepfather had fought all night. Breed had just shut his bloodshot eyes, and now they were open, again.

When he had gone to bed and the last rays of the orange setting sun had smiled through the open window and darkness surrounded him, he thought he would sleep until the morning sunbeams found his face and filled it with yellow warmth. But that didn't happen. The sunless night had been filled with the same cut down arguments of the past. His mother had gone through the counterattacks and insults, then dredged up things that happened years ago. And his stepfather had answered with smart

11

remarks. When stars faded from the predawn sky, Breed hoped his mother would run out of things that would add fire to the arguments. But she didn't.

If he could just get a few more minutes of sleep, he might be able to emerge from the, twisting horror-filled corridors of frustration and do something special today.

Finally, after the noise downstairs stopped, Breed gave up the pillow and rolled to his stomach. Lying on the lumpy mattress of his bed in front of the open window, he flared his elbows and propped his head on his hands. As a morning breeze stirred the faded curtain, he looked down over the rust-colored slate of the front porch roof. The green maple leaves on the branches of the big tree in the front yard of his shack were beginning to turn yellow. When a soft sigh of wind caused them to gracefully move in the cool autumn air, they resembled sad hands waving goodbye to the warm times of summer.

Muffled shouts and one gunshot, followed by dogs barking, came from somewhere down the street. Some of the mills were on strike, again. Where a couple of shacks looked so dilapidated that they would fall over in the next wind, loud and obnoxious arguments added to the woe of the rundown neighborhood. Breed understood he wasn't like the rich schoolboys with decent parents and television sets. Although those things were only dreams, he had sometimes mistaken for living, he planned to make them come true.

Exhausted, he let his head drop to the worn mattress and began to doze off. Bam! A door on the house next door slammed. He ignored it. But rumblings from a train, rattled the window and caused him to return drowsily to consciousness. Through half-open eyes, he lifted his head, peeked over the worn wooden headboard of his bed, and peered out the window. Outside was void of activity, but like an imprisoned kid in some kind of a controlled trance, from under the snugness of his blanket, he stared out the window and wished he were someplace else.

The sound of a car engine gearing down and backfiring grew louder. When the sound neared, the caved-in trunk and a gaping hole in the roof of a pink 1957 Ford could be seen chugging up the street. The bad-smelling kid with the wart on his pockmarked face who had hit Breed in the head with a brick, sat behind the steering wheel, tilting a bottle of beer to his lips. His fingernails were always wedged with dirt, and his hair was always oily. He was one of the many older kids who believed Breed and his friends were dumb-looking hoodlums who wandered the streets breaking street lights. To get revenge from the brick incident and other senseless beatings, Breed and his friends had not only crossed the spark plug wires in the kid's car, they had hooked one end of a chain around the axle of the Ford and the other end around an old, dead tree. After they got the kid angry enough to just about lose his mind, he floored the Ford and took off. When the chain went taut, the tree broke and crashed down on the Ford. Not only did the tree cave the trunk in, a broken branch poked a hole in the roof on the driver's side.

While the misfiring of the crossed-plug wires caused the engine to cough and struggled to get up the street, the kid deliberately swerved off to the side of the road, spun the tires in the gravel, and threw an empty beer bottle at Breed. As the bottle hit the porch roof and harmlessly rolled down the slate, pieces of dirty gravel shot from the spinning tires and showered the dirty white picket fence. The kid laughed and sped away in a great cloud of gray dust. Breed hoped he would never have to fight him.

With his head bent down and thinking, God knows what, freckle-faced Flick suddenly stood on the wooden footbridge that crossed over the sewage ditch in front of Breed's shack. With the back of his hand, Flick whipped the dust from the front of his loose flapping shirt that had ragged sleeves torn off at the elbows. Although he lived on the street where limbs of dead, dusty trees hung over broken bottles and cigarette butts, next to abandoned railroad tracks, in a tiny downtrodden shack with pictures covering up cracks in the plaster and a front yard covered with rubble and slag, he was tougher than the rest of Breed's friends, was a little wilder, and had the qualities of leadership with which a rare few are gifted. He usually had a twinkle in his eyes and an irresistible wiry grin, but today his grin had been replaced with an angry snarl.

Walking over the bridge, he jammed his hands deep into the pockets of his baggy pants. At the end of the bridge, he looked down and shuffled his clodhopper-shoed feet in the coal furnace ashes. Glaring with disapproval, he put a hand up to shade his green eyes and squinted toward Breed. "Goddamn dogshit," he moaned in self-pity and scraped the thick edge of his shoe along the ashes. After he walked in a circle with a pained expression on his face, he jerked his red hair to the side and whistled a slow, secret whistle. Then with one hand slicking his long, red hair back, he used his other hand to flash the usual obscene gesture at Breed.

The obscene gesture was a signal for Breed to come down, but Breed didn't want to hear about anybody's problems. He had just had had a whole night of problems, and didn't know when the shack would be quiet again. While he had the chance, he wanted to get some much-needed sleep. As if he were sleeping, he closed his eyes into slits and didn't acknowledge Flick's gesture.

Flick stepped out of the ashes, looked toward the big maple tree in front of the shack, and whistled again.

Flick wouldn't quit whistling until Breed came down. Disgusted, he let his eyes fly wide open and bent out the window.

With a questioning slant to one eye, Flick called up, "You comin' down?"

Breed swung his feet to the floor, stood up, and stared irritably to where the all-night noise had been coming from. He needed to get away from what was always happening here. But he didn't want to go through the shack and cause the all-night argument to continue and grow into an-all-day marathon. So he jumped into his ragged clothes, rolled out the window, and onto the porch roof, where he slid down the slippery slate and stopped at the edge. Then he swung his legs over and wrapped his ankle around the porch post. After he slid down it, he placed his feet onto the skinny top of the dirty-white picket fence.

While he balanced on the fence, Flick walked up to him. "You still goin' to the Rat House?"

Breed jumped off the fence. His foot landed on the only tuft of grass in the yard and mashed it flat. The Rat House was actually the Gable Theater, but had earned the Rat House moniker because of the many rats that ran around inside the battered building. He bent over, brushed his dusty hands on his pants, and looked up. "Heck yeah!" He straightened up. "Buddy Holly was a regular kid who made it big."

Looking worried, Flick walked onto the wooden footbridge and stopped next to the gravel road. Attempting to hide his worried look, he looked to Breed. "You think it'll be any good?"

Wondering what was bothering Flick, Breed stepped next to him and pretended he hadn't noticed. "You kiddin'? *The Buddy Holly Story's* gonna be the best movie of 1959."

For a moment the worried look fell from Flick's Face. "Buddy made some really good songs," he said, "but I think they killed him."

Breed furrowed his brow. "What do you mean, killed him? He died in a plane crash. Richie Valens and the Big Bopper did, too."

"They can set those things up."

Over the years, the people of Shitsplat had pulled many awful things on Breed and his slum neighborhood friends. The way he saw it, the people living in any place but Shitsplat were different. "Those guys in show business aren't like Shitsplat assholes," he said. "They ain't rotten enough to kill somebody who could sing a song as good as 'True Love Ways'."

"I don't know," Flick shook his head. "A lot of movie stars are getting killed in so-called accidents."

"The movie should tell what happened."

As if Flick didn't believe him, he looked Breed in the eye. "The good guys always get killed or something happens." He noticed Breed's torn shirt sleeve flap around his wrist. "You can't go dressed like that. They'll know you snuck in."

Although an occasional whiff of sewage odor from the ditch wafted into Breed's face, a clean bright sun was shining in his heart. "I ain't going like this." Glad he wouldn't have to feel the shame of wearing his usual ragged clothes, he puffed up with self-importance. "Today, I got new clothes to wear."

Flick stepped off the bridge and onto the road. "New clothes might help you look like somebody that paid, but you could still get your ass kicked out."

Breed stepped onto the road and hooked his thumbs under the front of his paint-spattered belt. Then as if he were a rich man who wasn't a problem of protocol and didn't have to watch long noses sniff at his shame until their faces stiffened, he leaned back on his heels. "I ain't sneakin' in today."

Flick's eyes brightened. "If you're the big man payin', you'll have to crack the side door and let us sneak in."

Breed's stomach growled. It was reminding him that he hadn't eaten since yesterday morning. If he snuck in, he could use the last of his money and buy a good piece of meat. He could carry it into the woods, gather up dry sticks, and build a little fire. With a little branch he cut from a tree, he could spear it through the meat, and hold it over the fire until it was perfect. And he could have it all to himself. Maybe it would stop that constant hungry feeling in his stomach. It was almost autumn. After he ate, he could walk to an open field of soft yellow hay and lie down. Without the constant banging of doors, he could take a nap in the warm sun. Maybe he could be like that boxer in the Jack London story about a piece of steak. But he wasn't going to box anyone. He was only going to a movie, and anyway, he had already made up his mind. It didn't matter if he were going to be hungry. He had been hungry many times before. For once in his life he was going to see a movie without being afraid the usher would check to see if he had a ticket stub. But before he could do that, he would have to sneak down the aisle and crack open the side door. There was no way around it. The gang had done it for him, many times. At the right exact moment, he would open the door. If he got caught, it wouldn't matter that he had paid to get in. He would be kicked out. If he didn't get caught, then he could stay in one seat and show any suspicious usher his ticket stub. He dropped his hands to his sides.

"Yeah, I'll do it," he said and tried to get out of opening the door. "But I never opened that door before. Just as soon as I open it, the ushers will see the light from outside."

"There ain't nothin' to it," Flick said and leaned on a stick he had broken off the maple tree. "Just don't open the door until the screen turns bright."

"Then what?"

"Then just get out the way. That bright light only blinds the usher for a few seconds. Before he sees us, we'll slip in."

Breed thought about getting caught. He shook his head with apprehension. "That usher with that purple bellhop cap is the one to watch out for."

Flick lifted his hand and hooded his eyes. "Sometimes when the screen goes bright, that skinny runt covers his eyes, but he's still a sour-faced creep who acts like he's got a corn cob stuck up his ass."

As if he felt a pain in his side, Breed cringed. "That's the kid that kicked Hog in the ribs."

"Did Hog tell you what he did to that kid?"

Although Hog sometimes had an academic air about him, he was a belligerent, muscular kid who had a malicious streak of a court jester. Being a kid who would not readily or agreeably give in to the desires of others, he usually smiled with an insolent grin, and his curly black hair was as unruly as his tendency to question authority. He lived in an unpainted ramshackle house sadly in need of repair. Even though he lived in a dismal place, where people were branded as poor and ignorant, there were few situations where he could not summon a

19

smart-ass remark. As a means of agitation, many times he would use words that were above other's intellectual level. When his agitating morphed into shouting bitterness, he was most happy. Whatever he did wouldn't surprise Breed. "What did he do this time?"

"He wouldn't tell me, just said he didn't want to appear facetious, whatever that means. And kept on laughing."

Flick reached across his chest and held his hand on the side of his ribs. "Hog might-ah got caught, but we ain't gonna."

Breed shot Flick a quick hard look. "I hope you're right." He stepped a pace off to the right. "Just as soon as you guys get in, split up."

"We know that," Flick said. "If that usher wants to find us, he'll have to look in every seat."

Breed imagined how the usher wouldn't be able to keep track of them all. If they wanted, they could keep him busy all day. They could make a game of it. Then that rotten usher wouldn't have a chance to kick anybody in the ribs. It would only take a fraction of a second to open that door, so Breed was pretty sure he wouldn't get caught. He told himself that it wasn't going to be a big deal and tilted his shoulders toward Flick. "I might even buy a bag of popcorn and pass it around to make it look like you guys paid."

Flick blew air out of his mouth and let out a low whistle. "You'll have to buy two, one to eat, and to keep the rats off your lap, you'll have to drop one on the floor."

As if he were swishing off an invisible rat, Breed brushed the top of his thigh with the back of his hand. "That ain't no lie. I've watched those big gray rats come up from the sewers in the riverbank. It's like their bodies are rubber. They slip right through the cracks in the walls."

Flick stepped away and pointed the stick at Breed. "If you hold still, those rats will eat the popcorn right out of your hand."

Breed felt the crow's feet form above the high cheekbones of his face, but remembering the constant gleam of laughter and mischief in Screwball's eyes, he ignored the sleep-begging call from his tired body and asked, "Is Screwball going?"

"If you get your ass in gear and quit standing there like a chicken with a broken wing, he's going."

"What's the rush? We got a lotta time."

"They're setting up the crane to knock down the Jones's house. Before we go to the show, we could watch 'em knock it down. Maybe make a little money."

The city had been saying they were going to tear down that house for years. Breed wanted to see how many whacks it would take the wrecking ball to knock the house down, but he really wanted to know how they could make some money doing it. He nodded. "I'd like to see that. But how are we going to make money?"

Encouraging Breed to hurry up, Flick jerked his thumb toward Breed's house. "After you change your clothes, I'll tell you on the way."

CHAPTER 2

With the sun baking steel mill fumes into a brown smog that burned Breed's throat, he jumped over the sewer ditch and landed in the yard in front of the shack where he lived. As if it were an omen, a stray ocean of wind roared against the walls of the dilapidated shack, and blew the fumes away. But he paid it no mind. He was thinking about *The Buddy Holly Story.* Buddy Holly was Breed's favorite singer, and now for the first time in his life he had found a way to stop the slow strangulation of the octopus of poverty. When his friends had tried to get people to pay to have their mailboxes painted, they were told they were too young. Although he was fifteen years old, being half Indian, with straight black hair, he looked older, and it caused people to trust him enough to pay him to paint their mail boxes. Not being old enough to drive, his friend Flick and he had walked to as many places as they could and painted mailboxes. With the money they earned, not only had they found a new freedom, Breed had earned enough money to buy new shoes, one shirt, and one pair of store-bought pants. And the purchases had caused his fierce pride of new possessions to flare. He wasn't going to the movie dressed like a bum. Instead of sneaking into the Rat House, like he had always done, he would walk right up to the worn-out, wood-framed ticket window, shove money under the half-moon opening at the bottom of the thick glass, and buy a ticket. Then he could leisurely walk right in the double-swinging front doors and stay in that theater and watch the movie as many times as he wanted.

When he tiptoed into the shack and into the kitchen, grease hung heavy in the air. A broken board from the cupboard door, his mother had slammed most of the night, was lying on the floor. Where the board was missing, sluggish flies crawled around and buzzed onto the shelf. Breed raised his hand and swished a cat-like swipe across the opening. The flies jumped away. He snuck his fingers through the missing board and pried a tin lid open. He looked over his shoulder. No one was watching. He dipped his fingers into the big blue lard can, scooped out a gob of white lard, and held it in his hand. To hide it, in case his mother was near, he dropped his hand to his side and then walked to the bathroom. He looked at his tanned Elvis Presley like reflection in the cracked mirror. Breed's hair was also black, but he didn't have the long sideburns, and his hair didn't look like Elvis' hair. If Breed used nothing on his hair, he wouldn't' look like Elvis, and his dull hair would show people he was poor. To fix the situation, he rubbed the lard into his hands and ran them along his long hair. Then he cupped some water in his hand, dumped it on his hair, and massaged it in. His hair turned jet black and gleamed like wet crow feathers. He combed the sides back over his ears and around the sides of his head, molded it up in back, and formed what resembled the shiny tail end of a duck. When he ran the comb down the center of the back of his head and felt the straight furrow that ran down from the top of his crown to the base of his sun-browned

23

neck, it felt like a perfect DA, which was jokingly called a duck's ass. Satisfied with his new Elvis look, he turned and dashed toward the stairs that led to the second floor. Taking strides long enough to skip three steps at a time, in an instant, he was upstairs, standing next his bed.

He took his new shirt off the dirty covers of his bed and pulled the straight pins out of the collar. Where a chunk of horse-hair plaster had fallen out of the wall, brown wooden lath showed through. It was an embarrassing thing that made him feel poor, and it reminded him that even though his stepfather was a mill worker, he couldn't even keep the walls in his own shack repaired because he had pissed all the money away with his drinking. Knowing that it was truth, and it wouldn't change just because he wanted it to, he sloughed off the feeling of being poor, and stuck the pins from the shirt into the lath. Then he unfolded the shirt, slipped it on, and stood erect. Being the first new shirt, he had ever owned, it felt good on his tanned skin, and it made him feel important and a step closer to being what he had always wanted to become: well-mannered, well educated, and well dressed.

He lowered his eyes and looked down at his old, torn pants. "These have to go," he said out loud and stepped out of the pants. As if they were hated insignias of poverty, he kicked them across the floor. They landed in the corner on top of cracked and peeling linoleum. He jumped into his new black dress pants and tucked his new shirt into them until it was straight and neat, but he needed a belt. He looked at the belt in his old pants. The scuffed old leather was a backdrop for the spatters of aluminum paint that seemed to scream poverty. He might as well wear a sign around his neck reading Slum Dweller, Inferior Social Status. Damn, he thought, If I put that old belt in these new pants, it'll make me look like a Shitsplat kid, but I could buy a new belt and not go to the movie. He shook the thought out of his mind. Not this time. No matter what, I'm going to the movie. I'll just let the shirt hang a little bit over the belt. I hope no one will notice.

When he looked at his new shoes, he remembered that people usually destroy presentable ensembles by wearing badly kept shoes, and they rarely look at their own feet. Today, that wasn't going to happen to him. But he didn't have new socks to wear. His old socks were torn at the heels. He could pull a piece of thread from his ragged shirt and sew them but he didn't have a needle. So he folded the tear in the socks under the heel of his right foot and held it in place with his finger. As he guided his foot into the shoe, he kept his finger on the torn fold, pushed, and pried with his finger like it was a thick shoehorn. His finger jammed against the stiff heel of the new leather and felt like it was in a vice. He pushed harder and his foot jumped in with the sound of a muffled drumbeat. He pulled out his finger and felt the blood rush back under his fingernail. When he stood up, the creased tear on the bottom of his sock felt like a wire on his heel, but Flick was waiting. It would have to do. He used his finger for a shoehorn again and jammed the other shoe on. He was ready to walk downtown and not feel the streets press through the soles of his shoes.

From outside, his mother's voice traveled through the opened bedroom window. "You goddamn drunk," she shouted loud enough for the whole neighborhood to hear. "You think you're going to go out drinking and whoring around, you're going to find out you're dealing with the wrong person."

With a drawn and haggard face, his stepfather wobbled out of the next room and teetered at the top of the stairs. "Aw, shut your damn mouth. I gave you money. I'll do what I want."

Breed shrank flat against the wall of his ramshackle room and cringed. If his drunken stepfather saw him, he would have to answer questions about where he was going, where he got the new clothes, and how much money he had made. If he tried to strike up a peaceful conversation, he might get his ass beat. If his mother caught him talking to his stepfather, there would be another fight. It happened so often that Breed wondered if it was normal.

He didn't want to stop and talk about rules of the so-called house that would change anyway. There was no time for silly hold-ups or ass whippings. He had places to go. He was going to see how it felt to go downtown without looking like a bum. He looked to the porch roof. If he went down that way, he would get his new clothes dirty and scuff his new shoes. He would have to go down the stairs.

Tensing with anticipation, breathing slow, and stepping like a whisper, he was almost past his stepfather. One more careful step would do it. But his stepfather teetered and bumped into him. As if he hadn't felt the bump, the master of the domain squared his massive shoulders and stretched out his arm until his work-worn hand rested on the opposite side of the stairway wall. Breed's path was blocked. Apparently not seeing him, his stepfather tipped a brown bottle of beer up to his lips. As the blue foil label glittered in the dull light, Breed ducked low, turned sideways, and as he slid past, a whiff of humid beer-breath-air cloaked his face like wet glue. He turned away from the odor. Knowing his young, sinewy legs could do it with comfort, he planned to leap down the stairs three or four at time. When he planted his foot on the top step to leap, the brown rubber that was supposed to be non-skid shot from under his new-shoed feet. He lost his balance and was about to take a tumble. In the middle of the stairs, he threw out his right foot and slowed his fall. He stopped momentarily, tilted sideways, landed on his rear end, and continued his downward descent. He jerked his foot out from underneath his butt, and stretched his hands out until they skidded against the walls. The braking almost put a halt to the impending doom, but just when he thought he was safe, the momentum of the fall caused him to lean forward. Before his head crashed into the stairs, he jumped. Thump! He landed at the base of the stairs and looked up.

His stepfather turned, teetered, reached with his calloused fingers, and gripped onto a hole in the wall for support. His arm muscles corded like a pumped-up wrestler, and he yelled down, "Don't be breaking up the goddamn house!" He waved the bottle of beer around in the beer-breathed air. "You ain't no son of mine. If you want to keep on living here, you better start bringin' some money into this house."

Breed ignored the drunken threat and brushed the stair's dust from his new pants. He walked through the kitchen and stopped at the back door. With his weight causing the rotten floor to sag, a spilt stream of beer ran across the worn linoleum floor, swirled, and formed a puddle in a low spot. On the kitchen table, a stack of empty beer bottles stood upright and others had been tipped over. The odor of stale beer and unwashed dishes hung in the air and wafted out the kitchen door. Like dope addicts trying to get a fix, green-metallic-bodied flies, waiting to get in, crowded the outside of the screen door.

On the tattered tablecloth, a constant swarm of buzzing flies landed, flew off, and landed again on what looked to be day old scraps of food Breed hadn't seen before. Big flies and baby flies crawled around like they were at a Sunday picnic. In the sink, the broken beer bottle, and three days of dirty dishes smelled like an explosion of stale ketchup and rotten eggs. It was a fly's paradise.

From the top of the stairs, his stepfather's voice thundered. "Did you hear me?"

"Yeah, okay," Breed yelled back and opened the screen door to leave. The rusted door spring twanged under the expansion. As if they were a squadron of happy pilots on their way to a beer party, fifty flies flew through the open door. Watching them hum in formation on their way to the lucky buffet, Breed didn't go out. He let the door close and watched the flies land next to an opened loaf of bread sitting on the table. Since the bread bag had been open all night, the bread's ends were dried up and crusty. For fear of being told not to eat all the goddamn bread, he was afraid to take any. But he figured if he took a few slices from the middle, they wouldn't know any was gone. He reached in and pulled a few slices from the center of the loaf. After rolling them in his hands, he jammed the dough ball into his mouth, turned his head, and as he opened the screen door, its spring slowly squeaked. More flies had landed on the screen. Now it looked more like a dirty fly barricade. Swallowing the bread, he stepped through and let go of the door. Behind him, it flapped shut. The hoard of flies on the screen jerked off like they had been shocked. They flew around for a second and landed back on the screen. It was as if they were too dumb to fly into the shack when the door had been open.

When he looked outside, he thought he had a clear path to the Rat House, and to make it more enjoyable, he would be walking under a sky suffused with pinks and gold. But when he looked next to the shack, a metal lawn chair that had been painted with thick white house paint sat there. The chalky surface of the chair was always dirty and attracted black dirt that wouldn't wash off. At times Breed thought he had become desensitized to the filth he had to live with, but the chair and his

29

mother sitting in it, washed out the unfeeling. The tattered housecoat she was wearing covered her beer-bloated belly and was just as dirty as the chair. Her hair was amiss, and she had her legs crossed, aggressively bouncing one leg as if she were waiting to do something to anyone she pleased. The fierce glare of her eyes reminded Breed that she was obsessed with a blind unreasoning hatred for anything that was different. And today Breed was exceptionally different, but she hadn't seen him.

Trying to sneak past, Breed tiptoed close. As his mother ran her fingers through her tangled hair, the odor of sour alcohol made him uncomfortable. She turned her head and looked at him. Even though her puffy, red-rimmed eyes flashed with anger, a sad stab of pity surged through his heart. Her once beautiful face was being washed away by the booze. He headed for the road and Flick. As if she had seen something new, her eyebrows soared suddenly. Then she snapped her head back in his direction, sat up in the chair, and shook her finger at him. "What are you talking to that drunk for?"

With his skin turning to gooseflesh, Breed stopped and felt the outside of his pockets to make sure he had his money. "I'm not talking to anybody." He turned to walk away.

His mother quit bouncing her leg and jumped up from the chair. "Hey!" She pointed a long, angry arm at him. "Hey! Rich Man!"

Breed turned back.

She stood with her arms akimbo, her eyes narrowing dangerously. "Give me some of that money you've been wasting on being a pretty boy. This ain't no flop house, you know."

Breed put up his nonchalant attitude shield. "Yeah okay," he said, and ignoring the fierce glow in her eyes, he walked onto the black dirt of the grassless yard and stopped. He had never gotten an allowance and never expected one. Now that he had made a few bucks and could do something besides be poor, his mother wanted to take it away. If she had needed it, he would have given it to her. But his doglike loyalty had limits. She would spend it on another case of beer.

"I don't have any money," he lied to avoid an argument.

"You had a lot of money," she shot back. "What did you waste it on?"

"I didn't waste it," he said and shifted his weight uncomfortably. "I spent it on school clothes."

She whipped her head around, hissing, "Don't lie to me." With her bare arm quivering with near-atrophy she held out her hand. "Hand it over."

Breed tried to maintain a placid demeanor, but blurted out, "What do you plan to do if I don't?"

As if he were dirt, his mother looked down at him. "Just wait and see."

The look was the same kind of look that teachers gave him when he didn't have decent clothes to wear.

He stared back.

His mother walked toward him and raised her arm in a threatening gesture. "Don't look at me like

31

that," she yelled with the fat under her chin vibrating.

To pantomime his helplessness, Breed held out his empty hands. "I don't have any money."

She gestured to his new clothes. "If you got money to dress like a goddamn hoodlum, then you got money for me."

Shaking his head, he watched the waving flab on her arm. It seemed to hypnotize him. He turned his head and took one step.

"Don't walk away from me," she roared.

Keeping his back to her, he stopped.

Loud enough to send pain into his ears, she screamed in a high-pitched voice, "Hand that money over, right now."

"I don't have any."

She turned, reached under the chair, and picked up one, of three glass jars of paint Breed used to paint mailboxes and held it in front of him. "If you're not making enough money to give me some, then you won't need this." She lifted her arm high and threw the glass jar of silver paint onto the sidewalk. It exploded sending paint all over the side of the shack.

As he stood in awe, she yelled, "And you won't need these." She picked up the other two jars of paint and threw them against the stone base on the shack. They crashed. Red and black paint spattered and ran onto the ground.

Horrified that his money-making business was gone, Breed stood in shock. But he didn't have time to be overwhelmed with shock. His mother was coming after him.

Heightened alertness poured through him. To protect his face, he lifted his left hand and turned toward her. But he had lifted the wrong hand. Slap! Like a sneaky left hook, her large hand pummeled his face, dazing the shit out of him.

"I didn't do nothin'," he yelled back. Then small blue streams of light ran before his eyes.

Slap! Slap! reported on his face. He backed up. She punched him in the stomach. The streams of blue light widened. He doubled over in agony, and his face made a perfect target for her jerked-up knee. Bam! She rammed her knee into his face. His head flew upward. Her fist thudded across his ear. Stunned, he didn't feel it. Blue light exploded into bright white stars.

He straightened and lifted his hand for defense and took a subtle step back. His foot caught on the edge of the sidewalk. He tripped backwards. His shining black-haired head painfully clunked on the cement. His mother went right to him, bent over, and with each word, she slapped him. "Don't," Slap! "lie to me," Slap! "Give me that money." Slap! "Right now!"

Breed was in a daze. His nose streamed blood, and his lips were smashed. His fuzzy thought was that his head had hit the sidewalk at a trigger knockout point. He knew he should fight back or at least defend himself, but he couldn't hit his own mother. The powerful, anger-filled slaps continued. "Don't lie to me." Slap! Slap! Slap!

The stars faded to black. He was out. Suddenly the earth had the smell of death, and he realized that in all the world there was no one to come and help him, and there would be nobody to ask or care where he had gone. As a bright light shone in the dark of his mind, he heard Flick's voice, "Let him alone. Ain't it bad enough you smashed all our jars of paint. Do you want to kill him, too?"

Breed looked up out of a dark fog. Panting from exertion, his mother held her flabby arm high and threatened Flick. "I'll break any goddamn thing I want. Get your thievin' ass outta here, or you'll get the same."

Although Flick's methods were not always strictly legal, he did have a sense of fair play. He grabbed Breed's mother's hand and held on to it. She struggled to turn it free, but Flick was too strong for her exhausted body. While he held her hand secure, Breed regained his vision, crawled a few feet, and pushed himself to his feet. As he felt blood run down his chin, Flick released the grip on Breed's mother's hand and stepped away. "Come on, Breed, let's get outta here."

His mother whirled around, rage clouding her face. "That's right! Just get the hell out and don't come back."

Breed staggered toward the road, and the toes of his new shoes bumped into the humped-up cracks in the broken sidewalk. Like a moving grinding stone, the rough edges cut into the new black leather.

Flick put his arm around Breed's shoulders, and as he guided him out of the front yard and around the fence, his mother stood with the fly-laden screen door open, and her words trailed behind. "Just get the hell out. Get out and stay out. Don't think you're gonna freeload around here." She stepped into the house and the screed door slapped behind her.

Standing in the grass and weeds next to the open sewer in front of the shack, Breed pushed his hair in place and looked to Flick, "I feel weird."

"That's from when you hit your head on the sidewalk. I was on the road and heard it all the way out there, sounded like somebody dropped a bowling ball."

Flick sat Breed down on the beat-down grass, and after they looked back and made sure Breed's mother wasn't sneaking up behind them, they leaned their backs against the dirty-white pickets of the fence.

Flick looked straight ahead. A faraway look settled into his eyes. "You gettin' the same crap I am?"

Slumped over with his head down, and gazing hopelessly at the ground, Breed didn't want to answer. He looked away in shameful exasperation. He had never wanted anyone to know how his drunken parents treated him. Now Flick had seen him being beat by his own mother. He tried to throw the deep sense of shame out of his mind. After the rich kids in the schoolyard had pointed and made fun of him because they had seen his stepfather drunk, he had learned to lie about it. Now he was like a trained dog. When it came to answers about his alcoholic home, he automatically didn't tell the truth, and now, everybody would know he had been lying. He reddened and jerked upright. "What crap you talkin' about?"

Flick leaned toward Breed and whispered in his ear. "You know we don't have to do what they say all the time."

Breed hadn't expected this. Staring wide-eyed, he shook his head in agreement and Flick continued, "My old man got drunk cause he got laid off again, says I have to pay rent or get the hell out."

"Are you going to pay it?"

"I probably won't live to pay anything. When I said I didn't have any money, he came after me with a board that had a nail in it." He pulled the sleeve of his shirt up and exposed a fresh puncture wound. "Before I could get away, he got me here."

Breed's eyebrows raised and he felt wrinkles form in his forehead. "That's insanity," he said, and blood ran down his chin. Out of habit, he wiped it on his shirtsleeve. "Damn!" He jerked the sleeve away from his mouth. "I ruined my new shirt."

"It'll be okay," Flick assured him. "It's red. It'll match."

Breed smiled and his battered face hurt. "Ah man, what the hell is going on? Before I give them money, I'll rent someplace that ain't a dump."

Flick picked the stick and poked it into the ground. "We finally figured out a way to make some half-decent money, and now everybody wants to take it off us."

Breed felt his resentment boil like acid. "People are like vultures. They swoop down and strip us of everything we have."

36

"We won't be able to paint mailboxes all winter," Flick lamely said and frowned in thought. "We got to find another way to make money."

Breed remembered how long it had taken him to earn enough money to buy his new clothes and a good pair of shoes. "Yeah, but that takes time." He threw his hands into the air. "Oh well, at least I got enough left to go to the movies." He looked at the fresh blood on his new shirt. "Damn it anyway."

Flick raked his fingers through his hair. "It doesn't matter." He stared straight ahead, his expression grim. "We ain't going to the Rat House."

Breed eyed him suspiciously. "What do you mean we ain't going? I got money."

Flick held the ends of the stick in his hands, placed it under the ball of his clodhopper-shoed foot, and pulled on it until it bent. "You *had* money." He looked to Breed's torn pocket. "When you were down, your mother ripped you pocket and took the money out."

In a panicked gasp, Breed reached into his torn pocket and felt around. He pulled his empty hand out, turned his palm up, and looked at it. Shaking his head in disbelief, it dawned on him. Not only was his money gone, his mother had torn the pocket of his brand-new pants. With his body going rigid with hate, he turned toward the shack and said through clenched teeth. "I should slap her around and see how she likes it."

He started to rise.

Flick pulled him back down. "The hell with that," he said. "If you do, they'll figure out some way to send us to jail."

Breed knew Flick was right. He turned away from the shack and unclenched his fist. "I know that," he said on the verge of crying and tried to hold his voice firm but it quavered. "Now I don't even have a pair of decent pants."

"That ain't no lie," Flick said and pulled on the stick. It cracked into a ball of fresh, white splinters, but the green wood didn't come apart. "I guess we forgot that in this shit hole, rat maze, playing fair is just a rumor."

Knowing Flick was right, Breed bit back an obscenity and stared at the broken stick. "We should figure out a way to get away from here."

As if he hadn't heard what Breed had said, Flick let out a dissatisfied sigh. "What the hell are they trying to do to us?" He flung the stick across the road. "We can't make enough money to pay rent?"

Breed looked back over his shoulder. Each day, the shack he lived in was crumbling and decaying a little more. The frame around his opened bedroom window was cracked, and the paint was peeling off in big slivers. He had wanted to paint it with his silver mailbox paint, but his mother had pitched a fit, said he didn't know what he was doing, and that she'd better not find one speck of his silver paint on the window. "Even if we paid, we'd still be living in a dump?"

Suddenly, a warm breeze surrounded them with the sickening odor of chemicals from a foundry.

Breathing shallow, Flick looked at the window and then back at Breed. "You got that right."

Lifting his arm and placing the sleeve of his shirt over his mouth, Breed nodded in agreement. Then he dropped his arm. "Let's get out of here."

Craning his neck, Flick looked down the road. "Hey, there's the Joneses."

Breed stepped to the side of the road and looked. "The Jones family was out. They were pulling their crippled grandfather in a red wagon. He wore a heavy black woolen coat with no buttons and a dirty baseball cap with a frayed brim. He waved his cane around and pointed to empty pop bottles in the sewer ditches. His inbred kids had weird glassy eyes, and when they looked at something, they never looked directly at the object. Whenever they stared at something that was a few feet away, it seemed as if their eyes had not been connected in a usual sequence that sent messages to their brains. They wore their pants high over their hips, and it seemed that their stout bodies made it difficult for them to bend at their waists. Three empty pop bottles lay in the ditch. When they saw them, under haircuts that looked like someone had placed a bowl on their heads and used it as guide, their faces broke into happy smiles. As if they were pieces of gold, they ran for the bottles, picked them up, and carefully placed them in the wagon between their grandfather's legs.

Breed and Flick walked toward them.

"I can't believe they're still around," Flick said amazed. "The health department condemned their house."

"Yeah," Breed echoed. "It's hard to believe, but their house is worse than our shacks. They have been trying to get them out of there for months."

A breeze traveled past the Joneses and toward Breed and Flick. It carried great fluffy fumes of human piss. Flick turned his head to the side. The fumes passed. "What's the big deal about getting them out?" he said and took a breath of good air. "That house is ready to fall over. There ain't even any windows in it."

Breed took a deep breath and huffed out the piss odor that seemed to be festering all the way down into his lungs. "Last week Screwball and Hog wanted to see if they were still in the house. They went over and pounded on the walls."

"How could they stand the smell?"

"I don't know. Those guys will do anything for a laugh, and the Joneses were still in there hiding. Screwball pounded on the side of the house, and the whole house shook. The Joneses ran around inside like a bunch of scared rats."

"The place stinks so bad, it's a wonder they didn't stink themselves right out onto the street."

Breed shook his head in wonder. "Maybe they hold their breath a lot. The old grandpa claims that the house is okay, says the city just wants to tear it down just to make room for a store or something that will make money."

Breed wondered if the old grandfather was right. From his own experience, the people of Shitsplat couldn't be trusted.

Flick picked up the pace. "Let's go and see how many hits it takes the wrecking ball to knock it down. After it's down, we'll be able to make some money."

"How are we going to make money on a knocked-down house?"

Flick walked faster. "There might be some scrap copper from the roof flashing. We could get it and sell it to the junkman."

Breed stopped in his tracks. "Good idea. I heard they're getting big money for it."

Together Flick and Breed hurried down the street.

A few yards before they got to the Jones family, Flick bent over, picked up a long cigarette butt, and walked toward them. "Watch this!"

He flicked the long cigarette butt. It landed on the ground, ten feet from the wagon. The Jones kids shrieked with joy and rushed toward it. The crippled grandpa's lips curled into a cruel smile. He jumped out of the wagon so fast that bottles flew out of the wagon. With the tail of his opened wool coat flying behind him, he raced toward the butt. Whipping his cane into threatening concentric circles, he warned, "Get away. Get away. It's mine!"

His kids backed away from the butt. He picked it up, put it to his lips, and jumped back into the wagon. Then he pointed to his lips and directed his kids to light the butt."

Breed shook his head in disbelief. "Amazing," he said. "How can anyone lose their mind over a stinkin' butt?"

Flick grinned. "It must be a fountain of youth. Did you see how that crippled old man made a miraculous recovery?"

Breed shook his head. "I just don't understand."

"Come on," Flick said, his grin growing wider. "They should be ready to swing that wrecking ball. There's money to be made."

At the Joneses' house, the wrecking crew had just hooked up the big steel wrecking ball. The crane operator checked the cables, climbed up into the cab of the swing crane, and started a little pony engine. When it was running with a smooth rhythm, he pulled a lever, and acting like a starter, the pony engine engaged, and the big diesel engine roared to life. The crane operator sat in the seat, and with his foot, he released the asbestos-lined hoist brake band. Right below him, the brake drum spun. A tiny whirlwind of asbestos particles blasted into his face. Squinting, he lifted his foot, and set the hoist brake. He wrestled with the controls and moved the big boom to the right. Then, to gain enough momentum to make the ball swing, he moved the crane's boom in the opposite direction. The ball didn't smash into the side of the house, but before the operator could get decent momentum for a good destructive swing, Tick! The ball gently touched the side of the house. Before the crane operator could get in another momentum moving swing, it was like the dilapidated house had been blown down with silent dynamite. It collapsed. Dense, dirt-filled dust slowly arose in a slow, choking cloud.

Below the churning cloud, years of collected garbage, backed up sewers, slimy overrun toilets, and green molds were covered with old splintering wood, plaster, and brittle shingles.

Like a billowing storm cloud, the gray dust engulfed Breed. He put the front of his shirt over his mouth and looked to Flick. "Let's get out of here."

But Flick was gone.

Blindly stepping through the thick dust, heading by instinct rather than sight, Breed stumbled and fell. Holding his breath, he quickly got to his feet and kept stepping, until he stepped out into the clean air, ran down the alleyway, and caught up to Flick.

Using his hand to brush the dust from his clothes, Flick looked up. "That Jones's filth crawled down my throat. We ain't gettin' any copper today. How about we saddle up and head for the river?"

Breed began brushing the dust from his new clothes. "We could, but that water's cold."

"It ain't that cold. Let's get in one last swim before winter."

As if it had the power of a graceful guardian angel, the river always seemed to make things right or made Breed forget about things that had gone wrong. He remembered the friendly, old man who had fished at the water's edge. He had always warned Breed that the river was tricky, and that if a person did not understand it, it could be a monster.

The river's deep undertows, drop-offs, and floods had taken many lives, but Breed figured the people had died because they couldn't swim, and if they could, they had always panicked and drowned, and the sad part was they were usually in four feet of water, and all they had to do to save themselves was stand up. Breed knew he wasn't going to drown. The river had always been his friend.

He looked up. On their way to some carnival in the deep blue sky, a few cotton candy clouds fleeced past. He reached into his pocket and wished his money were there. It wasn't. He looked to Flick. "Maybe it's like Screwball says, 'You're just like a leg. If you don't learn how to step out of the way, all the assholes of the world will just keep shittin' on you.'"

As they walked along, Flick ran his hand over the scraggly hedges that lined a yard next to the alleyway and chuckled.

Breed smiled. "I'd like to go swimming." He reached up and touched the side of his painful face. "But I ain't gonna go back in the shack and get my swimming suit."

"You won't have to. I got a spare one hid under the bridge."

"I don't know." Breed reached up and touched his face. "My face still hurts."

Staring at Breed's face that was becoming a distorted puffy, purple effigy of itself, Flick placed a comforting hand on his shoulder. "We'll find some Daisy flowers along the bank. We can crush 'em up and put 'em on your bruised face. It'll fix it right up. And besides, the cool water will help it heal."

44

Breed wasn't sure about the Daisies, but he was sure about Jewel Weed curing poison Ivy.

Smiling somewhat lamely, Flick pointed down the street. "The sun's out. Screwball's waitin'."

Even though the thinly-built, blond-headed Screwball lived in a broken-down shack bounded by the reaches of a dozen filthy streets around a central place of noise with scrambling children and drunken men, he derived pleasure from mocking people and laughing at many things that would get most people angry. He was also a virtuoso at the smart-ass remark, and he was casually leaning on a mailbox with his feet crossed, his long hair almost covering his one eye that had a perpetual squint.

Breed looked at Flick and grinned. "If he had to chop a hole in the ice, he'd go swimming."

Flick lifted his hand and patted Breed's shoulders. "Stop bitchin', Breed. We've gone when it was colder than this."

Flick was right. One New Year's Eve, the river had not frozen completely over. Just to be the first to swim in the new year, Flick had talked Breed and his friends into swimming. They had gone in wearing their underwear. After they had moved thin sheets of ice to make a swimming lane, they dove into the water, but didn't swim long. When they did, their arms jerked like comedians in old black and white comedy movies. It had been cold, and their hands and feet had turned blue, but they didn't care. They had been the first to swim in the new year.

Breed wiped the dried blood from his chin. "As long as the sun stays out, it won't be too cold."

45

"It's your Indian summer," Flick said with a grin. "You should know how warm it's gonna be."

Even though Breed was part Indian, he didn't know how long the warm weather would last. But he wished the long hours of basking in the sunshine on the bridge above the river would never end. Still feeling loopy from the beating, and hoping it had all been a dream, he reached into his pocket. In a furious attempt to locate the money that had been there, he shook his hand around. The pocket was still empty. His hand fell to his side. "If it were my summer, I wouldn't let it end." He breathed in. The dust from Jones' knocked down house stuck on the back of his throat like sticky flypaper. He turned to Flick. "Is there Joneses' dust still in your throat?"

"Yeah! Let's go," he said and coughed. "A few dives off the bridge will clear that shit right out."

CHAPTER 3

Leaning against the railing of the Clark Street Bridge with crushed Daisy flowers on his beaten-blue face, Breed looked through the steel grating beneath his bare feet. The rectangular shaped holes split the silver sun into long trapezoidal beams that traveled to the river far below, where they spread out like chunks of sparkling chrome, prancing on the water.

When Breed looked up, the tall, rivet-humped I-beams of the bridge slanted into the semi-warm sky. Breed was glad the river wasn't a public swimming place, where a sunken-chested lifeguard roosted on top of a platform built out of white two-by-fours and acted like some kind of idiot trying to take over the title of asshole of the world by trying to enforce some chicken-shit rules. If some flats gang kids didn't come looking for trouble, the bridge and the river below provided total swimming freedom.

After the Daisy flowers had dried and fell from his face, Breed leaned on the railing and surveyed the bridge.

As if they were sitting in reclining lawn chairs, Flick and Screwball stretched out on the bottom of the slanted I-beams and relaxed. Nobody asked about Breed's blue face, and he didn't volunteer any information. His friends knew he had been slapped but not into submission. It was just the way they were. Instead of showing pity they would say, "Shit, man, snap out of it."

Hog, a belligerent and agitating muscular kid, who was never one to do more work than necessary, lounged just under the catwalk railing on a cement ledge. From his position on the ledge, if he wanted to get into the water and cool down, he didn't have to get up. He could just turn toward the river and drop in.

Just as everybody but Breed were about to doze off, the tires of a shiny black Cadillac rolled onto the steel grating of the bridge and stopped right next to Screwball, and the pink Ford pulled up and stopped right behind the Cadillac.

With his nose wrinkling from the odor of the unwashed wart-faced kid, wafting from the Ford, Hog slowly got up, and without the wart-faced kid seeing him, he climbed to the top of the bridge and looked down into the hole in the Ford's roof.

The man in the Cadillac stuck his head out the window. His face was dark and narrow, and his green eyes stared at Screwball. The man said something but couldn't be heard. Screwball leaned over and placed his ear next to man's face. "What?"

As the man began to speak, Screwball flinched. The man's rancid breath caused Screwball's face to contort in revolution. The man raised his voice and pointed to the road ahead. "Where does this road go?"

Flick grinned the kind of grin that showed he knew Screwball was not only going to give the man a witty reply, he was going to delay him so Hog could do something to the kid in the Ford.

"It doesn't go," Screwball said, waved the odor from his face, and muttered. "Was there a sale of bad breath today?"

"Pardon me?"

Screwball spoke up, "The road doesn't move. It can't go anywhere."

The man squirmed uncomfortably. "That's not what I meant, smart ass. Where does this road end?"

"Does that road have an end?" Screwball asked with merriment. "All roads lead to other roads." Pointing to the road, he gave the man a cockeyed smile. "So all the roads in the world start right over there."

In quizzical disbelief, the man stared at Hog and Screwball. "You're not in your right minds."

Wart Face pounded his fist on the horn of the Ford's steering wheel and yelled at the man in the Cadillac, "Get your highfalutin ass out of the way?"

From high on the bridge, Hog broke out in caustic laughter. "Don't worry, everything is copacetic."

Not knowing where Hog's remark had come from, Wart Face craned his neck around, searching.

The man in the Cadillac leaned forward in a helpless heap and glared at Screwball. "You're just a goddamn wise ass."

Bobbing his head with laughter, Screwball raised one finger. "You're just full of cherry news."

"Just remember," the man replied, his eyes glaring with disapproval, "tomorrow is always another day."

49

"Tomorrow is not always another day." Screwball cocked his head discerningly. "When we turn our clocks back an hour, for daylight savings time, there are not twenty-four hours in that day. So tomorrow is not always another day."

In a voice slurred with fatigue, the man looked ahead and wagged his head from side to side, muttering, "Idiots, goddamned idiots." Then he yelled, "Stick that road and your twenty-three-hour day up your ass."

Wart Face held the horn lever down and yelled, "Get your filthy asses off the bridge."

Just before the Cadillac drove away, up above, Hog began to urinate. Urine streamed down and into the hole in the roof of the Ford.

Gaping at Screwball in undisguised befuddlement, Wart Face asked, "Is it raining?" When he looked up. The long stream of urine flowed right into his face.

With a lax mouth hung open in a perfect O, Hog said, "Oh! It would give us great pleasure if you would just leave."

Realizing what had drenched his face, Wart Face stiffened with resentment, opened the door, and jumped out. Looking up, he aggressively jabbed his finger toward Hog. "I'm gonna kick your godamn ass."

"What the hell you bitchin' about?" Hog yelled down. "That's the first shower you've had in years."

Flick stepped toward Wart Face, crossed his arms across his chest, and defiantly stated, "Why don't you try kickin' my ass?"

Screwball snuck behind Wart Face and silently dropped to his hands and knees.

Wart Face drew his fist back to strike. "I'll punch that smart—".

Before the last word was out of his mouth, Flick pushed Wart Face.

The back of Wart Face's legs rammed into Screwball's side.

Unable to catch his balance because of Screwball's body blocking his legs, Wart Face flew backwards. Windmilling his arms, his feet flew up, and his back painfully landed on the catwalk grating. He immediately rolled to his hands and feet, got up, and with a face purple with rage shouted, "You're all getting' your asses kicked."

There was no way Wart Face was going to beat four people. But instead of fighting, Breed and his friends jumped up on the railing, held out their hands, and Flick jeered, "Come on and get us, candy ass."

Red faced and cussing and with a pee-drenched head, Wart Face reached for Flick's hand. "I'll yank your dumb ass right off that railing."

Before Wart Face could grab Flick's hand, Flick lifted his hand away. "Screw You!" He jumped off the railing.

Ignoring Breed, Wart Face tried to grab other outstretched hands, but all he got was empty air. Confused and astonished, he whirled on his heel and faced Breed. The two faced each other, and for a silent moment, their stares streamed hate.

"If it's the last thing I do," Wart Face said in the disgust of intense irritation. "I get you for this."

He reared back to throw a punch. Breed easily ducked under it and jumped of the railing.

After taunting Wart Face with caustic laughter, Hog yelled sharply from the top of the bridge. "Hey pee face, how do you like us now?"

Wart Face recoiled with sudden shock. "It's not over," he threatened. "I'm callin' the police."

Forcing his mouth into a frown, and with pleading eyes Hog yelled down, "Please forgive us for the intelligence of our remarks."

Wart Face jumped back into the Ford, slammed the door, tromped on the gas, and sped away.

Minutes later Breed and the others were back up on the bridge, where Breed squirmed uncomfortably. "What if the police come?"

"We'll do what we always do, Flick said with victorious merriment. "We'll hide under the bridge."

A while later, the police hadn't come, but a big red Pontiac Bonneville came barreling onto the bridge and slowed. It was a real red boat, with chrome spotlights on both sides of a swept back windshield. The driver looked to be about sixty, was short and thin with a bald head, and a sharp nose sat between his hollow eyes. He rolled down his window and stopped the car. "Hey, you lazy bastards!" He wagged his head in grave admonition and yelled, "You ain't got no class. Quit playin' in that filthy river. Get a job."

Breed wondered why people who so fervently cut them down did it from a comfortable place and often after a good meal.

And Hog wouldn't hesitate to tell those kinds of people just how he felt about their criticism. After admiring the white chrome-encased white stripe that ran down the Bonneville's sides that accented the white leather interior, he lay back against the bridge beam, nonchalantly lifted his hand, and thrust his middle finger at the driver. "I'm glad you were awarded a gold star in your jackassification. However, we are not in the least influenced by your conceited suggestion."

Astonished, the other people inside the car jerked their heads in Hog's direction.

Making a dismissing gesture with his arm, Hog said, "Hey enema mouth, we're on the road to moral decay. Let's just forget the whole thing and take the afternoon off." Then he broke into a long peal of laughter.

Now the people in the big Pontiac were getting an eyeful of how their lifestyles clashed violently with the grimy fingers of the slum side of town. It was as if they had never seen or heard such a thing, and their twisted faces flashed with puzzlement.

To closely search the man's face, Breed stepped across the crosswalk and leaned forward. "Sorry about that!"

But Hog couldn't let it go at that. Giving a smiling nod to the man he said, "You're very astute, my good man. It's not that we're overly worried about you arousing the ire of the law. However, we will make a note of your dissent." He smiled big. "And we will place it in the 'Who the Fuck Cares What You Think' file."

While Screwball stuck out his lower lip in an exaggerated expression of sadness, the man's face filled with irritation. "You kids belong in a nut house." He rolled up the window and drove off the bridge.

The tomfoolery had caused Breed to forget he had just been beaten, but the pain was coming back. He walked to the catwalk railing and sat on it.

Across the river, the underground water pumps that led to the Westinghouse transformer plant high on the hill, groaned like a bellowing five-hundred-pound moose. Deep inside the hollow sluice pipe a floodgate squealed open. Although it was always followed by a chaotic mixture of disagreeable sounds that Breed and his friends were used to, all eyes turned toward the pipe. Pent-up dark water raced out of it. Like a cancer beyond control, black oil, acid, and whatever the stinking plant was flushing into the already filthy side of the river, swirled into a sickening stain that fanned across the water until it was sucked into the current and pulled downriver.

Breed found it hard to believe that the people of Shitsplat existed with such filth and ignorance. Although sewer and poison factory water flowed into the river directly upstream from the water treatment plant, which caused the town's drinking water to constantly be a derivative of sewer and poison water, it was an accepted process of making money. So it didn't seem to bother upstanding citizens of Shitsplat and it appalled him.

When Breed was on the side of the bridge where the cleaner water flowed, it was like a second home, and sometimes it caused him to forget about people's self-imposed ignorance. The sun-warmed steel beams and friendly water, beneath him, had not yet been polluted as bad as the other side of the river, and it had always made him happy, but today, the pain from the beating and getting cheated out of seeing the Buddy Holly movie pried at his mind. In Shitsplat an honest guy just couldn't seem to get ahead. He wondered if the whole world was rigged. He felt helpless. He felt poor. He didn't like it. He wasn't smiling.

In the distance, the mournful drone of a diesel freight train howled. It went right through him. That train was on its way out of Shitsplat. It was going to a better place. Breed wished he were going, too. But he wasn't. He would have to stay in Shitsplat, put up with drunken fights, sleepless nights, and pay rent, too.

He sucked in the cool autumn air and forced those rotten feelings out of his chest. As he watched the river sparkle in the sun, he tried to convince himself that it didn't matter. He was going to make the happy days of summer last just a little bit longer, at least long enough to get some sleep and go for one more swim. That was if the police didn't come.

The sun beamed down, warm, then hot. After a while, Screwball stepped up on the steel catwalk railing and dove into the water far below. Breed stepped up and teetered at the top of the railing. He looked back over his shoulder. Hog was on the rail, and Flick was reclining against the bridge beam staring at Hog.

"What the hell are you looking at?" Hog asked.

"Just wanted to know what you did to that usher that kicked you in the ribs."

Hog let out a roaring laugh. "I'm glad you want to get intellectual about it. However, at the moment, I really don't feel like launching a soliloquy about it." He lifted one finger. "Of course, you know, the description of what I did is a little too grandiose for you."

Knowing Hog was not going to tell what he did to the usher, Breed tilted his head toward the river below. "You guys going in?"

Flick jumped up, motioned to Hog, and pointed to Screwball who was treading water right below them. "Come on, he won't know what hit him."

Hog smiled and turned toward the river. They all jumped off at once. They bent their knees and held their ankles. Three perfect human cannonballs rushed toward the river water far below. Just a few feet from Screwball they bombed into the river. Each entry into the water caused it to rise up and form what looked like a miniature mushroom cloud. The sudden disturbance caused huge waves to slosh into Screwball's mouth. He choked and coughed. "Thanks for dropping in," he said and spit a stream of water toward Flick.

"A little water ain't going to hurt you," Flick said, and they all swam toward shore.

The water was lukewarm, and the air had the feel of an early winter, but it didn't matter. As they swam to the dock, no one voiced a candy-ass complaint.

Flick, Hog, and Screwball walked across the dock, dashed up the purple cinder path, and onto the bridge. Breed followed, but stopped at the top of the path and watched.

Hog pointed at the approaching pink Ford and yelled at Wart Face, "Here comes Pee Face."

While the Ford hummed across the grating on the bridge Wart Face bobbed his middle finger up and down and yelled, "I called the police. They're right behind me."

When Wart Face was gone, Breed joined the others in a warm huddle on the catwalk and kept an eye out for the police who would be there in a few seconds.

For a few precious moments the friendly sun was a heated gold coin. When its luster dulled behind a cloud, and the air cooled, signaling a dirty purple dusk, all their lips turned blue, and goose bumps formed on their bare skin. Even though a bat circled overhead, diving and fluttering about in an endless quest for insects, Breed turned his back to the light breeze and tried to suck the last rays of the late summer sun into his tanned body.

Hog shivered once and shook off the cold. "Where's those police? They should've been here by now." When the sound of a backfiring engine rumbled and cracked in the distance, he pointed across the steel grating of the bridge. "Get a load-a that!" he said with excitement in his voice. "Here comes Edward Carmichael."

Eddie liked to be called Eddie Chicago, but Hog called him Edward Carmichael just to agitate. Under a neatly combed blond head of hair, Eddie had a handsome face with blue eyes. Sometimes he blew off steam fighting in gang fights that he would start for no reason, and he had been arrested. When he felt like it, he had gotten drunk. He had no problem lying, cheating, or stealing. Breed knew Eddie's actions were a result of living outside, in the real world, where hunger, thirst, and cold waited. Because no one could know what Eddie would do at any given moment, he was a public dread, and not too many people liked to be around him. It was said that he had packed ten average lifetimes into one. He had always been full of big plans. Many times, in the past, people had underrated him. His outward appearance projected an image of an unfaltering person who looked the soul of honor. Although mysterious and charismatic, he had a mesmerizing effect on some people, but after knowing him for a long time, Breed realized the devious cunning that lay beneath the surface.

For a moment Breed stood in sudden silence, then said, "Looks like he lost weight again."

"Yeah," Flick said. "He says he skinny because he's always so busy that he doesn't have time to eat."

"Who cares about how skinny he is, "Hog said and pointed. "Look what he's driving."

Racing toward the bridge, the green six-cylinder car engine on the back of the go-kart, Eddie was driving, roared. As he raced alongside the dusty edge of the heat-baked asphalt, long trails of raising dust, loud thunder, and hot blasts of orange and blue fire shot out the ends of a big-holed exhaust pipe.

Flick shook his head in disbelief. "You gotta be kiddin' me."

Like a giant fly, the oversized tires on the go-kart buzzed on the steel grating of the bridge and, Zzzooommmmm! Eddie shot past. A trail of oily smoke followed. Breed blinked and Eddie was gone. A delayed echo from the thundering engine bounced around the tall beams of the bridge.

Screwball, who had been looking into the river, twisted his body toward the sound and jerked his head to see. His wet bathing suit slipped under him. He tumbled off the railing and landed on the steel grating of the catwalk.

As Screwball sat there, Hog made one of his usual snide remarks. "Sit much?"

Ignoring Hog's attempted agitation, Screwball pushed himself up off the grating, stood up, and brushed himself off. "I did that by popular demand. Repeat performance, tonight, seven o'clock." He jumped back up on the railing. "Was that who I think it was?"

Hog waved the blue exhaust smoke from his face. "You got it. It's Eddie Carmichael on a go-kart. The half-wit's got a car engine on the back."

Screwball, who always liked to inject off-the-wall antics into situations, held his blond, long-haired head high, kept his neck stiff, and in a maniacal frenzy, waved his hands above his head. "Maybe he just got out of the nut house."

No one laughed. They knew it could be true.

59

Screwball dropped his hands and gave an embarrassed shrug. "That crazy bastard doesn't have to go a hunnert miles an hour." He shook his head in amazement. "With that smoke blastin' out the back, he looks like a goddamn rocket."

Flick cocked an eye at Screwball. "Maybe he's trying to kill himself, like they said his uncle did."

The oily smoke was burning Breed's eyes. He blinked and squinted. "He's gettin' close to it."

Looking down the road, Screwball wagged his head from side to side. "I didn't see anything but a blur. You guys sure that was him?"

"That was him," Hog assured Screwball. "Eddie does not possess more than two speeds, off and on, and it looks like the switch is on."

"The best way to make Eddie turn the switch on is to tell him he can't do it," Flick said, lifted his arm, and pointed down the road. "Here he comes again."

Coming at them, Eddie crouched behind the steering wheel. As he increased speed, the wind rushed against his face, his eyes strained into slits, and his red, skinny tie trailed straight out from the back of his neck, flapping behind his back like an S-curling snake. The tailored small-cuffed black pants with the thin clean white belt looped loosely around his small waist, and the white vest that covered a light-blue sports shirt, he wore with the long sleeves rolled neatly around his arms and the front opened down to three buttons, stuck flat to his skin. Accented by his white socks, his shoes stuck out in front of him like two chrome hood ornaments. He always said, "Clothes make the man." It didn't matter that he was racing around Shitsplat in a greasy mechanical monster. He still dressed as if there were a pretty girl just around the next corner.

Behind the fire-spitting death machine, like black raindrops, a trail of slippery oil splatted the top of the gray pavement.

Imitating Eddie's squinted eyes, Screwball put his thumbs on the corners of his eyes and pulled them into slits. "He looks like he got Chinese eyes. If the cops catch him, they'll handcuff him and blindfold him with a piece of string."

The kart hit a rise in the road. Its tires left the pavement. The kart sailed a few feet into the air. Eddie let off the gas. The kart slammed back down onto the road. The sheet metal floor on the kart banged and with an ear-piercing screech on the pavement. A tail of orange-white sparks flew behind. The kart wiggled and smoothed out. Eddie tromped the gas feed. Black smoke poured out the back. The front tires lifted off the pavement. When they touched down, Eddie disappeared in a blue cloud of oily smoke.

"That thing's too low," Flick said and coughed. "If he hits a high place in the road, that thing will flip right over."

Hog dismissively flapped his hand. "That horse's ass doesn't give a shit. He's always doing something stupid. He doesn't even have a radiator or a fan on that engine. It'll be blowin' up."

"If his skinny necktie gets caught under those big back tires," Flick said. "He won't have to worry about the engine blowing up. He'll snap his neck right off."

Breed wondered what the big deal was. Eddie was doing something exciting. He'd do anything just to have something to do. He could ride out of Shitsplat anytime he wanted. But then again, anything Eddie seemed to do right was usually accomplished more by accident than by what he had planned.

Breed glanced in Flick's direction. "Eddie always said all he needed was a gas pedal and a brake."

"It looks like that's all he got on that death trap."

Jutting out his chin and imitating a person with an exalted station in life," Hog said in his best school teacherly tone, "That does not in any way violate the principles that have governed Mister Carmichael's life thus far."

Amazed at Hog's imitation, Breed gave Hog the once-over and shook his head with disbelief, and Screwball twirled his forefinger up around his temple in a Looney Tunes mode.

The sound of the engine on the kart faded, then got louder.

Eddie was coming back.

As he and the kart thundered close, Breed studied the splotches of oil the motor had blown all over the road. "If he hits that oil, he ain't gonna have no brakes."

"What's he got a bicycle strapped to the back for?" Flick asked.

62

"He stole that off fagot Burke," Hog said. "Says, he needs it just in case he gets a flat tire. Then he won't have to walk."

"I don't know why he's worried about walking," Hog said. "He's always going somewhere but never gets anywhere."

In the distance, a cop cruiser screeched around the corner. Its bubble-gum-machine-like light blinking like a mad red eye. The siren howled toward the bridge. Now Breed knew why the cops hadn't come after Wart Face had called them: They had been chasing Eddie.

As if he were a fan at a racetrack waiting for a wreck, Screwball sat on the railing. When Eddie zoomed past. Screwball snapped his head from right to left so fast, for a split second, he looked like he had two faces. The black and white police cruiser rallied behind Eddie. Its tires rolled over the oil splotches on the road and whirred across the bridge, leaving the whoosh of a tailwind behind.

But Eddie was out of sight.

Breed watched the taillights of the speeding police cruiser bounce down the road. "They ain't even close."

Flapping his hand dismissively, Flick said, "They'll never catch him. That thing's too fast. And Eddie's just plain crazy."

"I'm glad you explained that," Screwball said with a spasm of amusement. "I thought he was just nuts."

When the light on top of the cop car flashed red beacons into the breeze, Breed figured Eddie was gone.

Suddenly, looking like he was playing fox and the geese without the snow trail, Eddie appeared again, speeding around the corner. With the engine thundering and spitting fire, more oil blew out the wide-mouthed pipes. When the brightness of his full-toothed smile spread across his face, he waved to Breed. "I got away," he excitedly shouted and blazed by at a dizzying pace.

Hog tried to warn Eddie. "Watch out for Wart Face!"

But Eddie didn't hear the warning. Right before the bridge, Wart Face pulled the Ford onto the road right in front of Eddie. While Wart Face laughed with supreme egotism, Eddie cut the wheel sharp and just missed the Ford. Hog threw a rock at the Ford. The rock zinged past Wart Face's nose. He punched the accelerator and took off. But Eddie and the low kart doughnutted around on the oiled road, slid onto the brim and over the loose gravel. With yellow dust rolling around the tires, they kicked up circles of stones. When the kart careened back onto the road, the tires spun with awesome power. As if they were on a rosin-soaked roller-rink, they gripped the dry pavement. The kart and Eddie flew down the road like they had been shot out of a gigantic slingshot.

A ways down the road, Eddie shouted, "No brakes!" He hooked his thumbs around the steering wheel and whipped it hard and fast. The kart spun around and straightened. The front wheels lurched off the pavement, and Eddie was heading back toward the bridge. As he neared, the exhaust pipes spit fire into the air. Rushing toward the hill above

the river, Eddie was apparently going to turn into
the weeds and hide. But he would be turning into
the place where a truck had run into the river. Deep
wheel ruts that hid under the grass would make it
impossible for him to turn. Over the cacophony of
the blasting engine, spinning tires, and oily smoke
blasting high into the air, Breed Frantically waved
his arms and screamed, "Turn off, Eddie! Turn
off!"

The pink Ford seemed to come out of nowhere
and raced toward Eddie.

When Eddie was just about to run head-on into
the front of the Ford, he turned toward the grassy
ruts.

Breed warned him again. "Eddie, don't go in
there."

Eddie held his thumb up in an okay gesture and
smiled a big, white-toothed smile. But he kept
going toward the grassy ruts.

The kid in the Ford stuck his wart face out the
window, laughed, and sped away.

The big back tires on Eddie's go-kart fell into
the ruts. Even though he was squinting into the
bright sun, he must have figured he could speed up
and donut out of the ruts. He mashed the gas feed.
The tires spun with awesome power, cutting long
pieces of green grass into short curly pieces, and
like shattered clay pigeons at a skeet shoot, clumps
of mud slung high into the air. Eddie turned the
steering wheel to the left, but the guiding ruts kept
the speeding kart on its unwanted course. Like it
was on ice, the bottom of the kart tobogganed along
the slick grass. It didn't slow down. Eddie turned

the steering wheel to the right. It was useless. He was going too fast. The wheel ruts controlled the kart like it was a runaway train on a steel track. Eddie and the kart slipped to the edge of the steep cliff.

Above the roar of the engine, Flick yelled, "He's goin' over."

In the excitement, Breed hadn't seen the cop car stopped on the bridge. He turned his eyes from Eddie to the car. The officer sat inside, his eyes open wide.

With a backdrop of a misty blue sky in the distance, the go-kart and Eddie sailed out over the water. At the top of the arc, the go-kart suspended in midair. As it seemed to hover for a second, the bicycle flew off the back. But Eddie's foot stayed jammed against the gas pedal. The engine raced free. With the huge tires spinning stones and mud into windmill circles, and orange fire and black smoke blasting out the exhaust pipes, the go-kart fell. With one hand, Eddie held onto the side of the kart, and as he waved his other hand in the air like a cowboy on a bucking bull, the kart splashed into the water. The engine hammered, rattled, and smoked. Steam sizzled off the hot pipes. Eddie released his grip on the side of the kart. Like some angry river monster, the big back wheels bucked up and threw Eddie off the seat. He flew into the air. His feet dangled and his arms grabbed for support, but he caught nothing but oily smoke. The engine backfired three times, and the tires stopped spinning. Eddie hit the water, his feet running and his hands clawing at the water until he churned under.

Flick stepped up onto the railing, ready to dive in and save him. Like a hungry mouth the green water gulped the kart into its dark depth. The only evidence that the cart had existed were exhaust fumes and steamy bubbles puffing to the surface.

With a look of amazement, Screwball stared at the water and remarked, "That's entertainment."

The cop got out of the car and leaned over the railing. "Entertainment?" he questioned. "That's insanity." To get a better look, he thumbed his hat back on his head and watched the water.

CHAPTER 4

Standing on the Clark Street Bridge, Breed anxiously searched the surface where Eddie and the cart had crashed into the river. When it looked like he wasn't going to surface, Flick flexed his legs to dive.

Eddie surfaced, gasping for breath. Then using his skinny arms, he swam until he climbed up onto the dock under the bridge.

Shaking his head in awe, Flick stepped down from the railing.

With a questioning tilt to upper body, Hog looked at the square-faced cop. "Is he going to jail this time?"

The cop didn't answer. Laughing a humorless laugh, he pointed his finger at Eddie and said, "Dumb shit!" He turned and started back to his cruiser.

"Eddie ain't dumb," Hog added. "He just looks that way."

From beneath the bridge, Eddie's words, directed at the cop, echoed up. "After almost getting my ass drowned, you didn't have to be such a cheerful son-of-a-bitch."

Shaking his head and laughing, the cop muttered, "I thought the only thing that was going to beat that kid to the hospital was the headlights on the ambulance he would be in." The cop slid back into the cruiser, took one last look at Eddie, and said, "Goddamn kid's invincible," and drove away.

Breed and the others ran down the cinder path and stopped. Eddie stood on the end of the dock, hands on his hips, scowling in concentration. As if it weren't his fault that he had driven the go-kart into the river, he piped off, "Why didn't you tell me those ruts were there."

Flick cocked a questioning eye at Eddie. "Are you blind? "Those ruts were big enough for an elephant to walk through."

As if he were inviting Flick into a secret conference and imparting news of the greatest significance, Eddie whispered out the side of his mouth, "Ahh man, you know what I mean." He broke into a hopeful smile. "You guys are going to have to dive down and get that thing."

Screwball tilted his head to the side and looked right into Eddie's face. "*You* guys are going to have to?" he questioned with emphasis on the you. "No, *you!*" He jerked a finger at Eddie. "*You* are going to have to shit and fall in it."

As his hopeful smile faded, Eddie tilted his head down and looked to where his go-kart had sunk. "I think I just did that."

Standing with one hand on his hip and one leg cocked, Hog bobbed his head with mocking laughter. "Nice job, Carmichael."

While Eddie gave Hog a questioning look for calling him Carmichael, Breed told Eddie, "We can't get that thing out. It's in twenty feet of water. Why did you put a car engine on it?"

As if he were stunned by the question, Eddie leaned back and stated matter-of-factly, "Because that's the first time it's ever been done that man knows of, incidentally."

Breed ignored Eddie's off-the-wall reasoning. "Incidentally," he said and paused. "You'll need a tow truck and a crane to get that heavy thing out of there."

A pleading look appeared on Eddie's face. "If you guys can't get it out, could you at least get the bike off the back?"

"No problem," Screwball said. "It ain't on the back." Then he immediately ran up to the catwalk on the bridge, jumped on the top of the hand railing, gave out a Tarzan yell, and dove into the water. After three attempts, he snagged the bike from the river and dragged it up to shore.

"I'll go get a rope, and we'll pull the kart out," Eddie said. "I like that thing."

"You can get anything you want," Flick said. "Where that thing went in, it sunk to the bottom. It's stuck in the black sludge from the mill."

"I'll get it out myself," Eddie protested. "All you guys have to do is swim down and tie the rope on. Wait here. I'll be back."

Eddie ran down to the bike, picked it up and pushed it up the cinder path and onto the bridge. "So the grass can't grow under my feet, I gotta keep movin'."

"Yeah," Screwball said and squinted in Eddie's direction. "Keep movin'. It keeps the flies off."

Eddie snarled, jumped on the bike and pedaled down Clark Street. He stopped down the road at the intersection next to the Mobile gas station, looked both ways, turned the bicycle around, and started back without a rope.

70

As he pedaled, the front wheel of the bike zigzagged with an unbalanced rhythm. He wiggled down the road, waggled onto the bridge, and stopped at the catwalk railing.

Screwball lifted his hand and gestured toward Eddie's empty hand. "Hey, Eddie, where's the rope?"

Eddie nodded blankly, then tilted his head to one side, and shrugged. "I would have gotten one, but you guys are probably right, this time."

"We might not be able to pull it out," Breed said. "But if you tie a rope on the bumper of your car, you might be able to pull it out."

Eddie leaned over and rested his hands on the handlebars of the bike. "Maybe if that cop would have stuck around, he could have helped us pull it out with his cruiser."

"I doubt it," Screwball said with a careless flick of his wrist. "It takes ten cops to do one man's ordinary work."

Hog nodded in agreement and looked to Eddie. "Where's your car?"

Screwball cocked his head with suspicion. "Yeah! Why are you riding a little kid's bike?"

Eddie's face stiffened. "Don't have a car. Crashed into a pole."

"Yeah, those poles don't move," Screwball said, "even if you blow the horn."

Eddie laughed with surprise. "Yeah I found that out. The car just skidded into that pole and died. Man, it just died."

"What are you going to drive now?"

71

Eddie shifted uncomfortably then lifted both arms into the air. "What's the difference?" He wiggled the handlebars of the bike. "It doesn't matter what I drive, as long as it gets me there."

Breed remembered how Eddie only waxed the hood of his car. He claimed that was all he had to do because when he was driving, it was the only part of the car he could see.

Screwball must have remembered it, too. "Maybe you waxed the hood too much and the slippery wax made the car slide right off the road."

Grinning in agreement, Eddie adjusted the tie around his neck. "That might have done it," he said. "Never can expect anything to last when you take care good care of it."

"What are you wearing a tie for, Carmichael?" Hog asked and pointed to the red tie. "You don't make sense."

Eddie's face took on a look of excruciating discomfort. "You wouldn't make sense if you lived with my old man. That bastard makes me do all his work. I even have to sharpen the blade on the lawn mower." He pointed a finger at Hog. "And don't call me Carmichael."

As Hog ignored Eddie's pointing finger, his forehead wrinkled in comic disbelief. "Sharpening a lawn mower blade is a really hard thing to do. The next time you have to do it, Edward Carmichael, call me."

"Don't call me—," Eddie started to say, but instead he shrugged and said, "I'll do just that."

"Only one thing," Hog said with a devious smile. "When you call..." He pointed a finger at

72

Eddie. "Remember, I didn't say I was going to help. I just said to call."

Dumbfounded, Eddie's shoulders sunk down, and his face screwed up into a grimace of discomfort.

Breed couldn't understand why Eddie thought he had it so bad. When Breed cut grass, for a man who never paid him, he had used a mechanical push mower. Many days he had wished for a gas-powered lawn mower. If he had one, he would have been able to cut the grass in a fraction of time, and with a fraction of the sweat and effort. He scratched the back of his neck. "At least you got a lawn mower."

The grimace of discomfort faded from Eddie's face. "It ain't much easier," he said. "I have to cut that stupid grass even when it doesn't need cut. My old man says that I have to keep busy so I don't try to run away or commit suicide again."

Hog eyes widened, "Did You?"

Eddie rubbed his nose and looked down into the river. "I never tried to kill myself. When my old man locked me in my room, I forgot the window was down. I leaned against it and started to fall out. To keep from falling headfirst, I jumped, but he still thinks I tried to commit suicide."

Hog stepped close to Eddie and flashed him a toothy grin. "You rode your go-kart into the river. If you would have stayed home and tried to commit suicide, your go-kart wouldn't be in the river."

For a moment Eddie seemed astounded by Hog's reasoning, but shot back, "Oh yeah, it was better than doing nothing. And besides, that was freedom. While I was in the air, I didn't have to worry about anything but what I was doing."

Flick sat on the bridge beam, smiling. But when Eddie looked to him, he rubbed his chin with his hand and covered his smile. "I think you both lost your marbles."

"Yeah, Carmichael," Hog added. "You ain't playin' with a full deck."

Eddie looked to Hog and stiffened with resentment. "You're no flaming wit, either." He flared up angrily. "And don't call me, Carmichael."

Taunting him with laughter, Hog use his fake half-British accent, "Undoubtedly, Carmichael, my boy. That could be arranged."

Sluffing off Hog's agitation, Eddie leaned the bike against the railing and vaingloriously began strutting in a small circle. "Going into the river was nothing," he said. "Watch this." He stopped strutting, lifted the bicycle up, and placed the tires onto the skinny hand railing of the bridge.

"Big deal," Screwball said, his eyes slanting toward Eddie. "You're going to push your bike across the railing."

Eddie grabbed his skinny tie, swished it around his neck, and let it hang down the center of his back. "Just hold the bike," he sternly ordered. I'll ride across on the railing."

Hog gestured to the railing. "Go ahead, you goddamn nut."

Flick sprang up from the comfortable incline of the bridge beam and pointed to the river below. "Don't fall in there. The water's too shallow. If you get your head stuck in the mud, you'll die."

74

Eddie held his hand up, palm outward. "Don't worry. All I can do is get killed." He dropped his hand and looked to the bike. "Just hold this thing until I get on."

As if looking for intervention from above, Screwball looked up into the heavens, folded his hands, and bowed his head. "It's your funeral."

Flick and Screwball held the bike, and Eddie climbed on.

"Don't let go of him until he gets over the deep water," Flick said with concern. "If he falls in and drowns, the cops will have an excuse to close the bridge to swimming."

Eddie wiggled onto the seat, carefully placed his feet on the pedals, and with a determined expression on his face, he said, "Just push until I get going."

Screwball pushed him a few feet and let go. To everyone's surprise, Eddie not only pedaled across the railing, he kept his balance on the skinny steel rail, and reminded Breed of a circus clown but without the tiny umbrella in his hand.

Amazed, Screwball said, "I'll be damn."

Trying to create chaos, Hog grinned crookedly. "Looks like amateur day here in Shitsplat."

With an agitated look on his face Eddy rode the bike over the railing above the deep water, and yelled back at Hog, "You think it's amateur day. Watch this!" He lifted his hands from the handlebars. The front wheel cocked sideways. The bike fell off the rail. Eddie grabbed for the handlebars. He missed, but his fingertips nicked the bars. He swatted his arms, tried to grab the railing, and stay on the tilted bike, but like a drunken monkey, he tumbled. Screwball grabbed him by the arm but he was slipping. Flick reached over the rail and grabbed Eddie by the back of the pants. Eddie's pants wedged up his rear end, and his arms flailed in the air. The bike slipped from between his legs and fell into the water. Flick and Screwball pulled him up over the railing and dropped him onto the catwalk.

"Eddie Chicago, strikes again," Screwball said and dived in after the floating bike. He surfaced and caught it just before it went under. Then he towed it to shore, rolled it back up onto the bridge, and presented it to Eddie. "Bet-ya can't do that again."

Looking at the bike, Eddie squirmed uncomfortably. "I can't. That thing's just junk."

"I don't give a shit what it is," Screwball said and thrust the bike toward Eddie. "It's yours. Take it."

Eddie grabbed the bike and leaned on it. "If this was a good bike," he complained with an exaggerated whine, "I would have made it all the way across."

Screwball smiled right at Eddie. "If a frog had wings, he wouldn't bump his ass on the lily pad."

Eddie half smiled, laughed his whooping laugh, and kicked the bike out onto the road right into the path of an oncoming car. The driver of the car jammed on the brakes. The tires slipped on the fresh oil and skidded over the bike. The spokes bent and broke under the tire. The back tire of the car rolled onto the frame of the bike and pressed it into an obtuse angle. The rims squeaked and smashed into the rubber of the bicycle tires. Pop! Pop! The air blew out of both tires."

Hog looked to Eddie. "You didn't have to go public with your hysteria."

Screwball chimed in. "Do you practice that routine? You could take it on the road and make big bucks."

As Eddie looked at Hog in befuddlement, the driver of the car slowed to a crawl. Taking a hard drag on a cigarette, the driver looked back at the run-over bike. "You dumb ass kids better hope that piece of shit didn't give me a flat tire."

Walking beside the car, Hog gave the man an eloquent shrug, and using a heavily accented voice of a concierge at a five-star hotel, he said, "Kind, sir. If there's any damage, we'll be waiting at the airport in a limousine. Hand us the bill just as soon as you step out of the plane."

Still moving slowly, the man rolled his beleaguered eyes up toward the sky and shook an indigent finger at Hog. "What the hell's the matter with you?"

Bobbing his head like a happy simpleton, Screwball ran up to the window, and with immediacy in his voice, he yelled at the man, "Hey, Wait!"

The man jammed on the brakes. One screech of the tires and the car stopped. Talking with the cigarette dangling from his lips, the man growled. "What the hell do you want?"

Smiling, Screwball earnestly leaned toward the man. "Did you know that nobody smokes?"

Apparently wondering what Screwball was talking about, the man's forehead wrinkled with confusion. "What?"

Grinning, Screwball's face lit up with excitement. "The cigarette does the smoking. The person holding the cigarette just does the sucking."

With cigarette smoke encircling his face, the man hissed through his gap-toothed mouth. "You kids are nothing but a bunch of goddamn assholes."

After the man drove away, Breed glanced at the bike and turned to Eddie. "Now what are you going to do for a ride?"

"A ride? That's a cinch," yelped Eddie. "I can get a free ride anytime I want."

"If you can get a free ride outta here anytime you want," Breed said, "then why do you hang around Shitsplat?"

"I like Shitsplat," Eddie shot back with an exultant tone in his voice.

Breed was astounded. "How could anybody like Shitsplat?"

"Because Shitsplat's alive. I don't like the rotten people and the filth," Eddie went on, bent on completing his case, "I like Shitsplat because it's alive."

While Breed contemplated the notion of Shitsplat being alive, Eddie jammed his hands into his wet pockets. "I know where I can get a car."

Hog jumped off the railing. "You got money?"

With his shirttail hanging out, Eddie leaned back and displayed his usual nonchalant demeanor. "Not much, but I know a kid who's going out of town for a week. He won't mind if I borrow his car for a couple of days. It's an old car, but it's a free ride outta here." He smiled big. "You could call it freewheelin'. You guys want to come?"

Flick looked to Eddie. "You ain't going to steal that car, are you?"

"No way, man, nothing like that. The car's old. Only thing is, I have to wait until it gets dark, cause the kid's old man doesn't want him driving at night. The kid said I could take it, no problem."

Breed cocked his head with suspicion. "Free is the magic word, but how are we going to buy gas?"

"We'll get junk jobs, work for a few hours, collect the money, and quit."

Flick looked at Eddie in tortured wonder. "A lot of the mills are on strike. We can't make any money around here."

"That's right," Breed said without cracking a smile. "Those old mill guys scarfed up all the jobs. Even the rotten ones."

Eddie's mouth curled into a vehement sneer. "What are you guys afraid of?"

"We ain't afraid of nothin'," Flick snapped back. "We just ain't stupid enough to do the things you do."

"That's right," Hog chimed in. "Why don't you share the particulars of your *great* plan?"

"It *is* a great plan," Eddie retorted with an injured look. "All we can do is get killed, and I've seen enough death to know that being alive is a privilege. And we're all gonna lose it someday. So while I'm alive, I'm gonna get all the excitement I can."

"We would like to do that, too," Breed said and gave Eddie a hangdog, hopeless look. "But we still need money."

"What are you guys acting like a bunch of assholes in suits for?" Eddie's voice rose with excitement. "We don't need a job to go to where the next is."

Breed wanted to get out of Shitsplat, but he was suspicious of Eddie's motives. He had always thought Eddie was like a dog roaming around on a leash that was always getting into things, and was jerked back just before anything really bad happened to him. And he was a peculiar kid, with friends in many odd places. The fact that he would disappear for weeks and come back without a scratch, caused Breed to be interested. "What's the next?" he asked.

With a look of elegant amazement, Eddie didn't hesitate. "The next?" he questioned with excitement in his voice. "There's always something coming up *next*, something new, something cool, and we can be in on it."

"What are you talking about?" Breed wanted to know.

Eddie answered with a superior air. "The world's changing every day, and we're missing out on it."

Breed was skeptical. "I never see any great changes."

Eddie raised his hands to the width of his shoulders and jerked them into the air. "That's right!" He let his hands fall to his sides.

"Shitsplat's okay for a visit, but nothing changes here."

"Is that right?" Hog questioned. "Didn't you just say you like Shitsplat because it's alive?"

"Until my kart went into the river, "Eddie said, trying to look nonchalant, "it was alive."

While Hog gawked at Eddie in dazed amazement, across the river, deep inside the hollow sluice pipe the floodgate squealed open. Another sickening stain gushed into the river. Eddie shuddered at the sight. "I don't know about you guys, but I don't want to end up working in a stinkin' mill and gettin' drunk every night." His voice became sharp and ugly. "And then when I can't work no more, I won't even be able to tie my own shoes. I'll be pissin' myself, shufflin' around the streets with a cup beggin' for change." He stepped back and stared at Breed. "We gotta get out of this place, get out into the world. We gotta go where things are happening."

To let Eddie know he wasn't buying it, Breed defiantly thrust his jaw out. "Going with you could get us killed."

"So what? If we get killed, we'll die faster," Eddie echoed with joyful relief. Then we'll have less time to suffer around here."

Reliving the beating he had just been given, and the fact that if Flick hadn't stopped his mother, he might have gotten beaten to death, piqued Breed's interest. "That makes sense."

Screwball brushed a wisp of hair from his eyes. "Why do you think they call this place Shitsplat. It's just a splat of shit, everybody wants to stay away from. Everybody that stays here, stays the same."

Flick groaned. "Get with the program, you guys. It doesn't matter where we're going, we'll still need money."

"No problem," Eddie said, waving his hand around in the air. "I have enough money to get us on the road. You guys could come along, get a free ride out of here, then get a job at a farm baling hay." Eddie nodded in absolute certainty. "Make some really big money."

The idea of making big money made Breed's heart race. But going anywhere with Eddie could be dangerous, but then again, with a promise of big money, going with Eddie could be like jumping into a big unknown lake. It could be filled with old tires, sharp glass, or mill sludge, but then again, it could be clean, clear, and wonderful. "We were just talking about getting away from Shitsplat," he said. "What about this big money?"

"All we gotta do," Eddie said and went on excitedly, "is drive around the country and stop at farms. They always need somebody to bale hay or do farm work."

Flick's eyes sparkled with expectation. "We ain't got nothin' else planned."

"That's the spirit," Eddie said with a flourish of his hand and looked to Breed. "You comin'?"

With the vision of Eddie going into the river on the go-kart still fresh in his mind, Breed shook his head in confusion. "If that car's old, it might not take us very far. I'm not sure."

Eddie tapped his forehead with cryptic insight. "You might think I'm a fool for taking off in an old car, and that I'll end up cursing my luck on some deserted island, or with a knife in my back laying in some dirty alley, or a stomach full of lead. But I'll tell you one thing. If that day comes, I'll have lived it all. I'll have seen it all. I'll have tried it all." He took a step away from the bridge. "If you guys don't come with me, you'll miss a once in a lifetime opportunity."

Leaning toward Eddie, Hog let out a sigh. "What great bullshit opportunity are you trying to feed us?"

Eddie blew Hog off with a wave of his hand. "The opportunity for us to throw open a door and walk right in to a new and improved world."

Before Hog could reply with a smart-ass answer, Flick said, "I don't know. It sounds too easy."

As if he knew he were going to strike a nerve, Eddie shifted his eyes uneasily. "Don't you guys want to get away from this lunatic place and the *looks?*" As if it were the most ludicrous concoction imaginable, he dragged out the word *looks.*

Breed knew what Eddie was talking about. They all knew what he was talking about. *The looks!* The deadly mistrust! Shitsplat was a place for all forms of lunatics, whose looks on their faces said they didn't want Breed and his friends in their neighborhoods. Expectantly, they all looked to Eddie.

"Wadda you got to lose? Eddie pointed out. "It's a free ride. Are you guys coming or not?"

Hog turned and watched the sickening stain from the sluice pipe get sucked into the river current and gave a resigned shrug. "Balin' hay seems to have smatterings of a bucolic scene, and I'm usually not amenable, but anything would be better than this."

"I don't know what amenable or bucolic means, but this isn't exactly a tourist attraction," Screwball said, jerked his head, and looked away from the stain. "We could pool our money and maybe even have enough for decent clothes for school."

As if he didn't believe Screwball had said it, Eddie looked up toward the sky. "School?" He gave out a great whoop of laughter. "You won't have time to go to school, and once you're smart" — he pointed to his own chest — "just like me, you won't need no schoolin'. You'll be too busy making money."

Hog shook his head in amazement. "Modesty isn't one of your flaws."

Eddie ignored Hog's remark.

Breed liked the idea of living in a bucolic place, which he knew was a place of pleasant country life, but this was a big decision. He had never left home with an intention of never coming back. "I don't know if we should leave home."

Eddie's eyes glared with disapproval. "Home?" he questioned and strutted vaingloriously. "Our home will be anywhere in the world. You guys coming along for the free ride, or do you want to live with mommy and daddy the rest of your lives?"

"Hey, Breed," Flick said. "The side of your face is really getting black and blue."

Being reminded of the beating, his loss of movie money, and mailbox paint, caused Breed's beaten face to throb with pain. He looked to the sky. The sun was going down. "It'll be dark pretty soon," he said. "Let's go."

"Yeah," Hog agreed. "We ain't making no money here. When the cops change shifts and the new cops hear about Eddie, just for something to do, they'll chase us off the bridge."

"It gets cold at night," Eddie said. "Get your clothes and a jacket. I'll swing by my old man's house and change. By the time we get there, it'll be dark. But you guys will still have to watch for that kid's old man."

Breed and the others ran down the bank and jumped into their clothes. When Screwball looked at Hog's shoes, they had fishing string where the shoestrings should have been. He pointed to the shoes. "Hey, Hog, you going fishing?"

Hog knelt down on one knee, stopped tying his shoe, and looked up. "Yeah, Screwball, I'm going fishing all right. I'm going to see if I can catch you a brain."

Screwball's head bobbed with laughter. "Catch one for yourself, too." He ran up the cinder path, and Hog playfully chased him up onto the bridge.

Pretending to be struggling with the shoestrings on his new shoes, Breed stayed behind. He had changed his mind. He wasn't going anywhere crazy Eddie was going, but he didn't want the others to know. If he did, they would mock him until his dying days.

When Breed walked up onto the catwalk of the bridge, his friends were gone, and the sun was peeking over the horizon of a red sky, turning the water purple. The relaxing ambiance caused him to feel good about himself. As if out of nowhere, the kid with the wart on the side of his cheek that drove the pink Ford, walked onto the bridge and stood in front of Breed. As an ugly grin stretched across the kid's face, he shouted at Breed, "Hey, Blue Face, what are you doing here?"

Beed knew from the beginning of time, weaker people were displaced by stronger people, and he knew he couldn't beat the older, bigger kid. And being called Blue Face caused the pain in his face to throb. As he swiveled his head around in every direction looking for help, and not seeing any, every trace of his feel-good feeling vanished. He bucked up and hoped he could talk his way out of having to feel more pain.

"I'm sorry," he said, trying to appease the kid and avoid another beating.

The kid clenched both of his fists and spread his legs apart. "You thought your buddy pissin' on my head was funny." He nervously looked around. "Just get the hell off my bridge."

Squirming uncomfortably, Breed shrugged, hunched over like a whipped pup, and turned to go. "Okay, I was leaving anyway."

The kid punched Breed in the back so hard it caused him to stumble forward.

Watching Breed use the railing to catch his balance, the kid laughed with caustic laughter, but stopped long enough to say, "I should punch you right in that smart mouth of yours. But if I do, you won't be able to tell your buddy I'm gonna kick his ass for pissin' on my head."

Breed felt new pain, but he didn't look back. Trying to get away, he let loose of the railing and walked faster. Sounding like a threatening nightmare coming after him, the kid stood in one spot and clacked his steel cleated shoes on the bridge. Scared, Breed broke into a trot and then into a desperate run. The kid hammered his steel cleated shoes on the bridge again, and in victorious merriment, he laughed, louder.

A few shacks down from his shack, Breed stopped running. Above his head the streetlight twinkled in the twilight. As he breathed deep and walked toward the shack, a rotten feeling came over him. He had actually chickened out. He knew he should have done something to cut that kid down to size. That kid was stupid. A few well-placed words could have done more than any beating or fight. He could have made that kid feel embarrassed about his appearance. He could have pointed to that wart on his face and said something to make that kid feel inadequate. Something like, "Where did you get that third eye?" But he just didn't have the desire to physically or mentally deal with the kid. Now that it was too late to do anything, he felt ashamed. He didn't want to play the same old game anymore. And it caused him to decide to do something radical, something startling, something desperate, whatever it took. He was going to rise up out of this dismal place. He was getting a free ride out of Shitsplat. But it would be in an old car.

CHAPTER 5

When Breed reached for the handle on the back door of his parent's shack, the flies were gone from the screen. After he stepped into the dark kitchen, light from the next room illuminated a stack of dishes in the sink. They had been washed. The shack was quiet. He wished no one were home. Maybe they weren't. But that could change at any moment. It was a crazy place.

If he went with Eddie, it would be different. He could make some real money. It would be great to be like other kids, go to a new school, and wear new clothes. When rich kids made fun of him by guffawing and poking each other's ribs in unison with know-it-all winks, he wouldn't have to make excuses for his old worn clothes. He already had a pair of shoes that he didn't have to cover the holes in the bottoms by putting cardboard in them. With more money and more clothes, he wouldn't have to wear the same clothes day after day. He wouldn't have to pretend that he didn't care about having new clothes. He wouldn't have to lean indifferently against a wall and make those snappy comebacks. He wouldn't have to lie and say, "What do I have to wear good clothes for? It's only school. I don't want to be here anyway. I ain't dressin' up for a bunch of overeducated, whiny assholes trying to impress their friends and neighbors and teach me something I don't need to know."

Breed worried about Eddie sometimes being crazy, and for a moment, he was not absolutely sure he was going to go with Eddie, but he was giving

Breed a chance for a free ride away from a crazy shack and a shit hole of a town. Determined to go, he leaped up the stairs and grabbed his thin cotton jacket. Suddenly, a blinding rush of tears burned his eyes. His room seemed dearer than all the rest of the shack. He looked at his worn tennis shoes and decided he wouldn't need them. Until he could make enough money to buy another pair, he'd wear his new shoes. For a couple of days, he would just have to be careful not to scuff them up. But for some reason, it was hard to leave. His last look was magnified, transformed. With a swelling constriction in his throat, he whispered, "Good bye." At the head of the dark stairway he paused a moment and thought of changing into his old clothes, but when his stepfather yelled something unintelligible up the stairs, Breed figured he wouldn't have time to change. But it wouldn't matter. Better things would be coming his way. He would just buy new clothes. Before his stepfather or his mother could stop him, he threw his jacket on, and with bowed head, he slowly descended the stairs.

Just before he could step out the door, his stepfather grabbed him by the back of the neck, and roared, "Where the hell do you think you're going?"

Without warning, he grabbed Breed's long hair and bashed his head into the wall.

Luckily the rotten plaster and the front of his head took most of the impact. When his mother reared back to grab him, he dropped to his hands and knees. With his mother's and stepfather's hands grasping at empty air, pushing off both hands and feet, Breed sprang out the door.

Sprinting away in the semi-darkness, with his heart racing and his adrenaline running full tilt, the last thing he heard was his mother yelling, "Get back in this goddamn house."

After Breed joined Eddie and the rest of the crew, his heart slowed, and everything was going just fine. That was until they walked through a backyard, thick with white frost, and disturbed a brown dog on a long chain. Snarling and baring its sharp teeth, the vicious dog came charging at them. They took off running. With his heart racing again, Breed looked back over his shoulder. The dog charged to the end of its chain. The chain went taut. The dog flew sideways, landed on the paw-hammered ground, and gave out a painful yelp.

When they crossed the road at an intersection, Hog threw a rock at a streetlight.

He missed.

Screwball shut his eyes, turned his back to the light, and threw a rock up over his shoulder.

"Bulls Eye!"

The bulb arched blue, flashed white, one time, and went black. They ran down the road and snuck into a patch of woods a ways from the car. Once they were under the shielding trees, darkness deepened, but there was no white frost on the ground. Stepping onto a log, covered with dry leaves, Breed slipped and started to fall. On the way down, he caught the elbow of Eddie's outstretched arm, but still hit the ground.

"Ahh, man," Eddie whined, "you made me drop the keys."

Breed looked up. "I didn't see you. It's dark in here."

Shifting his eyes about uneasily, Flick whispered, "If you guys don't shut up, you'll wake up the whole neighborhood."

Breed picked himself up, dropped to a knee, and searching for the keys, he ran his hands through the dry leaves that covered the ground.

"We'll never find that key," Eddie said, his voice a shade hard.

Breed reluctantly lifted his hands from the leaves. "Does that mean the trip's off?"

"No way, man," Eddie said with a superior air. "I don't need a key to start any car."

Breed stood up, shook his head, and vowed to be more careful. In the silence, his mind wandered. He thought that anything had to be better than living in Shitsplat. At lunchtime in school, he never had the store-bought cakes and cookies, other kids had. He didn't even carry a lunch. The old question, "Do you ride the bus or carry your lunch?" didn't apply to him. He didn't have a lunch to carry, and he didn't have money to buy one. But that was about to change. If they made enough money, he might even go in with Flick or Screwball and share an apartment.

No wait. He argued with himself: Those guys are okay, but it would be better if I lived on my own money.

He didn't spend money like they did. He could have everything. No more surplus food. No more living on mill-filth-strewn land that wouldn't let anything grow but a few stinking weeds. Maybe he could find a place that had a little patch of land where he could make a garden. Eddie had said they could make a lot of money, and quick. Breed hoped he could earn enough money to get an old car and work on it until he was old enough to get a license. Maybe even sneak it out and drive it before he was. It would be better than making money just to have his parents take it.

CHAPTER 6

Under a sky filled with a dome of twinkling stars, Breed cat-footed through the darkness and tried to be as quiet as he could. But Hog and Screwball splashed each other with an occasional puddle that marred the path. After they quit splashing each other, Breed stopped at the base of a fat oak and leaned against its side. To magnify his night vision, he darted his eyes and created rapid eye movement. Attuning himself to the night noises, he peered into the cold dark. A slender maple branch waved in the breeze, letting a glimmer of light flicker on a 1950 red Mercury coupe. To Breed's surprise the Mercury didn't look old. Through the trees and beyond the Mercury, he could see the house. Except for a waving American flag on a stand, the house looked abandoned. But when a strong wind thundered among the house's three roofs, a powerfully built man with thick shoulders and huge arms, opened the door.

Alarmed, Breed pulled away from the oak, hunkered down onto his heels, and watched. The man flicked a spent cigarette into the dark. It flew into a rock, and orange sparks jumped like a tiny explosion.

After the man stepped back into the house and closed the door, Hog and Screwball sat on a stump. Screwball looked bored, and yawned to prove it, but his face betrayed his admiration for the Mercury.

Hog leaned back, cocked an ankle on his knee, and in his best British accent said, "Hey, Carmichael, old boy." Lifting his chin, he pointed to the red Mercury. "Is that transportation included on your itinerary?"

Irritated by Hog's pompousness, Eddie snapped back, "Don't call me, Carmichael."

"What? I didn't hear you," Hog shot back to agitate.

Eddie jerked a thumb at Hog. "What are you, deaf?"

"Eddie, old pal," Hog said. "I can assure you that my auditory faculties are excellent."

"With disgust in his voice, Eddie replied. "If you don't keep quiet and the kid's old man comes back out, the trip's off."

Hog snapped to attention. "Please forgive me, Edward." He gave Eddie a snappy hand salute. "Being quiet, sir!"

The expectation of riding away in the Mercury caused the adrenaline to rack Breed's body. When he shuffled away from the oak, leaves that covered the ground rustled. He stopped, stepped back, and leaned against the oak, and with an assurance he did not feel, he said, "We'll hear the kid's old man before we see him."

Shaking his head, Eddie crept toward the Mercury and muttered, "I hope I'm not with a pack of ninnies."

The others stood in the dark of the tall trees, waiting tensely and watching for the kid's father.

Although the brick house and the Mercury created an atmosphere of good taste, somewhere in the secret silence, fine smoky soot from a coal-fired furnace crawled up a chimney and swirled into the cold night air. Raw black specks of unburnt coal dust wafted around the night and funneled into Breed's nose. It stung the back of his throat and created an instant sore throat that the best drawn up hawkers in the world wouldn't clear. He didn't try to hawk the irritating mucus out of his throat. It would make too much noise. He swallowed the sickening snot. It didn't matter. He had done worse.

Crunching like bags of chopped ice had been strapped to the bottom of his shoes, Eddie tramped onto the limestone gravel next to the car. The night wind snuck up and tousled the treetops, causing the dark waving branches to look haunted.

Eddie paused, ran his long fingers through his hair, and opened the door of the Mercury. The dome light clicked on. He closed the door. The light went out. He motioned for Flick to come over.

Knowing what to do, Flick went to the door and waited. Eddie opened the door, again. The light went on, but this time Flick reached down and pushed the dome light button in and held it. The light went out. Inside the Mercury, while Eddie lay on the floor with his knife in his mouth and dug out wires from under the dashboard, his feet dangled over the rocker panel and scratched in the limestone gravel.

"Goddamn new wires," he cussed and pulled down a rope of braided wires. He cussed again, uncoiled three different colored wires, and stripped the rubber insulation from the ends and connected them into the correct starting sequence.

When his feet stopped moving, copper-orange sparks flashed like high speed Morse code signals, firing machine gun light into the darkness. Breed snapped his head sideways and stared at the flashes. The orange light stutters flashed the image of Eddie's face and caused his sun-cured features to project like the sputtering frames of a hand-cranked motion picture of an old-time movie.

The sparks quit.

The car started, but the starter stayed engaged.

Eddie pulled the starter wire from the other two wires. The starter stopped.

He had hot-wired the ignition.

When he pushed the accelerator, the glass packs of the dual exhaust roared like a wild animal. The engine slowed to an idle and purred with a throaty bellow. The AM radio lit up and blasted the voice of Dick Biondi, the famous disc jockey, broadcasting out of WLS in Chicago. Known as the Wild I-tralian because of his Italian accent, Biondi played the good records, and Breed liked him. The owner of the Mercury had left the volume control knob wide open. But this was no time to be blasting rock and roll music into the night air. If the kid's father heard it, and they didn't get away, and fast, huge fists could be pounding on their bodies, or they could be running from a blasting shotgun filled with buckshot.

Eddie scooted out from under the dash, but his knee hit the sharp gravel. He bumped into Flick and knocked him away from the light switch. The dome light in the car flickered on. Pain showed in Eddie's face, but escape and shutting off that loud blasting radio was more important than a scraped knee. He sprang behind the wheel, reached over, and snapped the radio knob to off. But the radio kept right on blaring. He reached under the dash and pulled the wire to the radio. It broke. The radio went off.

Walking toward the car, Hog pointed to Eddie. "Hey, Carmichael, you look like a one-legged man in an ass kicking contest."

With both hands busy, Eddie ignored Hog, used one hand to hold the twisted wires away from the metal dash and the other hand to wrestle the floor shift into gear. His feet pushed in the clutch and feathered the gas pedal. When he let loose of the bare copper wires, they hit the metal dash and sparked into the naked flesh of his hand and burnt his fingers.

He let go.

The wires quit sparking and dropped away from the dash.

In great haste, and with a jerk of his head, he motioned for Breed and the others to get in.

The wires sparked apart.

The engine backfired and began to die.

Eddie reached down, twisted the wires back together, and pumped the gas pedal.

The engine smoothed.

As if it were an evil sign, cool wind stirred Breed's hair, but he didn't care. He was getting out of Shitsplat. He bolted from the oak tree and ran toward the car. Flick reached for the door handle on the passenger side. His fingernails clawed at the smooth metal surface, and slid on the shining paint, sending out a toothache squeal. The handle wasn't there. It had been switched to the other side. It was called a suicide door. Flick laughed at his

98

temporary stupidity, reached across, and opened the door from the inside. Breed ducked under Flick's arm and dove into the back. He didn't know a lot about cars, but he knew a little bit about a 1950 Mercury.

The transmission was usually a three-speed manual. The engine, a V-eight, two hundred fifty-five cubic inch, with one hundred ten horsepower, could take the Mercury to a top speed of eighty-three miles an hour. But if the engine in this Mercury had been worked on, and the transmission had been changed to a four-speed, it could do well over one hundred miles an hour. Although the Mercury was old, it would take them anywhere they wanted.

As a final parting gesture, Breed turned toward the direction of Shitsplat, lifted his hand in farewell, and whispered, "Good riddance." Then he skidded across the red leather seat and scrambled to regain his upright position. As he stretched his neck until he could see out the front windshield, Screwball slid in beside him. Flick jumped in the front. Hog plopped in next to Screwball and Flick slammed the door. The wires came apart. The engine stalled.

"Maybe we're out of gas," Screwball said.

"We can't be," Eddie said and pointed to the dashboard." The gauge says full."

The wires sparked.

Flick bent down and twisted them together. They stopped sparking. The engine started but the starter whined.

Eddie jerked his finger toward the tangle of wires. "Take the red wire off. You'll burn up the starter."

Flick pulled the red wire out of the twisted connection. The starter stopped whining. The engine rumbled to life with a mean nasty growl. This was not the original one hundred ten horsepower engine. Deep inside, a racing cam opened valves that fed the high compression cylinders where secret gas and air mixtures exploded and pulsed vicious echoes out the two exhaust lake pipes that ran beneath the rocker panels. The engine beat in three-quarter time and reverberated with a mean, unmistakable boulevard rumble. This engine was tuned for racing. Eddie pushed the pedal. The engine roared loud and powerful.

"Take it easy," Flick warned. "This thing will wake up the whole world."

Eddie slacked off and gave the powerful engine as little gas as he dared. He let the clutch out, slowly. The tires spun in the loose gravel. With the engine panting hollow like a powerful pent-up dog under the insulation-free metal hood, Eddie eased the rumbling Mercury out onto the dark highway.

The bright flash of sparks from the ignition wires had night-blinded Breed. Blinking and watching over the seat, he knew it had blinded Eddie, too. Eddie was steering the car, but it was weaving on and off the side of the road, and the tires were kicking up gravel.

"Use the hood ornament as a guide," Breed suggested. "Line it up with the side of the road."

Eddie hunched forward and peered through the windshield. "There ain't no hood ornament." With quizzical disbelief, he blinked his eyes. "It's been shaved off."

"Yeah, customized," Screwball said.

"I don't care if it's shit-tom-sized," Flick said. "We can't see."

Eddie laughed his whooping laugh. "When Fast Eddie Chicago's at the wheel, you don't have to see."

Before the words were out of his mouth, the Mercury kicked up a long stretch of fine gravel at the edge of the road, slid sideways, and the rear quarter panel slapped something. Eddie wiggled the steering wheel. The Mercury bounced back onto the pavement.

Flick leaned his head close to the windshield. "Hey, Mister Chicago, why don't you turn on the lights?"

"Yeah," Breed jumped in, "you wanna run this thing into the river?"

"The radio probably woke up the kid's old man," Eddie said and ran his fingers through his hair. "I don't want him to see the lights going down the road." He paused and added, "Can you dig it?"

Screwball leaned back and muttered, "You have to have a shovel to dig it."

As Eddie moaned at Screwball's remark, the tires hit a pothole. Breed and the others were lifted out of their seats and back down.

Readjusting himself in the seat, Breed felt a cold draft run up his back. "What do you have to do, to turn that heater on?"

101

Eddie's eyes flashed in the rearview mirror. "It's on, man. It's on. Let her warm up."

A mile down the road, as Breed's eyes adjusted to the darkness, Eddie turned to him and shouted, "We're blowin' this pop stand." He switched on the headlights and pushed the pedal to the floor. The engine roared with radical force. The back tires screamed on the pavement and rolled in a blue band of smoke. For a brief second, the front of the car lifted into the air. As darkness soaked up the headlight beams, Breed could picture the front fenders and the chrome-teeth of the grill, looking like a windblown face rushing into the night and fire shooting out the chrome exhaust lake pipes.

The tires heated up and gripped the pavement. The Mercury dug in and launched on down the highway.

In a surge of excitement, Eddie banged his fists on the steering wheel. We're going to where things are happening. We're freewheelin', man. We're freewheelin'."

Hog leaned back in the seat and muttered, "So much for aberrant behavior."

While Eddie wondered what Hog was talking about, they passed stores with lighted windows then several dark houses and a gas station. When Breed looked out the back window, dimly lit by the chemical yellow of one lone street light, the reflection of the car appeared in a storefront window. Like vanishing blue embers, the frenched-in red taillights with blue-glowing dots faded and disappeared. Breed was on his way.

CHAPTER 7

When the Mercury crested a gentle rise in the road, Breed popped his elbow onto the back of the seat and stared at the back of Eddie's neck. It was wet with sweat. Like they were frozen to the steering wheel, his hands moved woodenly. At times, Eddie could be weird, and Breed didn't really know if he were just putting it on, or if he would really go off the deep end and turn into some kind of nut house thing. And there seemed to be an undercurrent of tension in the air. But Breed didn't care. He had to ask. "Hey, Eddie, where are we going?"

Eddie didn't answer. He only let out a deep throaty laugh.

As if he'd been sleeping upright and was only now recognizing his surroundings, Screwball sat up, leaned over the seat and stared at Eddie. "If you don't know where you're going, you'll end up someplace else."

Again, Eddie didn't answer.

Up ahead, little yellow eyes glowed. At the crook in the road, the headlights flashed into a weedy lot. A lone rat, as big as possum, blinked and ran into a sewage ditch.

Breed looked to Hog. Hog usually would jump at the chance to agitate someone who wouldn't answer, but he was sleeping. Breed gave up asking Eddie where they were going, leaned back in the seat, gloriously relaxed, and through the side window of the Mercury, he watched the black and white night sail past. Like flipping channels on a television screen, side streets and crossroads zipped past. Carley Street came and went. The Clark Street Bridge buzzed under the car's tires. The turn-off to the Orangeville Road and the sharp curve at the top of Myers Hill, flitted past in a gray night-maze.

When the Mercury slowed, a lone, yellow-bug light bulb sent warm light down on a white and blue sign hanging on the front of a clapboard grocery store. Dirty-white cases of empty, green Seven-Up bottles sat below a green and white tin sign nailed next to the door. As the Mercury churned past, Breed looked out the back window. The yellow light caused the blue and white sign to blur to green and yellow. Up ahead, an odor of Sulphur coming from a cloud of red smoke appeared. Then dimly-lit buildings, in various forms of dilapidation, paraded past. After the odor and cloud past, the black and white night returned. Breed was getting pretty far away from Shitsplat. But he still wanted to know where they were going. He nudged Screwball and whispered, "Ask Eddie where we're going."

Screwball leaned forward and talked over the back of the front seat. "Hey, Eddie, do you have to take a shit?"

A confused look appeared on Eddie's face. "What are you talking like that for?"

"You won't tell us where we're going, so I figured that you have to shit so bad that you can taste it, and you don't want to talk because it intensifies the taste."

"Intensifies?" Eddie questioned. "Pretty big word for a little kid." Looking like he had gotten something over on Screwball, Eddie smiled a satisfied smile. "I never tasted shit. You're the shit expert. What's it taste like?"

Screwball smiled big. "Shit."

Eddie giggled. "Oh yeah, how do you know what shit taste like?"

Screwball was amazed at how fast Eddie had sucked in to an old trick. "Shit tastes like your breath," he said and waited for some kind of a comeback.

Not having a comeback, Eddie shook his head in numb astonishment and said to no one in particular, "Who invited him?"

"You did," Screwball gloated and broke into a merry laugh.

Eddie's mouth curled into a vehement sneer. "I don't remember that."

Breed didn't know how far Screwball could push Eddie, but he figured the only thing Eddie could do was throw him out of the car, and being close enough to hitchhike back to Shitsplat, Screwball would only get out and make a joke of it. Eddie always acted like he knew everything. If Screwball kept it up, it would be a game of wits. Breed didn't want Screwball to get thrown out of the car, but if he did, it might be a good time for Breed to go with him. If he were going wherever Eddie was going, he wanted to know if Eddie had any wits about him.

Screwball smiled big and looked right into Eddie's eyes. "If you don't remember inviting me, then you probably don't remember when you were born."

105

"Nobody does," Eddie said with a hopeless look. "We're all too young to remember anything like that."

Screwball snapped his fingers. "I remember," he flashed a huge smile. "When you were born, your mother was constipated. The baby died and the shit lived."

Eddie's face grimaced with the pain of being outdone by a younger person. "If I have to stop this car, you're going to be constipated." He jerked his head around and stared at Screwball. "I'll kick your ass up, so high, you'll have to shit out your neck." He slowed the car, opened the door just a crack, and asked Screwball, "You want out now."

Breed leaned forward. "He's only messin' around, Eddie."

Hog opened his eyes. "Don't be a dip shit, Eddie. Quit gettin' excited about nothin'."

"You won't tell us where we're going," Screwball said to Eddie. "I just wanted to get you to talk."

"Yeah," Hog added. "Where in the hell *are* we going?"

As if he were enjoying the suspense, Eddie still didn't answer. He only laughed that hollow laugh.

So he wants to play the I-ain't-saying-anything game, Breed thought and gave up.

Screwball moved his thumb and finger like a mouth, and pointing to himself, he signaled that he would get Eddie to talk.

But Eddie saw what he was doing. "You're just a half-wit." He leaned forward, staring out at a dark stretch of road and the steadily rising glow of

106

the sprawling suburbs beyond. After the car motored around a steep bend and down a hill, a big blue bridge appeared in the dark. Because Eddie wouldn't say where he was going, Breed figured Eddie wasn't going anywhere. They would all probably be back home before the predawn chill of morning. He wondered if it would be warm on the Clark Street Bridge tomorrow. If it were, he could squeeze in one more swim.

The Mercury buzzed onto the blue bridge that resembled the blue bridge that crossed the Shenango river in Sharpsville. The scent of Sulfur from an unseen filthy foundry spewed into the open wing-window of the car. Breed held the front of his shirt over his mouth, but strong whiffs of Sulfur still stung his nostrils. As he fanned his hand in front of his face and held his breath, the Mercury carried them across the bridge and stopped at an intersection on the other side. A car pulled up to the opposite side of the intersection and stopped. Its headlights were on high beam, brightly flooding the inside of the Mercury.

Tooting the horn, shaking his fist, and squinting into the blinding headlights, Eddie yelled, "Quit shinin' that light in my eyes."

The car on the other side of the intersection didn't move. The light intensified. Eddie opened the door and jumped out. Waving his fist in the air, he yelled at the inconsiderate high-beam-blinding driver. "What are you? Crazy." Jerking and pointing his finger at the driver, he walked toward the car. "Turn your goddamn lights out."

Horrified, Breed let out a long moan. He figured Eddie would do something crazy. When he did, the guy would get out of the car and there would be a fight. If it lasted long enough, the cops would come. It would be the end of the ride. Eddie was the only one old enough to drive. The cops would take Breed and the others back to Shitsplat, maybe throw them in jail. If and when Breed's parents came and took him home, he would get the beating of his life.

The car's lights dimmed. Eddie stopped walking toward the car. The driver made a sharp right, and as if he were embarrassed and didn't want anyone to see who he was, he sped away.

Eddie jumped back behind the wheel and slammed the door. "Rotten bastards gotta sit there like some kind of retarded creep, shinin' light in my eyes and make me smell stinkin' mill shit." He shifted the Mercury into gear, tromped on the gas. As they sped away from the odor of the filthy foundry and the river it poisoned, Hog muttered, "Insanity, godamn insanity."

Breed sighed with relief and elation. He was still on his way out of Shitsplat.

After a few minutes of silence, Eddie loosened the frozen grip he had clamped around the steering wheel, leaned back, and relaxed in a new reality.

Breed glanced at Flick. He was sleeping. He always made things happen, and when he did, he took command of the situations. Breed figured it was about time for Flick to ask Eddie where they were going.

108

Strangely enough, Flick took a deep breath and opened his eyes. "Where are we going?"

As if he didn't know the answer, Eddie's hands fell dispiritedly at his sides. The car swerved toward the side of the road. Eddie popped his hands up, re-grabbed the steering wheel, and hooked his thumbs in the plastic cross spokes.

As if he had just woken up from a nightmare, Hog sat up with a horrified start. "Don't you know where you're going?"

Eddie wrapped his palm around the steering wheel and tapped his fingers against his thumb. "Don't get excited, Hog."

"I'm not excited," Hog lied. "You're the one that's driving."

Eddie's face clouded over. "To where?" he said and paused.

A possum's eyes glowed yellow alongside the dark road and blinked to black.

"Yeah, where are we going?" Flick wanted to know.

Eddie leaned over and fumbled with the chrome radio knobs.

"Hey dip shit," Hog said. "You pulled the wire to the radio off."

Still leaning over, Eddie jerked his hand away from the knobs. "Oh, I forgot."

As he leaned, he pulled the steering wheel to the left. The tires screeched over the centerline. He leaned back behind the steering wheel. "It doesn't have to be anywhere," he said as if nothing had happened. Then he adjusted the car back to center and combed the side of his blond hair back with his fingers. In the glow of the dashboard's instrument lights, a sunshine smile spread across his face. Like a man who had just raised his heartbeat and stepped out of the swimming pool, he looked to Flick. "Hell, man, we can just ride around and be free. Now we're equal with the whole world. They don't have a single thing over on us."

"Come on, Eddie," Hog said and lurched forward. "Your hypothetical suggestion may have some merit, but quit fartin' around. Tell us where these great hay balin' jobs are."

Screwball nudged Breed in the ribs. "Yeah, Eddie, if you want to fart around, get a whoopee cushion. That way you won't stink us out of the car."

"Don't start being a half-wit," Eddie snapped back. "We can go anywhere. That's what counts. We don't have to be snotty-nosed kids and do what everybody wants us to do."

Waiting for Flick to reply, Screwball watched Flick stare out the front windshield. He appeared to be looking into the future. As white strips of lines zinged under the car like fat arrows, he said, "Hey, that's right. We don't have to take their high flatulent bullshit anymore."

"Yeah, man, dig it," Eddie said with confidence in his voice. "Now we can go wherever we want and under our own power." Like a cowboy about to lasso a pony, he waved his fist in the air. "Yeah, man, we'll be one of the few guys in this great country who can do that. We'll be freewheelin'."

110

"We'll be freewheelin', all right," Flick agreed. "No more hitchhiking and walking backwards for miles."

Screwball reached up and messed up his hair. Then he shook his head until his hair puffed out like a shaggy buffalo. With his eyes crossed, he looked right at Flick. "What? You mean, you don't like begging some rich guy for a ride?"

"You're crazy," Flick said and turned away from Screwball's antics.

Eddie reached up and rubbed the side of his head. "Ain't this country great!"

"It's great all right," Hog agreed, "but you gotta be crazy to live in it."

With his arms crossed, Breed leaned his back against the seat. "It's supposed to be the land of opportunity, but I ain't seen any, yet."

"We'll get some of that opportunity," Flick said. "There won't be any more of that standing around waiting to get old enough to go into the stinking mill and turn into some kind of a stinkin' mill rat wishing our lives away."

"We're not measly kids anymore," Eddie said. "We don't need anybody." As if it were a pet dog, he tapped the dashboard. "We got our own ride."

"We might have a ride," Breed said. "But where are we going?"

Eddie made a sweeping gesture to indicate the vastness of the night. "We're going to some magic city"

"What do you mean, magic city?"

Eddie hesitated and a far-off expression, like someone about to have an epileptic seizure, filled his face. "A place where we'll live glamorous lives," he said dreamily as if he were a thousand miles away. "We'll go into terrific restaurants that have blond wood, shiny brass, and frosted glass that has expensive patterns on it. We'll feast on baked quail with chanterelles on a bed of sweet potato and a ruff of braised dandelions. Beautiful girls will scamper back and forth and attend to out every want and need." He cocked his head to the side. "But before we get there, we're going to bale hay." He jerked his hand into the air. "But it doesn't matter where we're going. We're going. Ain't that all that matters?"

"Amen," Flick agreed.

"Yeah," Screwball said. "But we didn't mean for you to spend an hour out of your life telling us about it. And what are chanterelles?"

"It's something rich people eat. It's just a fancy name for wild mushrooms."

Breed shivered. "I just want to know if we're going someplace warm. Turn up the heat."

"Screwball snapped his fingers in a steady rhythm. "Get the heat," he said, and as if it were a bass drum, he pounded his foot on the floor. "Turn," — thump! — "up," — thump! — "the," — thump! — "heat," — thump! — thump!

Breed looked into the rearview mirror. Eddie's smiling face appeared, but suddenly car headlights cut through the back window and blinked into the mirror. The reflected bright light flashed into Screwball's eyes. He stopped pounding his foot.

Eddie turned his head and talked over the seat. "That might be a cop. I wasn't going to tell you right off the jump, but we stole this car."

That wasn't something Breed wanted to hear. "What?"

CHAPTER 8

Slouching in the back of the stolen Mercury, Breed resented being steered like this, and it cause a rotten feeling to evaded his chest. He wondered why he had believed Eddie was only borrowing the car. As Eddie held to the right lane and allowed a few cars to pass and gawk at the shining red Mercury, Breed hoped the Mercury's great looks wouldn't attract the cops. If it did, his hopes for a better life would be blasted to smithereens. He still wanted to get away from Shitsplat, but he didn't want to be running from the police.

Up front, Eddie put both hands on the steering wheel. As a serious look filled his face, he looked ahead and spoke. "I've always had visions of racing across the country in a stolen car. I never wanted to care about the past or the future. All I wanted to do was chase a red sky and a setting sun." With a wild, reckless light flaring from his eyes, he grinned big. "Yeah, man, we stole our ticket. Now we're takin' a ride. Ain't it cool?"

Screwball's mouth spread into a sly grin. "It's not like anybody's gonna notice a nineteen fifty, shiny, red Mercury thunderin' down the road."

"Yeah," Hog added sarcastically, "It ain't any different from any car the police are looking for."

"That's right," Eddie said as if he believed it. Then in a show of malicious defiance, he tramped down on the accelerator. The Mercury fishtailed around a curve, picked up speed, and bottomed out on a hump in the road. A trail of sparks flew across the pavement sending a fluttering light into the black night. Watching the sparks, Breed figured the owner had put magnesium steel under the car.

He remembered knocking the key out of Eddie's hand just before he had hot-wired the car. Hoping Eddie was lying, he asked, "If we stole it, then how did you get that key?"

Eddie slowed the Mercury and smiled. "I never had a key. I was going to make up some kind of bullshit story about losing it, but I didn't have to. It was just luck when you bumped into me in the dark. All I had to do was say that you knocked the key out of my hand."

Breed felt a wave of intense dislike for Eddie. "You should've told us you were going to steal this car."

"Don't worry about it, Eddie replied. "When you bumped into me..." He grinned like a fool. "I knew our good luck was just starting. Since then, it's been with us."

Hog flashed Eddie a slight smile. "I think when you bumped into Breed, you knocked yourself goofy."

"Goofy or not," Breed said, "what if we get caught?"

"Wadda you mean?" Eddie exploded. Looking like some grim-faced wild man, he took one hand off the steering wheel and waved it in the air. "Why hell, even if the police catch us, you guys are so damn ugly and miserable lookin', they'll feel sorry for you." He dropped his hand and the Mercury slowed even more. "They'll let you go before you scare people and cause them to have heart attacks."

115

Screwball grinned at Eddie. "Thanks for the kind words. It's nice to know somebody cares."

The car behind them pulled up close. Eddie turned to the front. "Every time you try to do the speed limit," he said and tramped down on the accelerator, "some asshole has to get on your ass."

With the tires squealing and burning rubber, the Mercury lunged forward and sent them on a wild flash of speed.

The car's sudden performance was new to Breed. The quick force was so strong that it jerked his head back and pulled Eddie's relaxed hands away from the steering wheel. Smoke and the smell of burnt rubber filled the car. Breed's head jammed against the seat. It felt like the blood was being forced to the back of his brain, and it caused the thought of not liking Eddie to be put on hold. Now Breed wondered if he would live through the night, and he became afraid.

Eddie regained his grip on the wheel and adjusted his seating position. "Goddamn! This little son-of-a-bitch moves!" As if he had to make and agonizing decision, he gnashed his teeth and shook an indignant finger at the dashboard. "Man! Oh man! Slow down baby," he warned the Mercury and let off the gas. The speeding engine smoothed to a peaceful purr, and the Mercury slowed to cruising speed. Behind them, the road was dark again, and the car wasn't following.

Flick sat back and rested his head against the seat. "Looks like that wasn't the cops."

Breed had just felt the awesome power of the stolen car, and he was no longer afraid. Eddie has

116

shown that he could handle it with ease. There was no mechanical separation between man and machine. They had become one smooth working unit. Eddie drove like he was born with the car attached to his body and could step in and out of it and reclaim limitless control at any time.

On the surface Breed thought Eddie was okay, but deep inside where it really counted, he didn't know if Eddie was good or bad. Maybe he was a mixture of both. Some things taken at full strength taste bad, but if they're watered down, it's okay and even sometimes enjoyable.

At least Eddie wasn't talking about committing suicide. But that could have been Screwball's and Hog's fault for causing the crowning moment when Eddie was mad because his father made him do work when he wanted to do something else. Eddie had latched onto a metric wrench Screwball had slipped into Eddie's pile of wrenches, and he had tried to use it. Eddie said he might as well hang himself than work with a goddamn metric wrench. Screwball told him he couldn't hang himself because they only made metric-sized ropes, and they wouldn't work on his standard-sized skinny neck.

Eddie didn't like to be wrong or made fun of, and that day he had laughed his whooping laugh, and he would have beat up anyone else for such a remark, but he didn't punch Screwball. Breed figured it was because Screwball was always good for a few laughs. If Hog had said it, Eddie would have probably hit Hog, and it would have ended up in a knock down dragged out fight. But at that time,

117

a fagot who called himself Jonathan, just happened to be walking down the sidewalk. Eddie ran right to him, laughed that helpless hollow laugh, and like it was an everyday thing and for no reason, he poked Jonathan right in the mouth. As a bewildered Jonathan held his bleeding mouth, Eddie walked nonchalantly back into the yard, shrugged, and said to Screwball, "That fagot needed all the fun he could get."

In a way, Breed was glad Eddie had punched Jonathan. Jonathan was nice to a person's face, but when they turned their backs, he would imitate that he was having sex with the person, by humping his hips. There were other people in Shitsplat that were just like Jonathan. Their friendliness was phony.

Breed didn't care if Eddie went wacky and punched those kinds of people right in their lying mouths. But if Breed thought too much about those kinds of people, he would feel ill will toward other people and maybe hate them. Forgetting about them always made him feel better. And now because he was out of Shitsplat, he wouldn't have to think about those kinds of people anymore. Even that flats gang kid with the wart on his face and pissed on head could wait on the Clark Street Bridge forever. Breed wasn't going to be there. He wasn't going to be picked on anymore. He was going away from it all. He was going away from Shitsplat. As long as Eddie didn't go completely crazy, he'd never have to go back.

Up ahead, above a closed gas station, a lone light burned. Next to a whitewashed cinder block

118

wall, a shiny, chrome pop machine shaped like a box, set on a cement sidewalk.

Flick stuck his arm out the opened window and pointed. "Hey, let's stop and get a pop."

Eddie grabbed the floor shift, leaned forward, and downshifted. "You just read my mind. With all the crap I had to go through, I haven't eaten since yesterday." He let out the clutch. In protest, the engine wound down to a smooth purr that echoed out the lake pipes and created that familiar boulevard rumble. And the red Mercury slowed. Eddie pulled the two ignition wires apart. The motor moaned to a peaceful halt and the car silently coasted onto the station tarmac. With the headlights shining on the pop machine, the Mercury's tires grumbled over loose gravel and munched to a stop.

Eddie switched the car lights off. Doors flew open and thirsty kids bounced out. Flick tried to open the metal lid of the top-loading machine, but it was locked. "Hey, Hog, can you pick this lock?"

Hog fingered the lock and looked at the keyway. "No problem, I'll get my pick." He walked back to the car and lifted the lid on the toolbox in the back of the Mercury. Then he rattled around until he clanked a tire iron out of a pile of wrenches. Waving the tire iron in the air and walking to the machine, he said. "I got it."

He lifted the tire iron and whapped the lock on its edge.

It flew open.

Flick looked down at the broken lock. "Locksmith my ass."

119

Hog threw the tire iron on the sidewalk next to Breed's new shoes and yelled, "Snake!"

Breed jumped back.

The tire iron clanged once and fell silent.

"That lock ain't worth pickin'," Hog said. "It's just junk."

Eddie opened the lid and looked in. His eyes sparkled with anticipation. "Drinks on the house."

They all looked in. The bottles of assorted flavors of pop were imprisoned under rows of two-inch-wide, flat-metal bars that prevented the bottles from being pulled out.

Screwball placed his hands on the caps of the imprisoned bottles of pop and sneered. "Not drinks on the house, drinks in the machine," he said. "You still have to pay to get one out."

The necks of the full bottles stuck up only far enough to be held by the capped necks and moved. Once a bottle was selected, it would have to be guided through a maze of bars. If other bottles of a different flavor were blocking the pathway, they had to be shuffled around and moved until the chosen bottle was finally moved into the one slot that would allow it to be pulled through a release mechanism where money had to be slipped into the coin box slot to free the bottle.

"I'll wiggle one out," Flick said and shuffled the bottles around the metal maze until he had a bottle of cherry pop in the mechanism. It was ready to be pulled out. Although Flick pulled and changed bottle angles, the bottle wouldn't come out.

"Eddie reached over Flick's arm and dropped a coin in the coin box. Flick tugged on the bottle.

The release mechanism didn't move. "It ain't workin'."

"Let me try." Eddie scrambled the bottles around and got a bottle of Coke in the slot. He dropped another coin in the coin box and pulled. The release mechanism moved slightly and then locked up solid.

"Ahh, man!" Flick moaned. "It looks like we ain't gettin' any. This thing's broke."

Eddie looked at the caps of the bottles sticking up in rows. "Damn, those look good. We can touch them, but we can't pull them out."

"Yeah," Flick said. "We got openers on our knives but we don't have any straws. If we did, we could clean this thing out."

Hog looked at the Mercury. "Wait! Maybe we don't need straws." He picked up the tire iron.

"Ahh, man, that won't work," Eddie said.

Hog backed off, stepped onto the cement sidewalk, threw the tire iron on the ground, and placed his hands on his hips. "Okay, Mister Einstein, see if you can figure out how to get a bottle of pop out of the machine." He crossed his arms and leaned against the white cinder block wall of the gas station.

"Hey, Hog," Flick said. "See if you can pick the lock on the change box."

Hog bent over and tried to insert a piece of wire into the tumblers. He put the wire in his pocket and looked up. "Not this time, gentleman. Some asshole jammed gum in the keyhole. The tumblers won't move."

Eddie worked the bottle of Coke to the corner of the machine. It could almost be pulled out. There was just a small bit of the steel bar stopping it.

He looked at Hog. "I want that Coke." He held his hand out. "Hand me that tire iron."

With an I-told-you-so attitude, Hog picked up the tire iron and offered it to Eddie. Eddie snarled, grabbed it, and jammed it between the wall of the box and the restraining bar. "This will work," he said, and with both hands, he pulled. The bar didn't move. He re-gripped and braced his knee on the side of the machine. Breathing hard with his face flushing red, he pulled again. The steel bar didn't move. He put his foot down on the dirty-white gravel and looked up. "Let's all pull on this thing." With his knee bent, he planted his foot against the side of the pop box.

Breed and the others reached across the box, knotted their hands on the end of the tire iron, and pulled.

The strong steel didn't budge.

Eddie put his foot down and exhaled. "What in the hell is this thing made of?"

"Must be alloy," Breed said. "That stuff won't bend like regular steel. You can't even cut it with a hacksaw. It rips the teeth right out of the blade."

Hog took a step toward the car. "There's a rope in the toolbox."

"So... what are we going to do?" Screwball asked and leaned back against the box. "Tie it on the back bumper and pull it down the road like a trailer?"

Breed jerked his head toward the car. Before he could say anything, Hog started toward the car. "I'll get it."

Hog came back with the rope, and as Screwball watched him hand it to Breed, he questioned, "Now what?"

"You'll see," Breed said, and looked up at the horizontal light fixture attached to a pipe that was attached to the side of the gas station wall. "Okay, Hog, throw the rope over that pipe."

Hog threw the rope over the pipe and caught the end.

"Give me that end," Breed said and snaked the end of the rope around the stubborn bar in the pop box. He pulled the rope into a continuous loop that ran from the pipe and around the bar in the box and tied it in a knot. Holding the rope, he held out his hand. "Give me that tire iron."

Hog handed him the iron.

As Breed placed the tire iron between the rope and twisted it, Screwball put his finger to his lips. "Shhh, genius at work."

Like a rubber band on a wind-up model airplane, Breed twisted the rope. It grew taut. He stopped twisting, took a breath, and turned his head toward the others. "Help me turn this thing."

Hog and Flick reached up. Together they turned the tire iron.

As Eddie and Screwball watched what was happening in the box, "Eddie shook his head. "It ain't movin'."

The rope stretched tight. The tire iron gouged into Breed's hands. "It won't go any more," he whined. "Let's get outta here before the cops come."

Eddie reached in and grabbed the tire iron. "Damn it," he said. "I'll show you guys how to twist that thing."

Now three people were cranking on the tire iron. The rope twisted, more and more.

Screwball looked up from looking into the box, and like a traffic cop, he held up his hand. "Stop! It's bent enough."

"Not enough for me," Eddie said. "Two more turns., and we'll teach this machine to try and cheat us."

As they twisted the rope, Screwball looked up at the light fixture. "Quit! The pole's coming off the wall."

"Don't be afraid of a little light," Eddie said and grunted. "One more twist."

Under the strain, the machine began to buckle. Being that it was a rectangular chrome box, about three feet wide, four-feet-long, and three feet high, the rope should have easily lifted it off the ground. But the machine wasn't going to move. It had been bolted to the concrete.

The rope twanged. Screwball backed up. "Quit!"

Eddie made a winding motion with his free hand. "Wind it."

"Wind it, my ass," Flick said. "Get out of the way."

The rope went slack. Breed, Hog, and Flick let go of the tire iron and jumped away. Eddie didn't move. Holding the tire iron in his hand, he stood next to the pop box. The rope dropped down and coiled around him. The light went out. In a shower of flickering orange sparks, the steel pole and the light fixture came sailing down. The pole whooshed past Eddie's head and crashed right next to the box.

Now it was dark.

Flick ran to the car and pulled the headlight switch. The strong beams spotlighted Eddie. As if it were no big deal, Eddie stood there with the tire iron in his hand and the rope coiled around his body. Nodding and smiling, he said, "It might be twisted enough now." He dropped the tire iron, reached into the box, pulled out a bottle of Coke and opened it on the opener on the side of the box. Then in a toasting gesture, he lifted the Coke in the air. "The bar's open."

Hog went to the pop box, shuffled full bottles out of the maze, and passed them around. When everyone had arms full of the colorful bottled beverages, they carried them to the car and set them on the floor.

Pouring another bottle of Coke down his throat, Eddie pointed to the tire iron. "Hey, Hog, you want your key back?"

Hog nodded. "I better get it. Never know when we'll need to pick another lock."

Eddie walked to the tire iron, picked it up, and handed it to Screwball. "Put this back in the trunk. I'll get the rest of the Coke."

With the tire iron in the crook of his arm, Screwball picked up the rope, opened the trunk, and dropped the tire iron and rope in. The tire iron landed on a pair of greasy coveralls. To keep his hand from getting greasy, he lifted them up with two fingers. "Hey, Breed!"

Breed turned toward Screwball.

Making a sound like a sheep, Screwball said," Baa-baa! If you're still cold, put these on."

Thinking about how he would be like a member of a herd of sheep if he worked in a mill, Breed looked at the dirty coveralls. "No way! I ain't putting those stinkin' mill-worker things on."

Screwball pointed below the coveralls. Steeled-toed clodhopper work shoes with grease-soaked leather sat on the floor. He jerked his head in an animated giggle, and using one hand, he lifted the shoes up. "Baas-baa! Breed.

Breed looked toward Screwball.

Like a traveling salesman who had just pulled something out of his sack, Screwball lifted his other hand and pointed to the shoes. "How about those shoes?" he questioned. "They'll keep your little feeties warm."

To Breed, the shoes stood out like a warning. If he went to work in the steel mill, they would be the kind of mill worker shoes he would have to wear. To him they were like a prisoner's ball and chain. "How about nothin'," he said without cracking a smile. "I ain't puttin' those stinkin' things on, either."

Baa-baaing, Screwball dropped the shoes back into the trunk, paused, then reached back in and snatched up a semi-dirty baseball cap. Making a goofy face, he turned the bill on the cap sideways, quit baa-baaing, and set it on his head. "Look I'm a Little Leaguer."

Hog came back with his arms full of bottles of Coke. "Quit screwin' around. Close that trunk and Little League your ass over here and grab these."

Still wearing the baseball cap with the bill turned sideways, Screwball took the bottles of Coke and placed them on the floor of the trunk.

Breed closed the trunk, walked around the back fender, opened the door, and jumped into the back seat. Screwball looked at him with that cap placed sideways on his head and the bill hooding his right ear. The others jumped in the front seat. Eddie opened the bottle opener on his knife and passed it around. Bottles of Coke hissed open. Like some kind of a pointing clown dog, Screwball crossed his eyes and continued to stare at Breed.

Breed didn't care how stupid Screwball looked with the baseball cap setting sideways on his head, he still hated baseball caps. Caps were for the rich kids whose parents gave them money to buy expensive baseball gloves, so they could play on the Little League teams. And then they gave them more money to buy candy at the snack stands. Breed never had money for a baseball glove, and he never bought anything at a snack stand. If he had money, he would have played baseball. Half of the rich kids couldn't run around the bases without falling down. Breed just knew he would have been better baseball player than those candy ass kids, and he was angry that he could never play.

He looked at the pop box. "Hey, Flick, maybe the reason that machine doesn't work is because the coin box if jammed full of money."

Flick jumped out of the car and kicked at the coin box.

Headlights flashed down the road.

"That might be the cops." Eddie warned, reached down, grabbed the three wires to start the engine, and held them.

Hog held the door open, and with his arm rolling, he motioned to Flick. "We gotta go! Get your ass in here."

Screwball leaned over and stuck his head around the doorpost. "Close the lid on that pop machine, so they don't know we were here."

"Yeah, close it, and be a dumb shit," Hog said sarcastically. "They won't see the busted light pole layin' on the ground."

With a look of amazement, Eddie looked to Screwball. "You guys are actually crazy."

Flick kicked the coin box, one more time. It didn't budge. He looked toward the oncoming lights, slammed the lid down, and jumped in the Mercury. Eddie twisted the wires together. The engine ignited and roared to life. As the Mercury raced away from the pop box, Breed and Flick threw empty Coke bottles out the window and tilted freshly opened bottles of cherry pop to their lips.

The wires sparked and fell apart.

The engine stalled.

But the Mercury kept right on heading down the road.

128

Eddie bent over and twisted the wires back together.

The engine fired back up. Before Eddie could sit back up, the Mercury left the edge of the road. Its tires chattered violently over the roots of a fallen tree. Bouncing behind the wheel, Eddie steered back onto the road. The Mercury squealed through a sharp right turn, and after it raced through an intersection that was lit by one dull streetlight, it thundered into the night.

The heater still wasn't working, so Breed stuck his head over the front seat and searched for warmth. "Is that heater on?"

"It must be," Eddie said. "I ain't cold.

Screwball took the baseball cap off his head and offered it to Breed. "You want this cap to keep your little heady warm?"

"I ain't wearin' that fagot hat, and I don't feel no heat."

"Ah, Breed, quit your bitchin'," Screwball said and put the cap back on his head and turned it backwards. "The sun will be up soon and you'll have all the heat you want."

Breed sat back in the seat and thought about the situation he had gotten into. He was stuck in a stolen car with a broken heater on a cold night, and he was holding a cold bottle of pop. If that weren't bad enough, Screwball was trying to get him to wear a stupid baseball cap he hated.

Many bottles of pop later and miles down the road, Eddie turned left at a brightly illuminated billboard covered by a ragged picture of a 1957 Chevy parked on a paved highway next to a lake surrounded by pine-tree-covered mountains in front of an orange sky. Printed across the top, black dirty letters seemed to be speckled with white pigeon crap.

Breed figured that not enough traffic warranted the billboard's upkeep and it had been left to rot.

A ways from the billboard, Eddie stopped the Mercury at the top of a freshly blacktopped hill and opened the door.

Trying to keep warm, Breed sat in the backseat hunched over and listening. Under the hood, like a healthy animal, the big engine rumbled with raw power. In measured thumps, fire breathing exhaust exploded, then blasted into manifolds and raced into tuned, glass-packed, hollow metal chambers, where its resonance was enhanced into a rich low bass musical tone that was piped out the dual-exhaust, chrome lake-pipes, where it throbbed with a mellow beat and created a phenomenon comparable to a good rock and roll song.

Eddie opened the door and jumped out. "Piss race!"

"It's about time," Flick said. "My back teeth are hollerin' for a life preserver."

"Piss race?" Questioned Hog. Why we would have to be out of our minds to do such a childish thing like concentrate our energies on having such a thing as a urinating contest." He smiled. "However, on the other hand, if I don't enter, I can't win. When do we start?"

"I can't wait," Flick said. "Start right, Now!"

They jumped out and lined up, five abreast. They all unzipped their flies and waited for the signal.

"All right you guys," Flick said. "Whose ever piss goes the furthest downhill is the winner."

"On three," Eddie said. "Three!"

Five pent up streams of high-pressure piss arced high and came down on the smooth pavement. As they urinated and the urine flowed down the hill, Screwball began singing, "Yellow River," over and over.

With the headlights of the Mercury illuminating the strange night race, Breed and his friends cheered, and Screwball kept on singing, "Yellow River." It was a close race. Flick's and Eddie's urine battled for the lead. Breed was out of the running. Screwball dropped out, quit singing, and went somewhere into the dark. Eddie flowed into the lead. Flick zipped his pants up and coaxed his stream on. He motioned with his hands and cheered. "Come on, baby, come on. You can do it!"

Eddie's lead piddled out and Flick's stream could not be caught.

"And the winner is!" Eddie said and stopped talking and walked around in a circle, bent at the waist and his head up. With his butt sticking out, he wobbled his head from side to side like it was on a weak steel spring. After that, he stood erect and raised Flick's hand triumphantly into the air. "King Yellow River Racer!"

Flick lowered his hand, turned his palm up, and expectantly asked, "What did I win?"

Eddie looked around like a mother cat looking for a lost kitten. He searched his pockets for something to give Flick. He couldn't find anything. He stopped searching and turned toward the car. The headlights threw a wide strip of light on him. As if he were on a stage, he used light as a spotlight. "You," he said and pointed to Flick, "the coolest piss racer in the land, take a bow."

Flick bowed deep. "Thank you, thank you, ladies and gentlemen."

Holding his hand as if he had a microphone in it, Eddie waved it in an arc. "In the midst of all the magnificence of the Yellow River, you have just won a free turn at the wheel of this amazing chariot." He looked toward the Mercury and graciously signaled with his outstretched hands. "Your chariot awaits."

Trying to be funny, Breed held up one finger. "Was there a second or third place winner?"

"We're all winners," Eddie proclaimed. "For those of you who piddled out, you get a free ride"

Flick quit bowing, walked to the Mercury, and placed his foot on the rocker panel. He tied his shoe and bounced his foot on the frame. "That sounds like a good prize, but I don't have a license."

Eddie laughed. "What makes you think I got one? And besides, what's the difference. If we get caught, we'll be trundled off to jail for stealing the car. That license thing don't mean nothin'."

Flick smiled in agreement and stepped toward the driver's side of the car. "Hop in, you guys. I'm gonna see if this baby will fly."

Breed looked into the dark. Screwball walked out of a field carrying a head of cabbage under his arm. Breed pointed to it. "You ain't gonna eat that are you?"

"I didn't steal it for nothin'," Screwball said with a strand of grass clenched between his teeth and slipped it into the car.

Hog slammed the door and looked toward Flick. "I'd advise any interested party that you have never driven before."

"Yeah, I did," Flick said. "When I had to work on my old man's Buick, I drove it up and down the driveway." He placed his hand on the door and paused. "But I never drove on a main road."

"So what?" Eddie snapped back. "It doesn't matter. It's just like anything else. If you want to do something, don't sit around worrying about it. Just get off your ass and do it!"

Like a kid with a new toy, Flick sat behind the big red steering wheel and ran his fingers around it. Then he reached down, grabbed the shiny black shifting knob, and pulled the floor-shift lever into low gear. He revved the engine and let out the clutch. The Mercury didn't do the usual stuttering and bucking most cars do when an inexperienced driver gets behind the wheel of a car without an automatic transmission. The powerful engine would have none of it.

It roared.

The tires spun.

The car gracefully rolled ahead and took off down the road.

Flick caught on quick. It was a very good mechanically constructed car. The motor purred and the transmission shifted smooth and true. With no grinding of gears or burning of the clutch, the Mercury motored down the dark road like Flick had been driving it all his life.

A mile later, Flick stopped at an intersection, whipped around, and looked at Eddie. "Which way should we go?"

Eddie lifted his arm and pointed. His straight finger touched the windshield. "Right there," he said and jerked his finger to the road ahead."

As the Mercury pulled away from the intersection, a soft red glimmer of light caught the corner of Breed's eye. When he turned and looked out the back window, Screwball stuck his head over the front seat and talked in a high-pitched cartoon voice. "Just follow the yellow—"

Breed cut him off. "The cops are right behind us."

"They must have had some kind of an alarm at the station," Flick said.

"It don't make a rat's ass what they had," Screwball said, suddenly excited. "They're after us."

Eddie reached for the door handle. "Pull over, Flick. Let me drive."

Flick downshifted and let out the clutch. The engine rebelled and backfired under the strain.

"What are you slowing down for?" Breed screamed. "They'll get us for sure."

Just like he had done before he poked Jonathan in the mouth, Eddie smiled that weird smile and let out that whooping laugh. "Don't worry." He defiantly jutted his chin out. "We got it covered."

"If we get caught, "Screwball responded, "they'll be coverin' our bodies with blankets."

Flick steered to the side of the road and cut the wheels, hard. The car shot across the road. He stomped on the brake. The car jerked so hard that the steel coils of the seat pressed against Breed's back. They all lurched forward. Flick cut the wheels in the other direction, and before the Mercury stopped, it had slid twenty feet.

"They're to close," Eddie said, suddenly looking fretful. "No time to switch. Just do what I say. I'll get us out of this."

Flick drummed his thumbs on the steering wheel. "What now?"

"Turn around. Go the other way."

Flick jammed the gearshift into reverse. The engine stuttered. He pumped the accelerator. The engine overflowed with power. He backed up just enough to clear the other side of the road, pushed in the clutch, and stopped. With the heel of his hand, he rammed the gearshift into low and tromped on the gas. The engine bellowed like a mighty bull and shot orange and blue fire out the lake pipes. He let out the clutch. The wheels caught and the tires slung ovals of dirt and gravel across the highway.

"We're going the wrong way," Breed excitedly cried from the back seat.

As Flick steered the car down the center of the road, he stepped on the switch on the floor. The headlights went on high-beam.

Pointing a stiff finger at Flick, Hog cried, "Hey, you dumb shit. Can't you hear? You're going the wrong way."

"So what?" Eddie snapped back.

Breed realized what Eddie was going to do, but if he got Eddie excited, out of some cockeyed sense of obligation to do just the opposite of what he was told not to do, he wouldn't listen to anything. Breed tried to keep his voice calm, but a tremor of anxiety took over. He screamed at Eddie, "You can't play chicken with the cops."

"Why not?" Eddie asked with excitement growing in his voice.

"They'll shoot your lights out."

"Don't you know they're afraid of the dark," he replied with enthusiasm. "And besides, if they do, they won't see us coming."

While Breed stared at Eddie in quizzical disbelief, Flick jerked his finger toward the road ahead. "They're right down the road. Can't you see that red light?"

Eddie smiled a sly smile. "Just drive. I'll show you what to do."

With a look of excruciating discomfort, Flick shook his head and shifted into second gear. "I hope you know what you're doing."

"The main thing is," Eddie calmly said, "don't get excited."

The Mercury picked up speed. The engine was ready for another gear. Flick shifted into third, but the engine begged for still another gear. Flick swung the floor shift into fourth. The speedometer needle bounced over the hundred miles an hour mark.

"You crazy bastards," Hog cried. "You'll kill us all."

Eddie glanced back at Hog. "Tell somebody who gives a shit."

In front of them, the cop car blinked its headlights. Waaahhh! The siren whined like a baby.

Eddie laughed his whooping laugh. "If he thinks *we're* gonna be the one movin' over, he's in for a big surprise."

Breed reached for the door handle and thought that if he jumped out just before they crashed, he would be like James Dean in *Rebel Without a Cause*. But Breed was in the back seat. James Dean had been in the front seat, and he had a door to jump out of.

The time that Flick, Screwball, and he, had walked four miles to see two cars that had not chickened out, flashed in Breed's mind. Those cars had crashed head on. The front ends were smashed up to the front seats. Both drivers had been killed. That red speedometer needles on both cars were jammed over to the one hundred and twenty miles an hour mark. When Screwball had pointed to something inside one of the cars, a piece of the dead driver's scalp was stuck on the chrome overdrive handle. This human flesh had grayish hair, and a drip of some kind of human liquid hung down from it, like a sad drop of pain, suspended, just ready to drop, but held in time. It seemed to say, "I'm not dead yet."

137

Screwball had turned pale.

Flick had held his stomach and said, "Let's get out of here."

Breed thought he had forgotten all about that. Now he remembered it as if it had just happened. He didn't want any part of his head hanging on any part of a wrecked Mercury. He wanted to jump out.

He reached along the sides of the back seat and felt for a door handle, again. Again, there was none. There were only two doors handles, and they were up front. Real suicide doors.

Anyway, it was too late.

"Looks like pieces of our dead heads are going to be hanging all over this car," Breed said in a defeated voice.

Flick lifted his foot from the accelerator. The speedometer needle fell. Breed quit feeling for a door handle and waited. Even if he could get to a door and open it, the car was still going too fast to jump out.

"Blow the horn," Screwball excitedly said. "Maybe he'll get out of the way."

As both cars raced toward each other, red beams of light rotated from the top of the police car and flicked into the black night. From both of the speeding cars, headlights loomed bright and white. Eddie reached over the wheel and pressed the horn with his thumb. The cop car didn't waver. Now closer, four bright headlights blazed toward each other and bleached the glass windshields into a white glare. Breed opened his eyes wide. The bright hurt. The horn blared, louder. Breed couldn't see. He closed his eyes and placed his hands on the roof of the car and his feet on the floor. He figured if the car flipped over, he'd just keep his hands on the roof and do cartwheels as the car rolled.

Eddie stared into the bright, laughed his whooping laugh, and yelled at the oncoming car. "Move it on over, or bring it on."

Breed's eyes opened wide with alarm. The back of Flick's head appeared in full color. Breed pictured a part of it on the gearshift lever. He looked out the front windshield and then glanced down at the speed odometer. Now it was ninety-five miles an hour. It was a head-to-head death game, and he didn't want to play. From the oncoming police car, bright light was interrupted with flashes of red. The only thing left to do was crash and die.

Breed felt the car jerk to the right. The sound of the horn and the wail of the siren rushed into his brain until, flit!

The bright was gone.

The horn stopped.

The siren whirred away and died.

"What did you turn for?" Eddie asked. "They would have moved."

Flick rubbed the side of his head. "I didn't want my scalp hangin' off the gear shift."

"Pour the coal to it," Hog said.

"Take it easy," Eddie said with a satisfied smile. "They won't follow us now."

Screwball looked over the seat. The baseball cap on his head was turned sideways. "Yeah, if they wondered if we were crazy before, now they know we are."

CHAPTER 9

Traveling into the night, Screwball, Hog, and
Breed lay in various resting positions on the back
seat. Listening to the exhaust lake pipes on the
Mercury purring like a contented kitten, Breed tilted
his head back and looked out the window above his
head. Black telephone wires and sparkling stars
sailed across the glass. Up front, Eddie closed his
eyes and tried to get comfortable and go to sleep,
but only twisted and turned.

When Breed sat up and looked out the side
window, crossroads and route signs whizzed past.
Driving the car, Flick peered over the hollow steel
hood of the rumbling engine. As he sipped from a
bottle of Coke and concentrated on driving, Eddie
moved around and jerked like he was too excited to
sleep. He rubbed the palms of his hands together,
reached out, and batted Flick on the shoulder. "I
can't take it," he whined. "I gotta get the feel of
that wheel back in my hands."

Flick looked as if he were tired of driving. He
didn't hesitate to reply. "You got it." He
downshifted. The engine slowed. He turned the
wheel and pulled over to the side of the road.

When Flick opened the door to switch places,
Hog pushed the back of the seat over and jumped
out. "All that pop gave me a stomach ache," he
said. "I have to take a crap."

Screwball stuck his head over the seat. "You
mean you want to clear your throat?"

141

"Hog turned and snapped back. "No, I want to clear my bowels, so I can talk out my ass like you do."

Shaking his head, Screwball smiled a defeated smile.

Eddie and Flick switched places.

Hog cleared his throat, jumped back into the car, and Eddie drove away.

"We're freewheelin' to a new place," Eddie excitedly stated. "We're starting a new life. Damn, I love it." Smiling, he looked back over the seat. "Hey, Hog, if we have to play chicken again, don't let it scare the shit outta' you."

Hog lifted his arm from the cabbage he was holding and jerked his thumb toward the back window. "Hey, Eddie. Don't get excited, but the cops are behind us, again."

"Don't worry," Screwball said, imitating what Eddie has said earlier. "We got it covered."

With red flashes from the police car making red lines on Eddie's back, he gave Screwball a menacing look. "Smart Ass." He punched the accelerator down. The car roared into another wild spurt of speed.

Breed looked far down the black road. The red flashes grew smaller and smaller, until, like a little red eye, they blinked and disappeared.

Eddie looked right at Screwball. "Don't worry." He winked. "We got it covered."

No sooner were the words out of his mouth than the Mercury soared over a dip in the road and hit the ground so hard Breed wondered if something on the bottom had broken off.

Eddie shot Screwball a quick glance, shrugged, and let the car slow.

Screwball slouched back in the seat and waved off Eddie's reverse mocking.

"We better slow down while we can," Breed said. "James Dean got killed because he couldn't stop in time."

"Yeah," Eddie said, "but that was in June, this is September."

Screwball popped up and announced, "Turnipseed!"

Flick drew his chin in and turned his head in Screwball's direction. "What are you talking about?"

Screwball placed his hands on the back of the seat and leaned forward. "That was the guy's name, Turnipseed. He pulled a 1950 Ford right in front of Dean's Spider and didn't even get hurt."

Breed poked his head over the seat. "Dean almost made it past, but Turnipseed hit the car right in the side."

Eddie stopped for a country stop sign and looked in the rearview mirror. "Good old Dean was driving his silver 550 Porsche Spider."

"What's a Porsche?" Hog asked.

"I think it's a foreign race car, cost a lotta money."

"No, it ain't," Screwball said with a glimmer of mischief. "It's those little wooden things people build on the front and back of their houses, you know, front and back porches."

"Yeah, right," Eddie said and continued. "They said that it wasn't anybody's fault, but that Ford

143

pulled right across the center line to make a left turn and—"

"And what?" Screwball butted in.

"And Turnipseed hit Dean. His mechanic was in the seat right next to him. He said the last thing James Dean said was, 'You think he's gonna stop?' and the mechanic said, 'No, Jimmy, he's not gonna stop.'"

Screwball nodded gravely. "Guess he didn't."

"You got that right," Flick added. "I heard the mechanic was in critical condition but lived."

Screwball spoke up, but his tone was low. "Maybe he just wanted to take a ride in an ambulance."

Eddie pounded the palm of his hand on the steering wheel and jammed the accelerator to the floor. "Are you ever gonna stop that stupid kid stuff?"

Screwball moved his fists on the side of his eyes and cried, "Waaaa! Only trying to make you laugh."

While Eddie shook his head, Breed looked at the speedometer. It was climbing. "We can't keep hot rodding this car. The engine will blow up."

"That ain't no lie," Flick agreed. "If it blows, they'll catch us for sure."

Eddie eased off the accelerator. "Okay, any you Einsteins got a better idea how to get ahead of those cops?"

Screwball picked up the cabbage and put the baseball cap on it. "You guys should have told me you wanted to get a head," he said and lifted the

144

cabbage head over the seat. Here's a head right here."

"Goddamn it, Screwball," Eddie bitched. "Can't you stop that shit."

Screwball looked out the back window. Those little red flashes were behind them, again. "Can't you stop letting those cops catch up to us?"

Eddie tromped the accelerator to the floor.

Again, Screwball mimicked Eddie. "Don't worry. We got it covered."

Breed looked at the baseball-hatted cabbage. "That's it," he said and looked to Flick.

Flick reached over the seat, took the baseball-hatted cabbage, and examined it. "That's right," he said with excitement in his voice. "We can put this guy on the road." He looked around the car. "Who's going to donate their shirt and pants?"

Breed jerked his head back toward the trunk. "Nobody will have too. There's greasy coveralls and old work shoes in the trunk."

As if it were alive, Flick held the cabbage next to his face and talked to it. "Okay, Cabbage Head, you're going to get those cops off our ass."

Eddie slowed the car and leaned into a turn. On the other side, he straightened the front wheels and increased speed. "We still got the cops right on our ass. What are you guys talking to a cabbage for?"

Flick smiled and held the cabbage head toward Eddie. "If we put Mister Cabbage Head on a dummy and placed it right around a sharp curve, those cops won't see it until it's too late."

"Just like the time we put that dummy on the road in front of Pud's house," Screwball added.

"It scared those guys in that truck," Hog said and looked to Flick. "But I lost my shoes, and you lost your World War II pilot hat."

Pointing with his finger, Screwball made circles around the side of his head. "That girl that was with them probably had to go to the nut house. She kept screaming, 'He's dead. You killed him. You killed him.'"

"Yeah I miss that pilot hat," Flick said with a frown. "But I never thought they would get mad enough to pick that dummy up and throw it in the back of their truck."

"Okay, Eddie," Breed said, "look for a good curve. We know what to do."

Down the road, Eddie stopped at a right-angle curve, folded his arms across his chest, and leaned back. "The cops will be here any minute. Let's see what you guys can do."

Hog and Flick stepped out of the Mercury, jumped over a drainage ditch. landed in a field, and began pulling out grass and weeds. When Breed and Screwball got out, they went to the trunk and Breed opened it. He grabbed the coveralls, and Screwball grabbed the shoes.

Screwball threw the shoes on the road and placed the baseball-hatted cabbage head close the center of the road. Breed dragged the coveralls to Flick and Hog. Flick dropped an armful of weeds and grass into the coveralls and went back for more. Breed pushed the grass and weeds into the coverall legs. Hog brought another armful of grass and went back for more. Screwball came over, stuffed the arms and curled one under the dummy. Flick and

146

Hog brought another armful and stuffed it in the center of the dummy. Breed and Screwball buttoned it up and dragged it to the center of the road. Flick placed the cabbage in the neck opening and placed the baseball cap's bill toward the dark sky. Then they stepped back and examined the fake body.

Eddie stepped out of the car and stood next to Hog. "Looks pretty good," he said and nodded in approval. "You guys look like you've done this before?"

"Yeah," Hog said, "but this one's gotta be the best one we ever made."

As if he were some kind of inspector, Breed tilted his head to one side. "That grease and dirt on those coveralls make it look like grease from the bottom of a car that ran over him, but that cabbage head doesn't look real."

Screwball knelt next to the dummy. "Tell me when," he said and adjusted the head further into the dummy.

"That's it," Breed said. "I hear them coming."

Eddie unzipped his fly. "Wait, I'll piss next to it."

"What?" Flick questioned.

"In the dark, the wet road will look like blood."

After Eddie urinated around the dummy, they got back into the car, and Eddie drove a little way down the road and stopped.

"What are you stopping for?" Breed asked. "They're right down the road."

Eddie opened the door, but didn't get out. "When they see the taillights and the door open,

147

they'll think I stopped because I ran over somebody. They'll have to swerve to miss me."

Hog pushed against the back of the front seat. "I ain't stayin' in this death car." He squeezed around the seat and jumped out the door.

Eddie stepped out of the car. Breed pushed the back of the seat forward and looked at Eddie. "Ain't you gonna shut the motor off?"

Walking away from the car, Eddie waved his hand down. "Let it run."

They all ran into the field where they crouched down in the dark and waited.

Red razors of light reached into the sky and split the night into red and black lines. The motor of the fast-moving police car roared closer. When the headlights pierced the dark and beamed into the field behind the sharp bend, stands of little trees and tops of wheat were spray-painted with white light, but the dark behind the headlights made the car difficult to see. The speeding motor grew louder. And then, rumbling deep inside, it slowed.

"He downshifted," Breed said with disappointment. "Maybe he ain't going fast enough."

The car's lights came at them.

"The hell he ain't," Flick snapped.

Tires howled low and angry. The car jerked sideways. Tires stopped howling. One of the car's headlights lifted up on one side, and the red razors of light flashed at a different angle.

Flick stood up, took a step forward, and stopped. "He's going to flip over."

The headlights bounded to level. The car headed right for the dummy.

"No, he ain't," Hog said fast.

Trying to miss the fake body, all four tires locked up, screeched on the pavement, and sent sizzling smoke around the car. The front wheels turned to miss the dummy and the parked Mercury. But it was too late. The wheels hit the dummy. Grass, and leaves flew into the night. The cabbage head skidded across the pavement and shredded into a long line. The cop car swerved once and spun sideways. It kicked up dirt-filled gravel from the side of the road and skidded toward the field. At the edge of the ditch, it stopped and balanced on its center for a second. Then the front end shot up in the air and the back of the car dropped into a cement culvert. Almost like a bright-eyed dog sitting up, begging for food, the car's headlights pointed upward and beamed far into the sky.

Breed and the others walked back to the road and stood next to the Mercury.

Like he had just finished a job, Hog brushed his hands together. "That's that."

Screwball pointed the toe of his shoe and kicked up some of the shredded cabbage. "You guys want some coleslaw?"

Eddie turned toward the Mercury. "Let's get back in the car," he said and looked at Screwball. "They ain't gonna catch us now."

"Didn't we hear that before," Screwball said, ran to the Mercury, and leaped into the back, followed by Hog and Breed.

As if he had all the time in the world, Eddie slid behind the wheel and slowly drove away.

Like an owl, Breed snapped his head around, looked out the back window, and wondered if the cops had been killed.

With weird delight, Eddie pounded on the steering wheel. "Those stupid cops spun out." He laughed his hollow laugh and stared at Screwball. "Don't worry. We got it covered."

"Ain't you goin' back and see if they're hurt?" Breed asked.

Flick craned his neck and strained to look out the back window. "They're okay. I see them movin' around. If we were in that ditch, they wouldn't care about us."

Breed didn't want the cops chasing them, but he didn't want to let someone die when he could help. "How can you know that?"

Eddie opened the door a crack. The wind whistled in and rattled the latch. "Here, Breed, you wanna get out and go check?"

"Yeah," Screwball said with malicious glee. "You wanna go back and get that baseball cap?"

With disapproval, Breed looked up but did not reply.

Forget those assholes," Flick said. "They're like that teacher who tried to have Bull beat me up."

"What are you talkin about?" Breed asked.

"I had a stomachache from drinking homemade root beer. It must've had too much yeast in it. My stomach was swelled up bad. I asked old man Locke if I could go to the restroom, he said I could right after I went into the supply room and got

150

something for him. After I'd gone in—" Flick paused and looked at Breed. "You know Bull?"

Breed nodded. "Yeah, he's that that big muscle-bound kid."

"When I went onto the supply room, he came in behind me. Old man Lucko said, 'Get him, Bull. Teach him a lesson.' I heard the door slam and lock behind me. Bull wound up and was going to knock my head off. I saw it coming and ducked. Then he tried a wrestling move on me. We got tangled up in a big knot. I don't know how I did it, but I wrangled around and got his arms and a leg in a position where I had my ass right in his face. I let loose the best fart of my life. That room was little, and with that door closed it got really bad. Bull couldn't breathe."

Screwball moaned. "What about you?" he asked Flick. "Could you breathe?"

"After smelling Hog's farts all these years, I was used to it."

Hog sat up, lifted his chin and smiled proudly. "I knew those things would come in handy."

Breed turned the palm of his hand up and rolled it with encouragement. "And."

Flick shot Breed a crooked grin. "I was so pissed off at being tricked that I grabbed a broom and used the handle to stab Bull in the stomach. He bent over, and I beat the shit out of him. When Lucko opened the door, the stink blasted him right in the face. He jumped back, and I ran past him."

Like a little kid wanting to hear more of a bedtime story Screwball leaned forward. "Did Bull run after you?"

"I don't think he could." As if he were still in the room, Flick's face filled with anguish. "He was having a hard time breathing. But that little incident got me kicked out of school for a week. Dirty bastard set me up, and those cops are just the same." He pointed to the road ahead. "Let's just keep on going."

"In other words," Screwball said in a businesslike manner, "a fart saved your life."

Giggling, Eddie drove on down the road, and all was quiet for a few miles.

As if he were trying to think of something important, Eddie wrinkled his forehead and spoke. "I thought my old man was going to go to jail for selling those bulldog gambling tickets. You know the brown tickets with that picture of a bull dog stamped on them?"

"I've seen those," Breed said. "They have a string like the strings on a feed bag that are sewn across the top."

"Yeah," Eddie said, "that's so no one can pull the string, open the ticket, find it's a loser, seal it back up, and try to resale it. But you can win instantly."

"You mean lose instantly," Screwball said and cracked a smile.

"That's right," Eddie said with a look of amazement. "That's where the money is. You sell fifteen or twenty tickets and only one is a winner. Anyway, the cops came right up to the front door. They had handcuffs and guns drawn. My old man gave them a fist full of money and they went away.

You can't trust authority. Honest laws ain't for poor people."

Yeah," Hog agreed, "the whole system is rigged, we go back, we go to jail."

The wind whistled through the cracked opened door and blew on Hog. "Hey, Eddie, before you fall out, don't you think it would be a good idea to shut that door."

Eddie pulled the door shut. "I only know one thing," he said and laughed. "They won't follow us now."

"I'm glad you noticed that," Hog said and sat back in the seat. "But I'm tellin' you, we're going the wrong way."

"I think I know what happened," Screwball said, his eyes bulging with fake astonishment. "Maybe we were doing the Hokey Pokey and turned ourselves around."

Before anybody could laugh, Eddie's face flushed with discomfort, and he yelled, "You're crazy."

"Ain't we supposed to be going west?" Hog asked, keeping his voice calm.

"Yeah, so what?"

"That sign we just passed reads north?"

"You can't believe what those signs say. If we had a map, I could show that the road runs on a slant and going west is really shown going north, the route signs can't say north west."

With his face contorted in disbelief, Hog leaned forward. "You don't know what you're talking about."

153

Eddie's face tensed and he talked through clenched teeth. "I know what I'm doing."

As if it were a warning of bad things to come, weird dust devils danced across the road and spun into nothingness. Breed reached his arm over Hog's shoulder and pointed out the windshield. "Look, another sign. It says, north."

Eddie took his right hand off the steering wheel and turned his palm up. "See, I told you guys. We're going in the right direction." He put his hand back on the steering wheel.

Screwball shook his head. "I didn't hear that sign say anything. I think you guys need to go to a proctologist for a brain exam."

Completely missing Screwballs intended meaning, Eddie snapped back, "There's nothing wrong with my brain. And besides, some smart aleck kids changed the signs. If we turn around and go the other way, the signs will say just the opposite. If you don't believe me, just watch where the sun comes up."

Breed was amazed that Eddie didn't know Screwball had actually told him he had to go to a butt doctor because his brain was in his ass. Shaking his head, he looked at Screwball and smiled.

"I don't care what you say," Hog said and arrogantly leaned back. "You're still going the wrong way."

As if he had just been slapped, Eddie recoiled and stopped for a stop sign at a crossroads.

Like an idiot with his mouth agape, Screwball slid to the front edge of the seat and stared at Eddie.

154

His voice leaden with fatigue, he asked, "If you don't know where you're going, how are you gonna know where you are when you get there?"

"Hey Screwball," Eddie shot back, "don't you ever shut up?"

Screwball didn't answer.

"Well, do you?" Eddie asked and looked back over his shoulder.

Breed looked to Screwball. "He's sleeping."

Eddie made a right turn and continued on down the highway. "It figures. He's even a wise ass in his sleep."

CHAPTER 10

Waking up from what seemed to be a few minutes sleep, Breed squinted his sleepy eyes and watched through the windshield of the Mercury. The black sky was turning blue, and the horizon was just beginning to brighten to a golden glow. Like the folds of a brilliant fan, the sun's rays blinked at the end of the road, and a new morning splashed across the land. The fresh light charged Eddie with a new energy. As if he had just pulled a string on one of his father's instant bulldog tickets and won, he howled, "Oh, man! Oh, man! It's the beginning of it. We're actually riding toward the greatest times of our lives. Nobody in our neck of the woods ever thought of going on the road to make big money."

"You can't make big money in jail," Hog muttered in a hushed voice.

With the zeal of sudden inspiration, Eddie tilted his head to one side and talked out the side of his mouth. "I ain't going to jail for taking a ride in this little car. Those stinking, lousy sons-a-bitches can't pin a thief label on me." He pointed to his own chest. "I'll show 'em. I'll come back loaded with money. I'll pay 'em all off!" He lifted both hands off the steering wheel and threw them into the air. "We'll be rich, man, really rich!"

Breed glanced at the empty pop bottles on the floor and thought about the poor the Joneses scrounging the ditches, roads, and alleys for pop bottles to cash in for two cents apiece. "We ain't rich yet," he said. "How long's it gonna take us to get that big money?"

"Not long," Eddie said with all the confidence in the world, "maybe a couple of weeks. We gotta start somewhere." He looked back at Breed and smiled. "And we're on our way, ain't we?"

Flick turned back toward Breed. "Ain't this what we been waitin' on?"

Breed didn't answer right away. He still wanted to get away from Shitsplat, but the stolen car still bothered him. "We're on our way, all right," he murmured. "If we get caught with this car, we'll be on our way to jail."

"We are not actually stealing the car," Eddie assured him. "We're only borrowing it for a while. Matter of fact, we'll make enough money to buy this car, give that kid twice as much as he wants." With the palm of his hand, he hit himself in the head. His hair flew up out of place for a fraction of a second and jumped right back, neat and combed. Like he had just solved every problem known to mankind, he said, "Yes! Yes!" Then a sparkle came into his eyes. "We'll make enough to buy fifty cars. This scheme can't fail."

Breed thought about how he had felt when his motorbike had been stolen. It had given him a deep hurt in his chest. It was okay to take apple off the tree once in a while, especially when they were only going to rot. But taking the Mercury was different. Just like he had worked on his motorbike to get it like he wanted it, he could tell from the body work and smooth-running engine that the kid that owned the Mercury had worked on it to get it just like he

157

wanted. Breed had spent every cent he could scrounge on his motorbike. Judging by the work clothes and shoes left in the trunk, it was evident that this kid worked in a stinkin' steel mill, and had spent every cent on his prize possession, too. Someone had stolen Breed's motorbike and now, in one fleeting moment, he had helped Eddie steal that kid's car. He had not only stolen a car, he had stolen a dream the kid had made come true. Guilt stabbed him in the stomach, and he argued in his mind that it was too late to go back. He couldn't be like some candy ass cry-baby and whine, "I wanna go home." He wasn't going to get his face beat in again and pay rent to live in a dump shack. Those days were over. Things would work out. It would be like Eddie said it would be. Big money was going to change everything. They were going to have enough money to have the greatest times of their lives.

Eddie opened a warm Coke and took a big swallow. "It's gonna be great! Just great! Man, things are better already. Can you dig it? We already have a car."

Hog calmly held a warm bottle of Coke in his hands and studied it. "We have a car, but we don't have any cold Coke."

"It doesn't matter," Eddie said with a self-satisfied smile. "I love Coke. I can drink it warm all day."

He took a cigarette from the pack in his wrinkle-free shirt. Even though he had been up all night, had driven for miles, and had shifted his body into various positions, his clothes were still neat and

158

clean. They always were. They never got wrinkled, and he never got dirty. His father had said that he could fall in a pile of shit and come out cleaner than when he fell in. It was just the way he was. And sometimes Breed felt rumpled just looking at him.

"In no time, we'll make it," Eddie said, lit the cigarette, and exhaled smoke while talking. "This thing flies." He maneuvered the red Mercury into an S-curve. At the bottom of the S, the car swayed and gently forced them to one side. At the top of the S, the car forced them in the other direction.

With Flick gripping the top of the seat, the Mercury came out of the curve at the top of the S. "I heard the cops want to put you in jail," he told Eddie. "They said you stole that car engine you put on that go-kart."

Eddie flicked his half-smoked cigarette out the window. He didn't like to smoke. He said he only did it to look intelligent. It was the thing to do. "Yeah they *think* they want to put me in jail," he said. "My old man said they had a reliable witness, and that I would have to go work in the mill to pay for the motor or work it out in reform school."

Flick cast a sidelong glance at Eddie. "Where are they going to find a reliable witness in Shitsplat?"

Breed sat up and stuck his head over the front seat. "That asshole in that pink Ford probably figured you had money, and he could squeal to the cops and get you to pay for the motor and his car or something he messed up."

159

"That may be true," Hog added. "He would try to do it to us, but he knows he can't get any money off of us. We never have any."

"And he still thinks it was our gang they fought when we tricked them into fighting each other on the bridge."

Like he had just seen them for the first time, Eddie looked back over his shoulder at Breed and the others. "So you're the guys that set that thing up."

Flick pointed at Screwball. "It was his stroke of genius."

Screwball had told the upriver gang that if they wanted to fight, they had to meet him and his gang at the Clark Street Bridge. Then he told the flats gang if they wanted to fight his gang, they had to meet at the Clark Street Bridge. While Breed and the others hid in the tall grass and watched, both gangs met on the bridge and fought a blood-spilling battle.

Like slipping a flying punch, Screwball swished his head downward. "It kept me from getting my head beat in."

"Instead of us getting busted up," Breed said and let out a snide laugh, "they were the ones that got busted up, and real bad."

Looking thoughtful, Eddie nodded. "That was a big fight. They still talk about it."

For a moment, Flick pondered in silence then turned toward Eddie. "You know they're just using that jail thing to scare you."

Talking at a speed equal to the speed the car Eddie rapidly said, "So what! My old man will pay them off." He laughed a little hollow laugh. "And anyway, all those little shit problems might have meant something if we were still there. But we're not! Just dig it man! We're freewheelin'. You know, it just doesn't matter anymore."

Hog leaned over and whispered to Breed, "If he doesn't quit sayin' freewheelin', I'm gonna punch him in the back of the head."

Above a steep, tree-lined gully, Eddie slowed the Mercury and tracked around a sharp curve. "Never can tell what's just around the bend, could be something great." He steered out of the curve. As the road stretched straight, he thrust his head forward. "This road goes straight a long way." He leaned back and mashed the pedal halfway to the floor.

Screwball leaned forward, rested his elbows on the top of the seat, and peered out the windshield. Outside, the land stretched far and flat. "If I lived here," he said, "I'd have a dog."

Reaching up and rubbing the side of his head, Eddie asked, "What would be so great about having a dog around this flat land?"

"This place is so flat that if he ran away, I could watch him for three days."

As if he were trying to clear Screwball's words from his mind, Eddie abruptly leaned back in his seat, expelled a quick burst of air, and shook his head.

Hog jabbed a finger toward Screwball. "Would you care to expound on that?"

Laughing gloatingly, Screwball continued. "And after I couldn't see him anymore, you know what I'd say?"

Eddie averted his eyes. "Don't know. Don't care."

Screwball told him anyway. "I'd say, dog gone."

As if Screwball were boring him, Eddie stretched sluggishly. "Don' t you ever get tired of being a wise ass?"

"Don't you ever get tired of sayin' freewheelin'?"

While Eddie made a resigned shrug and shook his head in pleasant amazement, the Mercury flashed down the straight road and gobbled up quick miles. Eventually, the flat road was interrupted with crossroads, little hills, and cattle crossings, but Breed didn't see one dog.

With the sun hurling through the windshield and breathing fire through the glass, Eddie slowed the car. "This looks like farm country. I smell money."

Screwball held his nose. "All I can smell is horse shit."

When the pavement suddenly became a patchwork of various grades and consistencies, Flick pointed up ahead. A farmer with bib overalls and a sweat-stained baseball cap, stood next to a faded black pickup truck parked next to a field, and what seemed to be his sons, were throwing bales of hay onto a wagon.

"Look," Flick said, and pointed to the kids. "They're bailing hay. Ain't it a little early in the day to be doing that?"

"It doesn't matter, just as long as it's dry," Breed said.

"Here's our first chance," Eddie said, grinning. "Well stop and bail hay. I hear they pay good."

"Yeah," Flick said, "they say nobody wants to do that hard work anymore."

"Hey!" Screwball shouted and hunched forward. "Let's go bail some hay. Hey! Bail some hay today, or have a hay day. Hey!"

Ignoring Screwball's failed attempt at humor, Eddie said, "Let's see if they'll hire us." He downshifted, pulled the Mercury onto the side of the road, and like a jack-in-the-box, he jumped out and ran out to the pickup truck.

Breed was too far away to hear what Eddie was talking about, but he watched Eddie wave his arms and point to the Mercury. The farmer nodded and Eddie ran back to the Mercury. "We got the job."

"How much?" Breed asked.

"Buck an hour, maybe more, depends how good we are."

They hopped out of the Mercury and walked to the tractor and the wagon."

The farmer yelled over the roar of the thrashing hay bailer. "Just throw the bales up on the wagon." He pointed to the two blonde-headed kids on the wagon. "My boys will stack 'em. Then we'll ride to the barn."

Breed and the others walked along the slow-moving wagon and threw bales of hay on it. Breed

163

thought the work was easy, sort of fun. "This ain't nothin," he said and noticed the farmer's two boys. Dirty-white T-shirts covered their skinny upper bodies, and they looked to be about twelve, no more than thirteen. Their faces broadcasted a healthy red glow, but the tops of their forearms had bumps as big as hen's eggs. Breed figured, birth defect or something attested to the bumps.

When the wagon was piled high with heavy bales of hay, the farmer motioned with his arm. "Okay, fellows, hop on wherever you can. We're headed for the barn."

Outside the barn, a conveyer belt, brush-painted with thick red paint, sat like a huge steel monster waiting to gobble up the bales and send them up and into the open door of the huge third-story loft.

You boys go inside," the farmer said. "Climb up the ladders and stand in the loft. We'll feed the hay to you. If you want more hay, just yell."

Chewing on a piece of straw, one of the farmer's sons said, "Yeah, let us know if you city kids can't keep up. We'll turn the conveyor speed down to snail speed."

Flick glanced at the conveyer belt and then at the bales of hay. "You ain't going to keep up with us," he bragged. "This hay ain't nothin."

As if he didn't believe Flick, the farmer's son nodded and started the conveyer.

"Follow me," the farmer said, walked inside the big barn, climbed halfway up the ladder, and pointed where to stack the bales of hay. "We got a lot of hay left over from yesterday," he said, and as if he were studying Breed and his friends, he paused and then said, "We didn't get time to put it up. We'll feed that to you boys first." Skepticism filled his face. "Let us know if you want us to slow down."

"You ain't goin' have to slow nothin' down," Eddie said and scrambled up the ladder.

"Yeah," Flick said and climbed up the ladder, and two bales plopped onto the wooden floor of the loft."

When Breed climbed into the huge, airy loft, it smelled of straw, years of dust, and mice. If the birds darting in and out of the loft were twittering, they couldn't be heard over the sound of the conveyor.

The farmer turned to go, but turned back and yelled over the sound of the noisy conveyor, "We don't need any wasted space. So stack it neat. If you want to speed it up, just yell, more hay."

When Breed and the others climbed into the loft, Thump! Thump! Two more bales thudded onto the wood floor. Flick and Eddie threw them next to a small stack. Screwball and Hog snagged the other two off the loft floor and neatly placed them on the stack. Four bales thudded onto the floor. Breed picked up one and threw it. It landed short.

Eddie grinned at Breed. "Gettin' tired?"

"No way, man," Breed lied. "It just slipped."

Thump! Thump! Thump! Three bales thumped onto the floor.

"Step to it, men," Flick said and threw a bale to Screwball. The conveyer rattled and groaned but no bales dropped off.

Eddie yelled out the loft door, "More hay!"

Crowded end-to-end, bales came rushing up the conveyor. They flew a short distance, landed on the floor, and created small explosions of dust and chaff that flew into the humid air. Flick caught two bales before they ran off the conveyor belt. Using the force and the momentum of the belt, he swung them onto the pile. Eddie tried to pick up two, lost his balance, and dropped both bales. He recovered, picked them up and slung them onto the pile.

When the stacked hay began to tilt to one side, Hog stopped catching bales, put his hands his hips, and shouted down to the farmer, "Hey, slow down. We gotta keep it straight."

Behind him, giggling with delight, Screwball kicked the bales into a neat stack and yelled down, "More hay."

The conveyer sped up. As more chaff and dust billowed in the confined space of the loft, loud laughter from the farmer and his two sons mixed with the noise of the thrashing conveyer.

Breed's and his baling buddies' quick movements and strong hands weren't enough. The bales avalanched onto the floor and into a haphazard pile that all of them could not keep from forming.

As if they were tiny magnets, beads of sweat broke out on their foreheads and gathered chaff, but they kept working.

When the conveyer finally stopped, Breed and the others collapsed and lay on the scattered bales of hay. The farmer came up into the loft and smiled. "More hay?" he questioned, looked at the exhausted workers, and broke out into a huge barnyard laugh, "Haw, haw, haw, haw."

As the chaff and dust in the loft slowly dissipated, in long-climbing leaps, his sons came up the ladder and bounced into the loft floor. With a radiant, grinning face, one of them playfully picked up the scattered bales, and like they only weighed a few pounds, he tossed them with ease. His brother caught them, held each one briefly, and smoothly guided it into a neat stack.

Now Breed knew what had formed those bumps on their forearms. Years of bailing hay had developed their skinny forearms in one spot. That weird bump was a hay-bailing muscle. They could pick up two bales like they were empty cardboard boxes.

After the hay had been stacked and put away, the farmer smiled. "That was almost four hours," he said. "But you boys did good for city kids." He reached into his blue denim shirt pocket and pulled out a bill. "Here's five for the day. We'd invite you in for supper, but we gotta tend the animals first."

Eddie took the five-dollar bill. "Thanks."

With tiny bits of itchy hay trailing off their bodies, Breed and his friends jumped in the Mercury.

"Yawl come back next year," the farmer said, and waving his arm out the window, Eddie drove away.

Prickly sensations from the bits of hay attacked Breed's back. He reached back and scratched them. With surprise and irritation, he said, "I thought each one of us was going to get a dollar an hour, but he only paid a dollar an hour for all of us. Even though he gave us an extra dollar, we didn't do too hot."

Scratching, Screwball looked at Eddie and repeated what he had said earlier. "What are you talkin' about?" he said. "We made enough to buy fifty cars. This scheme can't fail."

Breed let out a tired laugh. "We made more money painting mailboxes, and it wasn't as much work."

Mocking Eddie, Screwball tensed his face and talked through clenched teeth. "I know what I'm doing."

Waving his hand in a dismissive gesture, Eddie growled. "That was only one farm. We could do three or four a day, build up our money."

Breed was thirsty and hungry. "Build up, my ass," he said and laced his hands across his trim stomach. "The little money we made will be eaten up by the gas we have to buy and the food we'll have to eat to keep working."

Itching from the particles of hay scattered over his body, Flick scratched the back of his arm. "That ain't no lie." He rubbed the side of his leg with the top of his foot. "Baling itchy shit ain't the way to go."

Hog took off his shoe and turned it over. Little sticks of hay drifted to the floor. "It's just a junk job."

"Yeah," Screwball allowed. "They just made itchy horse's asses out of us."

"Made us work for pennies," Breed added. "We shouldn't have to put up with those kinds of pikers."

With a voice filled with mounting tension, Eddie pleaded, "Come on you guys, we gotta give it a chance."

Screwball held up his hand. "He's right. We should stop bitchin'. At this rate, we'll be keeping up with the Joneses." He jerked his head toward the window. "Hey, Eddie, stop and go back. I think I saw a cigarette butt and a pop bottle in the ditch."

"Okay, you guys," Eddie said, and the tension visibly lifted from his face. "You're exactly right." Like he was searching his mind for a correct answer, he banged on the steering wheel. "You guys want to go back home?"

Breed felt the bruise on the side of his face and look down the long highway. "We can't give up yet. There has to be better a way to make good money."

As if he were looking for approval, Eddie turned toward Hog. "Okay, now we know baling hay is a junk job."

Reverting to his agitating voice, Hog told Eddie, "If you're expecting a little contrition, none will be forthcoming."

With a disappointed look, Eddie turned back to the front. The car increased speed, and Eddie smiled. "But just think of it, man. If we don't want to, we don't have to take those kinds of jobs."

"If we ain't gonna make any money," Hog said. "We might as well go home."

"Cry tomorrow," Eddie said with sternness in his voice. "Today, we're on the highway of opportunity. There's money right down the road, and we're gonna get it."

Screwball rubbed his itchy back against the back of the seat. "There's more itchy shit right down the road, too."

Eddie slowed at a crossroads. Off to the side of the road, in front of three dust devils, stirring in a field of grass, a hand-painted, cardboard sign with a rusty wire hung from a signpost. Purple letters read, CALIFORNIA GRAPES.

Eddie's eyes lit up. "That's *it!*"

Thinking Eddie had come up with another hair-brained scheme, Breed gave him a derisive look. "What's *it?*"

Eddie flashed an assured smile. "We'll work our way across the country. We'll chase a red sky and a setting sun all the way to California."

"California?" Breed questioned.

"That's right," Eddie said with sheer delight. "And we won't have to live in one of those housing projects where there are no streets or alleys or byways between the buildings, not even a blade of grass, where people use landings of the stairways to do everything.

Agape and bug-eyed Flick stared at Eddie. "Everything? Like what."

"Screw, smoke dope, inject heroin, have dice games, you name it, and more screwing."

"What do they do if they see you watching them?"

"In their happy state, nothing."

170

The car became quiet. Now that Eddie had said they were going to California, Breed was suddenly terrified at the thought of going so far and ending up in a housing project worse than Shitsplat. As if they were considering Eddie's words, no one talked.

Eddie raced the Mercury through the countryside. Trying to let the passing wind blow the chaff out of his hair, Breed stuck his head out the window and watched a blur of farmhouses pass by. After rolling green fields, peppered with bales of yellow hay to bale, came and went, he pulled his windblown head into the car.

Eddie broke the silence. "We'll dig the cars and movie stars and get good jobs and make good money. I'll even show you guys what clothes to buy. Not only will we be cool, we'll look cool." He laughed his hollow laugh. "Man, oh man, we'll be on Easy Street. What a team! Together we will see what's happening. We'll know what everybody's doing. We won't have to waste our lives away."

In a place where thick tree trunks of tall trees hugged the road on both sides, Eddie slowed. Traces of the sun's rays flickered through the dense canopy above. "The point is" — he squinted against the sun's flicking rays — "we know what we want to do and we're doing it. We're cool." The sun's rays quit flicking. He quit squinting. His eyes opened wide. "Things are going to work out really great." He banged on the steering wheel and rubbed his head. "We're headed west. We're going to California."

Screwball raised his head from the back of the seat where he had been resting. "If it's warm there, and things get bad, we can go back to painting mailboxes."

Breed stifled a yawn with the back of his hand. "Heck yeah!" He nodded. "We could paint them all year long."

"That's right," Flick jumped in. "We did do pretty good in the summer. But no matter what happens, we won't starve to death."

Without cracking a smile, Hog stared in an uncomprehending daze. "That's an interesting observation."

Cars appeared at crossroads. The itchy chaff under their clothes only attacked briefly. Cars backed out of driveways, and the traffic on the road increased. People in different colored cars were on their way to work on afternoon shift or were going to some other place they really didn't want to be.

Eddie turned his whole body toward Flick, clutched his shoulder, and whispered, "Look at those people in front of us. They're worried about getting to work on time. They keep bobbing their heads to look at their expensive wristwatches. They're counting the minutes, thinking about the beer they'll drink tonight, how much money they'll make if they work overtime, and which asshole of the day is going to make their job harder when they get there."

Eddie's whooping laugh filled the car. "He's fuckin' me!" His face took on an injured look. "He's fuckin' me! That's what they'll say when they get to work. And you know what? They'll get there anyway, and the guy on the shift before him will pass on the fuck of the day and make each oncoming worker's shift that much harder, because they all believe that they are getting fucked into doing more work than they have to. They just pass it on. And after work, they'll guzzle and piss beer, tell the same jokes that aren't funny, and laugh at them. The only way you can end the cycle is to shoot yourself in the head."

"What good would that do?" Flick asked compassionately.

"You could cheat them out of screwing you."

Screwball gave him a doubtful look. "It's a good plan, but you can only do it once?"

"Guess you got something there," Eddie said and laughed that hollow laugh.

A car zipped in front of Eddie. He swerved and missed it. "That guy must be nuts."

"He has to be," Hog said and watched out the windshield. "He didn't even look."

"Don't get excited," Eddie said and gestured toward the car. "Just look at him. He just has to worry and waste time with unimportant things like getting in front of another car. I don't think he would be happy doing anything else." Smiling, he nodded. "Of course, he doesn't really want to do anything else. The only thing those kinds of people like to do is work, so they have a reason to swill cheap whisky and screw low-priced women."

Hog leaned over the front seat. "What makes you an expert?"

"I don't claim to be an expert," Eddie shot back. "But when I had my paper route, I took papers into bars. I saw half-drunk people bragging about how much time they had in the mill."

The road curved sharply to the left. Eddie steered on around it and continued, "Every day when I dropped off the paper, I would hear the same thing. Some old drunken guy would say, 'Why I got more time in the shit house than you got in the mill.'"

A foolish grin spread across Screwball's face. "That guy must a stunk pretty bad."

"Probably had shit for brains," Hog observed with a rasping snort.

As if feeling disgusted, Eddie's face contorted into a grimace. "Every damn day that guy would reach into his pocket and say, 'Want to double your money?' and another guy would say, 'How?' The other guy would take a few dollars out of his pocket, fold them and say, 'Fold it.'"

"And of course," Flick added, "another guy would always say, 'Did you pass the fuck on?'"

Screwball lifted his hands and waved inward. "They could pass one my way."

"Wrong kind," Hog said without hesitation.

"That's for sure," Eddie agreed. "It was just a fuck 'em and pass it on routine. When you talk about anything but the mill, their expressions really change." Imitating the mill workers, as if he were confused, he made an ugly face. "Dah!" He wagged his head like an imbecile. "They live lives of shit and don't even know it."

"I think they got used to doing a lot of useless talking," Breed surmised. "But nobody is listening anymore. Maybe somebody should tell them about it."

"You can if you want, but I'm mighty glad it ain't up to me to figure out what they should do. I got enough on my mind without worrying about people like that."

Wondering if he could believe what Eddie was saying, Breed heaved a sigh. "You think we'll ever be like them?"

Eddie drew back as if Breed had slapped him. "We ain't ever going to be like them." His voice resounded with enthusiasm. "We ain't lettin' time fly by us. We're not gonna end our lives in a rotten mill." He jerked his finger toward the road ahead and roared, "We're going to California."

The traffic thinned out, and they threw the empty pop bottles at the road signs and called it Coke baseball. A miss was an out. A bounce was a double, and a broken bottle was a home run.

After each toss, Breed thought what would happen to the bottles. They would litter the ground below signs, and along the edges of the road, some would be broken, and some would stay empty until it rained or the water in a ditch filled them. They would stay there until a bum or a kid came along and picked up the good ones and cashed them in for the deposit. If not, they would be buried in the time of snow, sleet, salt, and just any kind of shit that storms off the highway.

After Eddie pulled the Mercury off the road and into a field of high grass, he stopped and they slept.

When they were back on the road, a gang of crows flew over the Mercury and landed in a stand of tall trees and constantly cawed.

Settling back lazily, Screwball asked, "Do any of you guys know why crows hardly ever get hit by a car?"

"Never thought about," Eddie said and glanced up at the crows as he drove past. "I haven't seen one dead crow on the road since we left."

"Okay great know it all," Hog grumbled in a voice slurred with fatigue. "Why don't crows get hit by cars?"

With a great expression of exuberance, Screwball replied, "Because every time a crow stands on the road to eat a roadkill, and a car comes, the other crows in the trees yell, 'Caw! Caw! Caw!"

While the others laughed in amazement, Flick looked at the gas gauge. "The tank's getting' low. We need gas."

As if he were astonished, Screwball stopped laughing and dropped his jaw. "Just brilliant! If the gas wasn't low, we wouldn't need it."

Eddie smiled at Screwball through the rearview mirror. "Very observant."

"Keep an eye out for some place to swipe gas," Flick suggested. "I don't feel like walking."

"Good idea, "Eddie agreed. "If we wanna get to California, we got to save all the money we can."

Feigning ignorance, Breed asked, "Do you think it would be a bad idea to steal gas in the daylight?"

"You never know when the time is right to relieve people of surplus gas," Eddie retorted. "You know what they say, 'When opportunity knocks.'"

Referring to the wart-faced kid in the pink Ford that had made his girlfriend pregnant, because Flick had poked holes in his rubbers, Screwball said, "Or when that stupid kid knocks up his rotten-mouth girlfriend and has an ugly bunch of little wart-faced kids."

Eddie cocked his head to the side and smiled a twisted grin, "Yes, yes, ah-uh, okay gentleman, look for one of those big green gravity fed gas tanks that they put around construction sites."

Flick looked at the gas gauge. "If we don't find some gas pretty soon, we'll be knocking our feet on the hard pavement."

CHAPTER 11

As the landscape flowed past outside the Mercury, Breed stared at the gas gauge. It hovered over the bottom of the empty mark. At the edge of a town, Eddie downshifted, threaded the car through a maze of traffic, and burst out onto a street lined with buildings that had storefront windows. Off to the right, a chain-link fence posted with Men Working signs blocked the sidewalk, a portion of the street, and a construction site. Slowing the car, Eddie leaned into the steering wheel and pointed to a big green gas tank sitting next to a mound of yellow dirt. "Look, there's some gas just waitin' for us to pull in and take it."

A sleepy-looking security guard wearing a blue shirt rubbed his eyes and peeked around a dirty-orange bulldozer. Like a warning light, his chrome badge flashed in the sun. Breed knew the bulldozer used diesel fuel, and usually there would be another construction gas tank near and it would be filled with regular gas. If Eddie knew that, he would probably cook up some half-assed scheme to keep the guard busy and try to steal the gas in broad daylight.

"It's daytime," Breed said. "There's a guard. He'll see us."

Eddie stuck out his chin, reached up and flicked his fingers toward the guard. "Don't worry about that guard. It's early in the morning. He'll probably take a whiz and go back to sleep."

To keep the guard from seeing him, Breed slouched down. "Yeah, but there are other people around."

"It doesn't matter." Eddie slowed the car, more. "People ain't gonna crawl out of bed just before their alarms clocks go off."

Staying slouched down in the seat, Hog grunted and opened his eyes. "How do you know?"

Eddie turned his head and talked over his shoulder. "They might wake up, but when they see they only have a few more minutes before it's time to get up, they'll pull the covers over their heads and go back to sleep." As if he had just guessed the right answer on a difficult test, he hunched over and nodded. "Yep, early in the morning is the best time to steal stuff."

That guard looked sneaky, and Breed didn't want to take a chance. "That's diesel fuel for the bulldozer," he said. "It won't work in this car."

"We know that," Eddie said and looked tolerantly at Breed. "Sometimes they use a lot of pickup trucks and generators and other little motor stuff that uses regular gas, and they'll have a different tank for that gas."

"Regular gas won't burn good in this hopped up engine," Breed told him.

"It won't run too good, but we can cram it in the tank anyway. It'll burn. It'll make us go."

Heck yeah," Flick said, "If we have to, we'll mix it with high-test."

Eddie lifted his foot from the accelerator and let the Mercury slow to a crawl.

179

Breed looked out the back window. A few people were walking on the sidewalk but no police were around. "Yeah we can steal it," he said, referring to the gas. "But if somebody sees us and we get away, then the cops will be after us for another thing. Don't you think we should try not to attract any more attention?"

"Hey! Dip Shit," Hog snapped at Breed. "Don't you think we'll attract more attention if all of us are walking down the street?"

Realizing skinny Eddie and four kids with long hair walking along the street would look like some sort of a gang, Breed lowered his head. "I guess you got a point."

Eddie stopped the car right next to the guard standing next to a bulldozer. Looking at them as if they were garbage, and with his hand on the handle of his holstered pistol, the guard walked toward the car.

Breed leaned over the seat and whispered in Eddie's ear. "I thought you said he'd go back to sleep."

As if he had just woken up, Hog jerked forward. "You dumb shit, it's not morning. It's afternoon."

Looking away from the guard's steady searching eyes, Eddie tilted his head, reached up and rubbed the back of his neck. In the process, he used his forearm to cover his face. "You might have something there, Hog." He pulled away from the guard and drove back on down the street. With a renewed upbeat attitude, he said, "Don't worry. Eddie Chicago's at the wheel. Everything's gonna

180

be fine." Smiling big, he hunched his shoulders, and huffed out of his mouth, "Yup, yup, yup. Everything's gonna be just fine."

Screwball lit up with fake excitement. "Sure, it is," he chided. "It doesn't matter whether you know if it's morning or afternoon. Everything's gonna be just fine."

Screwball's attempted sarcasm didn't bother Eddie. He seemed to be on an adrenaline excited high, living on the edge and feeling terrific.

A ways down the street, Eddie pointed to an alley that separated two buildings. "There's one."

At first Breed didn't see it, but when Eddie turned the Mercury into the alley, a hose with a gas nozzle could be seen. "I'll be damned."

Tucked inside the building, a gas tank, used to fuel company trucks, could scarcely be seen.

Eddie stopped the Mercury next to the tank and pointed to Hog. "Pick the lock." He pointed to Flick. "Get out and pump the gas. The nozzle is a big one. When I signal you to stop, stop."

"Why?"

"That gas nozzle is used for trucks, and the gas comes out faster than a car gauge can read it. When it reads three-quarters full, the tank will be full. If you don't stop when the tank is full, the gas will fly all over the place. And you know what happens then?"

Flick opened the door. "Yeah, we'll smell gas for days." Hog got out and had the lock picked before Flick dashed around the Mercury and unscrewed the gas cap. Hog handed the nozzle to

Flick and jumped back into the Mercury. Flick began putting gas into the tank.

In fewer than thirty seconds, Eddie lifted his hand and signaled Flick to stop. The tank was full. Flick quickly replaced the nozzle, replaced the gas cap, and jumped back into the Mercury.

***

Along toward evening, miles down the road, unable to hold the moisture, a feeble gray sky opened up. Like a thousand little rubber hammers, giant drops of rain plopped down on the Mercury's roof. The chest-penetrating thuds invaded a rare sanctity-like ambience inside the Mercury. After a puff of wind huffed past, the rain changed to a heavy shower, then small hail rattled against the windows. Eddie reached over and snapped on the windshield wipers.

They didn't work.

Screwball stared at the cascading hail stones on the windshield. It blocked the view of the road ahead. "Yup, yup, yup," he said mocking Eddie. "Everything's gonna be just fine."

The hail stopped.

Looking alert, Eddie lifted his arm, and blocking Flick's view, pointed to an abandoned ingress road. It was bordered with tall grass and bushes, and tree limbs almost covered it. "There's a little road," he said as he cut the wheel sharp. The car humped over the road shoulder, rolled into the tall grass, and stopped just before a low hanging tree branch touched the windshield. "We can fix those wipers." He looked back over his shoulder. "Hey, Breed, see if there's any string in the trunk."

182

Breed leaned forward to get out, but stopped. Outside a steady hiss of sizzling rain and a growl of thunder caused him to change his mind. "I ain't goin' out. It's raining."

Eddie pointed to his right. "Flick, check the glove compartment."

After reaching into the glove compartment, Flick thrust his hand into the air. He held a roll of kite string. "Here's some."

"Good," Eddie said, "unroll enough string to reach across the hood."

Flick did that.

"Okay," Eddie said. "Now hang on to the end of the string, reach around the windshield, and throw the roll over the hood."

Hanging out the window, Flick tossed the roll of string. Unraveling, the loose string waved across the hood and just missed the branch. Eddie reached out to catch the string, but it fell onto the wet grass. He jumped out of the car to get it, but the branch was in the way. To get it out of the way, he grabbed it and jumped back. But the branch broke so fast it caught him off balance. His feet flew into the air. His rear end plopped into a splat of mud, and Breed wondered if Eddie's rear end would be muddy.

As if nothing had happened, Eddie scooped up the ball of string and jumped up. Then he looped the string around the end of the windshield wiper blade, ran the end of the string through the wing window, and handed the roll to Flick. "Tie your end to this end."

Flick tied the ends together and pulled on the string. The windshield wipers didn't move. Flick looked at Eddie. "Now what?"

"Ahh, man," Eddie said and walked to the front of the Mercury. He lifted the hood leaned over the fender and disconnected the wiper motor. "Try that."

Flick pulled the string. The wipers moved and cleared the raindrops from the glass.

Eddie slammed the hood shut, jumped in the car, hooked the transmission into reverse, and let out the clutch. The tires spun, but the car didn't move.

Outside, sheets of silver rain danced on the Mercury, and in a dizzying, almost hypnotic display, flashes of lightning snarled and crackled under menacing clouds. Inside, Screwball bobbed his head and pointed a teasing finger at Eddie. "Yup! Yup! Yup! Just as soon as Eddie sticks his ass out the window and gets that mud washed off, everything's gonna be just fine."

"Don't get excited," Eddie said with sudden inspiration. "You guys will just have to get out and push."

"What-a-yah mean, *you guys* will have to get out?" Hog questioned.

"Just great," Screwball grumbled. "It's rainin' so hard that if we go outside, we'll have to jump in a river to dry off."

With a look of excruciating discomfort, Eddie clutched the steering wheel. "Ahh, man, don't make a big deal out of nothing'. A little mud ain't gonna hurt nothin'. And besides, somebody's gotta steer."

While Breed became amazed at seeing Eddie slipping into the mud and not coming out clean as he usually had always done, the rain slowed.

Flick opened the door, stepped out, and jumped back in. "A cop car just went past. Get down."

In a show of confidence, Eddie nodded. "See that? Our luck's still with us. A little inclement weather ain't stoppin' nothin'. We'll make it to California. We're gonna be rich, man." He threw his hands into air and shook them. "Rich!"

"If we're so rich," Hog said, "why don't you hire a tow truck and have it pull us out of here?"

Screwball muttered sarcastically, "Don't toe trucks only haul toes?"

For a moment, Eddie stared at Screwball in stunned silence. Then he roared at Screwball, "Get your toe truck ass out, dig your smart-ass toes in the mud, and push us out of here."

After Eddie sat behind the wheel a few moments, with the rain pouring down, everybody else got out and pushed. Tires spun. Flying bits of grass and yellow mud sprayed onto their ankles and feet. Water streamed down their faces. But they kept pushing. The wheels gained traction. Eddie backed out onto the highway, stopped, and waited for them to get in.

They piled in.

Flick bammed the door shut. "At least we got that chaff washed off."

Nodding, Eddie pulled the string to the windshield wipers. As the wipers swiped the rain away, Eddie looked to Flick. "So our arms don't get tired, we'll take turns and keep the windshield clear."

Driving down the road, Flick and Eddie took turns and moved the string back and forth.

Each time they moved the wipers, like an idiot watching a tennis match, Screwball moved his head from left to right. He stopped watching and shook his head. "That's stupid. Why don't we just stop and wait until the rain quits."

"The car's stolen," Eddie said and pulled the string. "Just like back there, the cops can't see us too good in the rain. And if they do, those candy asses ain't going to get out and get wet. They'll just let us drive right on by."

Flick pulled the string, the gas gauge ticked toward empty, and the Mercury continued on down the rainy highway.

When the Mercury passed through a curtain of rain and emerged out the other side, the road was dry, and the leaves on the trees alongside the road had been hit by an early freeze. They were dusty brown.

"We drove out of that one," Eddie said, and a gas station appeared in the distance. Eddie looked at the skinny white needle on the gas gauge. It indicated almost empty. All of a sudden, he shrieked with excitement, "Yessiree! I got it."

"If you got it in your mouth," Screwball said, "spit it out. It's mine."

"Ahh, Man," Flick said with an agitated tone to his voice. "Quit screwin' around." He leaned toward Eddie. "Got what?"

Eddie lifted his hand and hit himself in the forehead. "Why did I let it slip my mind?"

Flick jerked with surprise. "What?"

"Drain the hose, man. Drain the hose." Eddie smiled big. "The Great Eddie Chicago didn't forget. With Screwball always messin' around, my mind just wasn't in the right gear, had to shift into the thinking section that knows about draining the hose." He hit himself in the forehead, again. "Man, oh man!"

Eddie pulled the Mercury into a gas station, jumped out, screwed off the gas cap, and held it in his hand. With his other hand, he grabbed the gas nozzle and flipped up the worn silver pump control lever. The pump went on. The attendant waltzed out the door. Beneath the white, paper garrison hat, he wore on his black-haired head, his smooth brown face was expressionless. Eddie threw the nozzle into the tank opening and pumped in twenty-five cents worth of gas.

The attendant walked to the car and stopped. "Can I help you, sir?" He reached for the hose nozzle that Eddie held in the tank.

Eddie reached up with his free hand and turned off the gas pump. With the other hand he held the hose nozzle valve open and drained the gas that was in the hose into the tank. The small amount that drained from the hose did not register on the black and white metal numbers on the circular pump dial. As if Eddie were a thief, the young attendant glared at him. Eddie didn't give him time to speak. With one hand, he reached out and handed the nozzle to

187

the attendant. With his other hand he offered the attendant a quarter.

"Sorry. man," Eddie said, the gas gauge's broke. That's all she'll take."

The attendant replaced the handle to the pump opening, turned, and like a little kid being afraid his mother would catch him doing something wrong, he tensed his long-hooked nose. "The boss doesn't like people coming in and not buying anything. You want me to check your oil and clean your windshield?"

"No, but thanks anyway," Eddie said with an engaging smile. "You know what it's like to be on the road, don't yah, man?" He offered his hand in friendship.

The attendant reached out and snaked his limp hand around Eddie's. The young attendant's nose untensed, and his forehead smoothed out. "Yeah, man, I read *On the Road,* too."

Like a starving man trying to shake the last bit of ketchup out of a stubborn bottle of ketchup, Eddie pumped the attendant's hand and smiled.

As if he were Neal Cassady in some beat scene with the author Jack Kerouac, the attendant grinned. "I'm hip, man."

"Name's Eddie, Eddie Chicago. We're on our way to California, maybe even get into the movies. You can dig it, can't you? "

Eddie smiled and patted the attendant on the back. The attendant leaned on the gas pump. Like an awed kid looking at a movie star waiting for something to happen, he watched. Eddie twisted the chrome gas cap back on the tank opening, leaped into the Mercury, and slammed the door.

The attendant yelled after him, "I can dig it. man, wish I was going with you."

Eddie twisted the three wires together. The engine caught and died. He tried again. The starter turned and moaned to a stop. He opened the door, put one foot on the pavement and yelled into the car, "Get out and push."

Flick opened the passenger door. Everyone piled out. Breed, Hog, and Screwball went to the back of the Mercury and pushed on the trunk. With the door open, Flick pushed on the doorframe. Holding one hand on the steering wheel and the other hand on the doorframe, Eddie pushed. While Breed, Hog, and Screwball pushed on the trunk, Eddie jumped back behind the wheel, and the car rolled away from the pumps.

Breed turned toward Hog. "I think the fan belt's loose."

"Probably is," Hog said, "but it if you tell mud-assed Eddie about it, he won't check it out."

Breed's feet dug into the gravel and slipped. He regained his footing and pushed. "He just likes to be right."

"Yeah," Hog agreed. "He'll only give us a perfunctory answer."

While Breed wondered what perfunctory meant, the car increased speed. Eddie pushed the clutch in, hooked the transmission into second gear, and let out the clutch. Immediately, the engine fired up. The pipes roared in a smooth mellow tone. He pushed the clutch in, hit the brake, and motioned to the others. "Get in."

Breed, Hog, and Screwball, ran for the door. Before they could get in, Flick hopped in and slammed the door.

Eddie mashed the gas feed.

Tires spun and spit gravel and dust all over Breed, Hog, and Screwball. Standing in a cloud of gray dust, they watched the Mercury race down the highway.

Waving the dust from his face, Hog walked to the side of the road and picked up a rock. "If that mud-ass Carmichael comes back, I'm throwing this rock right through the windshield."

Screwball blew a puff of air and waved the dust away from his face. "And I'm gonna tell that dumb shit to clean the mud off his ass, so the ass doctor can examine his brain"

The dust cleared.

The station attendant stood next to the gas pump and watched, smiling.

But Eddie didn't come back.

Breed let his hands fall to his sides. "Let's start walking."

They walked a ways down the road, stopped, and stared straight ahead. The Mercury was stopped across the highway. Eddie and Flick were standing in the doorways pushing the car up a slight grade.

Hog looked at Breed and Screwball. "You gonna run up and help?"

In unison, Breed and Screwball smiled. "Nope."

Breed was going to tell Eddie about the fan belt, but figured that if he didn't and Eddie took off again, he wouldn't get far. So with Hog and Screwball, he stood at the side of the road and watched. The Mercury started rolling. Eddie and Flick jumped in. Eddie popped the clutch. The Mercury hadn't been going fast enough.

It stopped.

They got out.

Red-faced, they stood with their hands leaning on the fender, taking in deep breaths of much needed air, anxiously staring at Breed and the others.

Breed took one step and stopped.

After a few moments, Flick waved his hand down at Breed and they started pushing again.

The Mercury started.

They jumped in.

Eddie backed the Mercury up, pulled to the side of the road, and stopped next to Breed.

Flick stepped out and held the door open. "Thanks for the help pushing."

Smiling with revenge, Breed, Hog, and Screwball just stood there.

Flick motioned with his arm. "Okay, get in."

They piled into the back.

Flick jumped in the front seat and slammed the door. Eddie put the car into gear and drove back toward the gas station. The attendant was still standing next to the gas pump. Eddie turned left, made a wide circle, and headed back onto the highway. In a goodbye gesture, he waved his arm out the open window. Breed watched the attendant turn and go back into the station, and the Mercury purred on down the highway.

Breed could see Eddie's belief in his unlimited power to solve a problem had been renewed. Eddie pounded the bottom of his fists on the steering wheel and shook his head up and down with approval. "See, nothin' to it. We'll have all the gas we need." He held his finger on the chrome volume control knob of the radio and looked to Hog.

Hog couldn't resist. "Hey, dip shit!"

Before Hog could continue, Flick said, "We fixed it. Hant!"

Eddie turned the radio up full blast. He jerked his head to the beat and yelled over the music. "Keep an eye out for gas stations, Yessiree! Man, oh man, we'll drain the hose all the way to California!"

Eddie pulled in every station along the highway and drained the hose. And each time they stopped, the Mercury had to be push-started.

While the car was parked under an orange gas station sign, Breed lay back on the seat and looked at the clouds puffing past. "At this rate it'll take us a hundred years to get there."

"So what?" Flick said coolly. "We'll still get there."

Eddie snapped his fingers. "That's right!" He pulled out of the station.

"If that front tire isn't going flat," Hog said as the Mercury gained speed, "we might get there."

Wiggling the red steering wheel, Eddie said, "Dee wheel, dee wheel, she does seem to wobble a bit."

"It'll get us to California won't it, Eddie?" Flick asked and looked to Eddie for a positive answer.

"If it doesn't, the Great Eddie Chicago will figure something out. I always do."

"Heck yeah," Screwball said. "We'll take the engine out and get there on the go-kart we got strapped on the back."

Eddie winked at Screwball and snapped his fingers. "There's an idea. Instead of a spare tire we'd have a spare car. It'd be a little cramped, but we'd go so fast we'd think we were flying. Nobody would catch us."

As Breed took in the afternoon sights of the road, a few shiny, new cars roamed the roads. Inside one of the cars, a group of well-to-do pubescent-faced high school kids with pockets full of their parent's money, yelled out the windows with loud, horse-throaty voices. Breed thought they were just like the rich kids who lived on the outskirts of Shitsplat. Living pampered and sheltered lives, they screamed because they believed they were better than anyone else. They screamed because they had money, and they wanted the whole world to know it. They were just, "Hey look at me!" asshole rich kids, and it really wasn't their money. They had done nothing to earn it. They had no real right to it. By necessity they were smug and heartless, and they attracted more smug and heartless kids. Kids with small minds and big cruelty who didn't care about the people they believed were beneath them. They were sheltered kids out to conquer the world with their pubescent ignorance. Breed hated every one of them. He even hated the word pubescent.

Eddie slowed. The Mercury cruised past a string of suburban houses with green manicured lawns. An old man with a worn wooden cane, teetered to his mailbox. A roving band of adolescents, in a white Ford convertible, slowed. They hung out over the sides and spouted bubble-gum-breathed obscenities. As mean lines of hostility cramped the face of a blond kid with a football player type haircut, he threw a water balloon. It broke and wet the gravel drive in front of the man. Another kid with a chubby hand threw a half-eaten hamburger at the man. It bounced off the man's back and left a red smear of ketchup on his gray sweater.

"Hey Eddie," Breed said, and his voice grew fierce with anger. "Look what those assholes did to that old man."

Driving past the old man, Eddie slowed and looked in the rearview mirror.

Breed rested one hand on the back of the seat and looked back at the man. "Are they coming back?" He turned and looked ahead.

Eddie looked ahead, too. The white Ford kept on going. "They think they're really going somewhere," he said. "They ain't gonna stop."

Flick twisted around and looked back toward the old man. He was picking up the half-eaten hamburger and greasy papers. "Those phony bastards aren't going nowhere except back to Mommy and Daddy for more money."

194

"Who do they think they are," Breed wanted to know. "They got to throw garbage at that old guy, just because he came out to get his mail."

"They're just little high school punks," Flick said. "They have never gotten their hands dirty, and they're throwin' food away. You can tell they never gone a day without a meal in their lives." Eddie banged on the steering wheel. "What kind of assholes would make fun of a poor old man for no reason? Do they think it's funny?"

"Maybe they're practicing to be clowns," Screwball said in quizzical amusement.

"They looked like clowns," Breed said, "only not funny."

Eddie nudged Flick in the ribs with his elbow. "Maybe if I blew my brains out right in front of their dumb lily-white faces, they wouldn't laugh at anybody anymore." Eddie let out a weird, hollow laugh, and a look of excruciating discomfort filled his face.

The look caused Breed to wonder if Eddie would really shoot himself, but he kept it to himself.

Like a little kid shaking off a bad dream, Eddie shook his head and downshifted. As the engine purred deep and the Mercury slowed, Breed felt himself slide forward on the seat. He looked out the front window. On the railroad tracks, running parallel to the Mercury, a yellow railroad hand-car with two men pumping the levers, sailed alongside them. Breed reached over the seat and tapped Eddie on the shoulder.

195

Eddie whipped himself sideways and looked out the side window. His eyes bulged with astonishment. "Look at that!"

All heads turned toward the moving hand-car.

Hog made no effort to disguise his excited feelings. "I sure would like to ride on one of those things."

"Me, too!" Breed echoed with resounding enthusiasm.

Screwball leaned toward the window. "I'll ask them." He stuck his head out the window and yelled at the two men pumping the hand-car, "How about a ride?"

One of the men opened his mouth to speak, but before he could say anything, the hand-car followed a bend in the tracks and sailed away from the road.

With an injured look, Screwball pulled his head back into the Mercury and sagged limply in the seat. "If we had that, we wouldn't have to worry about running out of gas."

Miles down the road, and past a stretch of wind-churned mountains, Breed saw another gas station. "Are we gonna stop again?"

"We have to," Eddie said, slowing the car. "We don't need much gas, but I gotta check that front tire."

"I don't know about you guys," Screwball said. "But my stomach's sittin' on my back bone waiting for something to work on."

Eddie shook the steering wheel and let the car slow. "We ain't far enough away from those cops to be stopping for any length of time."

"That's right," Flick agreed. "We gotta get in and get out. That way, if the cops come around asking questions, those people in the station won't be able to remember what we look like."

Eddie slowed the car, more. "I can dig it, man. We need to check that tire, probably only needs air, but we'll stay long enough to get some food." A funny, crazed look came over his face. "After seeing what kind of assholes those kids were that threw that garbage at that old man, I ain't takin' no crap off nobody."

With the car moving at a snail's pace, Breed felt a pang in his stomach. He didn't know if it were Eddie's personality change or hunger. He shrugged it off and looked at the gas station. Up above, four crisscrossing stringers of sun-faded orange and blue plastic pennants snapped and flapped in the wind. "It looks like they got a little store in there."

Like a man with a terminal disease, Flick stared at the store as if it were a cure. "Let's stop and get some food."

CHAPTER 12

Sitting in the back of the Mercury, Breed peered out the window. As the gas station slowly neared, an uneasy feeling crept into his mind. Up ahead, cinders and stomped dirt spread from the station entrance to the side of the road, and old and rusting gas pumps sat on crumbling cement and looked like ancient ruins. This station reminded Breed of the gas station in Shitsplat, where the owner's son had hidden Breed's stolen bike. "That looks like a place cops would stop for free coffee, and the owner would kiss their asses."

"Come on, Breed," Eddie said. "Quit worrying. We're on our way to California."

"I'm not worrying," Breed lied. "I just don't want to do something stupid and get caught."

"We ain't gonna do nothin' stupid," Eddie assured him.

"Yeah," Flick said with confidence. "We got a lotta ways get gas that ain't stupid." He patted the dashboard above the radio. "And we got a radio to play. Ain't nothin' gonna a stop us now."

"Okay, you guys," Eddie said with authority. "Here's the plan." He used his hand and fingers to keep track of the unfolding details. "One. When we stop, I'll run in and see if they have some baloney and a loaf of bread. Two. Flick, while I'm in there, you can pump the gas and drain the hose."

"Can't," Flick said. "I have to piss."

"I'll pump the gas," Breed volunteered. "After I drain the hose, I can run in and take a quick piss."

Screwball lifted his hand. "Wait for me. I have to drain my hose, too."

Eddie flashed a look of disapproval in Screwball's direction but then smiled and nodded in approval. "Okay, that's three. It shouldn't take no time at all."

Flick held up his closed fist and popped up his thumb. "Team work."

"What's the matter with you guys?" Hog wanted to know. "It's only a gas station. Quit makin' a big deal out a nothin'. Just go in there get some goddamn food and take a piss."

"That's right," Eddie agreed. "We'll get in and get out. Before they even know we were there, we'll be back on the road." He paused to let his point sink in. "That sound okay to you guys?"

No one answered. Breed knew Hog was right. No use making a big deal out of stopping for gas and a couple of baloney sandwiches. He didn't want to act like a baby and spoil the plan. Maybe, once he got something to eat, that rotten feeling in his stomach and the foreboding feeling in his chest would go away. "Yeah, let's do it," he said and turned to Eddie. "Hey, Eddie, before we go in, shove those starter wires up under the dash so they won't be hanging down, if somebody sees them, they might get suspicious."

"If you piss your pants," Hog added, "somebody's going to get suspicious."

Yeah," Screwball grinned, "One, two, three, and Breed will have peed."

Hog leaned forward ready to spring out of the car the moment it stopped. "Not if I get in there first."

Eddie shut the motor off, guided the car beside the pumps, and stopped. Hog, Screwball, and Flick dashed to the side of the station. Before he opened the door, Eddie waited, his eyes constantly moving, his ears on high alert for the faintest hint of anything that could stop them from going to California. Breed crawled out of the car, unhooked the silver nozzle on the gas pump, and placed it into the tank opening.

Eddie opened his door, got out, and kicked the front tire. "It's just a flat spot, it's okay." He turned toward Breed.

Breed crossed his legs and held the nozzle. "I'll get it, Breed," Eddie said and took the nozzle from Breed's hand.

Breed turned and ran toward the station. When he caught up with the others, they were looking through the big plate glass window. Inside, a tall, skinny man who looked to be the attendant, appeared to have rough mannerisms and could be the type of person that if you said the wrong thing, would bite your head off. He was wearing one of those dirty-white paper garrison hats like the kid at the other station had worn, only this hat had green unreadable letters stenciled on the sides. While the others ran for the restroom, Breed ducked behind a pop machine. The attendant apparently hadn't seen him and trotted out of the stone-front gas station toward Eddie. "Are you fillin' her up?" the

200

attendant said in a loud demanding voice and forced a phony smile.

Eddie turned the pump off and drained the hose. "Yeah, already did."

The attendant lifted the hood. "Check the oil?" he said loud enough for Breed to hear.

Breed didn't want the attendant messing around under the hood. Last year Breed had hid next to the corner of the gas station in Shitsplat and watched the owner's kid cut fan belts and short stick oil readings to cheat trusting customers out of their money. If this attendant did that, it would set Eddie off. He wouldn't be able keep his mouth shut. It was one thing to cheat a little bit, draining the hose, but to out and out deliberately cut a belt or short stick the oil level and pretend to add a quart with an empty can was another matter.

Eddie hated people who tried to make him look stupid. If they tried to pull a fast one on Fast Eddie Chicago that was where he would draw the line. He wouldn't stand for being cheated. He would make a scene. The attendant would call the cops. They would probably be the same cops they had tricked with the dummy. They'd come and find the stolen car. Breed and his friends wouldn't be going to California.

Breed held his water and watched the attendant. He already had the hood open. Eddie turned his back, took the gas nozzle out of the tank, and clicked it back on to the pump. He screwed the gas cap on the tank, and the attendant reached under the hood and pulled the fan belt out. It had been cut.

Breed knew there would be trouble. Fear tightened his throat, but he had to go bad. He ran to the restroom and stopped. A dirty white sign taped to the men's restroom door read, OUT OF ORDER.

Breed couldn't hold it. He dashed around the back of the station where Flick, Screwball, and Hog had just finished writing their names in the oil-soaked dirt, next to five dirty-red fifty-five-gallon steel drums.

Breed stood next to a drum, unzipped his fly, and shrieked. "We're in trouble. So he could sell us a new one, that skinny attendant cut the belt."

Breed's statement sent an excited ripple through everybody around the barrels.

Flick gave Breed a puzzled look. "What?"

As Breed urinated, he looked down. A shiny dime had been tramped flat into the dark dirt. "When Eddie finds out, he'll be pissed."

Flick looked toward the station. "Where is he?"

"He was going inside, but I hope he's in the car."

Flick looked to the others, "Let's go."

After they were gone, Breed finished, zipped up his fly, picked up the dime, and put it in his pocket. Then he walked to the corner of the station and stopped. He could see the Mercury parked by the pump, but Eddie wasn't there. Breed looked through the glass and into the store part of the station. Eddie wasn't there either.

Behind Breed, a big man opened the restroom door just enough to shuffle out sideways. Once outside, he pulled his pants over his huge belly. At

202

the same time the door slammed shut, a chocolate bar fell from his back pocket and landed on the gravel. In a delayed reaction, the out of order sign banged on the doorframe and swung on the doorknob. The man buckled his belt and giggled. "Out of order, my ass."

As Breed stayed crouched behind the pop machine, the particularly bad odor of the man filled the air. It smelled like dried sweat, so old it had turned to vinegar. Apparently, the big man was too lazy to wash himself, and it was evident that he kept the restroom closed because he was too lazy to clean it.

Breathing in labored breaths, and walking with a penguin's walk, the man waddled past and headed to the back of the station. Breed moved away from the pop machine, looked through the glass and into the store part of the station.

A little gray cloud of hot air huffed around the corner of the station and danced through the open door that was held open with a little wooden wedge. Right behind it, Eddie walked in and stopped at the cash register. With his mud-splatted behind toward Breed, Eddie scanned the candy bars under the smudged glass of the worn oak-framed display counter and looked around for someone to help him. No one was around. He grabbed a loaf of bread off the shelf and looked at the gas pumps. The attendant was outside pumping gas into another car.

It was a perfect time for Eddie to get into that cash register. But the fat man was coming around the corner. Breed hoped Eddie would just buy some baloney and bread and get out of there.

Eddie looked down into the glass case. Although he couldn't hear him, Breed motioned with his hands and whispered, "That's it, Eddie, just hurry up. Forget about the baloney and bread. Buy a few candy bars instead."

Flick and Screwball came up behind Breed. Flick flashed a chocolate bar. "Look what I found."

Breed continued to watch Eddie. "Yeah," he said without turning around. "I saw the fat guy drop it."

Hog stepped next to Breed. "What's taking Eddie so long? We gotta get the car started and get out of here."

Breed jerked his head in the direction of the attendant at the pumps. "That's the guy that cut the fan belt. Probably wants Eddie to buy a new one."

Flick glared at the attendant. "Without a fan belt we ain't goin' far."

"Let's go, you guys," Breed said and backed away from the window. "I think I saw a spare fan belt in the trunk. We'll put it on."

As they ran toward the Mercury, a banged-up Chevy pulled up behind the Mercury and stopped. Breed looked down the road. Another car was coming. He turned toward Flick and held up his hand up in a stopping gesture. "Wait, maybe it's the cops."

Walking like weary travelers that had forgotten something, they walked back to the pop machine, and as if they were trying to decide what flavor to buy, they stood in front of it.

The door of the Chevy creaked opened. The lady inside was dressed in a dirty-blue checkered dress that looked like it had been made from a tablecloth. She adjusted her thick, dirty glasses and motioned upward with her thumb at the person seated next to her. The passenger door was apparently jammed. The lady stepped out, crossed her arms across her huge sagging breasts, and waited for her daughter to crawl over the floor-mounted gearshift and slide across the seat. After she did, she dropped her feet onto the pavement and stood up. She held a dirty hairbrush, and with nervous strokes, she brushed her long, honey-blond hair. It was greasy, and she had waited until the last possible moment to try and look presentable. Like a lady with a bladder about explode, her mother tapped her foot.

The attendant stepped to the lady, and hiding the cut fan belt in the front of his shirt, he asked, "Can I help you ma'am?"

Like a lady that had held it so long that the urine had backed up into her throat and was in terrible pain, the mother squeaked out, "One dollar's worth." She held her legs together, stepped around a pyramid of yellow cans of oil, and hurried her pinched ass across the station lot.

Eddie stopped looking for the baloney and watched the mother's daughter follow behind, picking knots out of her hair. She was a much better thing to look at.

Except for her top that showed off her beautiful breasts, she was dressed poorly. The smoking Chevy they had pulled up in and the dirty bare feet on the daughter showed that they were of meager means. Although she walked with a wiggle, her breasts were the only things she had to show off, and for all to see, she presented them like badges of beauty.

Mother and daughter looked like they were the same person separated by fifty years of time. The daughter was a younger image of her mother's past, and the mother was the image of her daughter's future. The time machine-like contrast made her daughter's beauty stand out like light in the dark. Breed thought her daughter's looks deserved more than her mother could provide, but it seemed that her mother sacrificed her own well-being and looks to make sure that her daughter had something decent to wear. Who knew? A lot of unfortunate people believe in fairy tales. A rich man might come along and marry her, take them right out of poverty.

The beautiful breasted girl distracted Breed. He knew she would distract Eddie, and more time would pass. And the police would creep closer. He looked through the window. Eddie was still inside, waiting.

Breed yelled through the window. "Come on, Eddie. Let's go!"

Before Eddie could acknowledge Breed's request, the attendant came in and yelled across the store, "Sir, your oil's fine. But your fan belt is broken."

As the attendant stood with his back against a shelf, the end of the fresh cut fan belt from the Mercury stuck out the front of his shirt.

Eddie glared at the attendant. "What?"

"Look for yourself," the attendant pleaded like a crooked trial lawyer. Behind his back he reached up and tried to sneak a different old, worn broken belt off the shelf.

But Eddie caught him in the act. "That ain't my belt," he said and pointed to the belt sticking out of the attendant's shirt. "If that cut belt's mine, I'll break your skinny ass."

Mopping his grimy, sweaty face with a dirty handkerchief, the fat man waltzed in. "You'll do nothing of the kind," he arrogantly stated. "We do not cut belts in this station." He tried to huff up his sunken chest, but his stomach barrel out. "We run a respectable business here."

Eddie pointed to the fat man. "Just because you're this skinny-assed attendant's pet penguin, you think you can call yourself respectable." Eddie laughed his whooping laugh. "You're nothing but scam artists and crooks. The only respectable thing you could run is dog shit. And a dog wouldn't work in this half-assed station."

"We didn't cut nothing," the attendant said, raising his hand to quell Eddie. "See for yourself." He held the old belt in front of Eddie's face and grinned. "See there's no clean cut. It just broke."

Eddie grabbed the belt and flung it across the store. "You ain't pullin' that shit on me! You probably used that same belt a thousand times." Waves of fury and hate beamed from Eddie's face.

The attendant crossed his arms across his chest and defiantly stood in front of Eddie.

"Eddie needs help," Flick said in haste and took a step to go in the station.

The roar of a car engine filled the air.

"Wait!" Breed looked toward the Mercury.

A police car pulled in front of it and stopped.

"They must've drove all night," Hog said and pointed to the car. "Look at the dents and mud on the bottom."

Breed winced. "Probably the cops that ran over the dummy."

"Those look like State Boys," Flick said and made a sour face. "If they are, we're in big trouble."

Grabbing at a glimmer of hope, Breed said, "Maybe they only stopped to get gas."

"Maybe, my ass," Hog said. "They're gonna see those wires hanging down that Eddie uses to start the car."

Breed nodded in defeat. "If Eddie didn't hide them, they'll know it's stolen."

With his palms back against the counter, Eddie glanced toward the door. The girl stood in the doorway, blocking his view of the police car. He faced the attendant. "I ain't got time to screw around with someone as dumb as you." He reached up and nudged the attendant out of the way.

Breed's heart grabbed at his throat. Trying to get Eddie's attention without letting the cops know, Breed whispered with great animation. "Can't you see the cops?" His hands made little flights in the air. "Get the hell out of there."

But Eddie didn't see Breed's warning. When Breed crouched down and watched through the window, Flick, Hog, and Screwball stood on the other side of the pop machine.

"That big tit girl's standing in the way," Flick said, almost whining. "Eddie can't see the cop car."

Breed knew they had lingered too long. If the cops found out the Mercury had been stolen, escape would be difficult. He froze in place and wished the cops would get some kind of emergency call on the radio and speed away.

A patrolman with a .38-caliber revolver, in a holster, with the handle facing forward, walked around the Mercury and looked into the front window. He looked toward the other patrolman, and gave him a quizzical look. "Is it hotwired?"

The other patrolman nodded.

"Damn it!" Hog said in a low voice. "Dumb ass Eddie didn't hide the wires."

The other patrolman stepped to the back of the car, took a notebook from his breast pocket and looked at the license numbers. "This is it!"

"Ahh, man," Flick whispered, "we should've changed the plates."

"We would have done that," Hog said, his voice quivering with annoyance. "But Eddie said we were only borrowing the car."

The attendant stretched his skinny neck out the doorway and pointed to Eddie. The fan belt that been in his shirt, dangled from his hand. Smirking, he shouted to the police. "Here he is!"

While the patrolmen watchfully walked toward the station, Eddie reached up and picked a red quart can of oil off the shelf, and screamed at the attendant, "You cheatin' son-of-a-bitch!" He banged the can down on the glass counter. The counter cracked but didn't break. He vehemently jerked his finger at the attendant. "I'll rip that smug look right off your ugly face."

Terrified, the attendant dropped the belt and leaped through the doorway.

Flick, Hog, and Screwball crouched and duck-walked until they were hiding behind the fifty-five-gallon drums. The attendant whizzed past the patrolmen and ran to the back of the station. Breed stayed hidden behind the pop machine and watched.

Inside, the fat man pointed at the cracked glass and thundered at Eddie, "You little asshole! Your muddy ass is going to pay for that."

"Oh yeah," Who's gonna make me? You're so fat, the only exercise you get is in the winter when you slip on the ice trying to get blubber ass to your car."

"You can't come in here with mud on your ass and talk to me like that!" The fat man lunged toward Eddie.

Eddie ducked under the fat man's huge gathering arm and picked up a Coke bottle. He lifted high and swung it down at the fat man. It missed and crashed into the top of the cracked glass counter. Glass splintered into long pointed shards, scattered into the case, and onto the floor. But the bottle didn't break. Still holding the bottle, Eddie lifted his hand high for another swing. Blood from his slit-open wrist pumped down the green bottle.

Outside, the older of the two state patrolmen shook his head as if he had just woken up, and placed his hand on his gun but didn't pull it out.

His younger partner looked to the gun. "He might be dangerous, aren't you going to pull your weapon out?"

The elder patrolman kept an eye on Eddie. "He's just a kid. You only draw your weapon if you are going to use it."

Breed knew Eddie was caught. He had been stupid enough to steal the car, but Breed didn't think he was dumb enough to get shot. Inside, Eddie was holding a yellow two-gallon can of oil over his head and yelling at the fat man, "Get the hell away from me." Jerking the can in abrupt threatening motions, his darted from side to side. "I'll bash your thievin' head in."

While the younger patrolman kept watch, the other patrolman took his hand off his gun. Then in an unthreatening gesture, thrust his hands in front of himself, sauntered through the doorway, and angled toward Eddie. "I know you're mad, son," he said slow and easy. "Before you get hurt, put the oil can down."

But Eddie wasn't mad. He was white-hot fucking livid. All the nice talk in the world wasn't going to control him. Eddie reared back, clasping tighter to the can with both hands.

Imitating a gun, the patrolman pointed his finger, lifted his thumb, and pointed at Eddie. "I'm not going to tell you again."

With fear in his eyes, Eddie stood hunched in the middle of the room. After a few tense moments, a look of relief filled his face. He lowered the oil can and set it on the shards of glass inside the counter. The glass crunched and squeaked under

211

the weight of the heavy metal can. The beautiful-breasted girl flitted past the front window. Eddie glimpsed her. Then as if he had had an afterthought, he lowered his head and raised his blood-soaked hands in the air. "Don't blow a blood vessel. I'm here. You got me."

With a disapproving look, the fat man slipped up behind him with a tire iron in his hand. Then, confirming he was low-bread scum of the earth, he reared back and blind-sided Eddie right in the side of the head. Eddie tumbled to the corner of the station and landed in the splintered glass from the broken counter.

The older patrolman jumped between Eddie and the fat man, "Back off!"

Breed popped out from behind the pop machine and stepped toward Eddie.

Before he could get to the door, sneering, the young state patrolman pulled his gun and pointed it at Breed.

Breed dropped down.

Eddie reached onto the floor with his bloody hand and grabbed a shard of broken glass from the pieces scattered on the floor. Like thick red water, blood gushed out his ear and ran down the side of his face. He jumped up. The front of his face was bloodless white. Waving his fists wildly with the bloody glass shard clenched in his fist, he stepped to the side and lunged toward the fat man.

The young patrolman pointed his gun at Eddie.

Breed stepped into the door and yelled, "He never killed anybody. Leave him alone!"

The young patrolman turned and jerked his gun at Breed. Breed thrust his hands into the air. "Don't shoot!"

Jerking his fist at Eddie, the fat man shouted, "He's trying to kill me!"

The young patrolman turned toward Eddie and fired. Eddie's hand was on his bloody chest, trying to stop the blood from spurting. Then he took his hand from his chest, and as if he were trying to fly to get away, he flapped his arms out to the sides, but he didn't fly. He fell to the floor, bounced, and with his shirt bunched up and his abdomen exposed, he rolled in a limp sprawl that signified death.

The patrolman whirled around and pointed the gun in Breed's direction. Breed bolted away from the door and ran around the whitewashed corner of the station. He stopped and tried to become invisible. Holding a gun, the skinny attendant ran toward him. Breed knew if he stood still, he would be shot or caught. He ran to the back of the station and zigzagged around the barrels.

Flick and the others were running away from the station and heading into the forest.

In what he hoped was a swift space-eating sprint, Breed raced after them.

Like a runner jumping a high hurdle in an Olympic track meet, Flick leaped into the air. "Electric fence. Jump!"

Breed hesitated and swung his hands back to propel himself over the fence. The attendant snagged one of Breed's hands, looked back over his shoulder, and yelled, "I got him, Officer."

213

Breed couldn't get free. Searching for help, his eyes shifted to the left and right. Flick jumped back over the fence and held out his hand. "Grab it!"

Breed latched onto Flick's hand. The attendant pointed the gun at Breed's head. "Stop, or I'll shoot."

Flick grabbed onto the electric fence. The current ran through Flick's and Breed's body and continually shocked the attendant. As he uncontrollably danced on the end of Breed's hand, Crack! A flame stabbed the air. The gun had gone off. The bullet zinged through the air. Soft flesh below Breed's eyebrow burned as if it has just been cut. Above, dozens of gunshot-frightened birds winged into the sky. Below, from constantly being shocked, the attendant danced around on the end of Breed's hand and dropped the gun.

With a jerk of his head, Flick motioned for Hog to get the gun.

Hog jumped over the fence, scooped up the gun, jumped back over the fence, and took off.

The young patrolman ran around the gas station pointing his gun, but didn't shoot. He seemed to be mesmerized by the skinny attendant dancing on the end of Breed's hand.

Flick looked at Breed. "When I let go, jump over this fence and run."

Flick ungripped the electric fence. The attendant quit jumping around and grabbed at his chest. Breed and Flick vaulted over the fence and caught up with the others. While the young patrolman stood with his mouth agape, they hopped

214

through the thick weeds, jumped over a shallow creek, and eased into a harvest colored forest.

Behind a tall tree, Flick bent over, rested his hands on his knees, and looked up at Breed. "Just before you ran around the station, we heard a whack."

"Yeah," Hog said. "But it didn't sound like a gun."

Breed stood next to the tree, gasping for breath. His chest heaved, his pulse hammered, and sweat poured from his forehead. Although he was terrified, it had been the greatest excitement he had ever experienced. Flick looked directly into his face. "Where's Eddie?"

Although he tried to hold it in, Breed started to cry. Not silently but like a boy with hysterical gulpings.

Flick repeated the question. "Where's Eddie?"

Breed shook his head once, quit crying, and regained his composure. "They killed Eddie."

A look of disbelief spread across Flick's face. "Are you sure he's dead?"

"Breed felt the tears well up in his brown eyes. "I watched him drop. I think he was dead before they shot."

"What?"

"When he wasn't looking that fat guy hit him with a tire iron. There's blood everywhere."

Hog's forehead creased. "Why did they shoot him?"

"Eddie tried to stab him with a piece of glass, blood everywhere. They shot him, then he dropped on the floor."

With a defeated look, Screwball looked into the thick brush and the tall trees. "It's a long way back home. Let's go back and give up."

Breed made a sour face. "We can't. They'll shoot us."

"I don't think they're after us," Screwball said, and edged toward the station.

Tensing to run, Breed looked far into the woods. "I wouldn't say they're not after us. After the cop shot Eddie, he pointed his gun at me."

As if undecided, Flick turned toward the station. Then he frowned and jerked a thumb over his shoulder. "Let's get outta here!"

216

CHAPTER 13

After running as fast as he could, Breed limply leaned against a tree and tried to get a grip on himself. He took several deep breaths, exhaling slowly until the fear subsided. His bullet-grazed eye had swollen shut. With the sleeve of his shirt, he wiped the blood from his eye. With his other eye, he looked into the forest ahead. It reminded him of the many times he had ran into the familiar forest around Shitsplat. That forest had been like a protective cradle. This new forest was bigger and probably stretched for hundreds of miles, and he couldn't see any well-beaten paths to follow. It would be rough going, but it gave everybody a better chance of getting away from those zinging bullets.

With one arm raised to ward off any pine branches that would reach out and slow his escape, Flick ran headlong into the new cradle of safety, and Hog, Screwball, and Breed followed. When they came to an open field, ground-hugging dewberry vines curled around their feet, and knife-like little thorns ripped at Breed's new shoes, snagged into his shoelaces, and caused him to trip and fall. With his one eye stabbing through the dimness of the forest, he got back up. He didn't want to go into what was becoming a cruel and unforgiving forest, but it was his only escape. Trailing behind Flick and the others, he kept on running.

In the dark shadow of a clump of trees, a skinny branch whipped across his face. The vision in his good eye blurred. He wanted to stop running, check his eye, and rest. But if he did, the police would catch up. If he let them, not only would it be an extra-added attraction to this fast-moving horror movie, he would have to outdistance a bullet. But even if he ran at full speed, he would not win that race.

The others ran further ahead. Gasping for breath, Breed slowed. What Eddie had told him a week before they left, flashed in his mind. "You have to be careful in places like the projects in Chicago. The cops can't protect you from the muggers, and the muggers don't protect you from the cops."

This wasn't the projects of Chicago, but Breed wondered what was going to happen when Eddie's father found out some hick-town cop shot his son because of a cut fan belt. His father was a big numbers man from Chicago who came down to Youngstown to work with Jimmy Hoffa and the Teamsters Union. What would those gangsters do if they found out Eddie had been with Breed, and he hadn't tried to help? Would they blame him? Youngstown was only a few miles from Shitsplat. The gangsters had blown up so many cars there that people called it Bomb Town. If the cops didn't catch him, and he made it home, would the gangsters blow up his parent's shack with him in it? Hog had the gun. Maybe they could take turns guarding each other's shacks, but there were too many gangsters, and Hog only had one gun. Trying to get rid the painful feeling of Eddie being dead, Breed shook his head and realized, if he wanted to live, he couldn't tell anybody anything about being with Eddie when it happened. Breed figured, if he and the others didn't get caught, the gangsters would never find out.

He ran faster.

After running across an open field, he slowed to a fast-paced walk and stopped at a stagnant pool of black water. The humid air of the dense place engulfed his face. Before he saw them, he sucked in a fleet of tiny flying bugs. They tried to fly into his eye that wasn't sealed shut. He closed his good eye into a slit, coughed the bugs out of his throat, and opened his mouth to breath. He breathed a half a breath and stopped. Like a million tiny black dots vibrating in midair, another fleet of bugs appeared before his half-opened eye. He waved the tiny dots away from his face, crashed through tall, jagged berry canes, and kept tripping over low brambles until the bugs were behind him. In a place where a small stream found its winding way among the trees, he splashed into the water. When it seeped into his new shoes and made a squishing sound, he muttered, "What can happen next?"

In sweltering air, under the thick green brush of a gully, Breed stood in the middle of the slowly flowing stream. The screech of birds and the buzz of insects became prevalent and energetic. And it seemed to be getting hotter and sunnier by the hour. His body felt sore and beat, but his mind hardly noticed it. Struggling to see out of his bloody eye, he called out, "Hey, you guys, "I can't see. I think I'm going blind. Wait up!"

The others stopped and splashed back to him. With the back of his hand, Breed wiped the blood from his eye. It smeared down his face.

Flick stepped next to him. "Stand still."

While Breed stood still, Flick bent over and dipped the frayed sleeve of his shirt into the stream. "You're not going blind. Most of that blood is dried. It's got your eye glued shut." Using the wet sleeve, he gently swabbed the reddish-brown blood from around Breed's eye. "We'll get it off."

Working on Breed's eye, Flick said, "That cut's pretty deep. I wish we had some methylate to put on to keep it from getting infected."

Breed opened his eye. He could see. "It'll be all right," he said with relief. "I'm not going blind."

Hog stepped close and looked at the cut above Breed's eye. "I'll be damned. If a bullet did that, it was so hot, it cauterized the cut. That's why it quit bleeding so fast."

They walked upstream to the mouth of a gray cement culvert that went under a road and was big enough to walk through.

Screwball stepped into the culvert. "Let's hide in here." His voice echoed through the roundness of the culvert.

Breed stepped inside. An eerie silence hovered in the darkness, and the dampness of the culvert reeked of cold death. It dredged up bitter memories of when he was five years old. The police and neighbors said that his godfather had hung himself in a tree, but everybody knew he had been murdered. The rope marks didn't match up with a hanging. He had been strangled and hung in the tree.

When Breed had looked up in the tree, he had been whisked away and told not to watch. However, without being seen, he slipped behind one of the many cars that had pulled onto the scene. Strangely enough, he suddenly remembered the car he had slipped behind, had been a 1950 red Mercury that he had peeked around and stared into the commotion.

Up in the tall tree, his godfather's body was black and blue. Nobody would climb up into the tree and cut him down. With urgency in his voice, Breed's real father asked for a spoon and said, "He might have swallowed his tongue. I saved a guy once. He might have just swallowed his tongue. He could still be alive."

Someone in the crowd gasp. Then, as if they were trying to make sure all efforts to revive the man were quenched, someone spoke out into the dead silence. "No!" a man said in a loud and stern voice. "He's already dead. You can't save him."

Breed's father ignored the man, ran into the kitchen of the house, got a spoon, placed it in his shirt pocket, and reached up for the first branch. "If I can get up there fast enough," he said, "I might be able to get his tongue out before he chokes to death."

Breed's father climbed the tree and used the spoon to hopefully pull Breed's godfather's tongue from the back of his throat. But he was dead. Breed wondered how his godfather, a war hero who had survived fiery plane crashes and marching gun bullets, had come home with a chest full of medals, and met his death at the end of a cheap clothesline rope. The disrespect for his body was worse. Voices mingled and rose above the chatter.

"Just cut him down," someone yelled from the huddle beneath the tree.

"Yeah, just let him fall to the ground."

"He's dead. It won't matter."

Police, firemen, constables, men of the law, and upstanding members of the community talked in conspiratorial tones and agreed.

A space in Breed's heart was empty, and the air hesitated and hung around before it rushed in to fill the void. His godfather wasn't even out of the tree yet, but on the ground, fake tears and dreams of taking his dead godfather's belongings flowed from the gathering crowd.

"What did he leave?"

"Is the house for sale?"

A friendly neighbor came over, and with the pretense of being helpful, asked, "What are they going to do with the house and the land? If they need money, to help out, I'll buy it, cheap." He looked into the tree and yelled, "Cut him down."

With his face flushing angrily, Breed's father yelled down from the tall branches of the tree. "I'll carry him down. No use making it worse than it already is."

And like some sort of secret joke against the rights of a human being, the real cause of death was never revealed.

Sagging limply beneath the weight of his despair, Breed thought about Eddie being dead, too.

But no one would have to carry him down from a high tree. That sneaky, fat bastard had hit Eddie with that tire iron, and it looked like his brains had oozed out the back of his head. The last time Breed had seen him, the cop had just shot him, and Eddie had been facing down, lying on the cold cement floor. Even though there had been no movement, Breed wondered if Eddie could have gotten the last laugh. That is, if a person wanted to call it a laugh. Breed could hear Eddie saying, "Screwball will never top this."

Now, like Breed's godfather, there would be a lot of things Eddie wouldn't be doing. The morning Breed's godfather had died, Breed was going to pick blackberries with him. After that day, his godfather was gone forever. There would be no more king-size Baby Ruth candy bars. No more berry picking. Being inside that dark cold culvert under the ground caused the sad silent feeling of death-laden air to run up Breed's back like slow flaps of air from black wings of an angel of death about to carry his soul away.

But Breed didn't have this feeling about Eddie, and it made him remember what his godfather had once told him: "A man lives by what he knows."

Did Breed's feeling about Eddie mean he was not dead? In his mind Breed went over what he knew. Even though he was sure Eddie was dead, a doctor had not pronounced him dead, and everything had happened so fast. But when he ran his go-kart into the river, everything had happened fast, too, and he should have been killed, but he had come out without a single scratch. When he had been shot, no dark cloud, no white light, and no storm had appeared on the horizon. There was just that weird silence of death and the void it creates. It was as if someone had stolen a piece of a living puzzle and thrown it to the winds. Now, Breed was not absolutely positive Eddie was dead.

With his voice sounding like it were coming out of a dark tunnel Flick said, "This place reminds me of a grave. Let's get out of here."

Breed shook the thoughts of death out of his mind, hurried out of the culvert, and jerked his head toward the road above. "Hey, Flick, let's check the road out."

"Now that you can see, again, go ahead up," Flick said and lifted his hand in the direction of the embankment. "There's less chance of them seeing one of us. We'll stay down here."

Breed turned, dropped to his hands and knees, and climbed up the grass-covered embankment. Near the top, he clawed into the soft ground with his fingertips, stretched his head, and looked through the slivers of space between the blades of tall couch grass. To his right, swift thudding hooves of a herd of deer galloping across the road caught his attention. With ears pricked and alert, they gracefully passed, and then they were gone. He turned his head and talked over his shoulder. "The station is right up the road."

Hog cocked his head in a disrespectful tilt. "Way to go," he said sardonically. "We're just a bunch of dip shits going in a circle."

Before Breed could reply, in the distance, the sound of a siren and flashing red lights threatened.

224

"Get down," Flick said with immediacy. "The cops are comin' right at you."

Breed dropped down. Between the blades of grass, he watched. A long, white ambulance with a blinking red light raced toward him.

Flick crawled halfway up the embankment and tugged at Breed's pants leg. "Are they slowing down?"

Squinting to keep wind-blown grit out of his eyes, Breed ducked his head down, and the ambulance zipped past. "No, it's an ambulance. It's going to the gas station." He lowered his head. "They're probably going to pick up Eddie's body."

Flick slid down the steep embankment and Breed followed, but the cuff of his black pants caught on the tall grass and slipped up around his knees.

Hog shook his head slowly. "Maybe Eddie's not dead."

"If he ain't dead," Screwball said, "he'll really be mad when he wakes up and finds all that dirt in his face."

Ignoring Screwball's attempted humor, Breed pushed the cuff of his pants back down to his ankles. Hoping Hog was right, he said, "Let's wait here. If the ambulance comes back and it's going fast with the siren on, Eddie's alive. If it comes back slow, he ain't."

Hog pointed up the embankment and told Breed, "Why don't you get your ass back up there and find out."

Flick and Breed crept back up the embankment. Watching, they stayed low and out of sight. Up on

225

the road, the ambulance pulled toward the gas pumps and stopped next to the Mercury. From the other direction, another police car pulled into the station.

"Keep an eye on them, Breed," Flick said. "My shoestring's broke, and there's only enough grass for one person to hide behind." He slid down the embankment. At the bottom, he sat next to the stream of water flowing out the big drainpipe. Tying his broken shoestring into a knot, he said, "Things are getting hot up at that station. We got to get as far away from it as we can."

Checking the chamber of the gun for bullets, Hog stood on a patch of saw-toothed ferns and leaned against the dirty-gray lip of the cement culvert. "Those state boys don't mess around," he said. "They'll shoot us on sight."

"Yeah but—," Flick started to say but choked up. He looked down, and rubbed the toe of his shoe around in a circle in the dirt. "Just to see if Eddie's still alive, we can wait a few minutes."

"Actually," Hog said and tucked the gun into the waistband behind his back, "Eddie *could* be alive."

"I don't think so," Breed said from above. "That was a lot of blood."

"Don't count on it," Hog pointed out. "Eddie's cut could be like the cut on your eye. It was bleeding a lot. Cuts on the face always bleed a lot. They always look worse than they really are."

Breed hoped Hog was on to something. His eye had only been sealed shut with dried blood, and he had thought he was going blind. Touching the cut above his eye, he checked the activity at the station. The rotating lights of the police cars and the ambulance flicked sharp red lines into the air. "I don't know," he said and looked down at Hog. "After he was shot, he hit that cement hard."

Staring at Breed, Hog wrinkled one eye until it was half closed. "You don't know for sure if he was shot. You didn't even know if you were shot. I'm tellin' you, he's alive."

"But the cop shot him in the chest, and he hit his head on that hard cement."

Screwball tapped himself on the forehead. "Eddie's got a hard head."

"They say you never hear the shot that kills you," Breed shot back. "Maybe I only saw something but didn't hear anything."

"All we heard was a whack," Flick said. "It didn't sound like no gun shot."

Breed looked toward the gas station and then looked down at Flick. "Ahh, damn it," he said. "Now, I don't know what it was. But I know my eye's cut, and nobody hit me." He put his elbow on the ground, propped his head up with his hand, and watched through stems of the tall grass. In the distance, the ambulance's red lights reflected off of the red Mercury and made it glow a maroon color.

Down the road, behind Breed's turned head, another police car burped its siren once and sped toward the station.

Breed jerked back.

They might have seen him.

He froze in place.

The police car passed.

He slid down the embankment, and they all ducked into the culvert.

Breed waited a few minutes. The cop car didn't come back. Cautiously, he crawled back up the embankment and watched. The white ambulance pulled away from the Mercury.

The red lights quickened.

The siren growled near.

The red lights brightened to orange.

"Get down, Breed," Flick commanded from the culvert.

"They won't notice," Breed said and lay flat in the weeds by the side of the road. "They're going too fast."

The ambulance howled close. Breed lifted his head and strained to see inside the ambulance. He was too low. He couldn't see. He jumped up.

Flick flared angrily, "Get down!"

Knowing a speeding ambulance with lights flashing and a siren whirring wasn't going to stop or slow down for somebody standing alongside the road, Breed stayed standing and watched the ambulance whip past. Inside, Eddie was sitting up. He was on a white-sheet-covered stretcher. Holding the side of his head with one white-bandaged hand and with his other hand, he was swinging his fist at the attendants.

A welcome tailwind from the speeding ambulance gushed into Breed's happy face. "He's alive!" he cried out and skidded down the embankment.

Disbelief filled Flick's face. "Are you sure?"

"He's the healthiest looking dead person I ever saw riding in a meat wagon," Breed said and broke out into a flood of excited speech. "I saw the crazy bastard trying to fight with the ambulance guys. I thought he got shot in the chest. But he had a bandage on his hand. He must have go shot in the hand, and when I saw him grab his chest, it looked like he had been shot in the chest."

Relieved, Flick clenched his hand in a closed-fist gesture. "All right!"

"After that cop shot, Eddie must have fallen to the floor and played possum," Hog said with a satisfied grin. "Told you!"

Screwball chuckled, a throaty sound. "What did-ya expect? That cop on the bridge said Eddie was invincible." Then as if it were an everyday occurrence, he shrugged. "We still going to California?"

"Aren't we humorous today?" Hog retorted.

Screwball tilted his head to the side and lackadaisically turned the palms of his hands up. "I just thought of something. If Eddie had died and we were standing too close to him, and he went to hell, would our feet get hot feet?"

Hog stared at Screwball in quizzical disbelief. Then he turned from Screwball and shrugged. "At least Eddie won't have to walk home." He deliberately stared at Breed and smiled an exaggerated ear-ear smile.

Breed didn't return the smile. No longer excited about Eddie being alive, his voice turned serious. "He won't be going home, "he said. "When they patch him up, he'll go straight to jail."

The sudden change of the tone in Breed's voice brought Flick's head up sharply. "If we don't get out of here," he said, "we'll go to jail or get shot."

Breed looked into the unknown woods. "Yeah, but we can't get far in that thick brush."

Fed up with the fear and indecision, Hog threw his hands into the air. "The hell with it," he said. "Let's just walk down the goddamn road."

Breed disagreed. "If we walk down the goddamn road, those goddamn cops will see us."

"If you guys don't quit swearing," Screwball said, "The cops will be after you for swearing, too."

Hog started climbing up the embankment. "No they won't," he said back over his shoulder. "They're too busy at the gas station." He reached around and touched the outline of the gun in his waistband. "They shoot at me, I'm shootin' back." He paused. "Goddamn it, Breed. Don't be one of those intelligent people with no brains. After you've had a brief respite come on up the hill."

Not knowing that respite meant a short period of rest from something unpleasant or difficult and pronounced ress-spit, Screwball stared at Hog. "Ress-spit?" he questioned and pointed to Breed. "He never spit in the first place."

Trying to ignore Screwball's antics, Breed looked past the little stream and into the thick brush. His new clothes were dirty, and his new shoes were wet. He didn't believe Hog would really shoot anyone, but the road seemed a better place to be.

Flick jerked his closed fist toward the road. "Let's saddle up." He followed Hog up the embankment.

Breed turned toward Screwball.

With his hand cupped to his ear, Screwball cocked his head so his ear was toward the forest and listened.

Alarmed, Breed turned toward the forest. "Do you hear something?"

"I knew a kid named Jack Burr," Screwball said in a tone of contrite amusement. "He had a brother named Tim. The last time I was in the forest, I heart somebody calling Tim Burr, and a tree fell. But I don't hear anything now."

While Breed spastically shook his head in disbelief, Screwball held out his hand in a welcoming gesture for Breed to go up the embankment.

Shaking off Screwball's ignorance, Breed thought about not going up on the road. If he went through the forest, he could travel a route roughly parallel to the road. That way, he would leave no obvious signs of his passage. It would be slower going through the brush, but it would be safer, and it would save him from taking unnecessary risks.

He didn't move.

"I'm not sure I want to go up."

Screwball's eyebrows arched in surprise. Shaking his head, he dropped his welcoming hand and climbed up the embankment. Half way up he turned. "Come on up, Breed. Tim Burr might be coming out of the forest."

CHAPTER 14

Breed walked through the water and took a few steps into the thick and unfriendly brush.

An owl hooted.

He froze.

To an Apache Indian, the hoot of an owl was a sign of death. Being part Indian, Breed automatically crossed his arms over his chest, assumed the traditional Indian stance, and listened. His Indian side wanted to believe the sign, but his other side told him to ignore the hoot. When he ducked down to slip under a low tree branch, a thorn-filled cane grabbed at his shirt. The more he moved, the more the thorns clung. The clinging thorns, the puncture wounds from when dozens of barbs had hooked in the skin of his arm, and the hoot caused him to say, "Screw this!"

He pulled the thorn-filled-cane from his shirt and decided that where he was had to be a much crueler place than being on the road.

He turned and climbed up the embankment.

At the top, he stood up and looked toward the gas station. The red Mercury that had brought him was still sitting in front of the gas pumps. There were no cops in sight. The Mercury had a hot rod engine in it that the cops couldn't catch. For a second, he thought about sneaking back to the station and stealing the Mercury. After all, it didn't need keys. But even if he did sneak in and hot-wire it, he would have to push it to get it started. If he did that, he could speed away, but even if he did, thanks to that rotten attendant, he wouldn't get far.

The fan belt had been cut. He turned, rushed down the road, and caught up with the others.

After they rounded a bend, tall pine trees shielded them from being seen by the people at the station, and the Mercury was out of sight, and the cops weren't coming down the road.

Screwball turned, stuck out his thumb, and walking backwards, he mimicked what Flick had said in the car. "Hey, Flick, now that we got this car, we won't have to do no more hitchhiking and walking backwards for miles."

Continuing to walk, Flick grumbled, "Yeah, right!"

The burden of distress faded from Breed's mind and other thoughts crept in. Eddie was alive but he was gone. Breed was mad at Eddie for the mess he had gotten them into, but he already missed him. As if he could see him in his mind, Eddie was right in front of him. He wondered if he would ever see Eddie dressed like he wished he could dress. But Eddie would probably go to jail and wear a typical jail suit. In jail, he wouldn't be wearing his tailored, small-cuffed black pants with the thin clean white belt looped loosely around his small waist, and he wouldn't be allowed to wear his black shiny shoes accented with white socks. The vest and the sports shirt with the short sleeves rolled neatly around his arms and the front opened down to three buttons, wouldn't be allowed either. Clothes did make the man, but they wouldn't keep Eddie out of jail.

They all tramped down the road. Every time a car came near, they leaped off to the side and ran into the purple and green forest.

On each side of the road, tall oaks, maples, and wild cherry trees reached into the sky and inhaled the sun's life-giving warmth.

As they walked miles away from the trouble at the gas station, time passed fast, and they felt safe. Now the sun was almost down. Soon it would be dark and cold. As Breed slung his cheap cotton jacket over his shoulder and continued on down the highway, he coughed and swallowed hard. His throat was sore. He wished he had worn his old clothes. They would have been warmer. Flick threw his jacket over his own head, and in one quick motion, he snapped it on. It wasn't the proper way to put on a jacket but it was different. It was cool. Eddie had taught him this old James Dean trick. Breed thought if he had a jacket that wouldn't rip in half, if he tried to snap it on, he could learn the trick, too.

The bottom of Breed's feet hurt, and the tears in his socks dug into his heels. He looked to Flick, and with a hoarse voice, he barely got the words out, "Why don't we try hitchhiking?"

"Flick turned and walked backwards. "We're not really far enough away."

"We could just hitchhike cars that don't look like cops," Breed hoarsely replied.

Screwball heaved a tormented sigh. "Yeah, what the heck. If we see the cops coming, we can always run." He looked toward the darkening forest. "They'll never catch us in there."

Breed arched an eyebrow. "That's true," he said with a clear voice, "but in the dark we won't be able to see where we're going."

"It doesn't matter," Hog said and waved his hand dismissively. "Nobody's going to pick up four guys."

"Somebody might feel sorry for us," Breed offered.

As if surprised, Screwball whipped himself around and stared right into Breed's eyes. "If you want somebody to feel sorry for you," he said, "just tell me when you want me to do it."

Not believing Screwball's never-ending wisecracks, Breed just stared at him.

Flick walked backwards, stuck out his thumb, and watched an approaching car. Breed and the others turned and stuck out their thumbs, too. The car zoomed past. In unison Breed and the others flashed the departing car their middle fingers.

Standing there with his finger still held up, Screwball said, "This is neat. Too bad nobody's watching."

Flick dropped his middle finger and turned forward. "Nobody's gonna stop." He looked down at the front of his dirty and torn shirt and pants. "Our clothes look like somebody just pulled them out of a cow's ass."

Breed took a few steps and stopped. "We need a place to hide until daybreak."

Hog cupped his hand to his ear and turned to the side. "We still might get a ride. A car's coming."

Everybody turned and stuck out their thumbs.

A bouncing carload of giggling, high school girls cruised toward them. Their amateurish excess dark eye shadow, bright red lipsticked lips, and powered faces made them resemble circus clowns, fresh from the makeup mirror.

Keeping his thumb out, Flick lifted his hand high and smiled.

The car screeched to a stop.

Surprised, Breed and the others ran up to the waiting car.

The girls had the doors locked. Like happy white-faced monkeys in a glass cage, they looked out the windows. A tall girl with a thatch of thick red hair and a pretty face rolled her window halfway down. The odor of cheap perfume and bubblegum floated out the window. A big-mouthed girl with short, ugly hair leaned over the tall girl's shoulder and yelled out. "Hey, let's rape these kids!"

Inside the car, the gaggle of girls erupted into titters and forced laughter.

With his face beaming, Flick walked next to the car and placed his hand on the door handle. With the girls flashing mocking smiles at him, Flick yelled, "Yeah! Let's rape these kids!"

The laughter stopped.

The girl's expressions changed from merry pranksters to ones of confusion and horror. They tried to make a snappy comeback, but only gasped and stammered.

The driver tromped on the gas.

Tires spun.

Dirt and small stones flew back, stinging Breed and the others.

"Evidently," Hog said. "The girls are not going to pick us up."

After the carload of girls roared out of sight, like a fragrant fart, the odor of overused powder, bubblegum, and cheap perfume hovered in the air.

Breed thought about Eddie and what he would have done. In his mind Breed could see the blood in his blond hair when he had hit the floor. It was messed up. It was no longer combed back on both sides. If Eddie wouldn't have gotten shot, he might have been here. Like a proud bird doing a sly mating dance, Eddie would have turned his head to one side. The partial DA that had no definite duck's ass running down the back would have gleamed like the bright sun. It was just a little different, not too radical. The girls liked it. They would have given Eddie a ride.

Breed's legs felt like they would collapse at any moment. But not wanting to be considered a candy ass, he didn't dare complain. As they walked on, Flick complained into the air, "Those goddamn rich people ride past with empty cars, and won't stop."

"Yeah, when I get a car," Breed said brightly, "I'm going to pick up every hitchhiker I see."

"Yeah, me too," Hog added. "Until that time, we'll have to put up with these intellectually deficient drivers who think they're too cerebral to stop."

Screwball's forehead wrinkled with quizzical amusement. "Hey, Mister Dictionary, you can stop using big words to bitch. When the cops come, they'll stop and pick us up."

Hog made a wry face, reached back, and felt the gun. "I don't give a shit if all the law

237

enforcement agency people in the world stop. I'm ready."

They kept on walking.

Under a darkened sky, the whisper of rain drops falling on the leaves filled the air. As the rain softly pattered on Breed, he knew his thin jacket wouldn't keep him dry for long. To make matters worse, the buttons on his new red shirt wouldn't stay buttoned. He would have to keep closing his shirt to keep warm. Flick and Screwball had thick jackets, too, and Hog's had a big rip up the back under the arm.

When the rain became a cold downpour, smug high-school kids drove past in parent's new cars with the wipers flapping. Through the rain, Breed sniffed. A sweet, stomach-upsetting, bubblegum and cigarette odor wafted into the damp night air. Screwball wrinkled his nose at the odor and flashed the kids the middle finger. "Those little assholes look like hogs eatin' shit."

Hog playfully turned his head to the side. "What's the matter with hogs?"

"Nothin' if they're the right kind, Hog."

Hog smiled and the kids yelled out the windows and threw hamburger and French fry cardboard containers out onto the side of the road.

Breed wondered if everybody in the whole world were like Shitsplat people. In their rich sheltered minds, they must have thought it was good to throw things out on the highways and roads, thought it gave the prisoners and road workers something to do. Thought it kept them working. Thought it was a useful thing to do, and believed the workers needed that type of work. After all, they

238

were just inferior laborers, and people who threw trash out windows were only helping the inferior laborers keep their jobs.

As the murkiness of evening thickened, the rain cloud continued to hide the sun, and its limited warmth dropped below the horizon. The rain fell, more. Breed closed his shirt and turned up his collar against the sheeting rain. It didn't help much. Water ran down his neck, onto his back and down the crack of his butt.

But no one complained.

Screwball held his shirt over his head and walked bent over with his butt sticking out. Walking next to Breed, he looked right into Breed's face. "How do you like the rain?"

Breed reached up and wiped the water from his eyes. He wanted to tell Screwball to stuff it, but smiled and lied, "I love it."

Screwball grinned happily. "Well, enjoy it while you can."

Breed smiled inwardly and continued to walk.

Giving a faint shake of his head, Flick pointed up ahead. A gray cement bridge stretched across a small creek. "Maybe we can stay under there for the night."

A car approached. Its high beam lights cut the semi-darkness and flashed down the road. "Maybe it's the cops," Flick said in great haste and leaped over the end of the bridge.

With the headlights barely feathering his back, Breed heard Flick's feet thump on the rain-covered path that led under the bridge. Screwball and Hog jumped. They landed with single thumps. If Breed jumped, he could slip and fall into the mud. He didn't want to get his clothes packed with mud. As he walked cautiously, the light from the approaching car nicked the top of his head. He came to life, ran around the end of the bridge, scampered down the path, and stopped.

In the semi-darkness, a ragged figure appeared.

"What the hell do you think you're doing?" the figure asked.

Breed jerked with surprise. Trying to make his eyes adjust to the darkness, he searched the outline of the figure. He could make out a man dressed in clothes that could have come from a Salvation Army store. As if he had been living on nothing but berries, the man was thin and looked played out. Like a little kid who had just woken up from a restless sleep, his hair was tangled in every direction. As Breed's eyes adjusted to the dark, he saw the man's face. It was haggard and deeply seamed with a three days growth of beard, peppered with gray, but a smile was there.

The man leaned forward and squinted. "Why you're just kids."

Hog gave him an acknowledging nod. "Very gallantly spoken."

The man ignored Hog and asked, "What are you kids doing out so late?"

Breed felt the man wasn't going to harm him and relaxed. "We're trying to get back home. What are you doing under this bridge?"

The old man reached into the pocket of his long dark overcoat.

240

Hog reached around his back and placed his hand on the gun.

The old man gripped something in his pocket. "I'm supposed to be here." His shoulders moved with a faint shrug. "I'm a hobo."

Remembering the fear from being chased by drunken bums along the railroad tracks next to the Clark Street Bridge, Breed defensively stepped back. "A bum?"

A bright flicker of lightning streaked across the sky. The old man's leathery face grimaced in the light. Beneath his coat, his body moved like it was rugged and ready to fight. "No, I'm not a bum," he said with agitation in his voice. "I'm a hobo. There's a difference, you know."

Studying the hobo, Breed remembered the close encounters he had had with the alcohol-drinking bums that frequented the field of huge cement drain pipes down by the Shenango River in Shitsplat. Remnants of what the town had called the Erie Gang, the bums were usually a sociable lot, and Breed had learned a lot from them. But he always had to be on guard when they started drinking Canned Heat, they had heated and strained through stale bread for the alcohol. After a few drinks they would lash out with knives and throw rocks. They were old leftover bums from the thirties who had jumped on trains when they were teenagers and had stayed on the rails. One ride had made them train crazy. They were hooked, couldn't quit. Back then you could get killed for your worn-out shoes. It was a brutal education. Bums were usually in a social struggle. Being somewhat secretive and down on

241

everyone, they had problems of their own and didn't want to be bothered with other people's problems.

Breed remembered the old bum by the river that he thought he had made friends with. Out of nowhere, the old guy just changed and snapped at him. "Don't make me pay for your mistakes," he had said. "I've got enough trouble tryin' to pay for my own." Breed found out bums could be unpredictable and dangerous, and he knew he should be cautious, but his chest hurt and his feet ached, and Hog still had his hand on that gun. Breed sat down under the dry bridge and looked around the area to see if another hobo might be lurking in the shadows. If he had to, Breed was ready to run.

Flick shook the water from his face and looked at the hobo. "What do you mean you're not a bum?" he said but kept tensed to run.

With rainwater dripping from his nose, the hobo nodded. "A bum won't work. A hobo will." Like a man who was nervous about something, he fingered the button on his dark coat. "We always look for a little work, and we won't steal like a bum." He turned toward the rain-lashed night. "Bums, you gotta watch them kind. But a hobo will help a fellow out."

Flick relaxed but looked leery. "How can you help somebody when you ain't got nothing yourself?"

"Nothing?" the hobo questioned with an air of objectivity. "Why, we got the whole world at our feet," he declared with vehement determination. "It's a way of life. I rode with the old Casey Jones.

242

We drove steam engines all over America. Had to shovel coal back then. Steam is still the most powerful force on earth, you know. Why, they still use it in the mountains. There's nothing stronger." He turned, spit tobacco juice into the creek, and continued. "We can show a fellow where to hop freight, tell him where it's going, and where not to go. But you got to learn to be careful. There's still railroad bulls out there. They got lanterns, rifles, and blackjacks. They'll pull out a blackjack and knock you in the head just as soon as look at you." A grumpy scowl formed on his face. "Those railroad bulls are a no-good lot, you know."

"You never stole nothing?" Flick questioned. "Weren't you ever so hungry that you took a little food?"

"Nope," the hobo said and pulled a paper bag with something in it out of his pocket.

Keeping his eyes on the bag, Screwball backed away.

Hog tensed, but kept his hand behind his back.

Knowing Hog had the gun in his hand and his finger on the trigger, didn't cause Breed not to be afraid. But he stepped back, anyway.

The hobo lifted a pint bottle of cheap wine from the bag and held it. Then he dumped a short, fat candle out of the bag. It landed on the dirt at his feet. He placed the bottle of wine back into the bag, twisted the cap off, and took a drink.

Stepping forward, Screwball pointed the candle. "Are you going to light that?"

The hobo reached into his shirt pocket, pulled out a match, and offered it to Screwball. "Here, go ahead. Light it."

Screwball took the candle, set it on a flat rock, and lit it.

Basking in its yellow glow, the hobo continued. "Excuse me, gentleman. I have to take back what I said about not stealing anything." With the bottle raised partway to his mouth he paused. "A little weariness or hard times will change a lot of things. I had worked all day from light until dark. The man only paid me two tomatoes. Said, 'Dat was a day's doe.' It was one of those mornings when everything glistened with silvery frost. The water in the pan, I had left on the fire had become solid ice. I needed a fire to warm my cold feet and take the sting out of my fingers, but I was too hungry to restart the fire. So I went into town and started begging for scraps like a skinny dog." He lifted the bottle and took a sip. "I spied a bottle of milk sitting on the front steps of a porch. Another hobo had marked the sidewalk. It had a solid circle with a line running through it. It meant stay away, but it was early Sunday morning, no one around."

Breed's feet slipped on the dry dirt. A stone rolled toward the hobo. The hobo glared at Breed. "Take it easy, young fella."

Nodding, Breed readjusted his foot, pulled his damp jacket around his chest, and looked to Hog. Hog relaxed and pulled his hand from behind his back.

Screwball stepped closer.

With heavy-lidded eyes, the hobo watched the yellow light coming from the candle flame. When he smiled a mellow wine smile, a look of calm radiated from his body. "Yes, that was the day," he said. "I had that bottle of milk in my hand and was walking down the sidewalk. I figured the lady wouldn't miss one bottle of milk. I was hungry, hadn't eaten anything but those two tomatoes for three days. I heard a baby cry and looked up to see where the sound was coming from. A cross in a morning beam of sunlight came right out of the sky, made the whole world look like a church, and the little baby cried again. I knew right then and there that I shouldn't take the milk from a little baby's mouth. God was showing me the way. I took the milk and put it back on the porch. And since that day, I never took nothin'."

The rain kept falling, but its roaring stopped, and the raindrops only freckled the water a ways from the bridge. Like a man searching for something, the hobo turned and looked into the night. "You boys stay on the rails too long, you'll get tough, end up shakin' walnuts for food. You might even learn to appreciate things better."

"Why don't you get an apartment or a house to live in?" Flick asked. "It would keep you out of the rain."

The hobo turned back toward Flick. "Because I don't want to. Train crazy, you know. You stay on the rails long enough, you'll be train crazy, too."

Lightning flashed one time. Rain rushed down and roared around the bridge. A faraway look came into the hobo's eyes. "Every time I got on a train, I used to hear that steam whistle blow. Only now it's a diesel horn. I wish I could stay in one place. But when I hear that horn, I feel good. It means I'm going somewhere, can't explain it. You'll feel it. You'll hear that clackety-clack play a hobo lullaby that will bring you back again and again." His expression turned woeful. "Used to wish I was rich. Hard times lasted nine years. Thought I was rich once, worked in a CC camp, made twenty-five dollars a month. Could send some home then, only let you stay six months. I knew a man who had a streak of luck and hit it big time. It didn't change him. He was an asshole when he was poor. When he became rich, he's became a bigger asshole."

Breed put his hands into his pocket and thought about the Shitsplat people. "We know a lot of people like that, only they're not actually rich. But they think they are because they work in a mill."

As if he were trying to shake a memory from his mind, the hobo shook his head, and stepped in a little circle. He raised his hand, waved it around, and talked. "God knows if I had stayed in a mill, life would have been much, much easier, but I just couldn't."

Out of the hobo's sight, Screwball was pantomiming him as if he were a comical hand puppet.

Flick ducked his head to hide his smile from the hobo, and asked him, "Do you have something against making money?"

"Some people prefer to make lots of money while they're young. Then when they're old, even if they don't deserve it, they are given awards and

246

things are named after them, and they are remembered as leaders of men. And the sad thing is that the only thing they did was make money." He paused. "Even if the people gave them the looks of not being wanted or not being welcome because they were different, money stopped all that."

Breed realized that what the hobo was saying about money stopping the looks could be true. After he and Flick had earned money painting mailboxes, a few people had begun to treat them differently.

Interested in what the hobo was saying, Screwball stopped pantomiming and asked, "Why do they do that?"

"Don't know and don't care." The hobo shrugged. "Maybe when you get older, you'll learn to ignore people that make fun of you when they think you can't see them."

Surprised that the hobo has seen him pantomiming him, Screwball's eyes opened wide. "Sorry, I was only kidding."

The hobo raised one finger. "And you'll find out that you don't have to ask why things are like they are. If you just accept things as they are, you'll live longer and relax more. Things don't have to have a reason to be what they are. Some things just are. It's like you boys being here. I don't care how you got here. All I know, or want to know, is that you are here."

As if he were making sure he standing where he was, Screwball tapped his body with his fingertips. "You're right about that. We're here, all right."

247

Water trickling from a crack in the cement bridge above, dripped on the hobo. He stepped away from it. "I don't know how to explain it to you boys. I'm a hobo because I don't want to be like everybody else. I don't want to make things that people don't need just so I can buy things I don't need."

The zipper on his Flick's cotton jacket was broke. For warmth, he sat on the dry ground next to a tuft of brown grass and clasp his arms around his knees.

The hobo took another pull from the bottle of wine in the paper bag. "I'd offer you some, but you're just kids. It's a bad habit to get into. I only take it for my gout, you know, strictly medicinal.

"Yeah, okay," Breed said and did not buy the lie because he knew that drinking and rich food caused the gout to get worse and was known as the rich man's disease. Breed didn't question the Hobo. He didn't want to take a chance and get the old guy mad at him. He needed to get dry. He needed to find a way home. They all needed to find a way home.

"Do you think you'll ever stop running around the country?" Flick asked.

The hobo smiled and wiped his mouth on his sleeve. "Only plants have roots. I have legs and I use them. If you jump on a train, that's another thing you got to watch out for. You let your feet hang out in the breeze, those switch stands will rip your legs right off."

Flick moved his legs in a restless manner. "You ever been to Shitsplat?"

The old hobo glanced at the tuft of brown grass next to Flick and sat on it. "I've been just about everywhere," he said and tucked the paper bag with the bottle of wine in it back into his pocket. He raised one eyebrow and squinted in Flick's direction. Reaching down like a man protecting a sack of gold, he placed his hand over the bottle in his pocket. He turned toward the rising water in the creek, and looked to be in deep thought. "Shitsplat," he said, coming out of his musings. "That might be where a guy was walking on top of a boxcar and a tiny turn in the tracks threw him off. His back was turned, you know. Didn't see it coming. Not sure, but Shitsplat could be the place where the last of the old Erie gang sit in those old cement drain pipes, down by the river. Nice and cool in the summer, a little hard on your back, but don't go in there in the winter time. That cement draws the cold, it'll stiffen your bones right up. Shitsplat?" he questioned.

"Yeah, Shitsplat," Hog impatiently said, "the place where they use farts for air-fresheners."

The hobo smiled. "Funny name for a place."

Breed got up, brushed the dirt off his rear end, and sat on a rock. He picked up a stick, and cleaned the mud off his new shoes. Somewhere in the distance, railroad cars banged and sent barely audible switching sounds into the night. Breed knew those familiar sounds. With excited realization and renewed hope, he stood up and turned to the hobo. "That's a switching yard. Could you tell us how to get to Shitsplat on a train?"

A frog croaked in the distance. The hobo stroked his salt and pepper whiskers. "Maybe," he slowly said. "Let me think about it." He repositioned himself on the tuft of grass, and like a railroad scholar in deep thought, he leaned over, put his chin on his hands, and rested his elbows on his knees. But he didn't answer.

As darkness deepened, the rain slowed to a fine mist, and bugs came out to dance around warm bodies in the rain-cooled air. Somewhere in the distance, musical frogs croaked. The night filled with noises, but the hobo sat silent.

After a while, Breed became cold, wet, tired, and miserable. In an attempt to stay warm, he lifted his knees to his chin and wrapped his arms around his legs. When it didn't work, he stood up, bowed his head down to the hobo, and asked again, "Can you tell us how to get to Shitsplat?"

Hog let out a low sigh. "Ferrona Yard's just a little yard in a shit splat town. He doesn't know where Shitsplat is."

With one eye open, the hobo looked up at Hog and gawked at him. "You say, Ferrona Yard?"

"Yeah, Ferrona Yard," Hog repeated.

"So, Ferrona Yard is the place you want to go?" Breed nodded.

Wagging his head, the Hobo said, "Ferrona being in a shit splat of a town slipped my mind for a moment. It's right next to the river there, nice little yard, no bulls there. A lot of hopper cars for the steel mills and a few empty gondolas for the pipe mills go there, not many boxcars. If they go, they usually need a little work at the repair shop there."

With sudden excitement, Breed's eyes swept the faces around him. "That's the yard right up from the Clark Street Bridge."

The hobo wiped the rainwater from his brow with the back of his hand. "Next to a river?"

"That's the place," Breed said with expectation.

The hobo gave Breed a knowing look. "Like I said, for a moment, it slipped my mind. I know about Shitsplat. Some hobos call it Shit Hole. In the steam engine days, I used to have to go through a long tunnel to get there, hot smoke could suffocate you, spit black coal dust for a month, if you lived through it."

The misty rain stopped. Fresh clean air took over the night, and all became still and quiet. Then the sound of railroad cars, being switched, called loud.

"We can hear that switching yard," Breed told the hobo. "Where is it?"

The hobo smiled an all-knowing smile. "Sound travels a long way at night, but I think we can find it."

"So what do we do if we find it?" Hog wanted to know.

Flick shot Hog a crooked grin. "We jump into a car and ride home."

"Oh yeah," Hog said, turned his head and stared at Flick, "how do we know which car to jump into?"

"Yeah," Screwball jumped in, "we could end up in California."

"You don't always know," the hobo admitted with a twinge of disappointment in his voice. "You

251

usually take an educated guess. But you'll get there, some time."

The hobo forgetting about Ferrona Yard being in a shit hole town called Shitsplat caused Breed to wondered if wine had begun to deteriorate the hobo's mind. "What do you mean educated guess?"

"Before you can make an educated guess," the hobo said, "you have to know how to grab onto a car." He grabbed a protruding block in the base of the bridge and tugged himself erect. As if he had hooked his arm around a grab iron of a moving car, he bent his arm and held it shoulder high. "I could show you," he said, and swaying on his feet, he pointed to his elbow. "You gotta hang on good, if you lose your grip." He thrust his arm out straight. Looking like he had fallen off the train, he threw his arm high into the air. "You'll die."

"We hopped freights before," Flick said with a self-satisfied smile.

"You don't have to boast about it," Breed said. "We always knew where they were going."

"Flick started to put his arm around the hobo but stopped. "This old timer will show us which car to get on, won't you?"

"I'm not going west, just yet," the hobo said, shaking his head. "I'm headed east, going out to meet a buddy and fatten up for the trip, then we're goin' to the hobo jungle outside Chicago, lots of good friends there. I know the jungle buzzards, all of them."

"Jungle buzzard?" Breed questioned.

"Jungle buzzards are the old guys that live there, run the place, you know."

"That's a good thing to know," Flick said tentatively, "but how do we get to Ferrona Yard?"

"How far east do you want to go?"

"We were going west to California," Flick said. "To get back home, we have to go east."

The hobo answered with sympathetic good humor. "You got a long ride. Buffalo is just a jaunt down the tracks, Ferrona is west."

Flick's face screwed up into a grimace of discomfort. "We were going north all that time," he whined. "Eddie kept saying we were going west, but all the time we were headed toward Buffalo."

Breed was dumbfounded. "Ahh man," he moaned and sunk down.

Screwball grinned with scornful satisfaction. "Eddie drove all night in the wrong direction. Probably got turned around when we played chicken." He clenched his teeth and imitated Eddie. "I know what I'm doing."

Hog shook an indignant finger at the others. "I told you guys he didn't know where he was going."

"If you knew that." Breed said, "then why didn't you get out of the car?"

"I didn't want to walk home." Hog cocked his head back. "You guys seem to forget that we didn't know nothin' about where we were, and I notice there were times when Eddie wasn't acting as crazy as he usually does. So I figure he was only faking being nuts. And besides, when you're lost, you ain't got no choice. You gotta follow the leader."

Breed wrinkled his forehead with confusion. "Yeah, but we still want to know how you knew."

"Yeah," Flick interjected somewhat testily. "We want to know."

"One clue was license plates."

"Why didn't you keep on telling us?"

"Because Pennsylvania and New Your license plates are both yellow and blue, I wasn't sure until we got to the gas station."

Breed had had his heart set on going to California, and was angry with himself for not checking license plates. "I must have been crazy to believe anything Eddie said."

Screwball continued to imitate Eddie. "You can't believe what those signs say. If we had a map, I could show that the road runs on a slant and going west is really shown going north, the route signs can't say north west."

"If you believe the accuracy of what Eddie says," Hog said with a superior air, "you'll believe California is up my ass!"

Amazed, Screwball stared at Hog. "Maybe while Eddie's in the hospital they'll get a proctologist to check out his brain."

"Maybe if you go, too," Hog said, "they'll see what you got rattlin' around in that head of yours."

Giggling, the hobo shook his head. "No need to fuss," he said. "It's almost time. I have to show you tonight."

Confused, Flick tilted his head to the side. "What's the big rush?"

The hobo growled into his beard and forcibly said, "If you try to hop on in the daylight, the bulls will see you."

"Won't they use flashlights and see us at night?"

The hobo nodded weakly. "They're supposed to do just that. But they just watch the yard for a couple of hours, then go to sleep."

Hog cocked a questioning eye at the hobo. "You sure we'll be able to see to grab on."

"You'll see," the Hobo said and waved his hand upward, "unless you want to wait until daylight and catch it on the fly, just outside the yard, that is, if it ain't goin' too fast."

Flick walked out from under the bridge and held out the palms of his hands. "It quit raining and it's not as dark. We can start for the switching yard."

"I hope you know where you're going," Breed said and stepped toward the hobo.

Slowly nodding, the hobo walked into the semi-dark, and broke into a flood of speech. "The old hobo camp is still in Girard, Pennsylvania, not Girard, Ohio. It's a good place to go north or south, east, or west. The Norfolk and Southern Railroad runs north and south. The P&LE is there, too. New York Central is there, Bessemer, too. Hobos come back every spring, make cardboard shacks a mile long."

Walking behind the hobo, Screwball exaggerated and imitated his movements. As Breed watched, he stumbled over a rotting log and slipped on something slimy, but managed to keep his balance. Walking in regretful amusement, Breed and the others filed behind.

CHAPTER 15

Leading Breed and the others over a beaten path of a deer trail that led to the railroad-switching yard, the hobo stopped at the edge of a field and huffed for air. In front of him, flooded with silver light from the moon, tall blades of soaking wet grass gently waved. Wheezing, the hobo regained his breath and pointed to the field of wet grass. "We can take a short cut right through there."

Flick bent at the waist and gestured with his arm. "Okay, Hog. You go first."

Hog stepped next to Flick and stopped. "Not me. I'm not gettin' my pants wet."

"Why not?" Flick asked with a wide grin. "I'm doing you a favor. The first guy sees the snake. The second guy gets bit."

Hog's face clouded. "Bullshit?" he spat. "It's too cold for snakes to be out."

Flick looked to Screwball. "You goin' first?"

Screwball bowed and waved his arm in the direction of the wet weeds. "Be my guest."

The hobo ignored them all and waded into the wet grass.

Screwball followed. "At least we won't have to pull that string on the windshield wipers."

Breed looked at his new shoes. Then looked at the wet grass. Walking through all that mud, and wet grass, would ruin his new shoes even more than they had already been ruined. They would end up just like his old shoes. Then he'd be wearing junk again. "It figures," he muttered to himself and stepped in line.

Even though Breed was last in line, wet whips of grass still beat against his thighs. The water soaked into his pants and made them heavy. It was difficult to walk.

But it didn't seem to bother the hobo. As if he were a fleet-footed angel waltzing through cotton candy clouds, he glided through the pants-whapping grass. But it was part of the hobo's world. He was used to it.

On the other side of the grass, trees hung over a shallow creek and cast a shadow over a little stretch of gently babbling water. Just above the still water, to the left, a mass of mosquitoes buzzed toward them. The hobo ignored the mosquitoes, walked right through the shallow water, and continued to talk. "You boys get up against it, you can go to the Salvation Army for food. But if you wanna eat, you'll have to listen to a sermon."

After watching four mosquitoes join three that were flying tight circles around his head, Screwball batted at them and asked, "How many more mosquitoes are going to join in the merrymaking?" He batted them away from his face, managed to kill one, and bitched, "You kill one and fifty more come to the funeral."

While Breed swatted the mosquitoes away, he remembered the last time he had gone into a Salvation Army store. It smelled like dirty clothes, and everything in the place reeked of other people's discarded filth. When he had gone outside, he had felt like he had bugs crawling all over his body. He shuddered. "I don't want to beg for food at no Salvation Army."

The hobo chuckled. "You get hungry enough, you'll go anywhere you have too." He tramped a big cattail down with the side of his foot, and kept walking. "Teenagers only get two meals and one night, and then you have to leave. When you get older, they give you six meals and two nights. They don't want young boys hangin' around. They say you're just wastin' your lives away, when you could be doing something useful, like joinin' the army."

Breed thought about joining the army, and wondered if it would better than working in a steel mill. If he had to work in a mill, he wouldn't be doing anything to put scum, like that gas station owner that had cut the fan belt, in jail. He wouldn't be doing anything to change the world. He would be making steel, and although the people of Shitsplat believed working in a mill was something useful, Breed felt he would only be wasting his life away. But then again, the Joneses did something useful, too. They made the streets cleaner. They picked up cigarette butts and pop bottles off the road. And they gave people house demolition jobs. Breed didn't want to end up in a steel mill, and he didn't want to keep up with the Joneses of Shitsplat, but he wasn't old enough to join the army. If they ever made it back home, he figured he could lie about his age and join. It would be a better way to live.

After the hobo led them up a small hill and stopped, Breed stood next to him and looked through a cleft in the ridge. Where a few broad leaf maple trees stood, a small beaten path led along a fine grass field. When he looked upward, the jagged shapes of the leaves were outlined against a clearing night sky. As they walked, the path zigzagged around a few large rocks left by the glaciers of the ice age. Then soft grass swayed around his wet legs, and like a gentle moving carpet of midnight gold, the grass fanned out across the land, and rolled into the night. Further on, a great variety of trees surrounded one butternut tree and looked like they had been planted to create a pleasing pattern. At the side of the path, a stream poured off a small incline, white in exposed places, and ran away from a small cabin of peeled logs. Yellow in the moonlight, the cabin jutted out over a steep valley. A stone chimney sat on top of a dull metal roof that kept out the rain. Bark-covered slab-wood, cut from the outer sides of the trees, waited to be cut and added to a stack of seasoned firewood that sat on the small porch. Soon, the firewood would be caressed with orange flickering flames and send out comforting heat.

Breed was cold and wet.

The cabin looked warm and inviting. He wanted to go inside, build a fire, stretch his cold hands out toward the flames, and dry his clothes. He tapped the hobo on the shoulder. "It looks like nobody's in that cabin. Why don't we go inside and build a fire? We could dry out and stay the night."

The hobo glanced at the cabin and stiffened with resentment. Moving in a nervous haste and violently shaking his head, he said, "No, no, we can't stop. Places like that a bum could've been eyeballin' all day. Looking into firelight is a comforting thing. Makes you dream. But it leaves your eyes unaccustomed to darkness, and that is not a good thing so close to the railroad. Come night, a bum could slip in, cut a throat or grab one of us, steal what little we have, and leave without disturbing anyone's sleep." He stopped and turned toward the cabin, and shook his fist at the heavens. "Hey! You rotten bastard. You're not going to fool me this time!"

Breed was surprised by the hobo's vitriolic response, but before he could say anything, the Hobo started walking. Making a hurry-up motion, he waved his hand next to his ear. "We have to go. The trains will be pulling out tonight. You'll see."

As they walked past the cabin, Breed wondered what the real reason was that the hobo didn't want to stay in the cabin. But he accepted the fact that a warm dancing fire inside the cabin, maybe with the hissing of frying meat, would bring no comfort tonight, and his stomach growled. Again, he tapped the hobo on the shoulder. "After you get off a train, what do you do for food?"

"You can beg at back doors, get a bag of food, that's a lump, get food on the steps, that's a knee slapper." He slowed and stepped over a small log that lay across the path. "Check for marks on the sidewalks. A circle not filled in is good for a hand out. If you don't smell too bad and you're clean, they might let you in for a sit down at the table."

Flick stepped over the log. "What about those hobo camps people talk about?"

The hobo giggled, but then turned serious. "Don't ever try to put your feet under the table at a hobo camp unless you bring something to put on it.

260

Show them a cabbage, some money, anything, and the jungle buzzard will let you have some mulligan. Gotta watch they don't run a con up on your ass, could end you up in jail, brute usually runs the place. He'll take everything you got, gotta hide it good, or he'll have it."

When they tramped down the long valley, it was easy going. So Screwball pulled a long piece of grass from the side of the path and touched the end of it on Hog's ear.

Thinking it was a mosquito or a night bug, Hog violently slapped the grass away. "Damn it!" he bitched, "I thought we got rid those mosquitoes."

Giggling, Screwball continued to touch the end of the grass on Hog's ear and Hog continued to bitch, until he caught Screwball in the act. "Keep it up," he threatened. "I'll shove that grass up your ass."

Screwball let out a taunting, "Hant!"

To which Hog replied, "Hant, your ass."

After Screwball dropped the grass, they tromped up the other side of the valley, cut through a narrow passage, and around large weather-rounded rocks, where it became steep and difficult to walk. At the top, the path ended. In front of them, lights flickered through the tall, dark outline of straight, black trees.

The hobo stopped and turned to Breed. "You're the one who hasta watch." A somewhat pitying look filled his ancient eyes. "In Texas, if they catch you, they'll drive you out of town and dump you off in the middle of nowhere. In the South, if you're colored, and they like you, you'll

261

be breakin' rocks in the hot sun, if they don't, they'll lynch you."

Breed's Indian heritage caused his skin to tan dark, and he had been called a nigger. He stopped walking and the thought about getting hung for no reason, made his neck hurt. He reached up and rubbed it. It seemed hard to breathe. He shook the feeling off and continued walking.

The hobo broke into a hopeful smile. "So you boys think you might want to be hobos?"

"Oh, yes," Screwball said sarcastically and let out a goofy giggle. "We'd love to be hobos."

Apparently, Screwball's sarcastic attempted humor didn't register in the Hobo's mind. Breed was beginning to wonder if the hobo didn't have enough brains to be unhappy. He acted like some great transient of the tracks, and continued to walk and talk like some kind of windup toy that wouldn't wind down.

"Most hobos are decent people," the hobo continued, "but there are thieves and murders and the like. People let you know you're a bum. They'll call girls away from you, embarrass you to your dying days." He reached up over his head, opened his hand, and gesturing to his dirty ragged clothes, he swept his hand downward. "When you look like a bum and smell like a bum, they'll treat you like a bum."

In the distance, the sounds of the railroad-switching yard caused a familiar friendly felling to come over Breed. "It sounds like we're on the tracks next to the river above Shell Island."

Breed could see the railroad cars in his mind. When they clunked loud and banged apart, he knew that the couplers between the cars had not been opened. He had heard the yard crews call them blind knuckles because the closed coupler couldn't see where it had to go in order to couple up to the other car. When cars had jolted forward and backward, they reminded him of a new kid, working on the railroad, who had been confused because he had been told to, "Go ahead, back up."

Breed and the others followed the hobo, and walked into a stand of thick trees, thrashed through dry leaves that blanketed the ground, and continued toward the familiar railroad sounds.

When the hobo tried to walk up the dark embankment next to a black tree line, he slipped on a wet spot and fell to his hands. Instantly, he regained his feet, scrambled up the small incline, and stepped into the world of the railroad-switching yard.

Breed and the others were right behind him.

When the night suddenly became silent, in a blocking motion, the hobo held his arm straight out to the side. "Wait!"

Breed and the others stopped and stared at the switching yard, washed with rain-dimmed light.

"We have to wait here and see what's happening."

"Oh," Hog said and smiled compassionately. "You mean like spectators at an arena?"

The hobo made a face at Hog but didn't answer.

Even though the welcome odor of creosote and diesel fumes filled their nostrils, they stood like spectators at an arena and watched. To their right, tracks lined with oil-soaked ground stretched the length of three railroad cars. Above that, trees, devoid of bark, supported a few gnarled, dead branches and attested to years of being enveloped with diesel fumes from parked and idling locomotive engines.

Rolling down the tracks to switch out switching lists, a red yard engine with yellow numbers burbled happily, throwing various cars down selected tracks and building up long drags of railroad cars that were destined for locations all over the country. Ear-damaging bangs and clunks of cars, being coupled, echoed up and down the dark tracks, and for miles the silence of the night became shattered.

A young yard clerk, with a handful of manila cards and a battery powered railroad lantern, briskly walked along the side of a string of recently set-off cars.

With a jerk of his head, the hobo gestured to the clerk. "See that kid?"

Flick nodded. "Yeah."

The clerk was writing big yellow chalk letters on the sides of the cars.

Although he was far away, and it wouldn't matter much, the hobo leaned forward for a better look. "He's marking the cars so the conductor knows where to cut them before the engine kicks them down the different tracks. He probably had to remark them after the rain washed the first marks off. The crew is working pretty fast. They must be behind, and that clerk looks mad because he had to do the same work over again."

"So what good are those marks?" Flick asked, peering into the night. "All I can see are letters, and they don't tell me nothin'."

The hobo chuckled. "You see, even hobos know something you can learn."

"I never said hobos were stupid," Flick countered. "What do the letters mean?"

"I don't know all of them, but the ones you need to find would be—". He stopped and thought. "I think, AB. No that's Hubbard, Ohio. NK is Youngstown. Those are close but you need Ferrona Yard, Shop. That will get you right into Ferrona Yard."

Breed's wet pants were making his legs cold. He wanted to get going. "So which car should we jump on?"

"You can never be sure. They might switch them again, or they could get lost."

With disgruntled suspicion, Hog eyed the hobo. The cars can just run off the tracks and hide somewhere. How can they lose a car?"

"That's what I used to wonder about, too. But I know where a whole line of old coal hoppers sat on a siding for fifteen years. Last time I checked, they were still there."

Breed imagined what would happen if they hopped on a car and it got lost up north in a snowstorm. If it did, they could starve to death, or their bodies could end up frozen somewhere, forgotten in the wilderness.

Screwball tapped the hobo on the shoulder and pointed to the cars the clerk was marking. "Why don't they just write where they're going in plain English?"

"Cause," the hobo said, "they made those codes to trick spies during the big war. I guess they never got around to changing them."

Breed gestured to the cars. "How will we know where we're going?"

The hobo pointed to the clerk. "If the markings are new, like that clerk is making, your destination is pretty well locked up. You'll get there. Oh yes, ON is a good one. It will get you to Ferrona Yard, too. That's usually coke, scrap, or ore from the lakes for the steel mills. They ship a lot of that, jump in one of them coke hoppers, you really get a black face. Sometimes those coke hoppers are red hot. In the winter you can get in one of those and stay warm a long time. But that coke dust blows all the way, make you cough really bad sometimes, too. I try to stay away from those cars." He stopped his flood of speech and lifted his hand. "Almost forgot. When ore season's in, a lot of ore cars go right past Ferrona and a ways down the tracks to Sharon Steel. Iron ore is heavy. It doesn't take much to overload a car. They put a little pile at the bottom of the car. If some spills out, it's like walking on marbles. You can fall, real fast. I rode in one of those once, my whole face and hands turned red. I stay away from them, too."

"I don't care if we get a little dirt on us," Breed impatiently said. "We just want to get home."

266

As if he were studying him, the hobo stared at Breed. "If I was your age, I would, too." He pointed toward the yard. "You wanna get home, watch that train."

Breed and his friends looked across the switching yard. A triple-header train made a double pickup, created a long string of cars, and began pulling out of the yard. The engineer in the lead diesel engine pulled the skinny air-horn lever. Two short, extra loud blasts filled the night.

Screwball put his hands over his ears and talked to the train. "I know you're coming. Quit blowin' that goddamn thing."

"The hobo smiled. "Two shorts. He's whistling off, just tellin' the crew that he's goin' ahead."

"We can see that," Hog said, clearly bothered. "Where's he going in such a hurry?"

"That's MC-3. He's headed east." The hobo tightened the belt around his baggy pants. "That's where I'm going. I got to get on."

Breed felt like he was drowning, and someone was about to pull the life preserver from his grasping fingers. He didn't want to be left in the yard without guidance. "Which car should we take?"

"Not to worry, young fellows, MC-3 will be stopping to get clearance and pick up the conductor. I got to get on before it gets moving, can't run as fast anymore, you know. You just wait for CM-2. It goes west, all even numbers go west. All odd go east."

"Where's CM-2?" Flick asked.

"He's right over there waiting for them to switch out number nine. Don't wait too long to get on. That track should have been ready for him a long time ago. He's probably mad cause he had to wait. To make up for lost time, that train will pick up speed fast. So he ain't gonna stop. Get a car marked ON, or better yet, FERRONA YARD, SHOP."

The hobo took a few steps toward his departing train. Breed stepped in front of the escaping hobo. "Even if the car's marked, it could be marked wrong. How will we know if it's the right car?"

The hobo stopped. "You won't, but you'll learn quick. Thanks for the chat. Try not to step in any guts from the gut cars. They make you stink real bad." Impatiently, he squinted at MC-3. "Someday, maybe we'll meet again."

"But what if we can't find a car marked, Ferrona Yard, Shop?"

The hobo reached into his pocket and pulled out a cylindrical object and offered it to Breed. "Here, take this piece of chalk. You can mark, Ferrona Yard, Shop, on the side of any empty Erie car you like." MC-3 began pulling out of the yard. Taking quick steps to get to the train before it was going too fast, he looked back over his shoulder. "But don't get caught."

Breed held the cylindrical object in his hand and watched. Stirring the tendrils of fog that were snaking out across the cobblestones, the hobo danced over the tracks, saying," The meek will inherit the earth." Then running alongside of the boxcar, he threw his bundle of belongings into the car, grabbed the side of the door, and gracefully flung himself inside.

The horn on the engine buzzed once, and the hobo was gone.

"I heard that shit before," Hog said. "The way I see it, the meek will inherit the earth after all the rich people die."

For a moment everybody stood in silence.

Then Flick turned to Breed. "Okay, Breed," he said with haste. "Let's mark a good car."

Breed held the cylindrical object up toward the sky. "Hey, this isn't chalk. It's a penny whistle."

CHAPTER 16

Looking at the penny whistle in Breed's hand, Hog waved his hand down. "It doesn't matter what it is," he said. "If we don't want to inherit another way home, we better find a car before that train pulls out of the yard."

"Hey!" Screwball held out his hand. "Gimme dat thing. Maybe I can learn how to play it."

Breed handed the whistle to Screwball. "Here, see if you can make a piece of chalk out of it."

Screwball lifted the whistle to his mouth and before he could blow it, Hog touched a piece of grass to Screwball's ear. Screwball blew once and swatted at the grass. "Maybe later. There're too many bugs around here. Let's find a car."

Hog getting back at Screwball for the grass on the ear, caused Breed and the others to smile for a moment, but then they frantically searched the cars in the darkness and tried to find a car marked Ferrona Yard, or ON. If they didn't hurry up and find one, the train would leave without them.

It started to rain.

As the MC-3 train began to pull out of the switching yard, Breed hopefully watched the cars coming down the track. Big drops of rain were spattering the big yellow chalk marks on the sides of cars. Soon the marks would be gone. Suddenly a dark, spooky gondola with a huge yellow "ON" marked clearly on the side loomed into view. "There's one," he excitedly said, jerking his finger toward the car. "Before the rain washes the letters off, let's get in it."

When they stepped over lines of the silver rails in the dark, Breed stepped into something soft between the tracks. He figured it was an old rag or something and paid no attention to it. When they got close to the moving string of cars, the car with the "ON" chalk letters was moving toward them, but it was quite a ways down the tracks.

The air horn on the locomotive buzzed. Its diesel engine pounded and labored under its heavy drag and sounded like the painting of a big Hunky dog. The locomotive's headlight flashed a dull yellow light and softly beamed down the waiting tracks. Breed and his friends could have run down the tracks and gotten on the car before the train picked up speed, but they were sure that just like MC-3 had continued going slow when the hobo had hopped on, CM-2 would keep going slow, too.

But to their surprise, just like the hobo had said it would, CM-2 didn't slow. It picked up speed. The hobo was gone. Breed didn't know how to get another train. They would have to get on this car, and right now. But the thought of not getting on haunted him. He froze with fright. He couldn't move. He watched Flick grab the grab iron on the front end of the gondola and swing on. He watched Hog reach across his chest grab on and fall onto the car ladder like a landed fish, and he watched Screwball ran after the tail end of the gondola and snatch onto the ladder as if he had done it every day of his life.

But Breed stood there in the dark.

Screwball yelled back over his shoulder. "Hey, Breed, do you think you're a statue waitin' for a pigeon to crap on you?"

The rain stopped and the engine's horn buzzed, two shorts. The hobo's words, "He's whistling off, just tellin' the crew that he's goin' ahead," flashed in Breed's mind. He jerked out of his trance and ran for the back of the car. He caught up, reached for the grab iron, but his wet pants slowed his reactions. He tripped and fell to the ground. When he got up, the car was moving faster, and it was three car lengths ahead of him. He sprinted and just barely snagged the grab iron at the end of the gondola. His shoulders weren't strong enough to take such a fast-unexpected pull, but he didn't let go. He swung around. His shoulder banged against the side of the steel car. Pain shot up his arm and screamed into his shoulder. He thought he had ripped his arm right out of its socket.

But he hung on.

He had to.

Now, the train was moving too fast to jump off. When the gondola hit a break in the tracks and swerved, it whipped him around and put more strain on his arm. Again, pain shot up his arm and shot to his shoulder. "Damn!" he cursed into the darkness. "Bein' a hobo hurts." Hanging on, he ignored the pain and watched Flick. He was sitting on the top lip of the gondola. He waved to Breed, turned, and release his grip. With a heavy thud, he landed inside the gondola.

To slow the pain in his shoulder, Breed kept most of his weight on one hand and worked his way up the ladder. At the top, he threw his leg over and gently eased down the inside wall of the gondola. When his feet touched the wooden floor, the gondola swayed and pitched like a ship on heaving ocean. He took one step toward Flick and fell.

"What's the matter, Breed?" Flick said with mocking laughter. "You lose your sea legs?"

Breed staggered to his feet and smiled tolerantly. "This is like trying to stand up in a boat going down the rapids in the river." He took a few steps, and walking with the motion of the moving floor, he held his shoulder and walked to Flick.

Flick stopped laughing and stared at Breed's shoulder. "You all right?"

"I'm okay," Breed said. "But my shoulder hurts like mad."

"You shouldn't have waited so long to get on."

"Yeah," Screwball said grinning. "The way you were standing there, I thought you were waiting on a train."

Shaking his head, Breed sat down beside Flick.

Flick made an ugly face and looked at Breed. "Damn this gondola stinks."

Breed looked into the darkness of the beat-up wooden floor of the gondola. "Maybe we're sitting in shit." He looked around. "But I don't see nothin'."

Screwball sat in the corner and tooted on the penny whistle one time, and looked down. On the floor of the car, round silver coins glinted. "Look, money."

All heads turned. Screwball picked up the coins and held them to his smiling face. His mouth

273

turned downward. "Scrap musta been in this car. They're just steel slugs."

"Yeah, Hog said, "but they might work in a pop machine, if we find one."

Screwball nodded, and his eyes brightened. "Maybe there's one in the next car."

Hog jerked his thumb toward the gondola in front of the one they were sitting in. "Climb over and see."

Screwball put the slugs into his pocket. "Maybe latter." He leaned back, and tooted the penny whistle.

Flick drew his knees up and encircled his legs with his arms. "I'm tired," he said and looked toward Screwball. "If you'll quit blowin' that thing we can try to get some rest."

"Yeah, Hog said and wrinkled his nose at the awful odor. "Maybe your playing is so bad it stinks."

Screwball put the whistle in his pocket, and to filter the smell, he pulled the front of his T-shirt over his mouth. "Something stinks all right. Maybe it's our breaths."

As a narrow break in the clouds admitted a stuttering cascade of moonbeams, Flick rolled over to his side, folded his hands, and used them for a pillow. "Shut your stinkin' mouths and go to sleep."

The traveling gondola buffeted and jerked beneath them. Huddling next to the wall of the car and looking into the strange unfamiliar darkness of the spooky car, Breed lifted his knees to his chin, wrapped his arms around his legs and squeezed them for warmth. "I wonder if that hobo told us the right car to hop into."

Flick sat up, stuck his hands into his jacket pockets, and held the broken-zippered front of his jacket closed. "It's too late to worry about that, now." He made a face and turned his head away from Breed.

Being that his face was close to his foot, Breed couldn't help but smell it. The odor overwhelmed him. "Uggh, I never smelled anything that bad."

"You dumb shit," Hog said and moved to the corner next to Screwball. "You stepped in a pile of guts."

Screwball playfully nudged Hog back toward Breed. "Get back over there and take a great big breath of clean, fresh air."

"Clean, fresh air, my ass," Flick shot back. Waving his hand in front of his face, he crawled away from Breed and to the corner, where Screwball and Hog were curled into a ball.

As the train picked up speed and settled into the rocking and roaring momentum of what they hoped was the trip home, Screwball looked up into the sky and sighed. "Wherever we're going, we're going now."

"Since I'm letting you sit next to me," Flick said and looked to Hog. "Why don't you tell us what you did to that usher that kicked you in the ribs."

"I'm too tired to tell you right now," Hog said and smiled. "Remind me later."

Too tired to care about what Hog had done to the usher, Breed stretched his stinking foot as far away from himself as he could, leaned back against the wall of the gondola, and watched the sky. He swallowed and his throat hurt more than before. He wondered how sore it would get. It had been a very busy day, and he had forgotten about the cut above his eye. He reached up and touched it. He was thankful that it was only swollen a little, but it was hot. A sure sign that it was getting infected. He shivered under his wet clothes and dropped off into a deep sleep.

But his sleep wasn't restful. He dreamed he was home sweating it out each time someone knocked at the door. The police had ways to make Eddie talk. Any day now, Breed knew they all would be caught. In his dream, the thought of not knowing the future disturbed him and made his chest hurt deep inside. In his tormented dream, someone knocked on the door. It was the police. Then an old bum jumped up out of the kitchen sink with a long sharp knife in his hand, ready to stab him. The bum stunk like something dead. Breed had never smelled anything like that before. He awoke with a jerk and looked up. One by one, stars in the black sky winked to life. The smell of the stinking rotten bum in the dream was still in the air. It was his gut car-stepped-in foot.

Breed's sudden jerk woke up Flick and the others. Flick cracked one eye, reached into his pocket and fished out the chocolate bar that had fallen out of the station owner's pocket. Like a counterfeit expert examining a thousand-dollar bill, he held the chocolate bar and studied it. "I was saving this for a real emergency," he said and let out

276

a breath of air. "But we'll be home pretty soon." He broke the bar into four pieces, reached over, and passed them around. "This ought to hold us until we get to the Clark Street Bridge."

The rain had soaked the bottom of the car. The only dry spot was where they were sitting. Screwball and Hog gulped their fourth of the tiny piece of chocolate and drifted off into dreamland. Flick folded his hands on the side of his head and lay on his side. Sitting quarantined in the far corner with his stinking foot, Breed let his meager bite of chocolate slowly dissolve his mouth and watched the wet night sail past through a gigantic gash in the railroad car's steel wall. They were going home.

CHAPTER 17

In the dark of night, the lead locomotive, pulling the long string of railroad cars moved on down the railroad tracks. Zipping past hunks of reeds and overhanging trees, the cars slashed past a placid lake where rushing noise from the train's panting engines and clacking wheels hushed the croaking bullfrogs that lived along the marshy shore. On down the line, right before many railroad crossings intersected the long straight tracks, the locomotive blasted its buzzing horn into the night, signaling drivers of thin metal automobiles that an unstoppable thick metal monster, pulling tons of freight, was smashing through.

But the buzzing didn't bother Breed. He was exhausted. It was as if the buzzing were whispering him into a deep, sound sleep. While the train rattled and lumbered over miles of rails, Breed slept in the open gondola and dreamed he was already home, and his tired, aching muscles finally had a chance to recover for whatever was next.

Miles away from any road or crossing, like some gigantic, hissing wild cat, an ear-piercing hiss shot into the night air, and the train shuddered to a heavily-braked halt.

Breed jumped to his feet, ready to fight.

Fists clenched; Flick jumped up right beside him. "What the hell's that?"

"I don't know," Breed said with his heart thumping wildly in his chest. "But it's right behind the end of this car."

While Screwball and Hog rolled over, turned their backs to the noise, and covered their ears, Breed looked through a crack in the railroad's car floor. The train's wheels locked up and screeched across the smooth steel rail. Like a thousand fireflies, orange sparks sprayed down the rail, illuminating the wooden ties below. The lead locomotives slowed. Taking up the slack that had been created when the locomotives had pulled the cars forward, one by one, the drawn-out string of cars lurched forward. In succession, they banged into their connecting couplers until all the slack was gone. Then the train stopped, and the engine's horn buzzed one short and one long.

Screwball lifted his drowsy head and opened his eyes. "Are we there yet?"

Flick cocked his head to the side and listened. The hissing of air seemed to slow. "Maybe," he said, puzzled, "but I don't know why they stopped so fast."

As if the only thing he wanted to do was go back to sleep, Screwball closed his eyes and let his head droop down.

Breed pulled himself up over the top of the car and looked down. Under the couplers, air rushed out of a crack in a black rubber hose. "Something broke and it's leaking right here."

Flick popped his head up over the side of the car. "There's two lights flashing down the tracks. Somebody's coming."

"Maybe they're railroad bulls," Breed said with alarm. "Before we get our heads bashed in, let's get out of here.

Hog jumped up and jerked the sleep from his eyes. "Now what the hell's going on?"

Breed reached up, grabbed the top of the wall of the gondola, and looked back at Hog. "Somebody's coming. Get Screwball up!"

Hog shook Screwball at the shoulder.

Screwball opened his eyes and closed them again. "We don't want any. Go away."

Flick whispered in Screwball's ear. "Come on, Screwball, get up."

Screwball opened his eyes. "Great people sleep late."

Hog pulled on Screwball's arm. "If that's a railroad bull with a club, he'll knock you on your great head, then you'll sleep forever."

Screwball jumped up, and everybody except Hog climbed up the wall of the gondola, hung over the edge, and slipped down to the ground. When Hog started to climb down the outside of the car, the gun caught on the lip in the car's wall, pulled away from his body, and fell. It bounced once and fell between the tracks. Lights from whomever was advancing, flashed toward the car.

Hog leaped to the ground.

Breed watched the lights. Each time the holders took a step, the lights lurched forward. There seemed to be two people, one coming from the front of the train and one from the rear, and they were in a hurry.

Hog bent over and looked for the gun.

The way Breed saw it, whoever they were, they hadn't seen them. But they were creeping closer.

280

"Come on Hog," he whispered. "Those guys are coming. We can get it after they leave."

Hog gave up looking for the gun, and they all snuck into the concealing dark of a small clump of trees. While the men with the light came close, Breed and the others squatted in the dark and became wide-eyed stone statutes.

Walking towards each other, two railroad men walked along the gondola. When they got close to the hissing hose, they stopped.

Both wore blue-and-white-striped bib-overalls and railroad worker's caps with the visor. One man had a double chin and a nose that could have been beat flat from boxing or street fighting. It reminded Breed of a frog's head, but the man not only had shoulders like crossbeams, he was as big as a refrigerator.

The stooped-shouldered man beside him looked to be the one who rode up front in the locomotive's cab, next to the engineer, the fireman.

The big man peered down his frog nose and bitched at the broken hose. "Goddamn rotten rubber has to break in the middle of nowhere."

"It figures," the fireman said. "I was just getting to sleep."

Frog Nose held the light on the hose. "There it is. Turn that angle cock before we lose all the air pressure."

The fireman took off his cap, and with greasy oily hands, he reached in and turned the angle cock. His corded arm muscles flexed, and the light shone in his bullet-headed face. It looked tough as shoe leather. The hissing hose stopped.

Frog Nose lowered the light. "In the caboose, there's another hose under the bunk." He turned toward the back of the caboose. "It's the conductor's job to change it. But he's probably sleeping." He started walking toward the caboose. "I'll get it."

The fireman held his railroader's cap by the bill and banged the dust from the side of his shirt and coveralls. "I'll go back up to the lead engine," he said and put his cap back on his bullet-head. "It'll be a while before we build up enough pressure to get us out of this big hold."

"Okay, tell Joe, after I get it hooked up, I'll give you guys a highball."

The two men walked apart, and Breed and the others eased back into the brush.

Like a man watching for a pot to boil, Flick stared at the broken air hose and whispered, "We'll have to wait until he's done fixing that hose."

Screwball yawned. "Why don't we just get in now?"

Flick shook his head. "There's a big crack in that car. They might see us."

"Yeah," Breed said nodding in agreement. "After he fixes it, he'll go back to the caboose."

For a while, the bouncing light, coming from the rear of the train revealed the frog nosed man carrying a black rubber air hose under his arm. When he got to the broken air hose, he stopped, stepped in-between the cars, and after much bitching and banging, he replaced the broken air hose. As he stood there, apparently waiting for the air pressure to build back up, Breed and the others waited for him to go back to the caboose.

He didn't.

"Now what?" Flick whispered.

No one answered. They only watched. So they could climb back in the gondola and go home, Breed wanted Frog Nose to go away

Frog Nose fumbled in his pockets until he dug out a pouch of tobacco. With the beam of light glittering off the steel rails, he jammed a big wad of tobacco into his mouth. As if he had nothing better to do, he stood around, chomping on the tobacco, waiting. He stopped chomping and looked between the rails. The light from his lantern beamed right on the gun. He leaned over and picked it up. "I'll be damned. How'd something like this get out here."

Hog looked like he had lost his best friend.

Chomping his tobacco, Frog Nose examined the gun for a moment, then put it in his pocket. Holding the lantern, he stretched his arm and rolled the lantern in an overhand motion. He had given a highball signal to the engineer.

With a combination of anger and defiance, Flick waved his hand in a sweeping motion, and with his voice barely above a whisper, he told Frog Nose, "Get the fuck out of the way."

Breed stiffened, ready to run for the car. "Yeah, go back to the caboose so we can get back on."

After a while, Frog Nose quit chomping on his tobacco, spit a slimy stream onto the ground, and shined the light toward Breed. But it didn't hit him. It bounced around the tree leaves and skittered across the railroad bed. Then a light flashed from the lead locomotive.

"It's about time," Frog Nose said and stood still, waiting.

One by one, the cars took up the slack, squeaked, and lurched forward, but Frog Nose held the lantern and didn't move. The cars of the long train passed beside him.

Flick stepped forward but stopped. "Ahh, man," he complained. "He's waitin' for the caboose. He'll catch it on the fly."

Breed stood up. "Let's grab on anyway."

Flick looked back.

Everybody got set to run.

"Okay, Now!"

They jumped up and ran toward the moving gondola.

Frog Nose jerked his head in their direction.

The light beamed on them.

They stopped.

Frog Nose reached into his pocket and pulled out the gun. "Get the hell outta here!" His voice was like iron. Boom! He fired the gun. A long orange streak of fire shot from the barrel. The bullet went somewhere into the night. "Make me shoot again, and I'll blow your goddamn hobo heads off."

Realizing that because of the darkness and their shabby clothes, Frog Nose assumed they were hobos.

Breed backed up.

The gondola that would have taken him home, rolled on down the line. Clacking on a cracked rail, the tail end of the train picked up speed. Frog Nose grabbed the trailing caboose, swung on, and shining the light on Breed, he traveled down the tracks and faded in the dark.

Flick let out a disgusted breath. "We'll catch the next train."

Breed felt relieved and disappointed at the same time. "Yeah," he said and let his hands fall to his sides. "No use taking a chance on getting shot."

Together they settled back into the trees and waited for another train.

A light beamed toward them.

A strong diesel horn blasted the night.

Flick stood up. "Here comes one now."

Breed edged back into the brush. "Let's hide till the engine gets past."

When the engines appeared, the throbbing from the diesel's five thousand horsepower motor, caused the ground to vibrate under their feet. As the lead engines of the doubleheader train hulked right on past, air blew and sniffed from its brake lines.

Breed and the others jumped up and got ready to grab onto a car.

Flick glanced at Breed. Uncertainty filled his face. "That son-of-a-bitch is really moving."

Like a man hitchhiking in a friendly town where the first car would slow down and pick him up, Screwball walked backwards and held out his thumb.

This puzzled Breed, but he reached out to grab a grab iron. Clunk! The moving train stung his open hand like the whack of a hammer, the grab iron slipped off the tips of his fingers. His feet jerked on the loose stones beneath his feet, and his hand flew off the iron. Shaking his hand as if it had just been hit with a huge hammer, he huffed out, "Damn!" Then he bent over, placed his stinging hand between his legs, and grimaced with pain. "That thing is going too fast. If it doesn't rip our arms off, it'll throw us against the side of the car and drag us under."

Flick waved everybody away from the train. "Let's just wait for one that's going slower."

Breed straightened up and blew on his bruised hand. "I can do that, but I'll need to find some Daisy flowers."

Screwball dropped his thumb. "Hey, he didn't stop."

Smiling, Hog shook his head in disbelief.

As they sat on the tracks waiting for another train, no more passed, but the gloom of dark faded and gave way to a gray and cool dawn with gold and pink beginnings in the eastern horizon. Somewhere in the wilderness, birds chirped their first songs of the day.

With a dry and thirsty mouth, Breed stood up and looked into the new day. "Let's scout around and see if we can find some water."

Flick looked at his hands. They were cover with grime from the gondola and the grab irons. "Good idea," he said. "There should be a crick or something around here that we can wash our hands in."

Hog looked expectantly down the tracks. "What if a train comes?"

"If one starts coming, we'll hear it."

286

Walking under a stand of tall pines, dry pine needles felt soft under Breed's tired feet.

Flick stopped, stood in one spot, and surveyed the ground. "No water here. I can feel it."

Breed ventured further into the stand of pines and looked up. "It looks like there might be something over that hill."

"If there's a low spot on the other side," Hog said, "it should have water."

"Yeah, I hope it's not stagnant," Breed said, and on their hands and feet, they climbed a dry grass-covered hill. Half way up, Breed picked one of three lone Daisy flowers and crushed it into his bruised hand. On the top, they looked down into a small stream. Making swift gurgling sounds, it slid down a little slope, flowed under the blossoms of a flowery vine, and wound its way along grass-lined banks on its way to a something bigger. The stream wasn't like the usual streams and waterways Breed was used to seeing in Shitsplat. There were no cans or bottles around the edges. No soapsuds floated on top of blue-fetid water. No dead, bloated carp were stinking up the air. This little stream was clean beyond Breed's belief. This wasn't water as he knew it. This was not Shenango River water or anything close to it. This water was clear and inviting.

For a closer look, Flick leaned forward. Where the stream spread out, it came tearing white and noisy over a rocky bed. "This water looks okay to drink."

"Try it," Screwball said. "If it's bad, all you'll do is break out in assholes and shit to death."

Breed walked down the grass-covered hill and surveyed the edges of the stream. Springs and signs of good fresh water flowed out of the ground. "It looks okay to me, too."

Flick stepped to the edge of the stream and took a good look at the water. "It ain't close to a stinkin' river, so it should be good enough to drink."

Screwball tilted his head to the side and looked upstream. "I don't see any turds floating down."

"We'll just drink a little at first, "Breed said. "If it's bad, then we'll just get a little sick." He dropped to his hands in a pushup position and took a small sip from the cool stream. The taste was good. Contrary to what he had just suggested, he couldn't help himself. He drank more.

The others dropped and drank, too.

Flick rose to a squatting position, reached into the stream, and washed his hands with dirt from the bottom. When they were clean, he scooped up palms full of water and drank. Wiping his mouth on the back of his hand, he slurred, "Now I'm hungry."

Squatting and washing his hands, Screwball tilted his head toward Flick. "You should be hungry." He shook with a muffled spasm of amusement. "A big turd just popped up where you drank."

Horrified, Flick held his throat and looked to the water where he had just drunk. "What?"

There was no turd in the water.

Screwball shook the water from his hands, pointed at Flick, and roared, "Hant! Just seeing if you're paying attention."

Originally Breed and the others had used ha, ha, as a jeer, a jest, or a tease. After ha, ha evolved into Hant, it had become an attitude, a way to make fun of one's troubles, a state of mind that kept Breed and his friends from getting angry or feeling sorry for themselves when things happened that they couldn't control or do anything about.

Hog smiled at Screwball's attempted agitation, but stopped abruptly, cocked his head to one side, and held up his hand. "Listen."

Another train blared over the hill. Breed turned toward the sound. "Let's get to the tracks and grab that one."

They scrambled up the hill. At the top, a great cloud of dust erupted and spilled over the hill. As they watched the tail end of the train go flying down the tracks, Flick changed a few bars from Hank Snow's song "Fireball Mail" singing, "We don't wanna watch her fly. We don't wanna let her sail. We don't care if it's the fireball mail."

With his face glistening in the heat, Hog threw his hands up in defeat. "I don't give a shit what you call it, those things go too fast for us to catch."

"Yeah," Flick said and gave Hog a look of exasperation. "Looks like they only stop when they have trouble."

Standing on a sunbaked incline of yellow dirt, Breed stared at the long ribbons of railroad tracks. On the top of the rails, steel shone silver, and the sides were dusted with dull rust. The perspective distance between the tracks grew smaller and smaller and disappeared into infinity.

Flick looked down the tracks. His face turned ashen. "That's a long way down there."

Breed shook his head in agreement. "If we can't grab a train, it's going to be a long walk home."

Hog scanned the edges of the tracks. "Maybe we could put something on the tracks to slow one down."

"Like what?" Flick wanted to know. "We ain't got no ax or nothin' to chop a tree down."

Screwball put his hand into his pocket and leaned back. "Maybe we could put a nickel on the rail and knock the train off."

Hog almost smiled. "You sound like a shit salesman with a sample in your mouth. A nickel ain't gonna derail a train."

With his head and upper back bent forward, Screwball's jaw drooped open, and he imitated a moron. "Dat's not what dah cop told me when I put dat nickel on the tracks to mash into a quarter. He said, 'It's gonna derail dah train.'"

Hog managed a thin smile. "If you believe that, you're as ignorant as you look."

The moronic look on Screwball's face was replaced with a wide smile. He stood up straight. "Just seeing if you're paying attention."

Breed reached into his pocket and fingered the dime he had found at the gas station. "That cop just didn't want you making nickels into the size of quarters to put on a candy machine."

"It didn't work in any machine I tried," Screwball said. "The train smashed it down too thin, almost big as a half dollar, ruined a good nickel for nothing."

Flick nudged Breed in the arm and looked at Screwball. "Where did you get a nickel anyway?"

"Off Jimmy," Screwball said.

Hog looked concerned. "Who's Jimmy?"

Kicking his foot back and dancing in a circle like a simpleton, Screwball wagged his head from side to side, and sprang into the song "Jimmy Had a Nickel".

Being caught off guard, Hog shook his head. "Quit pullin' that little kid shit on me."

Screwball stopped the simpleton act, put his thumb in his mouth, and like a baby, he sucked on it and crossed his eyes. "Yep! Yep! Okay, Hoggy."

Trying to divest himself of Screwball's antics, Hog turned his back to him. "Just blow it out your ass. You ignorant bastard."

Although he didn't want it to, the tune of the song "Jimmy Had a Nickel" went over and over in Breed's mind. "I wish we did have a whole lot of nickels."

"Wouldn't do any good," Hog said, shaking his head. "Out here, there ain't no candy machines to put them in."

"Speaking of food," Screwball said, rubbing his belly, "that train smelled like baloney. Let's try and find something to eat."

Flick cocked his head back and looked toward the sun. "Before we waste more daylight standin' around doin' nothin', let's baloney on down that stream. It might run into a big river or something."

Everybody but Breed started walking. Before he took a step, he looked down. An old piece of railroad car metal sat on top of a railroad tie. He held up his hand. "Wait!"

Flick and the others stopped, turned around and watched Breed.

He bent over and pick up the metal. As the aroma of old wood and creosote wafted into his face, he said, "Maybe we can make an ax or something out of this junk."

Flick tilted his head back a little and squinted toward the forest. "We might not need it. There might be a town over there."

Hog glanced over his shoulder toward the forest. "I don't see anything."

"Look close. You can see where there used to be a path."

Hog studied the overgrown outline of an old path. "That's pretty small. It could be a path used by deer."

Flick turned sharply, and started down the path. "Let's find out."

As Breed followed, he wished the path would lead to a green meadow and a grove of cool trees with a spring-fed stream, and maybe a small waterfall dropping over a little stone ledge, next a cabin like the one the hobo didn't want them to stay in.

Instead, a ways down the overgrown path, scorched trees with gnarled black limbs clawing at the sky, loomed over a field of dying grass. As Breed walked along the path, he was smacked in the face by heat and stink. When he squinted into the sunlight and looked beyond the trees, old wooden houses, blackened by time, had been built next to a dirty-red-brick street. Crusted with foggy grime, broken windows glowed red and looked like they had once detained ghosts of forgotten hobos. Rickety, tilting and broken fences, fenced in dirt yards and looked like they would fall over at any moment. At a high spot in the brick road, abrasive winds had polished the brick to a smooth finish. Here heat waves danced a queer rigadoon, producing distant shimmering mirages of shadowy figures that may have entered the world centuries before civilization began. As the ominous spirits danced along the fence, heat beat against Breed's face, and the fence wavered vaguely in the sun.

Screwball stared ahead, rubbed his eyes, and stared at the figures disappearing and reappearing behind waves of heat. "Do you see what I see?"

"I've heard of phantoms like that, "Flick said with an awed nod. "They say they're images of another world. After people looked at them too long, they got hypnotized and walked right to them. They were never seen or heard of again."

Not knowing if Flick was joking or serious, Breed took two steps back. "Maybe we should get out of here."

Hog picked up a rock and held it. "They're just heat mirages. What are you afraid of?"

Before Breed could answer, a rooster crowed, a pump creaked, and water gushed into a bucket.

Screwball inclined his head toward the sound. "That could be ghosts pumping water." He turned to run. "Let's go."

Holding the piece of railroad car metal as if it were a weapon, Breed stiffened.

Throwing the rock up and catching it, Hog said, "Don't you guys think you're a little old to be scared of a noise?"

"We're not afraid of the noise," Screwball said. "We're afraid of what could be making the noise."

With resounding scorn and authority, Hog stated, "I don't care what you say. If there's well water, I want some. If there's a rooster, we can eat it."

"He's got a point," Flick allowed. "If we can't catch a train, we're gonna haft to walk a lotta miles. We gotta eat something to restore our strength."

Hog threw the rock at the figures. The rock hit the fence. As if they had never been there, the mirages of the shadowy figures vanished. Hog lifted his hands in a helpless gesture. "Let's find that chicken."

With their eyes wide with hunger, they guardedly walked toward the place the figures had danced. The closer they got, the more dilapidated everything appeared. Skirting in the shadows of old, weathered buildings, they stepped as quietly as possible, but the crunch of their soles against loose gravel announced their arrival. When they stopped at an old green water pump, in addition to the area being cold as a meat locker, a dank odor of rotting wood filled the air.

As Hog leaned against a crooked old gate post, Flick grabbed the handle of the water pump and tried to lift it to pump water. It wouldn't budge. It was rusted solid.

Screwball pointed to a broken-down chicken coup at the side of the fence. On top of a pool of cracked mud, a dead chicken lay in the sun. It's feather-covered carcass, maggot-infested and putrefying. "Hey, Hog, do you still want to eat that chicken?"

Although Hog didn't acknowledge Screwball's joke, a shudder ran through Breed's frame. It felt like the hand of death. He looked around. Making ever-darkening and grotesque shapes on the ground, a squirming shadow seemed to crawl out of spider webs under the chicken coop. Everything reeked of death.

Indicating the strange surroundings, Breed slowly moved his arm in an arc. "Nobody lives here for a reason."

"Maybe there's poison or something in the air," Flick said with an anxious look on his face.

Hog stepped away from the gate post and defiantly crossed his arms across his chest, but it took only a moment for him to realize the implication behind Flick's words. He assumed an anxious look of his own. "If you want, we can sit here and breathe in poison.

"If there's ghost here and they only eat brains," Screwball said and looked to Hog. "You won't have anything to worry about."

Hog started to reply, but when a creaking sound came from the inside of the building, he stood stock-still, watching.

Breed had never seen anything like this. The hair on the back of his neck rose with suspense and dread. Something evil and grotesque seemed to be near.

Shaking their heads in unison, they all turned, ran from the ancient buildings, and ended up back on the tracks.

While they walked along the windswept railroad tracks, as if he were going to make a wisecrack about what had just happened, Screwball's mouth fell into a lopsided grin, but he said nothing about the figures, and neither did anybody else. They had learned very early to be wary of sharing any part of anything strange they had seen. Skepticism, resentment, and persecution, had always followed.

Where water flowed down a narrow gap, lined with distorted, old trees, black and brown, with dead branches, they hopped down a little hill and started walking along the murmuring water of a stream. It got wider and formed into a deep pool.

Breed searched the water for signs of life. "Hey, maybe there's some fish in here."

"Yeah," Hog said. "If I had that gun, I could shoot one. You got a string or a hook?"

Flick reached into his pocket. "I got a safety pin."

Like a hungry dog peeking into a butcher shop window, Breed stared at Hog's shoes. His shoestrings had broken long ago. He had doubled and tripled fishing line and braided it into shoestrings."

In a sign of surrender, Hog held up his hand. "All right! But just one." He bent over and unraveled a piece of line long enough to tie on the end of a stick.

While Flick fiddled with the safety pin and bent it into a hook, Breed used his penknife to cut a stick to be used as a fishing pole, and held the end of it out to Flick.

Flick tied the bent pin onto the string and tied the other end of the string onto the end of the makeshift pole. Breed handed Flick the handle end of the pole, and Flick stepped to the stream and cast the pin into the water. Trying to imitate a bug, he skittered the pin across the surface. "Nothing," he said, dissatisfied with his attempt and pulled the line from the water.

Hunching protectively over the water, Screwball hooded his hand over his eyes. "I can see the fish." He pointed. "That one, right there weighs two pounds and three ounces."

Hog looked at the fish and then looked at Screwball. "How do you know it weighs two pounds and three ounces?"

Breaking into triumphant smile, Screwball looked directly into Hog's face. "I can see the scales on its sides."

Hog's face screwed up into a grimace of acute discomfort. "More little kid shit."

Laughing with amazement, Flick gave a helpless shrug, then said, "Why don't you guys quit playin' grab-ass and look for some bait."

Just to agitate, Hog stubbornly shook his head. "Nope."

Flick's shoulders sagged somewhat in defeat. "No bait, no fish. No fish, no eat."

"No shit," Screwball said with a glimmer of mischief.

As if he didn't want to miss a chance of getting back at Screwball, Hog said, "No shit? Take Ex-Lax."

But the joke was old. No one laughed, but when Screwball turned his back, his shoulders jerked with tremors of silent laughter.

Flick didn't have to repeat that they needed bait. Abruptly, Screwball and the others appeared to take on a greater interest in the process of finding bait. They all stumbled around in the weeds, lifted up flat rocks, and searched for worms.

They didn't find any.

Breed looked into the water and wagged his head. "The fish ain't here anymore."

"Let's go further downstream," Flick said. "Maybe there's a river around the bend."

They tromped on down the stream. It widened. When deep pools appeared, the current and the water smoothed out, but no river was found.

On a grassy bank just high enough to be the height of a comfortable chair, they sat down to rest.

"If we go too far," Breed warned, "we won't hear a train coming."

Sitting on the bank, Flick squirmed uneasily and leaned back on his elbows. "We can't grab on anyway."

"If we could," Hog said with a faint shake of his head. "We probably wouldn't have enough strength to hang on."

"You may be right," Breed allowed and held his hand over his stomach. "I'm so hungry, I feel weak."

Flick stared at the stream. "If this crick goes into a river, we might be able to make a raft and float down on the current."

"If we knew where we were going," Hog added, "that would be a good idea."

"I don't think it really matters where we go," Flick reasoned, "just as long as we keep going."

Screwball hunched his shoulders, let his arms hang loosely at his sides, and took on the look of a simpleton. "Dah! If we don't know where we're going, how are going to know when we get there?"

Breed turned from Screwball's simpleton look, and shook the remark out of his mind. "We can't just stay here."

"We know dat," Flick said and stood up. "Let's keep moving."

"Yeah," Screwball said and wiggled his body. "If we keep moving, we'll never be able to stop."

They all pushed on down the bank of the stream, pushed on through unyielding rope-like weeds that tangled around their feet like tough twine, pushed on through grabbing, sticking, tripping, tearing, thorny branches, and pushed on through the sharp grass that attacked the ankles of their feet, on the way to where? It didn't matter to Breed. He knew his friends were not ready to wave a flag of permanent defeat, and he wasn't either. They struggled on down the side of the water ribbon.

Screwball stopped walking and looked downstream. It stretched as far as the eye could see. Like an employment manager questioning a liar auditioning for work, he glared at Flick. "Are you sure we can get out of here this way?"

Imitating Screwball's simpleton imitation, Flick stopped, bent his head and upper back forward. With his jaw drooped open, he said, "Duh! I ain't sure a nut' in. But dis here crick gotta go somewhere. Day all do."

Screwball returned the simpleton look, waved his hand toward Flick, and they kept walking.

Breed tromped into a thatch of thick jaggers growing along the shore, stopped, and pointed forward. "Maybe there's a house or something past those trees." He kept on going, but tall, thorn-laden jaggers tangled around his feet and clung to the back of his shirt. It became too much. He quickly turned and struggled to get out of the clinging plants. But a branch scraped across his back and snagged the seat of his pants. He twisted to unsnag them, but other branches gouged into his arms and shoulders. He felt like a porcupine had jumped on him.

Don't move so fast," Flick advised.

Breed stopped struggling. Most of the branches came lose. As he slowly turned, he fingered dozens of barbs, hooked in the skin of his arm and pulled them out. As he stared at his bloody arm, Screwball pointed to the jaggers stuck to his back. "Dumb shit!"

"You're right about that," Breed allowed. "Hant on me."

"These jaggers are tearing our asses up," Flick said disgustedly, and pointed his makeshift fishing pole at the water. "Let's just jump in the water and follow the crick."

Breed broke free of the thorns and looked at his new shoes. They were wet, and the leather was covered with little cuts. He figured a little more water wouldn't hurt them much more. "I can do that," he said and was glad to get away from those jaggers.

They waded up to their waists. Now that it was easier going in the water, they continued downstream, at a leisurely pace.

When a moss-green turtle stuck its head up out of the water. Screwball riffled the water and startled it. Breed watched it swim madly into the water and under the yellow mud bank. "There's supposed to be seven different kinds of meat in turtles. Let's catch him."

"Go ahead, Breed," Flick said smiling shyly. "Just reach under the bank and pull him out."

"Bullshit, he ain't snappin' my fingers off."

"Don't be afraid, Breed," Flick advised. "They always go in headfirst. Grab him by the tail and pull him out."

"No way!" Breed said, shaking his head determinedly. "The last person who told me that had three fingers missing."

As a corner of Screwball's mouth quirked upward, he looked to Hog. "You wanna pull that turtle out?"

"That's okay. I'll pass."

"Bunch of candy asses," Flick said and looked to Breed. "Here, hold the pole."

Breed took the pole.

Flick bent low. With his chest touching the surface of the water, he felt under the muddy bank.

Breed held his breath and waited for Flick to pull his hand out of the water with his fingers bit off. "When you do that, you give me the willies."

"Yeah, I know," Flick said and kept on searching. "But I'm hungry."

Flick searched and felt until he ran out of stream bank. He stood up. "He ain't here no more."

"Yeah," Screwball said, "I knew a guy that used to pull turtles out from under the bank. Maybe I misunderstood him, but the guy always talked off handedly."

Laughing with surprise, Breed held the pole and watched the surface of the water. "He has to come up for air sometime. Let's wait."

Reaching out for the pole, Flick said, "Let me have that pole, Breed. When he comes up, I'll snag him."

The turtle never came up. Wherever it was, they left it there, but Flick continued to cast the safety pin into the water. When the stream widened, and the bank became a grassy carpet, they sloshed out of the water and walked on the soft grass.

A noisy splash sounded in the quiet. Breed looked downstream just in time to see a fish jump. He watched the circling ripples make miniature

302

waves on the top of the deep pool and travel toward the shore.

He held up his hand. "Hey, Hog, if you and Screwball stay here, me and Flick might be able to sneak down there and catch that fish."

Hog lay on the grass. "The lavishness of this place makes me tired." He folded his hands behind his head, and watched the sky. "Knock yourself out. I need a break."

As if the meaning of the word lavishness was hardly worth knowing, Screwball dropped to one knee. And like a man giving directions to an airplane pilot about to take off from the deck of a carrier, he stretched his arm straight out and rapidly rolled his other arm in a circle. "Cleared for takeoff."

Shaking his head, Flick held the makeshift fishing pole in front of himself and started walking. "Maybe we'll have fish for dinner."

He crept up to the open clear pool of water, lay on his stomach near the water, and flipped the safety pin.

It hit the water.

Nothing bit.

Twitching the pin, he waited.

Still, noting.

Standing upright, Breed walked to Flick and stopped.

"Goddamn, Breed, stay down," Flick bitched. "You'll scare the fish."

"It doesn't matter. They won't bite on a bare hook."

Flick lowered the makeshift fishing pole. "Yeah, we need bait."

Breed tilted his head toward Flick. "Cut a piece of my hair."

"What?"

Breed lifted his hand. "Tie it on the pin with this red thread I pulled out of my shirt."

Flick studied Breed's hair. Yeah," he said and considered the idea. "It might look like a bug."

Flick used his knife to cut a small piece of Breed's hair and held it.

Breed picked up the thread and looked at the safety pin. "If the fish bite on this, they'll slip right off." He took out the piece of metal, bent over, put the pin on a rock, and with the edge of the metal, he curved the end of the pin into an offset S. He stood up and handed it to Flick. "This should work," he said. "I'll get a longer stick. Then you can get further out where the fish can't see us."

While Flick tied the piece of Breed's hair onto the pin, Breed tromped off into the trees, found a skinny ten-foot maple branch, and trimmed the small branches off. Then he walked back and presented the new pole to Flick.

"Holy cow, Breed, you'll need a crane to hold that thing over the water."

Tethering the string onto the end of the pole, Breed stated, "Just try it."

As if he were in deep thought, Flick flipped the hair bug into the water, rolled the stick in his hand, and jerked it. The vibrations caused the bug to skitter across the water like a dragonfly. A small mouth bass jumped and hooked itself in the side of its mouth.

The bass fought back and forth and jumped once. The long maple stick bent and snapped off at the end. Breed watched the stick float around like a miniature buoy until the fish swam under the bank and stopped.

"I'll get him," Breed said and waded into the water. He grabbed the broken stick, pulled in the wiggling bass, and threw it up on shore. "Catch him, Flick. We'll eat today."

Like a starving dog after a bone, Flick leaped to the ground on all fours and trapped the flopping fish. Then he pulled out his knife. "This one ain't gettin' away." He cut its head off.

Breed retied the line onto the shortened fishing pole and danced the bug across the water. Nothing hit it. He looked to Flick. "We probably scared all the fish out a here for a while."

Flick shoved the fish in his back pocket. "Let's move on down and try another spot." As they weaved around the next curve in the waterway, Breed looked into the sky. A flash of white on dark blinked out of nowhere. He moved his eyes in rapid jerks and concentrated on the flash. As if it were showing him where to fish, an old wide-winged eagle circled above a small pool of water. Breed walked to the edge and offered the pole to Flick.

Flick waved his hand down. "You catch 'em, I'll clean 'em."

Breed flipped out the hair bug and danced it across the water. A fish broke the surface and hooked on. The pole bent and sprang the line tight.

305

The fish swam to jump. Breed didn't wait for it to flop off the safety pin hook. He jerked the long pole. It sprung the fish out of the water. It sailed through the air, jerked off the hook, and landed on the bank, flopping. Before it could wiggle back into the water, Flick stepped on it.

Another roll of the bug and Breed had another fish. It was a white-mouthed rock bass, the size of a large sunfish.

These rock bass are easy to catch," Breed said. "They have no wits about them. They bite anything and run like hell."

As Breed kept rolling the bug, a feverish pitch and sense of immediacy overcame him. He flipped out the bug. The fish jumped. He panicked and jerked on the long stick so hard that it bent over like a huge metal spring. The hook set quickly. The pole rebounded and flung the fish out of the water. It came flying back, right at his face. He ducked. The fish slingshotted onto the shore and flipped off the hook. Again, and again, Breed snatched fish from the water and jerked them onto the bank. When the fish flipped and wiggled to get back into the water, Flick scurried around the grass and trapped them with his hands, feet, and any way he could.

When the fish stopped biting, Flick held two fish in his hands, and a pile of fish lay at his feet. "This is food."

Hog and Screwball walked up to Flick and stopped.

When they saw the fish, Hog asked, "Where did all those fish come from?"

Smiling big, Screwball stared at Hog. "They came from the water."

Breed laid the pole on the bank. "They did, but I think that's it. They just quit biting."

Gutting the last fish, Flick looked up. "Maybe you caught 'em all."

"That's okay, we got nine."

Flick gathered the fish into a pile. "While you guys get the firewood, I'll finish cleaning the last two."

Breed, Hog, and Screwball walked into the thick trees and snapped off the dead branches from the sides of trees, gathered them in their arms, and came back.

"How are we gonna light that wood?" Flick asked. "We ain't got no matches."

Breed reached into his pocket and pulled the piece of metal he had picked up on the railroad tracks. "Maybe I can spark up a fire with this."

"I don't think so," Flick said. "That thing's wet.

Breed waved the piece of metal around in the air. "The sun will dry it. See if you can find a piece of flint. I'll get some dry grass."

Flick waded into the water and searched for a shiny stone of flint. "None here, Breed."

Breed pulled some dry grass off the ground and looked back over his shoulder. "Look in the shallow part. I saw some close to the ripples."

Flick hopped into the shallow water, scooped up a handful of stones, and found one good-sized piece of flint. Sloshing back to shore, he handed it

307

to Breed. "Okay, Breed, let's see just what kind of Indian blood you got. Start a fire."

Breed hadn't done the flint and metal trick for a while. He wasn't sure he could do it. He searched the area until his eyes landed on a place where some animal had long since gathered little sticks for a nest. They were dead and dry. He grabbed them, carried them to the pile of branches, and set them aside. Then he dried the flint on his shirtsleeve and blew on it until it was dry. Reluctantly looking to Flick, he said, "I don't know if I can still do this."

Flick placed an encouraging hand on Breed's shoulder. "Come on, Breed. You can do it."

While Screwball arranged some rocks in a circle, Breed dropped to his haunches and crumbled the dry grass and made a fire ignition bed. He struck the piece of metal against the flint. Orange sparks flew but nothing happened.

Getting ready to feed the starting fire, Flick held the little sticks and told Breed to, "Do it faster."

Breed regripped the metal and set the crumbled grass on top of a flat rock. "Now that I got a good base. I'll hit this flint so fast, it'll make enough sparks to burn the whole woods down."

A succession of quick strikes made the sparks fall like miniature molten metal. Breed stared into the dry grass. A glow appeared like a little jewel. He bent low, and blowing gently, he teased it. The grass smoked and puffed into a flame. He kept his eyes on the infant fire and motioned to Flick. "Bring on those sticks. I almost got her going."

Flick piled on the little sticks.

308

They sparkled, crackled, and burst into tiny flames.

Fanning the fire, Breed stated, "We got fire. Bring on the big stuff."

Hog reached into his pocket and pulled out a wooden match and held it in front of his face. "I guess you won't be needing this."

"Why didn't you tell me you had a match?" Breed asked in disbelief.

Hog stared at Breed. "You didn't ask me. Hant!"

Flick set a stick of wood on the fire and was about to add more, but Screwball held up his hand. "Wait!"

All heads turned toward him.

"The cops are looking for us." He grinned like a happy simpleton. "If we start a fire, the flames will give away our position for miles."

With his lips curled back, Flick bared his teeth into a snarl. "What the hell's the matter with you? There ain't anybody within a hundred miles."

With a bewildered look on his face, Hog spun around and faced Screwball. "I don't know why you're worried about the police taking you to jail," he said. "If they did come, they'd take you directly to the nut house."

Nodding with delight, Screwball replied, "You're just saying that because it's true."

Wagging his head, Flick placed bigger sticks over the small fire. For a few moments they didn't catch. They only sent white smoke into the air. Then they caught. The fire roared. The sticks crackled and gave off a curling plume of smoke.

As if the smoke had been a signal, Screwball and Hog stepped next to the fire and held their hands over the welcome heat.

Flick cut sticks and ran them through the cleaned fish. He poked the bottoms of the sticks into the ground around the fire, and like offerings to a god, the fish hung near the flames.

"Roast fish," Screwball said and rubbed his hands together, "what a treat."

Better than nothing," Breed said. "If you don't want any, I'll eat yours."

"Naw, that's okay," Screwball said. "I think I can manage to eat a few."

Breed fed the fire and repositioned the fish until they looked done.

"Check one out," Flick said, "you caught 'em."

Breed pulled a stick from the ground. The fish were dry and shriveled on the outside. Breed picked off a piece and put it into his mouth. Inside it was moist and tender.

"Well how is it?" Flick asked with a mouth full of fish.

"Perfect," Breed said and tore off another piece

Screwball puckered his face, and his mouth turned downward. "It don't look too good."

"Maybe not," Breed said, "but it tastes good."

Yeah," Hog agreed, "any food taste good when you don't have any."

Breed chewed the last of his share of the fish and went into the woods with Flick for more wood. "That couple of bites of food just made me hungrier," Flick said, and a rabbit jumped up. Flick kicked at it with his foot and Breed jumped for it.

It ran free.

After Breed fed the fire with the pile of wood, they all took their wet clothes off and placed them over the roasting sticks to dry. With a sense of relaxed well-being, they lay around the fire, and steam pillowed from the wet of their shirts, pants, and shoes that were being roasted dry over the heat of the yellow fire.

There goes the leather on my new shoes, Breed thought. They'll dry but they're going to be as hard as cement. If we ever get out of this place, I might be able to polish them back into shape.

The sun fell from the blue bird sky and lit up an orange horizon like it was a coming attraction of a better day.

"How about we make a shelter from sticks and grass?" Screwball suggested. "It's going to rain."

"No it isn't," Breed said and cast a furtive glace in the direction of the horizon. "We'll be gone tomorrow, and we don't have an ax. It'll be a bitch to cut branches with our pen knives."

"You're probably right," Flick said, "but if it rains, we'll be sorry."

"Then you'll be sorry," Screwball said. "I saw the Big Dipper in the sky last night, and it was tipped over. That means it's going to rain."

For a moment, Hog appeared to be puzzled. Then asked, "What kind of crap are trying to start now? I see that Big Dipper tipped down all the time. It doesn't mean anything."

"Yeah it does," Screwball protested. "It means the water is pouring out, and just as soon as the water gets to the earth, it'll rain."

Breed smiled and gestured to the sky. "It ain't gonna rain. Red sky at night, sailor's delight."

The clothes quit steaming. Flick leaned over, shook his shirt, and felt it. "The sky's red, but that ain't always true."

"Might be true here," Breed countered. "There ain't no steel mills lighten up the sky with its red smoke."

Flick stood up and rotated the clothes. Now they steamed from the other side. "At least we got our clothes washed."

Breed looked toward the stream. In the flare of the sunset, a clear blue-opal sheen glowed on its surface. "That water is really clean. We must be somewhere really far out."

After he dropped to the ground, Flick sat back, leaned on his elbows, and looked deeply into the flickering flames of the fire. "We should find out tomorrow. We got all day to go down this crick."

"Come on you guys," Screwball said with his goofy giggle. "Cheer up! Tomorrow everything's gonna be just fine"

"What are you talkin' about," Hog wanted to know.

Not missing a stimulating opportunity to throw open one of his dazzling witticisms, Screwball beamed urbanely, "When we wake up in the morning, the sun's gonna be shining out of a clear blue sky. A slow-moving train's gonna come down the tracks. We're gonna jump on and before we know it, we'll be home."

Hog discerningly cocked his eyebrows. "You're out of your goofy mind."

312

As the shadows of the trees were thrown farther and farther over the water, they all put their clothes on and lay down on the grass next to the fire. Frogs trilled and one cricket chirped, and thousands of bright stars seemed to peer down on them. With food in their bellies and warmth at their faces, they closed their eyes.

The dry clothes covering Breed's body made him feel better, but he couldn't sleep. He was still hungry. He figured he was too tired to sleep. But he had to sleep. If he didn't, tomorrow will be worse than today.

He shut his eyes tighter and tried to force himself doze off. It didn't work. He gave up and rolled over with his back to the fire. When he finally fell asleep, a big night bass jumped and splashed water right into his hungry face. In fright, he sat up.

Screwball woke from a deep sleep and called out, "Hant!" Then he rolled over and sniggered.

"It figures," Breed muttered to himself.

Bah-Womp! A bullfrog echoed from the water. Breed waited for it to croak again. It didn't. He thought about putting more wood on the fire, but he decided he was too tired. So he watched it flicker and go out. When the moon smiled down and dark clouds gathered and covered its face, he finally fell to sleep.

Craackk! Boom! came from the sky.

Flick jumped up with his knife in his hand, eyes darting every direction.

Breed rolled away from the sound. Grabbing at the empty air, he scrambled to his feet. "Damn!"

He exhaled with surprise and irritation. "That thunder scared me half to death."

"How'd you like that alarm clock?" Screwball said with laughing amazement.

"It ain't bad," Breed lied, holding his heart-thumping chest. "But it ain't daylight yet."

Screwball sat up and stared at the knife in Flick's hand. "It might still be dark," he said smiling, "but there's never a dull moment with a sharp knife."

While Screwball sat there like an idiot laughing, a great rain hissed and roared through the trees.

Flick looked at Breed. "Naw, we don't need to build a shelter."

With a look of excruciating discomfort, Hog looked up into the gray sky. "Courtesy of 'It ain't gonna rain. Red sky at night, sailor's delight', we're getting our asses soaked."

Screwball tilted his head back and shook it from side to side. "That Big Dipper doesn't mean nothin'."

"Yeah okay," Breed said and flashed an injured look. "The red sky wasn't a sailor's delight. Let's go into the woods and get under a tree."

When the ozone odor of lightning filled the air, Flick advised with a sweep of his hand, "If we do, we'll attract lightning."

"Oh that's just terrific!" Screwball said. "Lightning should add to our life expectancy."

Breed felt the rain soaking his clothes. "We just got dried off. I don't care if I attract the whole goddamn sky. I'm getting under something."

314

Zing! Crraack! Lightning lit up the area and was followed by a rolling boom of thunder that caused the ground to vibrate under their feet. As the sky brightened to signal a new day, a muskrat crawled up onto the bank, right behind Flick. He saw it and jumped with fright. In a terrified rage, he yelled at it, "You scared me half to death, you little creep!"

Breed looked on the ground for something to throw. "If we had something to kill it, we could cook that thing."

Flick stepped back. "I ain't gonna grab it. It'll bite my fingers off, maybe even go for my throat."

"What I wanna know," Screwball said, "is what happens if you get scared to death twice?"

Flick started to laugh, but lightning flashing and causing the sky to look like shiny tin foil, stopped that.

Shivering in the predawn chill, they walked into the woods and stopped under a fat oak tree and waited for the rain to stop. The morning sun tried to shine down, but was blocked by gray clouds.

The rain stayed.

Breed and his friends broke long straight sticks from trees and sharpen them.

"These will make good spears," Hog said, poking his stick into the air. "If that muskrat jumps up again, we'll get it."

Flick took a few steps toward the stream, and his feet loaded up with yellow mud. In the distance, the moaning of a train's horn echoed through the trees. "I didn't know we were so close to the railroad tracks," he said and looked toward the

315

sound. "Let's get back there. This stuff's like quick sand."

Hog looked to Screwball. "Cheer up! When we wake up in the morning, the sun's gonna be shining out of a clear blue sky. A slow-moving train's gonna come down the tracks. We're gonna jump on, and before we know it, we'll be home."

"Maybe I had the wrong morning," Screwball said with a superior air.

Shaking their heads at Screwball, they squared their shoulders, rubbed sore, aching muscles, and with faces jeweled from the rain, they headed for the tracks.

CHAPTER 18

A while after the rain stopped, Breed and his friends were greeted with a sun-scorched day. A fast-moving train raced through a shimmering heat-haze and on down the tracks but was going much too fast to grab onto. After it was out of sight, for a moment all was still. Then it was as if someone had turned a water spigot on in the heavens. Big raindrops plinked on the steel railroad rails, and a threatening wind gushed out of the forest. To keep the roaring rain from pelting Breed's and his friends' faces, they bent their heads down. Using pointed spears for walking sticks, they walked along the railroad tracks, until overhanging trees and bushes forced them to walk on the ties. Sheeting rain obscured the tracks, but the thought of a town or a road that could show them which way they had to go to get home, kept them slogging on down the tracks.

Just before a bend in the tracks, the rain stopped, the clouds cleared away from the western sky, and a rainbow curved down and buried its exquisite hues into an area around a bend in the tracks.

Pointing to the rainbow, Breed shook the water from his face. "Look! A rainbow. There should be a pot of gold or something around that bend."

"Here's what's around that bend." Hog lifted his leg and farted.

As the odor wafted into Screwball's face, his nose crinkled, and he looked like he was about to throw up. "You rotten bastard," he yelled with a trapped feeling of terror. "That's the worst thing I ever smelled in my life."

Showing no remorse or shame, Hog tilted his head toward Screwball and graciously replied, "Thank you!"

With a look of comic disbelief, Flick stepped up his pace. "My feet are about to fall off, but if you wanted me to walk faster, instead of releasing a toxic bomb, you should have just told me to speed up."

"Quit your bitchin," Hog said to agitate Screwball. "Don't you see that rainbow? When we wake up in the morning, the sun's gonna be shining out of a clear blue sky. A slow-moving train's gonna come down the tracks. We're gonna jump on and before we know it, we'll be home."

Screwball moaned and they all walked faster.

When they rounded the bend, the rainbow and its promise were gone. The land surrounding them was dry, and there were no overhanging trees or bushes. Breed could see a long way down the tracks.

He stopped.

Screwball brushed his wet hair from his forehead. "If we would have gotten her sooner, we would have never gotten wet."

Ignoring Screwball and looking at the unpromising miles of tracks, Breed shook his head. "The rain stopped here, but there's no end to these tracks."

"That's for sure," Flick said and pointed to the steep side of a little mountain. "Let's go up there. We'll be able to see a long way."

Hog wiped the rain from his face and looked toward the mountain. "Good idea. There might be a road or something on the other side."

Together, they cut away from the railroad tracks and filed up the steep side of the mountain. When they were gathered together on the top, standing in the gray dirt and shale, looking down into an abandoned strip mine, Breed shared the apprehension of his friends. At the bottom, a clear blue body of water sat still and deep.

While Flick waited at the top, Breed, Hog, and Screwball spilled down from the top and swarmed down the side, causing loose, gray shale that hadn't been disturbed for years to shuffle under their feet. Halfway down, a stand of scrub pines leaned out of a thick brown blanket of sharp pine needles. Breed saw the needles and tried to step carefully. He had tied his shoestrings in his low-cut shoes tight enough to make his feet turn blue. But it didn't matter. With each step, like hypodermic needles, random pricks from the sharp, dry needles pierced the thin sides of his worn socks and poked into the tender skin around his ankles. He ignored the pain, stepped into the dry shale, shuffled the needles off his socks, and tromped on down the incline. Each time his feet struck the earth, tiny puffs of gray dust exploded up around his knees, and wafted up into the air and into his nose. It smelled like snakes.

Swinging his stick in the air, Flick yelled down, "If you smell cucumbers, watch out for copperheads. They hang around places like this."

Always being the one to rush ahead, Screwball quickly lopped down the hill toward the water. In

319

the process, he created a miniature landslide. At first only little dust-devils rose in gray funnels and scampered behind him. Then they grew, sending a boiling cloud of gray dust toward Breed. At the shore line, Screwball picked up a crooked black stick and threw it up the hill. As it sailed through the cloud of dust and headed toward Hog's feet, Screwball yelled, "Snake!"

Hog looked down. In the haze of dust, the dull-black, snake-like curves of the stick rolled over his feet. Damn!" He jumped away. His feet caught a curve in the stick. He tripped and fell into Breed, but landed unharmed on the ground.

Trying to catch his fall from being knocked over by Hog, Breed thrust his pointed walking stick forward. It plunged into the soft shale powder and snapped in two. To see where he was falling, he jerked his head forward. Threatening pieces of sharp, gray slate loomed up in front of him. Pulling his hands back, he squatted and ducked his head until his chin touched his chest. Rolling on his right shoulder, he flipped onto his back. In an attempt to stop his downhill momentum, he straightened his legs. He had avoided the sharp slate cuts to his bare hands, but now he was sliding like a sled on a snow-covered hill. With gray dust streaming all around him, he sailed down the steep bank. Bracing his feet in the powdery dirt, he tried to stop, but his feet plowed in. Slowing, he slid over little pieces of shale. They shoveled up the back of his shirt, and dirt funneled it into his pants. His right foot slammed into a big rock. His knee bent. The heel of his shoe wedged in between the rock and the dirt.

Like a mighty mechanical hand had grabbed his foot and was holding it secure, it caused his body to slide sideways. He kicked his foot free, rolled over to his stomach, and then back to his back. Gray dust rooster-tailed off the side of his foot. With his belt scooping dirt into the back of his pants, he continued down the hill until he careened sideways and stopped at the water's edge.

Flick called down from the mountain of slate and shale. "You all right, Breed?"

For a moment, Breed squirmed uncomfortably. Then he checked his body for cuts. He found only a few scratches. "Nothin' to it," he said, stood up, dropped his pants, and let shook the dirt out.

Sitting on the ground, smiling with merriment, Screwball said, "Hey, Breed, I missed that. Could you do that again?" He took out the penny whistle and played, Cuck-oo! Cuck-oo!

"It figures," Breed replied back, pulling up his pants. "You finally learn to play one thing and it has to be something stupid." He smiled inwardly and felt his not so new, new shirt with his hand. Small tiny pieces of slate stood out amidst his dust-covered red shirt and stuck to it like tiny magnets. He brushed them off and looked at the sight before him.

To his right, like sharp hatchets thrown into lifeless mounds of yellow dirt, ends of gray slate stuck out. On his left, like scenery in an oil painting, veins of dried, gray clay blended into a yellow dirt background. Right in front of him, a little way from the shore line, chunks of soft coal littered the ground. Just about everywhere around the water, scrawny pine trees, with sickly branches, stuck up between huge rocks and created a heaven for copperhead snakes. This was strip mine territory.

It looked like it had been a busy place at one time. If people worked here during the war, they probably worked like victory was just another double shift. Breed looked back up the mountain of slate. A dragline as big as a house could have been there. Strung-up lights might have floodlit a place crawling with workmen in overalls and sweat-stained shirts, digging coal all night long. He looked at the scattered gray coal. The coal strippers had taken all the good hard coal and left the soft stuff. It was called kennel coal, and it burned too quickly to efficiently heat homes. That was why it was everywhere.

Now that the dust had settled, the air was sparkling clear, and the sun shone through the cover of the pines. Its rays penetrated deep and lit up the clear blue strip mine water. Breed bent over, and brushing the dust and dirt off his shoes, he discovered deep scratch on the back his shoe. He figured it must have happened when he got his foot wedged between the rock and dirt. He tried to assure himself that it wouldn't matter much. The scratch was in the back. He tilted his head toward the water and looked down through its surface. Old sunken branches rested on the bottom. Among the algae-decorated branches, three big bass sat, suspended and still. They moved their front fins and opened and closed their gills. Breed stood like a man who had just landed on another planet. He

322

had never seen fish in water as clear as this. It was crystal blue, looked good, and was deep.

When a gaggle of Canadian geese paddled around the bend, a metallic-green sheen accented their white-striped necks, and their black eyes, accented with golden dots, gleamed out into the day. Unruffled, preened and primped feathers adorned their graceful bodies. They were clean from their bills to the end of their tails. They looked ready to win a blue ribbon at a county fair. When Breed looked to his right, a series of deer tracks ran up the steep incline. All these mountains and hills were friends to the deer. Here they could walk around the sides of the steep mines and be free from the threats of drunken weekend hunters.

A shadow ran across the water. Breed looked high above. A bird flew in the sky. Its brown body was separated with a white head and a white tail like a reverse exclamation point.

It dove.

Its white tail flashed in the sun.

It was an eagle.

Breed wondered if it would crash into the water and dive to catch a fish. He watched and waited. The elegant eagle swooped down, delicately dipped its talons into the water, and in one motion, plucked a fish out of the water, sailed back up into the air, and disappeared over a tall blue spruce tree.

Standing intoxicated by the clean beauty presented by the strip mine, Breed couldn't get over the clarity of the water. Now that the dust had settled, the air was a joy to inhale, and it reminded of Screwball saying, "Take a great big breath of the

323

clean fresh air." But this time, the air was clean and fresh.

As Breed continued to stare at the water, a big bass moved once and stayed suspended. Being clean water, Breed was sure the bass didn't have the white worms that curled out of their fillets, like the fish from the river. And they probably didn't have that black sewer taste.

When he looked back over his shoulder, like a baseball pitcher, Hog lifted his leg, wound up, and threw a rock. It zinged through the air and plopped into the water with a loud, Chook!

With instinctive fright, the peaceful geese flared their wings, thrashed the water, and paddled their webbed feet. Like airplanes with pontoons instead of wheels, their speed increased. When they pumped their wings to fly, they skimmed across the calm surface, creating a moving sheen of spray that traveled alongside their bodies. Just before clearing the water, their feet gently kissed the surface, and their wings pumped their bodies skyward. Honking like bicycle horns with rubber bulbs, they flew around the bend.

Behind Breed, Flick shambled down the hill, shuffling dirt, stones, dust, and shale, and causing it to avalanche on down the incline, forming another great cloud of gray dust.

Waving the dust from his face, Flick looked to where the geese had flown around the bend. "They'll be back," he said and kicked a stone into the water. "They're just practicing to see who'll lead them south."

Dusting gray dust from his pants, Hog looked up. "How do you know that?"

Flick pointed to the geese. "Just watch." The geese flew around the bend but stayed in the sky. "They'll take turns at the lead point of the Vee and come back."

Screwball jabbed his stick toward the sky. "I'm still hungry. They can take turns sitting on the point of this stick."

Like a hungry dog in a meat shop, Flick stared at the flying geese. "Good idea, Screwball, but you'll never get close enough to stab 'em." He held his stomach. "We'll have to make a trap or something."

Breed stood near a sunken tree and pointed into the clear blue water. "There's bass in here. You can see them, clear as day."

"Hey Flick," Screwball said, "get a long stick and make another a fishing pole."

Like a crowd at a free sample stand, everyone converged on the spot where the fish were.

Flick moved his head back and forth searching. "Where?"

Breed pointed to the suspended bass. "Right there."

"Damn," Screwball said, "they're just sitting there."

"Get that pole working," Hog said. "I'll gather up some of this coal for a fire."

Give me a chance to catch one," Flick said and searched the trees for a branch to cut. He snapped off a long pine branch, skinned the branches off, sat down in the dirt, and rigged up the line and the hair bug. Then he stood up and looked for the bass. "Hey, they're gone."

Screwball pointed to the fish deep in the water. "No, they ain't. They're right there." He jerked his finger toward the fish. "Throw it right there."

Flick flipped the bug onto the top of the water and twitched it. "Come on, fishy, snack time."

The bass didn't budge.

"Look at those things," Screwball pointed out. "They just sit there, moving their gills like they're chewing gum."

As if he were casting a fishing pole, Hog made a motion with his arm. "Throw it again. Maybe they're sleeping."

"Sleeping?" Screwball questioned. "How can they sleep? They never close their eyes."

Flick cast the bug out, again. "When I catch him, he'll sleep. I'll close his eyes permanently."

"Yeah, if he comes up," Breed said, watching the bass. "But he isn't moving."

"You can watch them all day," Hog said, scrunching his face into a frown. "They won't bite."

Screwball talked directly into the water toward the fish. "That's it. Just sit there, you big bastards. Don't waste any energy. Just sit there."

"Won't bite nothin', my ass!" Hog said. "Stab the goddamn thing. I'm hungry, and the coal's right here."

"Flick skittered the bug across the water again and again. The big strip mine bass would not bite. They wouldn't even move. Flick pulled the bug from the water. "They won't play fair. Spear one of 'em, Hog."

"Give me that line," Hog said holding out his hand. "I'll tie it on the end so we can pull it in after I spear it." He tied one end of the line on the end of the long sharp stick and wrapped the other end around his hand. He reared back and speared the stick into the water. It didn't even come close. Apparently realizing his ignorance, he laughed out loud. "Hant on me! Those bass are too deep. That clear water makes them look closer than they really are."

Screwball threw flat rocks into the water. "Eat this, you lazy fish." The rocks splashed into the water and zigzagged down past the bass like big gentle snowflakes. One rock fell close to the biggest bass. It stayed suspended, opened and closed its gills, and seemed completely unconcerned.

"Hey, this sucks," Hog said, seething with anger. "I gotta get something to eat. The coal pile is ready to light. What are we going to cook?"

Screwball smiled a mischievous smile. "Well lighten up," he said and giggled. "Enjoy the hunger while it lasts."

Shaking his head, Hog turned a cold eye on Screwball. "It'll be better than enjoying your half-assed jokes."

Screwball put the whistle to his lips and blew out a soft, Cuck-oo!

"The main thing is," Breed said like a man about to say something great that would go down in history and paused in mid-sentence.

327

"Well what?" Screwball said with an impatient tone of voice.

"The main thing," Breed said and paused again, just long enough for Screwball to start to speak, and then he interrupted him with, "The main thing is, don't get excited."

"I'm not excited," Screwball protested. "Not one of those bass will bite. Let's figure out a way to catch a goose."

Feeling a hunger pain in his stomach, Breed studied a stand of reeds in the water. "I think I got it."

"Flick's eyes shifted toward the reeds. "Way to go, Breed. We can hollow out one of those reeds. While we're breathing through it, we'll sneak right up on those geese."

"That's right," Breed agreed. "Before they know we're there, we can grab one."

Breed and Flick went to the water's edge and pulled out a few long reeds.

"They're already hollow," Breed noticed. "But it doesn't look like we can get much air."

Like a genius in deep thought, Screwball clenched his lower lip between his teeth. He let go of his lip. "In the movies, cowboys do it all the time."

"Yeah," Hog said flatly, "but we're not cowboys."

Flick cut off the reeds, tipped them up toward the bright sky, and looked through the holes in the ends of the small, dark-green cylinders. "This should do it." He handed the reeds to Breed.

Breed looked at the reeds and put one in his mouth. He tried to breathe. "Not enough air with one." He held up three fingers. "Maybe three." He put three reeds into his mouth and took a breath. "Ahh, yes, this should work."

"Okay, great inventor," Hog said and pointed toward the water. "Get your ass in there and catch our supper."

Breed handed the reeds back to Flick. "No problem."

While Flick held the reeds, Breed took off his shoes and set them next to the water. "I'm sick and tired of getting these things wet."

Screwball stepped toward the water. "The best thing to do when you're sick and tired is to take a rest, then you'll only be sick."

Squinting at Screwball, as if he were crazy, Breed closed one eye, stripped to his underwear, and eased into the water. When he was waist deep, Flick reached out and offered him the reeds. "Not yet," Breed said, looked to Hog, and held out his hand. "Hey, Hog, throw me that spear."

Hog flipped him the sharp stick that had the fishing line attached to it. "What are you going to do stab 'em?"

Breed examined the sharp stick and stabbed it into the water. "Maybe if I dive down, I can spear one of those bass. They're still not moving."

Breed tied the stick to his wrist, pushed away from the shore, and glided on the surface until he was just above the suspended bass. Then bending at the waist and thrusting his legs straight up toward the sky, he straightened his arms, flared his hands, and pushed them away from his body. With his body perfectly straight, he stroked one powerful stroke. Rapidly descending, his feet were the last part of his body to slip below the water's surface. His perfect surface dive sent his body toward the deep bass. To his surprise, the deeper he dove, the colder the water became. He opened his eyes. The fish were a blur, but he was close. Just as he was ready to spear that big bass, ice-cold water attacked his forehead. Instant pain screamed in his brain. He turned, dropped the stick and burst through the surface.

Ready to catch a fish, Breed had speared, Hog was standing on the bank, bent at the waist. "Did you get one?"

Breed breathed in deep. "No way, man, that water's ice cold down there." He rubbed his forehead. "That stuff gives you an ice-cream headache."

Hog's face fell. "Looks like we go to plan B."

Snorting with amusement, Screwball said, "Let's go to plan E, for eat."

Flick ignored Screwball's jibe and stepped next to the water. Then he extended his arm out full length and handed Breed the three hollow reeds. "Here, take these. Get over by those cattails and hide until the geese come back."

Breed nodded in agreement and dog-paddled toward the cattails. Once he was there, he stopped, placed the breathing reeds in his mouth, went under, and tried to breathe. One breath and he came up spitting water. "I can't breathe without getting water down my nose."

330

Hog wagged his finger at Breed. "Don't be a candy ass. Get under that water and wait for our supper."

Breed tried again. This time water rushed into his ears and nose. He came to the surface spitting and blowing snot. "This doesn't work," he said and felt a stabbing pain in the back of his throat. Trying to ease the pain of his worsening sore throat, he swallowed and plowed toward the shore, but before he got there, he stepped on a sharp rock. He ignored the pain, but knew he would have to put his shoes back on.

Flick waded waist deep into the water and stopped in front of Breed. "Give me those reeds. I'll show you how to do it."

Breed shook his head and cleared the water from his ears. "Here." He handed the reeds to Flick. "Be my guest."

While Breed stood on shore watching, Flick tried over and over but couldn't do it either. He gave up and sloshed toward the shore. "Those cowboys are full of shit." He flung the reeds out over the water. They landed with a gentle splash, floated for a few moments, and sank just beneath the surface.

Hog sat on the shore with his elbow on his knee and his chin resting on his fist. "Hey, Breed. You got any more bright ideas?"

After Breed slipped back into his shoes, he searched his brain for a solution. When it came to his inventing abilities, he couldn't let Hog get one up on him. So he asked, "Why do we have to hide under the water to catch those geese?"

With a look of amusement, Hog laughed. "If you're invisible, you don't."

Screwball dawned his simpleton look. "Good idea. Got any vanishing cream."

Breed walked to the reeds, grabbed a handful, and broke them off. "Let's make a helmet out of these," he said. "We can weave one and put some cattail leaves in the holes. I'll go in up to my neck, put the helmet on and wait."

Flick's eyes lit up. "Those geese won't even know you're close."

"Let's try it," Hog said and gathered more reeds.

Hog and Screwball searched the shore and scrounged up a few cattail leaves, and with the geese honking around the bend, they presented the cattail leaves to Breed.

"Okay, Breed," Hog said, "make your great helmet and get back in there. Those geese are trying to land."

Like a caveman making a basket, Breed weaved the reeds into a green helmet and filled in the open spaces with the light green cattail leaves. Then he put the helmet over his head, crept back into the water, and waited.

Flick and the others walked a few yards away and crouched down to watch.

In fifteen minutes, the first goose landed. Breed watched it swim and scrounge for food along the shore, but it was too far away for him to catch.

He waited.

Another goose dropped out of the sky and water-skied across the water. It stopped a few feet in front of him. He held his breath and kept his body perfectly still. The goose turned its head and stared directly at the camouflage helmet that covered Breed's head. Breed raised his hands to get closer to the goose. It juked and swam a few feet away. Breed dropped his hands, held them just under the surface, and waited.

Another goose dropped out of the sky, but this time, twelve followed the leader. Honking and raising a ruckus, they all skidded across the top of the water. When they swam toward him, he opened his hands and flexed his knees. Three geese glided right to his helmeted head. He couldn't decide which one to catch, or better yet, maybe he could catch two, or maybe three.

He waited.

One goose glanced at him. In a panic, it honked a warning to the others and flapped its wings. But it was too late. Like a hungry crocodile, Breed leaped out of the water and dove on the wing-flapping goose. He had it by the neck. It flipped over and beat Breed with its powerful wings. The bones in the wings were harder than Breed had expected. They hurt, and he was surprised how strong the goose was. But Breed's survival instinct was stronger. Like a hungry dog clamping onto a last scrap of food, he held on tight.

With speed fueled by desperation, Flick and the others jumped up like a horde of vultures. They sailed toward Breed. Breed wrestled the goose to shore. It flapped and kicked at Breed's bare stomach. He held the goose below his knees and squeezed. The goose crapped all over his shoes.

He relaxed his grip. The goose escaped, turned away from the shore, and into the water. Flick pounced into the water and grabbed it. It flapped its wings and fought to go free. Holding it by the neck, Flick carried it up onto the shore. Screwball and Hog jumped on the flailing bird. It flapped a few times, but under the many hands that now controlled its fight, it quit.

They had caught supper.

Hungry, Hog didn't hesitate. He picked up a heavy rock, and commanded, "Put his head on that flat rock."

Flick and the others positioned the goose. It seemed to know its fate. It willfully stretched his head onto the rock. Hog picked up the rock, reared back, and slammed the rock right into the head of the goose. "Fly away now."

Bending over the little pile of coal, Breed looked up at Hog. "You still got that match?"

Hog thrust the match out toward Breed. "Here."

Breed struck the match on a rock. It did not ignite. He tried it until the match head was scraped clean. "So much for that."

Figuring that little bits of coal would start as easily as little sticks, he threw the useless match onto the pile of coal and pounded the steel and flint, but the coal would not ignite.

"Coal's harder to start than wood," Flick said. "Get some sticks and grass going first."

Everybody scrambled for wood sticks and grass. They heaped it onto the little pile of coal. Breed started the offerings, and before the coal had caught, the goose was ready to roast, and a spit had been fashioned out of green sticks.

Black smoke came from the coal and wafted into Breed's nose. The smell reminded him of the cold winter days in Shitsplat, when chimneys sprinkled the black coal soot across the white snow.

The goose sizzled and dripped fat juices into the coal fire, and a weird odor enhanced the area. Breed and the others stayed downwind from the fire and waited with hunger in their bellies and impatience in their minds.

Breed walked to the edge of the water. The heels of his new shoes were broken over and were covered with black and green goose crap. He picked his shoes up and swished them around in the water. That's it, he thought. I give up. These shoes have had it. No use trying to save them, now.

He put the shoes next to the fire to dry and looked at the goose. "This thing is getting pretty black. You think it'll be any good to eat?"

"No problem," Flick assured him. "We'll just take that black skin off and eat the clean meat underneath."

"Yeah," Hog said, "if it ever gets done."

With a toss of his long blond hair, Screwball told Breed, "Check it and see if it's done."

Breed stuck a splintered piece of green stick into the goose. "It ain't even close." He sighed.

They waited, more.

As time passed, they sat around the fire and constantly checked to see if the goose was cooked, but when they added more coal to the fire, the goose grew blacker. When it was pronounced ready to eat, it looked like it had been carved from coal.

Flick rubbed his hungry hands together. "Get that thing off the spit, so we can get that skin off and eat."

"I guess we could," Hog said, standing up and stretching like he didn't have a care in the world. "We ain't doin' nothin' else."

Ignoring Hog, Flick pealed the black skin back. Underneath the aroma of dark and white meat steamed into the air, and drove a hidden hunger, Breed never realized he had.

Flick pulled off strips of meat and passed them around.

Breed ate like it was the last meal on earth. He bit and wolfishly gulped the goose meat. He swallowed quickly, and like a savage, he bit again. In his hunger-fueled haste, he bit right into his fingers. Looking at his bleeding fingers, he felt his face contort in pain. "What the hell," he said out loud.

Screwball grabbed at his mouth. "Man!" he mumbled, "I got a broken piece of bone stuck right in my tong."

Hog talked with goose meat in his mouth. "You're not supposed to eat the bones."

Flick looked up from his slow and deliberate bite. "Take it easy, you guys. We got more."

Breed looked at his bleeding finger. "Now I know why hungry dogs hurt so bad when they bite."

Hog looked at Breed's bleeding finger. "You guys gotta be crazy. Screwball's eating bones and Breed's eating his fingers."

Breed finished his goose meat and reached for another piece. Suddenly a bad taste came alive in his mouth. "This thing tastes like tar."

"Yeah," Flick allowed, "but it's food."

They all ignored the tar taste, ate their fill, and then, awed by the scope and splendor of the pristine strip mine, they lay back as if they were lounging around at a swimming pool on an expensive cruise.

Breed looked at his shoes and tried to convince himself that they weren't damaged too bad. He could still clean them up. A little bit of polish would make them shine again. They were the best shoes he ever had. He would just have to be more careful.

Just then, a faint glimmer of something silver appeared in the dirt. Flick bent over and scraped the dirt away. It was an old aluminum can. He picked it up, held it, and using his hand, he brushed the dirt away.

Screwball lit up with excitement. "If that can's here, it means we must be close to a town or something."

At first, Breed entertained the thought that Screwball could be right, and that civilization could be just a short walk away. But then he frowned. "I doubt it," he said. "If that thing were a tin can, it would have rusted away years ago."

"So?" questioned Screwball.

"So, it's aluminum, probably left over from when the strip mine workers were here."

With a hangdog hopeless look, Flick lifted his arm to throw the can into the water, but when a mischief suddenly filed his eyes, he lowered his arm and looked to Hog. "Hey, Hog." Flick offered the can to Hog. "Those bass are still there. Why don't you use this can and cook up some way to catch those big things?"

For a moment, Hog stiffened with resentment. Then with a sly look, he said, "I'll cook something up, you'll really appreciate." He grabbed the can. "Cheeseburger coming up!" He held the can over his ass, farted, and immediately covered the can with his hand and held it secure. Then he thrust it in front of Screwball's nose and pulled his hand from the top of the can. "Here's a present for throwing that stick and yelling snake."

The odor from the can escaped right into Screwball's nose. With his face twisting in grotesquely tortured wonder, he gasped at the sudden smell. Then in a sudden and uncomprehending daze, he whirled and raged at Hog, "You goddamn Hog!"

With a look of sophistication, Hog leaned back. "Yes, that's my name." With a look of delight, he asked Screwball, "How do you like me now?"

Sinking down dumbfounded, Screwball only groaned.

Flick straightened his back and took on a look of adult objectivity. "Save those canned farts for the future," he advised, holding in laughter. "I don't think those geese are coming back. You'll have something to eat later on."

"Instead of catching farts in a can," Breed said and drew a sniff of greatly agitated air into his unsuspecting nose, "why don't you just shit in it?"

338

"Cause it ain't like gas," Hog said. "Why with this new invention you will be able to crap on up that hill and farty on down the railroad tracks."

While Screwball goggled with amazement, they started back toward the tracks.

CHAPTER 19

Although they wanted to get home, Breed and his friends had no idea where they were going. Hoping they were heading in the direction of home, they walked down the tracks that narrowed to a pinpoint and disappeared on the horizon.

Walking to the end of the tracks or even coming to a bend, seemed to be as impossibly remote and as unattainable as Breed and his friend's chances were of making the high school football team, where players were selected not because of their abilities but because of where they came from or whom their parents were. Breed felt no feverish hurry to walk down the long and unpromising railroad line.

But it didn't seem to bother Screwball. Making it look like a bandage, he tied a bandanna around his head. Then using one hand, he put the penny whistle to his lips, and marching with his knees stepping high like a Civil War drummer boy, playing a drum, he swung his wrist on his other hand and went toot-toot-tootling down the tracks.

Shaking his head, Flick smiled, and with his teeth gleaming in the bright sun, he turned to Screwball. "One good meal and you think you're a soldier boy."

With a cocky, lopsided grin, Hog added, "Seeing that we only have about a thousand miles to go, that's an interesting observation."

"I don't mean disenfranchised Screwball," Hog said, "But once you've heard Screwball's tune, you've heard them all."

340

Breed let out a little laugh, but burped up the greasy goose, and the taste of stomach acid clung in his throat. "I don't know if that was such a good meal. I don't feel so good."

Screwball stopped playing the penny whistle and quit marching. Then he placed his hands on his knees and bent over. "Disenfranchise this! Yeak!" he belched and threw up on the side of the tracks.

The sight triggered Breed's queasy stomach. He felt it roll and clench with a threat of voiding its contents. With rivulets of cold sweat forming on his face, he bent down and tried to hold it in, but partially digested goose meat gushed from his stomach to his throat and flew out his mouth. Talking between gasps, he managed to blurt out, "Everything taste like tar." When the disgusting odor of vomit drifted to his face, he felt weak-kneed and heaved again.

Watching the others, Hog defiantly thrust his jaw out and wagged his head, saying, "What's matter with you guys? I'm not sick."

Even though he looked queasy, Screwball gave Breed a sly, conspiratorial wink. Then he surreptitiously cupped his hand on his own ass and stepped behind Hog. Then he farted in his hand, closed it, and held it in front of Hog's face. Hog's eyes opened wide with alarm. He tried to turn away from Screwball's fart-throwing hand. But he was too late. Screwball opened his hand. "Here, put this in your can."

With a look of horror, Hog spun away, leaned over, and threw up.

Screwball laughed hysterically. Then they all leaned forward in a helpless heap, placed their hands on their knees, bent over, and heaved until the coal-tar-tasting goose meat was out of their stomachs. Then they straightened up. Trying to get rid of their sour and tar-tasting mouths, they wiped their mouths on the backs of their hands, and wiped their hands on the tall grass alongside of the tracks.

After they had cleaned up, felt better, and the cramping in Breed's stomach subsided, behind them, what seemed to be a dust devil dancing in the heat waves, turned out to be a lone figure walking in the distance. It was coming their way, and fast.

Breed thought about the stolen car and the gas station. He tensed to run. "Maybe it's the cops."

With his forehead puckered, Flick stared down the tracks and concentrated on the approaching figure. "It ain't the cops. They'd never walk this far. It's some guy carryin' a suitcase."

Breed sighed with relief. "Let's ask him if he knows where these tracks go."

"Yeah," Hog said, and his mouth twitched with a smile, "maybe we can quit walking all damn day."

"Dee-da, do-da," Screwball sang, "all the dee-da, do-dam day."

No one laughed.

No one talked.

Mesmerized, they all watched the approaching man.

In the distance, as the man walking toward them tramped on the ballast stones between the dark-brown creosote-soaked ties, he became taller,

342

and the crunching sounds, his feet were making, grew louder.

Looking like an imaginary character, the man edged forward. As the others stood still and stared, Breed squinted into the early-afternoon haze and recognized the man. "That looks like the same guy we saw walking on the tracks next to Shell Island."

"I doubt it," Flick said, "Shell Island's a long way off, and that guy kept saying he was going to Canady."

"Oh yeah," Hog said, with a trace of resentment, "that guy had a paper suitcase, and it looks like this guy got one, too."

Squinting at the approaching man, Screwball said, "I can't see what kind of suitcase he has, but when he gets close, ask him where he's going."

As the man loomed close, Breed studied the man's face. It was lean and wrinkled, and seemed to have seen many decades of strife and disappointment, and his bony hand hung onto an old fake leather suitcase. "That's a hobo," Breed whispered and waited.

With a long-striding, space eating walk, the hobo seemed to glide toward Flick. When the hobo neared, he didn't stop or break his quick stride. Flick smiled at him. "How you doin', old timer?"

The hobo didn't attempt to turn or slow.

Flick stepped out of his way.

Like a gentleman tipping an imaginary hat, the hobo reached toward his forehead and tipped his hand. Smiling, his rugged face lost all expression, but he kept on walking with his lanky legs and looked over his shoulder. "Howdy, boys, can't

343

stop. Headed for Canady." Smiling a great gap-toothed smile, he motioned for them to follow.

A confused look appeared on Screwball's face. He called after the hobo. "What did-jah say?"

"Headed for Canady!" the hobo repeated and kept walking with those long strides.

Almost tripping over the railroad ties, in an effort to catch up to the hobo, Flick and the others ran until they were briskly walking next to him.

Gasping for breath, Flick asked, "Do you know where these tracks go?"

The hobo didn't miss a stride. "Why they go to Canady."

Flick stayed next to the hobo and kept on walking at the awkward pace. "We ain't goin' to Canada. How far is the next town?"

"Oh, there's a town all right." The hobo shook his head so fast it looked like he was trying to shake it off his skinny neck. "You don't want to go there."

"Why not?"

"That's the place where an old lady sat on the tracks with a bottle of wine. With loaded cars, the engineer couldn't control the speed of the train on a downhill run. Ran right over her legs. Cut them clean off."

"We're not going to sit on the tracks," Hog assured him.

Breed hastened his step and walked close to the hobo. "How far is it?"

"The Erie Interchange to go south?"

"No, the town?"

The hobo lifted his eyebrows. "Oh, that's where they start setting up cardboard shacks in the spring. Some stay all winter. There's a little town around the bend where they buy wine and some stuff." His face took on an injured look. "You won't want to go there."

"How come?"

"We'll be in heaven before then." The hobo lifted his face to the sky and let out a triumphant whoop. "Why those peaches are just hanging off the trees."

"Peaches?" Breed asked with hunger in his stomach and expectation in his heart. "I could really go for a peach right now."

Like a little kid asking about a special treat, Flick looked into the hobo's eyes. "Are you sure they're there?"

"Sure, they are," the hobo said and smiled. "Those peaches are just waitin' for someone to come along and pick 'em. It might as well be us. If we don't, they'll just go to rot. Seen them do it many years, when I couldn't get there soon enough."

The hobo lengthened his stride.

Breed and the others struggled to match his steps.

Almost running, Breed was at the hobo's side. "You sure you're goin' in the right direction?"

Keeping time with the rhythm of the strides of his long legs, the hobo swung that paper suitcase faster. "Yep, I know right where I'm goin'." Like a fruit farmer holding a big juicy peach, he lifted his hand, turned his palm up and examined it. "Gotta skedaddle on down the tracks and get there before they get too ripe." He dropped his hand. "Don't want to miss heaven again. Missed it a few years now." He slobbered brown tobacco juice down his chin, then reached up with the dirty back of his hand and wiped a long smear across his weather-beaten face. After he swallowed, like an old dog, he yelped out a loud, "Yep!" and continued his banter. "Gotta keep on goin'. Goin' to Canady, you know."

Wondering if every hobo walking on the tracks was going to Canady, Breed looked up ahead, and the thought fled his mind. He could almost see what looked to be a stand of trees. "Look there," he excitedly said and pointed. "Those little trees look like an orchard."

Flick hunched forward and strained to see. "I can already taste those peaches."

"Yeah," Hog said. "They gotta be those big white ones. They're the only ones that get ripe this late."

Breed reached up and rubbed his eye. The swelling had gotten bigger and the infected flesh around the cut was hard. Keeping his good eye fixed on the trees, he dropped his hand, and walked closer. But the trees didn't look like peach trees. "There ain't gonna be no peaches," he said in a tormented tone.

"I'm still thinkin' they're peach trees," Flick said with hope. "Are you sure there ain't?"

Breed looked at the hobo. "It's just too late in the fall for peaches. Are you sure those aren't apple trees?"

346

The hobo flashed Breed an admiring smile, but didn't answer. When he kept on stepping with those heart-pumping strides and pulled ahead of Breed, Breed said, "Maybe he doesn't know the difference."

Appearing puzzled, the hobo tromped toward the trees almost like a circus clown on stilts.

Shaking his head, Breed looked to the others.

They panted with anticipation and struggled to keep up with the hobo's lanky-legged body.

When they could see what kind of trees were ahead, they stopped. A grove of poison sumac trees covered the land.

Breed clenched his fist in anger and directed his voice at the hobo. "Goddamn it. You dumb shit. You made us walk our asses off for nothing."

Showing no expression, the hobo just kept on walking.

Hog put one foot on the railroad rail and threw his hands in the air. "Hant!"

Screwball pulled out his penny whistle and blew a taunting, Cuck-oo!

With his eyes darting in search of a single peach tree, Breed raised his voice, "Cuck-oo, my ass." He turned to Screwball. "There ain't no peaches. There ain't no apples. There ain't no food. There ain't nothing except poison sumac and more of the same shit we just busted our asses to get away from."

"What are you bitchin' about?" Screwball said and his face split into a wide grin. "We've never had so much fun in all our lives."

Deadly tired and hungry, Breed wanted to cry. He tried to disguise the torment of thirst and hunger with a laugh, but when he looked ahead, he couldn't disguise anything. Irritation piled on irritation. More never-ending nothingness appeared. More endless creosote and ballast stones appeared. More infinite lifeless toxic-smelling brown and black railroad ties appeared, and the shiny continuous steel rails ribboned their long way across the country.

When he looked down. The railroad ties were uneven and had deep drop-offs along the edges. He lifted his head, and with probing distrust, he watched the hobo. As if the uneven ties and drop-offs weren't there, under a merciless sun, in a merciless land, the gangling hobo never stumbled or tripped, he just kept right on racing away. "Just around the next bend," the hobo said loudly and pointed down the tracks. "I know they're there. You'll see, we'll be in heaven. Then we'll go to the cabin."

With a sudden spark of rekindled hope, Breed and others ran and caught up to the hobo.

"What Cabin?" Breed asked, huffing for air

The hobo's eyes sparked with delight. "Why there's a little wooden cabin on an island in the middle of the river. Best place I ever been in all my en-tar life. Why, you can catch fish right off the back porch." Like a man on vacation holding a fishing pole, the hobo held out his hand. "Yep, that cabin even has a little stove. And there's a big black skillet hangin' on the wall to fry them fish in."

"What if the fish ain't bitten'?" Hog pointed out. "Then what will you eat?"

"When the fish weren't bitin', I ate many a salad when I stayed there. All kinds of watercress grow along one side of the island. Maybe there's still a little garden there with red tomatoes. I don't know why they get so big, but they do." To demonstrate how big the tomatoes grew, he made a big circle shape with his fingers. "Matter of fact, just one tomato will make a meal. And the taters. They're in the ground all the time. They never rot. You always got something to eat there." He paused for a moment. "You won't have to worry about the dog," he said and kept on walking.

Flick eyes opened wide with alarm. "What dog?"

"The old dog that used to sleep on the porch. He's probably not there anymore."

Breed didn't feel like running from a vicious dog. "Does he bite?"

"Only if you stick your hand in his mouth and jump on his head."

Laughing, Screwball nodded in approval.

Breed smiled a half smile and thought about going back home, but the beating and paying rent still left a sour taste in his heart. He still wanted something better. "Hey, Flick, maybe we could just live in that cabin."

Flick's eyes widened. "You might have something there."

Breed's hopes soared. "It would be better than going back to Shitsplat."

349

"I can see it now," Flick said with a far-away look in his eye. "Out on that little porch, we could sit back on easy chairs. Anytime of the day or night, we could throw out our fishing lines, set our poles right on the banisters."

Breed imagined what it would be like. The fragrance would be sweet. In an atmosphere of unhurried time and solitude, birds would be singing in the trees and bees humming in flowers. "We could live like kings," he said. "We would never have to look for firewood. We could put out nets and catch driftwood coming downriver, then stack it up and have enough for the rest of our lives."

"We could use some of that driftwood and make a dock," Flick added. "We could swim anytime we wanted, maybe even put up a diving board."

As if he had just hooked a fish, Breed jerked his hand. "We could catch fish, eat from that garden, and at night, we could make a fire in that little pot-belly stove and cook the day's catch. We would never be hungry. And on a warm night, we could sleep out on that cool porch under the clean stars."

"Sounds pretty good to me," Flick said. "That would be the way to live, no rent to pay and no stinkin' steel mill to die in."

"What I don't like about steel mills," Breed said, "is that after people who start to work in one and make a little money, they suddenly become experts on everything known to mankind." He paused. "Damn steel mills."

The hobo's eyebrows arched in surprise. "Steel mills," he said. "You go into one of those, your

350

unlimited opportunities will end. Your obituary will already be written, it just wouldn't be in the papers yet."

Nobody replied.

They walked on in silence, until the hobo spit a wad of tobacco onto the side of the steel rail. "Yep, you boys would like that cabin." He pointed ahead. "It's there, just around the bend. Last time I was there, there was a bushel basket hangin' on the front door. Somebody must a put it there just to pick those peaches."

Hog kicked at a rock and waved his hand down. "Peaches just around the bend?" he questioned. "That sounds like a big bullshit story, if I ever heard one." He paused in thought. Then as if he had just thought of something he said, "If there is a cabin, somebody has to own it. If we go in it, we'll just get kicked out."

The hobo, glared at Hog. "Nobody owns that cabin or the island it sits on. It belongs to God. If somebody thinks they own it, they don't. They're just renting it from God." He skipped a step, and glanced back at Screwball. "Maybe you boys don't know what it means when you can go home and have food on the table and extra in the house?"

"Yeah," Screwball said, "it means you're in the wrong house."

Like a man who had just been told he was stupid, the hobo spit and kept on walking.

"That's about right," Breed said and rubbed his empty stomach.

"Maybe he's right," Flick said with a glint of hope. "Maybe there are late fall peaches, and we can pick 'em."

Hog usually had smugness around him. Now it came out strong. He waved his hand down toward Flick. "Maybe we'll shit and fall in it, too."

As if he were a lawyer who had lied and wanted to get away from the truth, the hobo squirmed uncomfortably, quicken his pace, and used strides that seemed to be five feet long.

With sun bearing down, he pulled ahead of Breed, and Breed noticed that the hot surface of the dark creosote-soaked ties was cooking the soles of his feet. He stopped, stood on the cooler dirt at the side of the tracks, and wiped away the sweat from around his neck that had trickled from his chin. "If we don't stop, we'll be going around the next bend the rest of our lives."

Screwball stepped next to him. "And there won't be any peaches. It's too late in the season."

The hobo stopped and looked back. Obviously, for dramatic effect, the hobo lolled his eyes in dazed bewilderment. Then he said, "At least I'm going somewhere." Then he turned and continued walking.

Flick stopped chasing after the hobo and stopped. The others stopped, too. Flick turned toward the others. "Hey, that's right. That old bastard had me going."

Sneering arrogantly and referring to Eddie's failed scheme, Hog pointed at Flick. "I told you, Eddie."

Breed watched the hobo scurry away. For a brief moment, he turned back and smiled. Then he continued walking and become small. It seemed like he didn't care where he was going. He just had to be going, and his many travels and misfortunes were like badges of honor that no one would ever know about because they were hiding behind a smile.

Breed watched the hobo until he became a tiny man walking away in the distance. "Yeah." He sighed. "When you're hungry, you do strange things."

"Don't these tracks ever end?" Hog asked with disgust. "It's the same thing, over and over."

A sly look gleamed in Screwball's face. "Maybe they go all the way around the world and join again where we started."

A tight smile curled on Flick's lips. "Maybe your stupid jokes go around the world and never stop."

Hog picked up a rock and held it in his hand. "We've walked for miles. It doesn't end. It doesn't change, just more tracks that that lead to untouchable infinity."

Tap dancing on the ties, Screwball opened his arms wide and held them open. "Welcome to the railroad life, folks."

Ignoring Screwball's antics, and chastising himself for falling for the hobo's story, Hog lifted his arm and held a rock. "That old hobo thinks his nefarious bullshit is going to drive us crazy." He yelled after the hobo. "You ain't putting me in the nuthouse. Here's a goddamn peach for your ass,

353

you old fucking goat." He threw the rock toward the escaping Canady hobo.

It didn't come close.

"You seem to be somewhat irritated," Screwball said to Hog. "After all, I thought we were only walkin' for the exercise." He pulled out the penny whistle. Cuck-oo! Cuck-oo!

Too angry to reply with a few highbrow words from his encyclopedic arsenal of words, Hog waved his hand down, "Stick that whistle up your ass."

As Breed and his pals stood in the middle of the tracks and watched the hobo blend into the narrowing distant tracks, no birds chirped in the trees, no wind tussled the treetops, and there was no sound. In the heat, the leaves of trees along the tracks hung dead-limp. As Breed and his pals watched the hobo become a prospective dot and disappear, they slid into a hypnotic-like stupor.

Apparently thinking about all the things that had happened since the sun had come up, Flick let out a discouraged breath of air. "All of our plans have been blasted to hell. How much shit can be heaped on us in one day?"

With his head bobbing, Screwball looked at Flick. "We don't know. The day ain't over yet."

Flick flashed Screwball an injured look. "Don't you think this shit heaping on us has to stop sometime?"

"Actually," Screwball said with a tone of contrite amusement, "it did stop, but it started again."

With his head down, walking slump-shouldered, and his eyes on the hot railroad ties,

Breed cursed silently until a sudden realization offered him relief from his anguish. He looked to the others. "Hey, that hobo can stop anytime he wants to."

Hog snarled, "So what?"

With a zeal of inspiration, Breed said, "He doesn't want to stop. And he hasn't died or starved to death."

Flick swung his hand down and whooped in triumph. "Exactly! If we keep on walking, we won't either."

"It's our call," Breed excitedly added. "We can just quit or keep on going. One way or another, it stops when we want it to stop."

"That's right," Screwball agreed. "We can stop any time we want, too."

"We can stop and die," Breed said. Or we can be just like that hobo and keep right on walking." He looked down the long unending tracks. "I just know those tracks are not a thousand miles long and don't go on forever."

Standing there with his thumbs hooked in his belt, Flick nodded in agreement. "That's right. Those trains gotta come from somewhere."

"So what if those trains come from somewhere," Hog said and dropped his arms helplessly. "That Hobo could be just a suck on guy with that piece-of-shit, paper suitcase makin' us do shit we don't need to do."

"You're probably right," Flick agreed and unhooked his thumbs from his belt. "Just to make you hungry, all he did was move his skinny-ass legs a hundert miles an hour and talk about peaches just up around the next bend."

Screwball's face tightened, then relaxed. "It's only food," he said, then smiled. "Don't you want to be in heaven?"

Hog replied with the usual, "Blow it out your ass."

And Screwball replied with the usual, "Hant!"

Hog pointed to the tops of a distant clump of hardwood trees. "Look up there."

A stream of light blue smoke curled from a break in the branches.

"Somebody's there," Flick said with enthusiasm. "Let's go."

Hog muttered sarcastically, "It's probably just another dumb hobo."

Impelled by a curiosity that robbed them of caution, they hasten their weary steps and huffed on up toward the wafting blue smoke.

After they left the tracks and rushed toward the smoke, they passed thick thorn bushes that meandered to their left and were eventually intersected by a lush growth of wet skunk cabbage plants. When they trailblazed through clinging vegetation, Breed struggled to keep up. But once they had crashed through some old dry underbrush and stopped a few feet from a tall oak tree, his struggle ended.

Screwball stared at an oak tree stump that had a large growth clinging onto its side. "Hey, Flick, What's this?"

Flick stepped next to the growth. "It looks like a sheepshead mushroom."

Hog rubbed his chin. "You seem momentarily flummoxed, but it might be poison."

"Take it anyway," Flick said. "Sheep-heads grow on oak trees, so it should be okay. If we get hungry enough, we'll take a chance and eat it."

Breed walked up to the mushroom and looked closely. "Maybe those guys that have that fire will know. Then we won't have to take a chance and get poisoned." He bent over took out his penknife, cut the mushroom off at its base, tucked it under his arm, and following the others, he ducked under a fallen tree.

Then everything became quiet.

"Pay attention," Flick warned. "I think somebody's coming."

Screwball cocked his head and listened. "I don't hear nothin'."

"That's right, you don't. Think about it."

Apparently realizing that when everything is too quiet, there is always a good chance that someone could be silently waiting in ambush. Screwball stared at Flick for a moment and nodded. "I get you point, but—" He jerked his head to the right. "I see something over there."

On the other side of the tree, car batteries sat lined up in neat rows. Skinny, colored wires were wrapped around the terminals and twisted into two long wires that ran under freshly dug ground.

"Somebody's using these batteries to run something," Breed said.

Hog began pulling the long wires from the shallow dirt. "Let's follow the wires."

357

The wires ran a few yards into the grass and were covered by a layer of leaves, but sections of it could be seen. Hog quit pulling the wire and walked along its length. It weaved through wagging goldenrod and stopped at a single baldheaded car headlight nailed to the rough-barked trunk of a tall maple tree. Between the maple and another tree, red tail light lenses from cars, were strung out on a skinny steel wire. As if they had been yanked out of the cars, some were cracked around the screw holes. Clear little light bulbs hung from bare wire sockets and ran back to the batteries.

Screwball reached up and shook the line. "If we come back here when it is dark, it'll look like Christmas."

When they walked past the line, the odor of burnt cardboard filled the air. Hog sneezed and pointed. They all looked in unison. The orange flame of a fire blazed before them.

Beyond the orange fire, mirrors, hanging on branches, decorated a little grove of trees. Breed pointed to them. "Somebody must use those mirrors to shave by."

A hint of cunning expectation crept into Screwball's face. "How do you know that?"

"Because when you shave you have to see what you're doing."

"Oh, yeah!" Screwball laughed ecstatically. "Do you use a mirror when you wipe your ass?"

Even though Breed stared at Screwball in quizzical disbelief, it caused him to recall what an old bum a ways from the Clark Street Bridge had told him. "Don't get caught in that hobo trap. If

358

you do, you'll be like those old bums that hang up mirrors at their hobo jungles. They're defeated bums who have given up on life and think they have found a better way. They'll always be imprisoned by hard times and going nowhere, but going, always going." Breed figured, except for the money, being a bum wasn't much different than wasting his life in a steel mill. He decided he didn't need to look into a mirror to shave, and he surely didn't need one to wipe his ass. He wasn't ready to become one of these bums.

But when he stared into one of the small mirrors hanging on a branch, he could scarcely recognize the lean and repulsive image of his face. His black hair dangled down his face and ears, and his deep brown eyes were circled and etched with jagged red blood vessels. He looked at the others. Like himself, they looked to be travel-stained, worn out, and well on their way to becoming bums.

They all walked past the mirrors, stopped, and huddled shoulder-to-shoulder next the fire in front of a big, steaming iron kettle that was hanging on metal teepee supports.

With hungry eyes, Flick stared at the pot. "Maybe they got mulligan stew."

When Breed looked down, dirty white cigarette butt filters, with absolutely no tobacco in them, accented old and new tin cans that littered the black, cement-like ground. Off to the left, a few empty wine bottles blinked alcoholic colors into the sun.

Standing close to the pot, Screwball moved his head from right to left. "No one's around."

Feeling intense heat from the fire, Breed stepped back. "Maybe they all went to town."

Hog stepped back and turned his head toward where they had come from. "Somebody has to be close. The fire's still going."

"It's a mystery to me, my good man," Screwball said, pompously imitating Hog, "how you get through a day without my assistance."

"The real mystery," Hog fired back, "is how I put up with your smart-ass remarks."

Looking wounded, Screwball put the penny whistled to his mouth, hesitated, and said, "Maybe because great intellect like mine, is hard to come by." Cuck-oo!

While Hog shook his head in disbelief, Flick cupped his hand to his mouth and called, "Anybody here?"

Screwball cupped his hands to his mouth and shouted, "If anybody ain't here, tell us."

No one answered.

"Yeah, okay," Breed said.

The fire burned and the big black pot boiled.

Breed stepped close to the pot and peeked in.

"What's in it, Breed?" Flick asked. "Anything good to eat."

An awful smell came from the vaporizing mixture. "I don't know. If it's mulligan stew, it's pretty mangy."

Screwball stepped up and took a whiff. "Damn that stinks. "Maybe somebody's sterilizing shit."

As if he were going to throw up, Hog groaned, "Goddamn it, Screwball. Just what I need on my stomach, tar meat and shit stew."

As if he were going to throw another fart into Hog's face, Screwball reached around and grabbed his own ass.

"Hey! you glorious pain in the ass," Hog said and his mouth curled into a vehement sneer. "Don't even try it."

Moving his fists at the sides of his eyes, faking he was whimpering, Screwball backed off.

The bottoms of Breed's feet burned hot. He looked down at his shoes. He was standing in the hot coals. He jumped back. The mushroom fell onto the ground. He slumped to the ground, sat down, and tore off his sizzling shoes. "Damn, I ruined the bottoms of my shoes."

"Stand in the fire some more," Screwball muttered sarcastically. "It'll keep your shoes looking just like new."

Waving his shoes to cool them, Breed grumbled to himself, "Dumb ass."

Flick picked up a flat wooden stick that had been hanging from one of the teepee's supports and dipped it into the kettle. He looked up from the steam rising from the kettle and stared at Breed's shoes. "That's what stinks. Anything will be better than your stinkin' gut car shoes." He held his nose and guided the stick toward his open mouth.

From out of the bushes, "Hey!" rang loud and threatening.

Flick dropped the stick.

It fell into the dirt.

From the cover of the thick brush at Breed's right, a gruff whiskey voice stirred. "What the hell do you goddamn kids want?" A lithe, dark-skinned man who moved like an animal wanted to know.

Another bum, broad at the shoulder with a pot belly hanging over his belt, stomped out. "Get the hell away from that stew before I bash your heads in."

Another bum, a tall bald man who carried a revolver in a holster high on his left hip, seemed to appear out of midair. Flashing a rotten-toothed scowl, he wore a white shirt, yellow with filth and was too small to cover his narrow shoulders. Although the man had a degenerate slouch, and his eyes were sunk deep into dark craters, his sleeves were rolled up revealing a pair of huge wrists and hands.

Then more bums appeared. Unshaven and dirty, they came out of concealment like pop up figures in a horror show.

Breed's sweeping gaze took in the whole scene, and his strange impression was that these bums resembled ghouls who had lived in the dark holes of mud. He hadn't noticed him before, but just beyond the trunk of a big oak, a bum sat on a flattened pile of straw around which the ground was muddy. The bum raised his head. His face became a scary flash, his eyes piercing black, staring, deep, full of terrible shadow. His blood-caked fingers and bark-like knuckles seemed like they never healed.

Flick turned and held up his hands defensively. "We only wanted a taste."

Forcing his shoes back onto his feet, Breed jerked his head toward the mushroom on the ground. With a heavy expulsion of breath, he said, "We brought a sheep-head for the buzzard."

"Yeah," Hog said, "we're hungry."

The bums didn't answer. They converged like zombies. Their dirty, toothless faces showed no expression. They walked slow and threatening. When their dark figures stopped, they hovered for a second, then with bluish, bony hands clutching heavy clubs, they crept toward Breed and the others.

Breed stood next to the big black pot and stared at the dead looking skin on an approaching bum's fingers. It looked worn and thin. He wondered if the bum's years of throwing back bottles of cheap wine and holding them securely to their thirsty purplish lips had caused their brains to become worn and thin, too.

The broad-shouldered bum, using a metal pipe for a walking cane, reminded Breed of Grandpa Jones, sitting in that wagon pulled by his inbred kids. He had appeared to be crippled, too. But when Flick threw that cigarette butt and grandpa Jones's kids ran after it, the crippled grandpa miraculously came to life. He charged into his scrambling kids, whipped his cane into threatening concentric circles, fought them off, and came up with the cigarette butt.

So the bum with the pipe might not be crippled, either. His eyes shifted uneasily. Then he lifted the pipe and pointed to the sheep-head. "That was our sheep-head," he protested angrily. "We could've ate for a week, but, no! You son-of-a-bitches cut it off too soon."

Breed didn't know if the bum was going to use the pipe, and he didn't want to get mauled by the other bums. He reached into his pocket and pulled out the shiny dime he had found by the pop machine at the gas station. He looked at the dime. It seemed that he had found it a very long time ago. It was a link from the past when things had been easier. He didn't want to do it, but he pitched the dime toward the oncoming threat. It fell onto the black flat ground. The bums saw it, but didn't rush after it.

The broad-shouldered bum lifted the pipe. "You boys lookin' for trouble?"

"You look like the one that has the trouble," Screwball said, matter-of-factly.

The bum's face filled with confusion. "What?"

"Check your teeth. You look like you got asshole rectimentitis."

The bum looked to the other bums for an explanation.

"Don't look at them," Screwball said. "They're too dumb to know asshole rectimetitis happened when their eye teeth grew up around their asses and caused them to have a shitty outlook on life."

Enraged, the bum swung the pipe.

Breed jumped back.

The pipe zipped right in front of his face.

As tension filled the air, Breed and his friends cautiously backed away, Screwball looked at the dime, and then looked at Breed. Breed nodded once and pointed to Screwball's pocket. Screwball reached into his pocket, took out the silver metal slugs, he had picked up off the gondola's floor, and tossed them onto the ground. As they scattered in a wide display, the pipe dropped from the bum's hand and hit the ground so fast, Breed didn't even see it. Just as Grandpa Jones had come to life, the bums did, too. As if they were the last coins on earth, pushing, elbowing, and shoving each other, they scrambled after the blinking coins. Like a train wreck, they piled into one another. Breed thought the bum's urge to get money for more alcohol was a strange motivator for man or bum.

With the bums arguing and fighting over the dime and slugs, Hog shouted out some very uncomplimentary suggestions as to what the bums could do with them. When he looked up and saw Breed and the others running from the camp, he took off, too.

Huffing from the run, they slogged their way up a strip mine mountain. At the top, before they stopped for to rest, Hog picked up a rock and threw it toward the bum's camp. "That goddamn Canady guy and that hobo under the bridge are both full of shit. There ain't no peaches and the great buzzard of the camp won't share a damn thing."

Screwball lowered his head and pointed to Breed's foot that had smelled so bad after he had stepped in a pile of guts from a gut car. "Hey, Hog, how do you know they're full of shit? Maybe you were just smelling Breed's foot?"

Before Hog could reply, Screwball's eyes flung wide open. "Look, a town."

In the distance a dirt road lead to a stretch of blacktop between rows of little buildings with signs on top.

"Piss on those Hobo's and their shit stew," Flick said. "This is it."

Screwball crashed down the side of the mountain. Follow me.!"

CHAPTER 20

On top of the strip mine mountain Breed looked at Flick. Flick was watching Screwball, running down the mountain.

Flick turned to Breed and Hog. "What are we waitin' on?"

They started down the soft side of the gray mountain. As they gained speed, slate, small stones, and dust avalanched under their feet.

When they stopped at the bottom, the dust behind them was crawling up the side of the mountain. Hog looked toward the town. "They'll have food." He waved his stick in the air like a triumphant gladiator. "We can finally eat something decent."

To Breed, the town gave off an aura that it should be flying Gadsden flags, the yellow banners flown by colonists during the Revolutionary War, that were emblazoned with coiled rattlesnake with the words "Don' t Tread on Me." It gave Breed an intolerable woe. "We ain't got no money for food."

"Shut up!" Flick snapped. "If we have to, we'll steal it."

And off they went.

They jogged through the thick dust alongside of a yellow dirt road, and when it met a paved road, they stomped dusty footprints onto the black top and slowed to a walk until they stopped in front of a small clapboard movie theater.

Breed squinted his eye that wasn't swollen. On the marquee, big black letters read, THE BUDDY HOLLY STORY. He looked down at his shoes.

These were the same shoes he was going to wear to see the movie before he had jumped into the red Mercury, the same shoes he had worn when he thought he was racing across the country toward California but ended up in Buffalo. Now the shoes weren't new. The leather was scuffed past their original shiny black sheen. It had cuts and nicks that the thickest shoe polish would never cover or fill in. Now they matched his old socks that still had the holes in the heels that painfully rubbed the heels of his feet.

Trying to ignore how his shoes looked, Breed swiveled his head around and surveyed the town. Box-like houses nestled in rows. Flat-roofs on top of twenty by twelve-foot buildings sloped slightly forward in the direction of the back of buildings. A few had a fenced-in enclosures, containing outhouses, but no people were in sight, no cars lined the street, and the air was still. Except for the smoke from a tall chimney, going pencil-straight into the sky, the town looked almost like a ghost town. As if it were a warning, a stray blast of a knifing wind whistled across the roofs of the buildings, and gave Breed a foreboding feeling. "Where are we?"

Waiting for somebody, anybody, to answer, Breed remembered what Eddie had once said, "Always know where you are. If you can't know where you are, try to look cool."

Breed didn't know where he was, but his worn shoes and shabby clothes made it impossible for him to act or look cool, and it bothered him until Screwball said, "If you really want to know where

368

we are, why don't you go on over the hardware story and by a compass and a map. And while you're there, get some matches and a flashlight."

While Breed starred into the sky as if he were looking for divine intervention, Hog almost smiled and said, "You sound like one of those intelligent people with no brains."

Flick tilted his head and looked along the side of the movie theater. "I don't know where we are," he said. "If I wasn't so hungry, I might try to sneak in."

Breed studied the side of the building. Like the Rat House Theater in Shitsplat, there was a side door. They could possibly sneak in, but seeing a movie wasn't important anymore. The hungry feeling in his stomach took priority. And to top it off, his throat was so dry that when he swallowed, the back of it felt like an open wound that was being rubbed with sandpaper.

As they walked past the movie theater, the tinkling of a piano came from somewhere down the deserted street and reminded him of better days.

When they stopped in front of a grocery store, memories of those better days were replaced with something more important. Just below the store's cracked front window an unpainted, wooden shelf had been built with rough sawmill lumber. Like the store's front porch, the shelf's wooden boards had been weathered to a dark brown with course jagged grains. But on the shelf, bushels of apples, bright with the kiss of the sun, shined with the color of huge juicy cherries. Breed light-footed up the steps and peered into the fly-speckled, dirty window.

When he didn't see anyone inside, he grabbed as many apples as he could and waved the others to come up.

Flick and the others cat-footed up on the wooden steps of the storefront, and as if they were getting giant juicy cherries, they grabbed apples, jammed them into their pockets. Then lifted the fronts of their shirts and piled more apples into the makeshift carriers.

The tinkling piano stopped.

A board creaked.

An astringent taste and smell of chlorine filled the air.

With the front of his shirt full of apples, Breed jerked his head up.

Wearing a white apron spattered with blood, a compactly built man with bulging muscles of steel stood with his foot resting on the first step. As if he were ready to defend the honor of the town, he projected a hard-jawed defiance. Staring murderously at Breed, his unshaven face filled with lines of evil, and two other men with deadly expressions on their faces stood at his sides.

With the knowledge they had entered a dangerous place, Breed's heart accelerated.

Looking like he suffered from constipation, the man with an apron pressed his thin lips tightly together and spoke abruptly, "You boys going to buy those apples?"

In an attempt to dazzle the men with his use of language and put them at ease, Hog struck a pose and used a most eloquent voice to say, "Although we may have a common dissimilarity in our

370

vernacular, we would never consider taking something that doesn't belong to us." Then he flashed the man a wide friendly smile and held it.

Appearing perturbed, the man with the apron turned from Hog's bedraggled appearance. With a gawking stare of fascination or hidden amusement the man spoke again. "If you smart-ass kids are tryin' to steal those apples, we have a constable who will be along any minute."

Clutching the apples in his shirt, a pitiful smile formed on Breed's face. "We don't have any money."

Referring to Breed's dark skin, the man waved his hand in a dismissing gesture. "Would somebody get this breed out of my sight?"

The thought of being hung caused Breed to rub his neck, but the man turned his attention to Hog.

Like a dog making sure he got at least one bite before his food was taken away, Hog took a bite out of an apple. "We're hungry," he said with his mouth full and flashed a look of appeal.

The face of the man with the apron screwed up into a grimace of acute discomfort. "It's not our problem."

Stiffening with resentment and hostility, Hog snapped back. "You mean to tell me that you self-righteous assholes have so much nihilistic bitterness that you have no compassion for people who have had nothing to eat for days?"

The man with the apron gaped at Hog in undisguised befuddlement and replied, "Don't be tryin' to used big words to impress me. You ain't gittin' no apples."

Lifting his chin and looking down at the man, Hog told him, "Your claim that our hunger is not germane to this situation does not impress me. You are not a good citizen."

While the forehead of the man with the apron wrinkled as if he had a headache, the man with a military haircut and a bony skull with a nose jutting out like a buzzard's, stood next to him at parade rest. Using a long searching look of condemnation, he studied Breed and the others.

Next to him, a cadaverous-faced man with clammy skin, eyes like a ghoul, and fingers quivering like those of a palsied old man, pointed with the cane in his hand and stuttered to the man with the apron, "T-t-t-t hose mua-mua- ust be those dirty hobo kids that are st-st-st ealing our car batteries."

Apparently surprised at the man's stuttering, Flick lifted an apple to his mouth but didn't bite into it. He cringed and spat out, "You're lyin' out your ass. We didn't steal your goddamn car batteries. A bunch of bums did."

While, the shifty-eyed man tried but only sputtered and stuttered, so angry he could not speak, a mean-looking man in a brown trench coat with a silver badge pinned to his chest nonchalantly stepped out of the store and adjusted the Stetson hat on his head.

Breed gasp.

It was the constable.

"It's getting a little warm out here," the constable said and took off his coat. When he did, his muscular chest and arms bulged under his tight-

372

fitting T-shirt that covered most of his tall frame. His very presence was intimidating.

"Constable," the shifty-eyed man said, stopped stuttering, and stated matter-of-factly, "These are the hobo kids that keep stealing our car batteries. Now, they're stealing our apples."

Hog's face filled with resentment. "You're just saying that cause you too cheap to give us a few apples."

The shifty-eyed man began sputtering and stuttering again.

Laughing as if Hog had told the funniest joke in the world, the man with the military haircut quit standing at parade rest and tipped his hand back and forth. "If you ain't got no money" — he picked up an apple, took a bite out of it, and chewed with his mouth open — "you already ate." Looking at Hog with malevolence, he broke into a huge horse laugh.

While Breed wondered if the man thought Hog was a member of whatever particular ethnic group, the man blamed for all the problems in his shitty life, the other men joined in the laughter.

But Hog waved off the man's attempted humor. "People like you don't have enough sense to know how dumb they are."

That remark not only stopped the men who had joined in the laughter, it stopped the man's apple halfway to his mouth. "You sayin' I'm stupid?"

With an affectation of levity, Hog whirled his index finger beside his temple. "You're not smart enough to be stupid."

The man's face darkened to scarlet, but Hog continued. "You're a fucking embarrassment to the human race."

The constable stiffened with bitterness. "Why you're just a bunch of malcontents, ignorant hardheads that ain't got enough brains to know when they're whipped." The flash of the badge on his chest winked in Breed's bad eye. He knew there would be no staying here. He backed away.

But Hog seized the opportunity to agitate. With a neutral grin, he turned toward the constable. "I daresay, quite the bit of excitement, here."

"You can't talk to me like that," the constable said with surprise and irritation.

"Why not?" Hog said, "Are you someone special?"

The constable puffed up with self-importance and jerked his thumb toward his own chest. "I'm not only a constable, I'm a sheriff and a judge."

"Well, don't feel too bad about it," Hog replied. "You have to start somewhere."

For a moment, the constable's face took on a look of an intellectual condemned to a mental institution, but then he turned serious. "I'm a man of distinction who holds many positions of high authority."

"Constable, Sheriff, Judge, my ass," Hog retorted. "You're just an undereducated, under experienced bribe-taking whiner who has no real enforcement arm or mandate to do what you promised to do when you lied to get elected."

374

Apparently amazed at Hog's total disregard for authority, the constable stood stone still and stared at Hog.

Staring at the Stetson hat on the constable's head, Hog said in a most pleasing voice, "I apologize, sir. I was wrong."

Surprised, the constable slightly nodded.

Hog continued, "When I first saw your hat, I was under the impression that someone had shit under it. But upon closer examination, I can see that it's your head."

As Flick and Breed made no effort to refrain from laughing, Hog continued to pile it on. "Are you having a rare moment of lucidity?"

Screwball reached into the basket. The man with the military haircut whipped himself around and yelled at Screwball. "Are you trying to steal another apple?"

As if they were poison, Screwball slowly set one apple back into the basket and wiped his hands on the sides of his pants.

While the constable stood stunned, the man with the military haircut pointed at Screwball. "Ain't our apples good enough for you?"

"From the way you guys smell, they might be infected with Zackly."

All heads turned toward Screwball.

The man with the cane stopped shifting his now wild looking eyes, glared at Screwball, and quit stuttering long enough to ask, "What the hell are you talking about?"

Giggling, Screwball edged to the side of the porch, and used his stick to point at the man. "Your breath smells zackly like your ass."

The jaw of the man with the cane dropped in astonishment.

While Screwball laughed, Hog stared at the man with the military haircut. "I wonder if God's looking down and smiling at fools," he said, shaming him. "Cause he sure got a bunch gathered here. I hope he sends them to hell, cause they ain't got any class. After they get there, Satan can bend over and let them kiss his ass!"

The man's mouth stayed gaped open, but he did not move.

Although he was uncontrollably sputtering and stuttering, the shifty-eyed man's eyes darted from person to person. Like a kid caught with his hand in the cookie jar, in a delayed reaction, he realized he had been the brunt of Screwball's joke. Enraged, he raised his cane, shook it at the Screwball, and yelled, "That's not funny, you snot-nosed little bastard."

Smiling a huge mocking smile, Screwball let out a loud, "Hant!"

Before Screwball knew what was happening, the constable reached out, grabbed him by the head, and placed him in a headlock. Holding him secure, the constable began pounding his huge fist onto the top of Screwball's trapped head.

"Let him go!" Flick shouted.

But before Flick could do anything to help, Screwball reared the stick in his hand back and jabbed it into the fleshy part of the constable's ass.

The constable let out a yelp and immediately let go of Screwball's head.

Screwball dropped to his knees. The constable reached for him again. Screwball rammed the stick through the constable's pants and on up into his ass.

The constable squealed like a little girl.

Screwball let go of the stick, and took off running.

While the stuttering man and his friends watched Screwball's dust, and the constable was pulling the stick out of his bleeding ass, Breed and the others seized the opportunity. They clutched the apples in the front of their shirts and took off. As the constable and the man with the apron ran after them, the constable yelled, "Come back here!"

Hog looked back over his shoulder. With uncompromising resentment, he shouted, "No!" One apple fell from one of his pockets, but he kept on running.

Infuriated, the man with the apron and the constable ran after them.

Way ahead of everybody, Screwball stopped at the top of the strip mine mountain and watched the chase. Still clutching the apples, Breed lagged behind. Although he had left the man with the apron in the dust, the constable was not only grabbing at his back, he was trying to stab him with the stick.

To avoid getting stabbed with the stick, Breed ran around the back of the theater and ducked down behind a trash can. When the constable tried to ran past him, Breed stuck his foot out.

The constable tripped.

He hit his head on the hard ground.

The stick flew from his hand.

He went limp and did not move.

As the odor of garbage caused Breed's nose to wrinkle in distaste, he stared at the theater window that seem to stare blankly at the shale mountain. Just below the window, a bum with a veined nose and the fogged eyes of a habitual drinker, grabbed the stick and held it. Grinning as if he had the instincts of a rat, he stared at Breed.

While Breed's stomach roiled from the stench of the garbage, a drunken bum who looked like a remarkable specimen of something preserved in alcohol, sagged against the wall of the theater. As a slow trickle of blood came from the corner of his mouth, he went lip but stayed sitting.

The fogged eyes of the bum with the veined nose, flared with hate. Keeping Breed at bay with the point of the stick, the bum moved like an animal, reached down, and took a wad of money from the drunken man's pocket.

With an amused expression directed toward Breed, the big bum lifted the pointed stick and thrust it into the drunken man's stomach. The man burped and the fumes mixed with the garbage odor and damn near knocked Breed over. As the man's face turned deathly pale, the foggy-eyed bum bragged, "Easiest thousand we ever made."

Breed's eyes widened. There was a lithe, dark-skinned bum standing over him. With a face sharp with triumph, he pushed his baseball cap back and pointed to Breed. "And you're gonna get blamed for it."

Before Breed could react, the side door to the theater flew open. Ablaze with light and choking on a big mouthful of food, a round-faced bum about as round as he was tall, loomed in the doorway. After he painfully swallowed, he darkened angrily and stood with his hands on his hips.

Looking at the extremely round bum, Breed said, "I didn't stab him." He pointed to the big bum. "He did."

"Don't make us get rough," the round bum said with a menacing expression.

Breed protested, "You can't kill somebody and blame it on me."

The bum waved a casual hand. "We'll do anything we want, and nobody will be the wiser." He stepped out of the light, and like a shadow of death, he merged with the shadow of the building. Moving one finger in a come here gesture, his voice cracked like a whip. "You're comin' with us."

With the air suddenly sour with vehemence, Breed hurriedly looked for an avenue of escape.

Before he could move, Flick walked around the building. "He didn't do nothin'".

The round bum's face purpled, and his eyes turned mean. "Don't try to tell us he didn't kill Rudy." He pulled the stick from the drunken man's stomach, and with a faintly amused look, he shook the bloody end of the stick at Breed. "We just saw him stab him with this stick and throw him on the ground."

"If he threw him on the ground," Flick reasoned. "Then why is he leaning against the wall?"

"He isn't," the round bum said, reared back, and kicked the drunken man. The man slammed down, hard to the ground, twisting in the dust.

As little whorls of dust slowly rose around the lifeless body, a fly landed on the body, crawled around the blood coming from his stomach, flew up, and buzzed around the round bum's ears, but he didn't seem to care.

Flick flared up. "You ain't blamin' us for something you did."

Trembling, the round bum tossed the stick at Flick's feet. "There's your chance. If you want a quick slide into the grave, pick it up."

Flick wasn't asking for trouble, however there was something in him that resented being pushed around. If he had to, he would fight, and Breed would be right by his side.

Wondering if he and Flick could overpower the three bums, or if the constable got up, four people, Breed studied the situation for a fraction of a second, but there was no time to reason or wait, they had to get out of there, and fast. They needed a diversion. Before he could think of one, a long gray rat slipped out from under a loose board and headed toward a drip of water from a leaking facet attached to the wall. Breed pointed to the rat. "We're not the only ones who saw you kick that man. He did too."

The bums turned toward the rat.

It was just enough time for Flick to knock over the full can of garbage and kick it toward the round bum. With garbage spilling out, it rolled toward the round bum's feet. The round man tried to jump

380

over the rolling can, but he was too fat. His feet hit the can. Falling with his arms windmilling, he brought the other man down with him. Breed and Flick ducked under the lone standing bum's grasping arms and dashed away.

Breed was outrunning the bums, but the constable must have been playing possum. He was grabbing at Breed's back, again.

"Come on, Breed," Screwball yelled from high above and waved his hand with encouragement. "He's right behind you."

Leaving a trail of apples behind him, Hog scrambled up the mountain and slipped just before the top. After he crawled to the top, he stood up, reached into his pocket, took out an apple, and speared it onto the end of his stick. Then he reared back and flung the apple toward the constable.

It whizzed past the constable's head.

The constable ducked down, but he kept on reaching for Breed.

Hog took his last apple and put it on the end of the stick. He took careful aim and flicked the apple.

It flew straight at Breed.

Breed saw it coming.

He jerked his shoulder away from the incoming apple.

The apple smacked the constable on the forehead and cracked in half.

The constable stopped in his tracks, grabbed his head, and whined, "You dirty son-of-bitches, you stuck me in the ass, and now you're trying to put my eye out."

381

Mocking how the shifty-eyed man had stuttered, Hog shouted back. "Wh-wh-wh-who, gi-gi- gives a shit?"

With a look of excruciating discomfort filling his face, the constable shouted back, "You can't make fun of my friend, you little son-of-bitch."

Hog quickly shot back, "Hant! Yes, I can. And I still don't give a shit!"

"You'll give a shit when you go to jail for assaulting an officer of the law."

"Why don't you try to stop bitchin' about it," Hog hollered down. "It's your lucky day. If you would've had your head up your ass, like you usually do, the apple would have missed."

Standing there wiping the spatter of apple off his head, the constable muttered, "You can run now. But you won't be running after I blow your goddamn hobo asses off." He reached for his gun, but it wasn't there.

While Breed made his way to the top of the mountain, like unflinching machines, Screwball and Flick stood tall and threw apples at the other men at the bottom of the hill. The constable tried to run up the hill of shale, but he huffed like an old potbellied steam engine. At the bottom of the hill, the man wearing the apron motioned with his arm and yelled, "Come on down, Constable. When you dropped your gun, dirt got jammed in the barrel. After we clean it out, those little cocksuckers are gonna pay for killing Rudy."

The buzz of a locomotive's horn came from somewhere. From up high on the mountain Breed and the others strained to see where the sound had

382

come from. Far off in the distance and beyond a straight line of trees, a train waited on the railroad tracks. Breed looked hard and fast. The train was so far away that he could scarcely see it. But he managed to make out what was between two gondolas. A miniature dust storm whirling around like a little whirlwind gone wild. It blew into dry dirt and made dust fly right in front of two railroad men.

Screwball tugged at Breed's shirt sleeve. "Wh-wh-wh, What's that?"

Even though Screwball was making fun of the stuttering man, Breed could scarcely believe what he was looking at. "It's air from a broken air hose," he croaked out his sore throat. He turned toward the others and hoarsely shouted, "Hey, that train's stopped."

The little whirlwind between the gondolas stopped. Flick jerked forward in sudden realization. "The air's stopped. Those two guys just fixed it. Let's get to it before it builds up air pressure and takes off." He jumped over the ridge, and in a rolling cloud of gray dust, he lost his balance and began to stumbled down the strip mine mountain. To keep from losing his balance, he slowed to a safer pace.

Screwball jumped down the side of the mountain in big leaps, but he was nowhere near the bottom.

The others followed.

Breed wasn't even halfway down the steep mountain, and he couldn't see the train, but in the distance, the train's horn buzzed two longs and a

383

short. He gasped. Somehow the train had already gotten enough air pressure to start moving.

"We'll be ready this time," Hog said and kept on stumbling down the hill. "He can't get up that much speed."

Breed looked through a break in the trees. The big engine panted and hunkered. Its great wheels grabbed and bit into the steel rails. It picked up speed, fast. It was still a long way off, but now it seemed like it was right in front of them, coming right down the track, looming big and monstrous. Breed knew if he took the apples out of his pockets, he could run faster, but they had missed a train before. If they missed this one, he wanted to have something to eat.

Flick was still stumbling down the mountain, kicking up a rolling cloud of dust. As if he were close enough to grab on, he held up his arm. "Here she comes."

The diesel engines strained and churned. On top of the engine compartment, black exhaust smoke blew out the exhaust ports. Raw mechanical power fed the generators, and electric current buzzed into the electric traction motors. Physical power surged to the wheels, and the mighty shadow of steel thundered toward them. The train was getting closer.

Screwball slowed but kept hopping toward the bottom of the mountain. "That goddamn thing's gonna be gone before we get there."

Stumble-running and looking for something to throw, Hog shook his head from side to side.

"Throw a rock. Hit that engineer in the fucking head."

Doing a complete turnabout from his usual treasure house of puns, wisecracks, slanders, and dazzling, ignorant sayings, Screwball roared, "That cocksucker should know we are stuck out here in the wilderness a million miles from civilization with a bunch of bums down on our ass."

Through the gray dust, they stumbled and tumbled on down the hill. When they stopped, they were just shy of the tracks, but the dust clouds that had been boiling behind them caught up and enclosed them. Squinting through the settling dust they realized that even if they could see, the train would be moving too fast to grab onto.

As if he were wishing it were true, Flick said, "He might slow down for us."

"And you might eat mulligan shit stew and fall in it, too," Screwball said in a mocking child's voice.

Fifty yards in front of them, the engineer stuck his head out the window, waved, and blasted the buzzing horn.

"See that? He sees us," Hog said with hope in his voice.

The horn buzzed in one long blast. The engineer leaned out the window and waved to them. "He's going to slow down," Hog excitedly said.

"He ain't slowin' for nothin'," Screwball disagreed.

Another blast buzzed into the wilderness. The train didn't slow. It picked up more speed, rushed toward them.

"The asshole's just gonna go right on by," Screwball bitched.

The diesel engines whined to a fast idle, and the engine pumped more black smoke out the stacks.

Flick cursed silently and slumped his shoulders. "He's pourin' on the coal."

When the train was right beside them. The engineer leaned out the window, took off his gray and white striped hat, and waving it at them, he yelled over the roar of the engine, "Get the hell away from the tracks, you little ass holes."

The engineer and the engine zipped past.

For the benefit of the bitching engineer, Flick thrust his middle finger into the air. "Here blow on this."

The others all followed suite and flashed middle fingers for an extra added attraction, but the engine was way down the tracks, and the engineer was gone from the window.

As the speeding train humped on the rails and ran clackety-clack past, Hog let his arms fall limply to his sides. "He ain't stoppin' now."

True to form, Screwball reverted to his old self. With his head bobbing with laughter, he said, "That's an interesting observation."

A faint smile formed on Flick lips, but when it faded, he lowered his head in defeat. "Ahh, the hell with it."

The train's horn buzzed once more and weaved out of sight.

Hog kicked at a rock. "If I wasn't so hungry, I'd think that guy was some kind of a clown."

"Maybe there's some kind of a clown of the railroad," Breed said. "He's playing a big joke on us, rolling the tracks in a circle that wraps around the earth like a big hay conveyor belt. We're walking on it, but we ain't getting' into the barn." He looked to Screwball. "We don't even know where we are."

"Well, the way I see it," Screwball said and smiled. "If you don't know where you are, you could be nowhere."

Breed ignored Screwball and looked to Flick. "What are we gonna do now?"

Flick looked to Breed. "Got any ideas?"

Breed had been so engrossed in trying to catch the train that he had forgotten he still had four apples in his pockets. "First thing we're gonna do is eat some apples." Offering the apples to the others, he stepped forward. After each of his friends had taken an apple, he held the last apple and bit into it. As he chewed, he didn't know if it were his imagination, but he was sure he could feel the life-giving effects of the apple.

Chomping on his apple, Flick walked in a circle and spoke. As he talked with his hands and stabbed the air, his face beamed with energy. "Look, you guys," he said, "we've been in worse situations than this. We ain't no candy asses that need to suck up to anybody. Life isn't fair, but we're going to get out of this."

Breed realized he had been feeling sorry for himself. He didn't want anything to do with being an ass-kissing candy ass. That's just what I am becoming, he thought. A baby-fied, whiny-ass-

387

kissing candy ass. "Yeah, you're right," he said to Flick. "And this time we ain't got those flats kids breathing down our backs."

As if he were trying to suppress the mistaken hope he had felt when he had believed they would get on the train, for something to do, Hog rolled one end of the spear stick in his hands and the other end on the inside edges of his shoes. As the stick spun, he said, "Look! Automatic drill."

Screwball bent over and swung his arms like he was ice-skating. "So we can slide right on out of here, we should drill for oil."

"Hey!" Flick shot back. "Cut the wise cracks?"

Slouching over like a simpleton, Screwball faked a sad look. "Yeah, okay."

"Come on you guys," Flick said. "Those bums came from somewhere. All we gotta do is follow these tracks to a road crossing. Then we can hitchhike home."

"We can't hitchhike anywhere, if those assholes" — Hog pointed behind Breed — "are on the roads."

Breed looked back over his shoulder. The town constable and a gang of men with guns avalanched down the mountain. "Ahh, man!" Breed cried. "Those assholes are coming. Let's get outta here."

CHAPTER 21

Slouched over, Screwball jerked his head in the direction of the mountain. The gang of men were half way down the side. He instantly came out of his slouch and pointed across a field of grass. "The tracks curve. If we go across there, it'll be a short cut." He broke into a ground-covering lope. In a few seconds, he was in the tall grass.

The others followed.

Following in the path Screwball had blazed, the others caught up. But the yard-high grass became dense and stiff. Like dull knife blades, it seemed to be trying to slice into their clothes, but they kept on running. They had to.

Just before a clearing next to the railroad tracks, a wall of tiny insects hovered over a stretch of swamp. With mud building up on their shoes and grabbing grass clinging to their knees, they slogged forward. Out the other side, they ran for the tracks. Once they got there, they kept to the side of the rails and sprinted around a bend.

Breed glanced back over his shoulder.

No one was close.

He slowed.

The others slowed.

They all stopped.

With their hands on their knees, they sucked in needed air.

"We gotta keep going," Breed panted. "Those bullets go a long way."

Screwball lifted his hands from his knees and did a quick imitation of a traffic cop motioning traffic to come ahead. "Bullets always have the right of way." He stopped, looked back over his shoulder, and tensed to run.

Hog looked down the tracks. "There's a shed down that side track," he said, and they ran toward a rusty steel shed."

Right after the switching stand that lead into the shed, Breed examined the powdery rust on the top of the rails. "A train hasn't been here for a couple of weeks. If it had, this rust wouldn't on the rails."

Screwball stood in front of the door of the shed. "Maybe we can hide inside."

"Yeah," Hog said, "then they can trap our dumb asses in there."

Flick gave Screwball a gentle push. "Don't just stand there. Open the door."

Screwball stepped off to the side, grabbed the big brass lock and shook it. "These locks are bullet proof and this one's locked."

Hog reached into his pocket and pulled out his lock pick. "Get out of the way."

Screwball let go of the lock.

"These big locks might be bulletproof," Hog said, "but they're the easiest ones to pick. He slid his lock pick into the padlock and turned it. "No problem." The lock swung open.

Breed and Flick pulled the heavy door open. Inside, sitting on the tracks was a cab-less railroad hand-car. On the platform of the yellow car, a hand pump that could be pushed up and down to propelled the car down the tracks waited to be used. Under the front of the car behind a hole for a starting crank, a motor that when started could power hand-cart and take railroad crews to their work sites was a welcome sight.

Flick's eyes brightened. Referring to the hand-car they had seen when the Mercury had driven alongside of one, he said, "It looks like you guys got your wish."

"All right," Hog said and rubbed his hands together. "A hand-car. Let's start that motor and go home."

Breed's feet hurt, his knees didn't want to bend, and he was weary of walking. The hand-car would end all that. He was so happy to see the hand-car that his brown eyes filled with tears. He wiped the tears away with sleeve of his shirt, stepped to the front of the car, and looked into the hole where the starting crank slid in. "Where's the crank?"

"It ain't in the shed," Flick said. "All that's in here are old stinkin' oil rags."

"Just like those railroad guys take the reverse'er lever with them when they leave the cab of the engines," Hog said, "somebody probably took the starting crank with them."

"That's right," Flick said. "If they don't take it, and someone takes off with the train, they get in big trouble."

"Breed looked at the hand pump on the platform of the car. "Maybe we can pump it."

Flick jumped upon the hand-car. "Come on, you guys. We'll pump this thing on down the tracks. They'll never catch us."

Breed jumped on the other side of the hand pump handle and pushed down. His feet left the floor of the car. "I'm not heavy enough." He jerked his head toward Screwball. "Get on the other side."

Screwball grabbed on and pushed. His feet came off the floor of the car and the handle didn't move. "Some days you get the elevator and sometimes you get the shaft."

"Come on, Screwball," Breed said. "Quit screwin' around. Those guys are coming down the tracks. We can't run as fast as you. Push!"

"It ain't goin' a go," Flick said. "Let's try to push it first to get the handles moving in the right direction like the pedals on a kiddie car."

Hog jumped down and put his shoulder to the end of the hand-car. "Probably a little rusty. Maybe we can loosen it up."

Breed and the others jumped down and pushed. The hand-car squeaked once and rolled out of the metal shed. It moved freely and the handles pumped up and down.

"I think we got it now," Flick said. "Let's get her out on the main track." He pointed up the tracks. "Breed, run up and throw that switch."

Breed ran up, put his foot on the switch pedal, and tried to lift the weighted square at the end of the switching lever. It didn't move. He looked at the switch locking mechanism. A big brass lock had it locked in place. He motioned to Hog. "It's locked."

Hog ran up and kicked the lock. It fell open. Breed looked at Hog in disbelief.

Hog beamed with a superior look of confidence. "How'd you like that, Breed?"

Breed looked at the lock and flashed a skeptical grin.

Hog slipped the lock off the switch. "I get better all the time."

Breed threw the switch, and a train buzzed in the distance. "Get that car back in the shed, A train's coming." He reached down, threw the switch back to where it had been, and Hog looped the lock back in place. Breed ran to the end of the hand-car and helped push it back into the shed. Screwball and Hog closed the door, and they all ran into the woods along the track.

Breathing heavily, Flick crouched low. "If that thing's goin' slow enough, we're gettin' on."

Breed leaned forward and watched the train. "It might slow down," he said. "Maybe a train crew is checking the hand-car to drop off a track gang to repair the tracks."

"You might have something, Breed," Flick said and glanced toward the tracks. "We did see some loose spikes and some of those ties were moving up and down when those trains went by."

As Breed and the others watched and waited, the big steel locomotive buzzed its horn. A passenger flyer thundered toward them.

Screwball stood up and looked at Hog. "It's only going seventy miles an hour. You jumpin' on?"

"Be my guest," Hog said and jerked his thumb toward the rapidly passing cars. "Those passenger trains don't stop for nothin'."

After the blur of cars flicking past came to an end, the train's end car zipped past and disappeared down the railroad tracks. As if it were an afterthought, a tailwind from the swift train blasted into the trees, and the green and yellow leaves waved bye-bye.

Breed tilted his head and looked down tracks where the train had come from. "Now we know a train ain't coming."

With a worried look, Hog looked back up the tacks. "No train, but those assholes with the guns could be right around the bend."

"We can't let those knuckleheads surround us," Flick said and motioned with his arm. "Come on, you guys, let's try to get that hand-car going."

Breed ran up, took the lock off the switch and threw it open. Flick and the others pushed the hand-car out of the shed and onto the main track. Breed threw the switch back, and a boiling noise of many voices, rose from around the bend.

He looked back up the tracks.

Here they came, packs of men and a few angry-faced women, their eyes fastened on Breed and his buddies. The constable carried a rifle at port arms, and other men held shotguns, ready to fire, and none of them were smiling. Breed threw the lock on the ground, ran to the moving hand-car, jumped on, and yelled, "They're coming around the bend."

Before the words were out of his mouth, a keening crack of a shot pierced the air, but didn't appear to hit anything.

"They're just trying to scare us," Hog said.

Another shot rang out and howled along the side of the shed. Then shotguns boomed. Snarling and snapping, bullets zinged through the air, and hit the ties and rails just in front of the hand-car.

For a moment, Flick stared at the advancing rifle-carrying constable. He stood with his legs spread wide and his arms held his rifle at his chest. Although his face was set with grim determination, he wasn't pointing the rifle at anybody. "Maybe they're just trying to scare us with buckshot."

The constable put his chin down. In a way that was pure menace, he shook his head slowly. Then he lifted the rifle and began firing. Bullets zinged past Flick's head and thunked into the metal shed.

"If they're trying to scare us," Hog said, "they're going a good job. That ain't buckshot."

"They're shooting to kill," Breed said. "They think we killed a guy named Rudy."

"One good thing," Screwball said, "the bums aren't with them."

"Everybody in town must be after us," Flick said looking toward the constable leading the mob. "Those bums are probably looting the town."

Breed grabbed the pump handle next to Screwball and pushed.

With his eyes wide with alarm, Flick latched onto the other end of the handle. "Let's pump this thing."

Coming forward in a stumbling run, Hog leaped onto the hand-car, teamed up with Flick, grabbed the other end of the handle, and they pushed. With a shower of buckshot falling on the metal shed, the drive wheels bit the rails, but the wheels whirled full circle several times, before they lurched forward and rolled down the tracks. Breed pumped the handle and watched. The gang of armed marching men grew small and finally disappeared.

"We're on the way now," Flick said, shaking his head in pleasant amazement. "If we can pump down the tracks for the rest of the day. "We'll be home before the sun goes down."

Breed slowed his frantic pumping pace. "My arms are tired. Let's take a break."

They sat on the floor of the car and rested until the car slowed to a stop.

Breed looked under the floor of the car. The end of a hand crank stuck out of a gap in the back of the car. "Hey, those railroad guys hid the crank under the floor."

Flick jumped off the car. "Let's get this thing started before a train comes."

Breed pulled out the crank and handed it to Flick. Flick slipped it into the starting hole in the front of the car.

Breed jumped back up on the car and moved the throttle lever.

"Here she goes," Flick said and cranked the motor.

It didn't start.

Breed looked over the end of the car. "Check and see if there's a gas valve."

Flick bent over and looked in. "I can't see."

Screwball flashed Flick his simpleton look. "Do you need a mirror?"

"Damn it, Screwball." Flick reached in. With his fingers, he searched around the gas line that lead to the tank. "Here it is." He turned on the valve and cranked the crank again. The motor backfired. Breed pulled the throttle lever back. Flick cranked faster. The engine caught and slowly putted to life. Flick pulled out the crank and hopped on. Coaxing the engine to increase speed, Breed pulled the throttle lever out. The engine began to stall. He pushed the lever back in. The engine smoothed and ran in a steady beat, but was running too slow to pull the car. "Maybe the reason the car was in the shed was because the engine was wearing out and doesn't have enough power."

Frantically waving his hand in a negative gesture, Flick said, "No! No! Let it warm up."

After a few moments, Breed pushed the throttle lever out. The engine increased speed, but this time, it not only ran smooth, its rpms increased. He engaged the hand clutch. The motor's speed changed. Now powerfully putting, the little engine picked up speed and chugged on down the tracks.

Screwball stood on the front of the car like a hood ornament and moved his arms like a half-wit trying to direct traffic. "Move over big trains, little hand-car's comin' through."

Breed looked ahead. Now that they were moving at a good rate of speed, the long distance down the tracks didn't seem so far. He looked down at the little putting engine. "I wonder if we got enough gas to get us home."

With the agility of an Indian, Flick dropped to a cross-legged position and rapped his knuckles on the gas tank. "I checked it. We got a full tank."

Breed felt relief and excitement. "Nothin' can stop us now."

CHAPTER 22

Relaxing on the putting hand car traveling down the railroad tracks, Breed shook his head in amazement. "I can't get over how that round that big bum was."

"Yeah," Flick said. "I never seen anybody that round."

As if he were disappointed, Screwball leaned forward in a helpless heap. "I just wish he would have run to the top of the hill with us."

Hog reached over and shook Screwball's shoulder. "Hey, you glorious pain in the ass. He was too fat to get up that hill. And if he did, what good would he have been?"

"We could have rolled his round body down the hill and knocked over all those assholes that were chasing us."

Before anybody could respond: Waaahhhaa! A diesel locomotive's horn blared behind them. With his arms akimbo, Breed defiantly turned toward the sound. Just coming around the bend, a fast-moving triple-header freight train was coming right at them.

"Screwball held up his hand. "Maybe he'll see us and slow down. Then we can get on."

"Don't be stupid" Flick snapped back. "That looks like an ore train. They don't stop for nothin'."

Breed didn't want to lose the hand-car. He took his hands off his waist and lowered them into a lifting position. "Let's pick this thing up and take it off the tracks."

"Right," Hog snorted. "We can't even pick up one wheel of this thing."

The train buzzed again. Flick flexed his legs to jump. "We ain't gonna outrun it."

Breed hated to let the hand-car get hit. He pushed on the throttle. "I'll give it more gas."

Flick smiled. "It's already wide open."

The train was a hundred yards away and coming fast.

Flick looked back at the speeding train, then at the others. They didn't get up. "Come on you guys. When that thing hits, this car's gonna fly. Maybe a couple hundred feet. We gotta jump off and run."

Breed had wanted to ride the car as long as possible, but he jumped to his feet. "I didn't think of that."

The horn on the locomotive buzzed again.

Hog and Screwball stood up.

The train wasn't even slowing.

Hog stood at the edge of the hand-car. "See you guys later." He leaped off the car.

Screwball followed.

Flick reached over and shook Breed's arm. "Come on, Breed. Let's go."

Breed looked at the approaching train. Feeling like he was losing his best friend, he took one last look at the hand-car and jumped. When he hit the ground, his knees came up and hit him in the chin. He rolled down the embankment and stopped. Flick scrambled toward him. "Get up and run."

Breed scrambled to his feet and ran toward the woods. Behind him a loud clunk filled the air. He turned toward the tracks. The hand-car shot forward and sped down the track. Its wheels spinning and sparking at a hectic pace.

"We should a stayed on," Screwball said. "It's still going."

The hand-car slowed. The big diesel locomotive towered over the little car and hit it, again. This time the little car buckled under the force and turned sideways, sending white sparks along the steel rails and flinging off bits and pieces of shrapnel until it was nothing but scrap metal strewn along the tracks.

"Maybe they'll stop the train," Hog said with hope.

"Even if they stop," Flick said, shaking his head, "they'll arrest us for killing Rudy."

"Not only that," Screwball said. "They'll put us in jail for driving a hand-car without a license."

Ignoring Screwball, Breed nodded in agreement. "Let's get out of here."

They took off into the pleasant surroundings of the concealing woods and waited.

The train didn't stop.

With his elbows on his knees, Screwball sat on the ground. "Hey," he said. "Let's see what's further into the woods." He pointed toward a light spot through the trees. "It looks like there's lake or something over there."

They all got up, and as they made their way through the trees, dark vines and thick tree limbs blocked the sun. Moving saplings out of the way, they weaved their way through the gathering darkness. When they came out the other side, a clear meadow, with soft, blond grass lay ahead.

"Ain't no lake here," Flick said and jumped back. At his feet, a huge black snake was coiled up with its gray scale-covered underbelly turned up toward the sun.

Hog walked up to the snake. "Maybe it's dead."

"I don't know," Screwball said. "It's not moving."

Hog picked up a rock. "I'll find out." He wound up and zinged the rock. It shot into the black snake with a painful thump. Like a broken wind up spring, the snake immediately uncoiled. Its six-foot-long body vacillated in angry waves.

It rushed toward Breed.

He took off running.

Flick let out a laugh.

The snake turned and rushed toward him.

He took off running.

They all took off running and didn't stop until they were back on the railroad tracks, walking past the remnants of the hand-car, walking on stones, and walking on new railroad ties, where the black smelly creosote built up on their feet and caused the bottoms of their shoes to burn with the friction of the sun-heated surfaces.

With the threats of the towns people with guns and the threat of railroad police coming to investigate the demolished hand-car, pushing them onward, they kept walking. When a train buzzed, their hearts filled with anticipation. But all the trains that had zipped past were going too fast to grab onto, and this one was, too.

Exhausted from the arduous walking, Breed looked ahead. The tracks stretched across the land until they vanished in a hot haze.

With growing weariness and exasperation, they walked and walked. The tracks just didn't want to end.

"This place looks like the place we just left this morning," Screwball grumbled with a voice slurred with fatigue.

Hog wagged his head around, looking. "Maybe it is. Are you sure we're walking in the right direction? I don't think those bums would walk this far for a bottle of wine. Maybe we should go back."

"There was probably a path right behind their camp," Screwball said with fake enthusiasm.

"You wanna go back and check?" Hog echoed. "There might be some mulligan stew left."

"Don't start that Buffalo shit now," Flick warned him, referring to ending up in Buffalo instead of California. "I don't even want to know if we have gone the wrong way again. I'm too tired."

Almost falling asleep walking, Breed's foot hit a protruding rail spike. He stumbled but caught his balance and didn't fall. When he looked up, a blue bird sky was turning orange on the horizon. "We better start a fire and get ready for night."

"If we are going the wrong way," Hog said. "It doesn't matter. We ain't getting out of here today."

Breed jerked his head forward. "Maybe it's better up around the bend."

And they walked some more.

Around the great bend, they found the same tracks with the same nothingness to nowhere. "Maybe they built this railroad in a box and we're boxed in," Screwball said.

"Maybe they built your brain in a box," Flick said. "We'll get out. You just gotta have a little faith." He pointed to a small clearing a about fifty yards from the tracks. "Before we have to face the night, let's make a camp over there behind that big dead tree."

Screwball stuck his chin out. "If we build a fire, won't those people chasing us see it?"

"We're too far away," Breed said. "And if they do come, we'll know it's them."

Flick clasped Breed on the arm, and wasn't surprised to find it heavily muscled. "Oh great Indian, how would you know that?"

"People don't make sounds like an owl does when it is catching a rat or a rabbit. Unless they're scared and running, most animals in a forest do not step on twigs or branches. People, like the ones chasing us are the dumb assholes that step on twigs and branches."

For a moment, in the faint light, as if he were amazed because of what Breed had just said, Flick studied him closely, then turned and walked toward the tree in the clearing.

When Breed looked down at his shoes, they looked older, and with each step he took, puffs of blackish railroad dust exploded and covered his pants legs. "Yeah," he said and looked at the dead branches jutting off the trees surrounding the

403

clearing. "We can use those dry branches for the fire."

At the tree, Breed started a fire, and its bright-burning wood warmed him just as the sun hit the bottom of the world. He was tired. They were all dead-tired in every part of their bodies. And there was no water. There was nowhere to fish for food. No animals were in sight. Like refugees bedding down around the fire, they made themselves comfortable. With the firelight flickering against their faces, in a blaze-lit circle, shut in by darkness, they immediately drifted into a deep, hungry sleep and dreamed of food.

With the fire smoldering in the wet morning haze, Breed awoke with fog breath. The misty air and the damp chill struck through his clothes and caused him to shiver. Looking like a bedraggled-looking bunch, the others began rising stiffly.

"Get that fire going," Hog said, flapping his arms at his sides. "I'm freezing my ass off."

Announcing its arrival, a train buzzed, and a long string of ore cars buffeted and swayed on their way to where Breed wanted to be.

"Your ride's here," Screwball said and paused. At great speed, the train rushed past and was gone. Then he said, "Now it's not."

"Let's forget about the fire and go on down the tracks," Breed suggested. "Maybe there's some water. This fog has to be coming from somewhere."

Imitating what the hobo had said, Screwball wagged his head like an imbecile. "Why, water's just around the bend right next to those peach trees,

404

and there's a little cabin where we can fish off the back porch."

While Screwball bobbed his head with laughter, Breed kicked the cold ashes of the fire, turned toward the tracks, and blurted in exasperation, "We ought a be able to find that cabin easy. There ain't but five-hundred million tracks to walk." He started walking.

Like starving prisoners of war, the others gave him grim looks and followed.

With endless, lifeless lines of railroad tracks leading to nowhere, the day began and was just like the day before. After the sun had burned off the fog that had promised water, the air became furnace-hot, oppressive, and so exceedingly dry that Breed's lips smarted so that he had to continually moisten them. All sides of the dreary, parched tracks stretched as far as the eye could see.

When Breed and the others stopped to sit down on the rails and take a rest, something splashed in the background.

Flick jerked his head toward the sound. "Did you hear that?"

"Water?" Breed said and he hoped it was.

"Check it out," Hog said and waved his weary hand down. "I'm too tired to be fooled again."

CHAPTER 23

Breed and Flick walked up over a tall grass-covered hill and peered over the top. At the bottom of the hill, a swift little brook ran clear and musical. Places with flowery banks were open to the sky, and willows hid places where birds sang in little thickets.

"I think we found some water," Breed yelled back over his shoulder and looked at the shoreline.

Screwball and Hog scrambled up the hill. When they saw the water, they ran down the other side of the hill, and Breed and Flick followed.

At the crick, they dropped to their hands and drank directly from the crick.

After Breed had gulped in a few mouthfuls, he held water in his mouth and let the dry tissues absorb the water.

Hog rose to his feet and looked around. "Somebody was here," he said and gestured to the ground. "Look at all these tin cans."

"Grab one," Flick said. "We'll wash it out and make some sassafras tea."

Hog took a few steps back and pulled a small mitten leafed tree up by the roots. "Good idea. There's a tree right here."

"Might as well," Flick said. "We'll have something different to drink."

Hog offered the roots of the tree to Flick. "Go ahead make some."

Flick dropped his hands to his sides. "I would, but if I don't take a good break, my legs are going to fall off." He sat on the ground, lay back, and closed his eyes.

Staring at the willows, Breed felt the soreness of his throat. If he peeled back the bark of one of the willows and got to the inner bark, he could scrape some off and chew it. Being part Indian, he knew it would be good for pain and fevers. For the pain in his sore throat, he wanted to do that. He turned toward the others. "Let's make a lean-to, crawl under, and rest all day. That way, that fog and wet shit won't soak us in the morning."

Hog looked to Screwball. "What's the Big Dipper doing?"

Screwball lifted his finger and started to answer.

Flick jerked to sitting position. "Don't start that shit again." He started to lay back but stopped himself with a sharp gasp. "I'm too hungry to rest." He sprang to his feet. "I'm going after some fish. While I'm gone, get that lean-to built."

After Breed scraped some inner willow bark and began chewing it, he started snapping branches for a shelter. The long walk and the lack of food had weakened him, and the once easy task was more difficult than he had thought. His feet were sore, and his whole body ached. Between great throat-rasping gasps, he forced himself to continue snapping branches and setting up the sticks against a strong oak tree.

Screwball gathered long grass and weeds for the roof and weaved thick armfuls into the sticks. "I don't know why they call it a lean-to," he said. "The branches really lean on the tree."

"Yeah, maybe they should call it a lean-on," Breed mechanically replied.

Hog threw a few sticks onto the side and walked off in the distance. "Something has to live in this crick," he said. "Maybe we can get some minnows for bait."

"Check for some watercress while you're out there," Breed suggested.

"No shit, Breed, I would have never thought of that."

"If you're so smart," Screwball said, "how about getting some of those chanterelles?"

"I would," Hog said back, "but those wild mushrooms only spring up in the spring."

After Breed and Screwball finished the lean-to, they lay back and watched. In the distance, Flick was whipping through tall grass. When he came near, he waved his hands around like a man who had just found a fist full of hundred-dollar bills. He had a fish in each hand. "Get that fire going, Breed. We got food."

Breed jumped up so fast he hit his head on the roof of the lean-to.

"Don't knock it over," Screwball said. "We'll have to call it a lean-over."

Amazed at Screwball's never-ending half-wittedness, Breed rubbed his head and picked up some dry twigs. After Screwball cleared a spot for the fire, Breed piled the sticks in a pointed apex and crumpled up a handful of fine dry grass. He took out his flint and steel and hit the flint against the steel. Sparks came but nothing caught. He struck the flint faster. Sparks flew and the grass smoldered. He bent down and blew gently until a fire appeared. He placed the small fire under the sticks and waited. "It sure takes a long time to make a fire when you're hungry." He waited, more. The sticks briefly smoked and caught.

Hog proudly stepped up with a tin can and sassafras. "We'll have tea and fish today," he said and reached into his back pocket. "And this." He pulled out a wad of tender watercress, and displayed it like a prize trophy.

While the fish roasted on long sticks place above the fire, the inner bark Breed had chewed began to work. The pain in his throat began to subside. Feeling better, he and the others nibbled at the watercress and sipped the unsweetened tea from the can.

When Screwball was handed the can, he gave Hog a suspicious look. "I hope this isn't the can you were farting in."

"Ho, ho, ho!" Hog faked a laugh. "You're talking really stupid. You're not even old enough to know what a real fart is."

"Oh," Screwball said as if completely surprised. "So now you're a fart expert?"

As if he were astounded, Hog leaned back. "That's an interesting observation."

"I'm so hungry," Flick said, "I could probably eat a fart." He looked to Hog. "Of course, it would have to be inspected by an expert."

"Hey!" Breed squawked out with a mouthful of watercress. "The fish are done. If you guys quit yacking about farts, I'm gonna try to eat."

"Okay," Flick acquiesced, and the others shut up and silently picked every last bit of the fresh nourishment off the fish and sucked on the bones. They felt better, and enjoying the contented feeling that was settling over them, they lay back. But just before they were about to doze off, Screwball sat up. "Hey, Hog?"

Hog growled. "What do you want?"

"Did you ever find that box?"

Looking into the dancing fire, Hog's forehead wrinkled with puzzlement. "What Box?"

"The Box you stood on to kiss the elephant's ass."

"If you don't shut up, and get some rest. I'm gonna shut you up."

"Yeah, okay," Screwball said, lay back down and rolled over, giggling.

As encroaching drowsiness dulled Screwballs halfwittedness, the sun set red over the trees and dusk fell, shrouding the weary travelers like a friendly blanket. They sank to sleep. And the drowsy hours of that golden autumn day continued without them.

When Breed awoke and stepped out for a whiz, it was dark, and even though the fire had died down to coals, when he stared up, millions of stars speckled the sky. There were no street lights, no glow from a nearby city, and no automobile headlights washed out the tiny flickering lights that shone in a velvet black sky. It was one of those silent nights when a stick could be heard breaking a half a mile away. A night owl flew overhead and didn't make a sound. As if they were stopped in time, the stars stared motionless. They didn't wink. They didn't twinkle. For a moment, Breed felt refreshed, but he was still hungry. Although he knew there would be no food there, he expectantly looked to the coals. Their red glow reminded him of the spooky mirages they had seen next to the rickety fences that enclosed the old wooden houses with the glowing red windows. He didn't really believe in ghosts, but hoped a ghost of a forgotten hobo wasn't going to cause him to believe there were.

Suddenly the swish of walking feet behind his back caused him to whip around in fright.

It was Screwball.

He smiled a sleepy smile. "Did I scare you?"

"No," Breed lied. "Did you get up to take a whiz?"

Screwball let his hands fall to his sides. "No, I got tired of sleeping, so I got up to take a rest."

Breed felt his forehead wrinkle with confusion. "Oh," he said, went back into the lean-to, and slipped back to sleep.

When the morning sun warmed the top of the lean-to, its rays filtered through the grass roof and shined on Breed's face. He woke and watched Flick stretch and yawn. Then he reached down and tightened his belt. "Down a notch," he said. "I'm ready for a fill up."

Hog sat up and leaned his back against the oak tree. "Me too," he said. "But I don't wanna be walkin' down those goddamn tracks, again."

Breed gestured to the crick. "Let's shit can the tracks and follow that crick. It has to go into something bigger."

"Hey," Flick said and looked to the crick. "If we have to, we can swim and float until that crick pans out."

"I'm ready to give it a whirl," Hog said, dusted off his hands, and stood up. "Anything will be easier than walking down those tracks."

"I don't know about you guys," Breed said and shot them quick look, "but my feet are killing me. If we find that cabin on the island that hobo talked about, I'm gonna prop my feet up on that railing and just relax forever."

"Smells good to me," Screwball said and wrinkled his nose. "No more walkin' and waitin' on a million-mile-an-hour train that we can't catch."

Hog raised a skeptical eyebrow. "I don't believe there's a cabin is on any island. That hobo lied about the peaches. He's lying about the cabin, too." He lifted his hands and lightly jerked them upward. "But if we stay near this crick, we stay close to food."

"Let's see if the fish are jumping this morning," Flick said, gathered up his stick fishing pole, and tromped off.

Hog picked up the fire-blackened tin can and walked in the other direction.

Breed refreshed the dying fire with new wood and it roared to life. Screwball stepped up, stood around the flames, and soaked in the heat.

Flick came back with three fish. "I think I cleaned them out. These rock bass bite anything."

412

"They didn't bite this," Hog said and walked in with handfuls of something that looked like the green, slender tops of scallions.

Flick stared at the green tops. "What are those?"

Hog shook the tops and smiled. "Ramps."

"What's ramps?"

"Wild onions, they taste like onion and garlic."

He passed the mild garlic-smelling ramps around.

Screwball took one bite. As if he didn't like the taste, he made a discussing sour face and shook his head irritably, but said, "Good!"

Munching on the ramps while the fish roasted, Breed lifted a finger. "Hey! I just thought of something."

"Oh yeah?" Hog said to agitate. "Whoever told you, you could think?"

Breed continued, "When the constable and people got back and found out the bums looted their town, they would know we didn't kill Rudy."

"I hope that's true," Flick said and reached for the fish.

Although the fish only amounted to a few bites each, they wolfed them down.

Still hungry, Breed used the back of his sleeve to wipe his mouth and pointed downstream. He envisioned a wide sparkling stream that would lead to a boat, but said, "Let's get on down the crick and get back in that movie of the world."

"Yeah," Screwball agreed. "I could go for some popcorn right about now."

They left the endless tracks and the strip mine dust behind and plodded on, each step drawing them closer to a place unknown.

CHAPTER 24

Slogging wearily, Breed and his band of friends made their way to the crick and waded into water. In an effort to avoid weeds, trees, dense-vegetation, and any obstacles that would block their progress, they walked in the water next to the bank of the stream, and to their relief, navigating this way, the little crick was much easier than walking the rails. The crick wound its way around bends and under fallen trees. Here and there, a cotton-mouthed water moccasin would crawl around and search for heat under the bright autumn sun.

When an unusually large cottonmouth appeared to Hog's right, he snatched a rock off the bank and threw it at the sunning snake. But he only threw one rock. It missed the snake but scared it into the water. Breed realized because Hog's body was tired and undernourished, it had taken the edge off his habitual rock throwing accuracy, and each step Breed took was a mind and body straining effort.

Hunger and fatigue had also slowed Screwball's half-witted antics. They only surfaced now and then. Breed felt he was hungrier than he had ever been in his life. A wind moaned across the crick and made him think of death. He imagined himself huddled in his worn clothes, shivering in a fetal position. The lack of food, the cold, and little rest had drawn his strength until he was only a dank shell of his former self. He shook the thoughts out of his mind. But when he watched Flick's footsteps begin to slow, he said, "I wonder how long it takes to starve to death."

Flick forced a cheery face. "I think it's three days." He quickened his pace. "We ain't even close."

With the water pulling at his feet, Breed struggled to keep up. "It takes three days, then why am I so hungry?"

Screwball rolled his eyes upward. "If you're hungry try eating your words."

Breed's voice came out weak and unexcited. "If I could, I would."

"Quit your whining like a bunch of candy ass little kids," Flick said with a flat finality. "We just ate a few hours ago. Nobody's gonna starve to death."

Feeling weak, Breed rationalized. "It might not take us three days to starve to death. I don't think those people who starved to death after three days had to walk down a long railroad track."

A devilish grin crept onto Screwball's face. "I knew a guy whose doctor told him he only had six weeks to live."

"What did the guy do, take a trip around the world before he died?"

"No, he had a big ranch. Sold everything off and gave all his money away. And then he sat of his front porch and waited to die."

Hog shot Screwball a questioning look. "What happened?"

Screwball shrugged. "He's still sittin' there."

Being caught off guard by one of Screwball's stupid jokes, Hog's eyes bored into Screwball's. After a brief moment, he smiled and shook it off. "You're a half-wit."

And Screwball's little theatrical performance had caused Breed to forget he was hungry. He stopped in ankle deep water and rubbed his foot. "Hey, let's take a break."

Flick splashed through the edge of the stream and motioned with his arm. "Come on. If there isn't another bend" — he pointed to the bend ahead — "after that one, we'll take a break."

Breed knew Screwball looked forward to stopping, but after they had gone around the bend Screwball was rewarded with another bend. He stopped and stood with his hands on his hips. "I'm gonna give this crick just one more chance to quit going around another bend."

"Oh yeah," Breed said, "then what are you going to do?"

Screwball craned his neck and looked downstream. No use wasting all the steps we've already taken. "I'll just give it another chance."

A stray wind with an icy touch whisk around bend. Breed took one step. He could see around the next bend. He took it in with one sweep of his eyes. "You won't have to," he said. "Look!"

Welcome as a cool drink of water, a big blue river appeared. Breed walked closer. Like a puny kid standing before a God, he stopped and stared at the river. Huge rectangular stones with rounded edges lined its banks. Upriver, the blue water made magnificent plunges over falls, blowing mist that created a cool temperature. Years of fast water had worn down the river's bottom. Now it was deep and smooth. In small eddies and slower bends, long fingers of dark green algae clung to the smooth stones and waved gracefully. Breed knew fish hid there like they had done for years, waiting for prey. Maybe they would jump for Flick's hair bug.

Breed bent over and reached into the water. It was cold, much colder than the stream. He drew his hand back. It was too cold for autumn, and it was too cold for a rock bass to come to the surface and bite on Flick's hair bug. This river had to have been here for thousands of years. It had been here before he was born. Good people would die, and bad people would die, but this river would still be here. It would go on and on.

He looked toward the top of a tall, white-barked poplar tree. A fierce autumn cloud cruised behind its branches. When the cloud peeked around the other side, it became a soft pink light. The leaves on the popular were beginning to die. Soon leaves, grass, and bushes would hang on to the last ounce of life and stay green, even if was only a few more days. Then they would die in the first killing frost, and all the trees except oaks and pines would become baldheaded and stay baldheaded until spring.

After a dark-purple cloud blocked the light and warmth of the sun and the air turned colder and held the threat of snow, Breed shuddered at the thought of trying to find his way home through a baldheaded winter forest. It would look dead, but even worse, thick ice would cover the cold river, and snow would lie on top of the ice. He hoped he'd make it home before that happened. If he didn't, and somehow, he lived through a long winter, the ice would melt in the spring. The river would renew itself with fresh mountain water. It would be a beautiful sight. But he didn't care how nice it would be, he didn't want to stick around to see it. A visit would be okay, but he didn't like the idea of being stuck on this river. But then again, the summer sun would come again. It would shine long and hard. It would shine into the darkest depths of the water, and the feeding light would make the long seaweeds and grasses grow again. The river would become a quiet place again. Breed shook his head. What am I thinking about? The lack of food must make me stupid. My throat hurts more every day. When the river freezes over, there will be no fish to catch, and it will be hard to walk in the deep snow. I don't even have a decent winter coat. There will be no dry grass to start a fire. We'll all freeze to death. We'll all die.

Breed shrugged off the thoughts of winter and spoke. "That cold water gives me the creeps. Let's build a raft."

Screwball put his hand in the cold water. "If we wait a few days, we could make one out of ice."

Flick spread his arms wide and drank in the expanse of the big blue river. "It might be cold" — Breed began nodding before Fick was finished talking — "but this big baby has to go somewhere."

Still impressed with the mighty river, Breed replied, "It ain't gettin' any smaller."

Flick looked across the great width of the blue river. "That current looks strong. Maybe there's an undertow. If there is, it'll suck us under."

"If we build a raft," Breed said, "we won't have to worry about that."

419

Flick's brow puckered with certainty. "There should be some old logs or something around here we could use to make one." He turned upriver and walked through the green leaves of the lower branches of the tall trees that lined the hillside next to the river.

Searching downriver for a dry fallen log he could break up and use to build a raft, Breed found small sticks, good for a little campfire, but nothing big enough for a raft.

After a few moments, Flick looked back over his shoulder and yelled to Breed, "See anything?"

Breed reluctantly shook his head from side to side. "Not even a big stick." Hoping he could chop it down, he stopped at a tree, and using the little piece of metal he had picked up off the tracks, he hacked at its trunk."

Screwball smiled and pointed to where Breed was hacking. "You're not even making a decent dent."

Flick stepped to the tree. "At this rate we'll be here all winter."

With each whack, the scrap metal dug into Breed's hand. He quit. "No use cuttin' up my hand up for nothing. This green wood won't float worth a crap anyway."

Like a boxer getting ready for a fight, and unconsciously building up his courage, Hog rapped the knuckles of one hand into the palm of the other. "Ahh, quit bawlin' about it," he said, and then, referring to the deep holes, called drop-offs, in the Shenango River that people were afraid of falling into and drowning, he said, "Next thing, you'll be crying about fallin' in a drop-off."

Flick stood back, folded his arms across his chest, and stared downward at the river. "Hey, that's right," he said with renewed confidence. "We've been in deeper water than this."

Breed didn't believe it, but he felt Flick's confidence. "Yeah," he said, encouraging himself, "the Shenango River's drop-offs are deeper than anything in this river, and the rapids in the Shenango River are faster and stronger than this river, not as wide, but harder to swim in."

"Let's just jump in," Screwball suggested. "We could tread water and let the current take us downriver. If we have to, we'll drift to Texas."

The purple cloud swayed away from the sun. Sunlight reflecting off the water's surface, give it an inviting, clean look. Flick stuck his foot into the water and yanked it back out. "Hey, this thing's really cold."

"Don't be a candy ass," Hog chided. "Jump in. Your jacket will keep you warm."

While Breed contemplated the possibility of his jacket keeping him warm, Screwball turned sideways, bowed at the waist, rolled his hand in front of his chest, and gracefully directed Hog toward the water. "Be my guest."

Hog waded into the water. When he was waist deep, he stopped.

Breed looked at Hog's thin jacket. It was dry but Hog's face broadcasted sudden shock from the sudden drop in temperature.

Screwball smiled a crooked grin in Hog's direction. "Hey, Hog, is that water cold?"

Before Screwball had a chance to say it, Hog butted in, "Yeah, Screwball, I know, enjoy it while you can."

Screwball bobbed his head. "Yep, yep, enjoy it while you can."

Hog ignored the cold and snarled through his clenched jaws. "Goddamn, candy asses." He walked into the river until the water was up to his neck. "See nothing to it. Get your candy assess in here. I'm going downriver."

Unlike Polar Bear Club members on a New Year's Day swim, Breed and the others waded into the big cold river with their clothes on.

Breed eased into the water up to his chest, stopped, stood still, and shivered. Hog laughed at him. "Weren't you ever in cold water?"

Breed wanted to reply that his jacket wasn't doing a damn thing to keep him warm, but before he could speak, Screwball butted in. "Well you are now."

Their bodies became accustomed to the water, and they let the current carry them around the big bend, where an undertow, stronger that any of the Shenango River undertows, they had been accustomed to, pulled them down, tugged at their jackets, and threatened to take them to the bottom.

Fighting the draw of death, Breed kicked and stroked powerful strokes. Tiring quickly, he watched the others. Their faces revealed they were tired, too.

422

"Don't quit now," Flick said for encouragement and huffed for air. "A couple of good kicks should get us out.

The others kicked clear of the undertow but Breed didn't. "Don't fight it," he told himself and huffed for much needed air. "You're almost out." He huffed again.

"Yeah," Flick said. "Just let the current take you downriver. That's where we're going anyway."

Breed breathed like a man having a heart attack. His chest hurt and his arms cramped with pain. It was a struggle just to keep his head above water. Then he went under. He tried to swim for the surface. Vertigo set in. He twisted in liquid space not sure which way was up. With the sensation of whirling and falling, the thought of drowning invaded his mind. He kicked hard and thought about the friendly old man who had fished at the water's edge on Shenango River. His warning flooded his brain. "The river is tricky. If you get excited, it will turn into a monster. Its deep undertows, drop-offs, and floods have taken many lives."

In his mind, Breed argued with the old man's warning. People drowned because they couldn't swim, and if they could, they had panicked and drowned themselves. Some even drowned when all they had to do was stand up in four feet of water.

Breed felt the mighty river pull him down. He kicked harder and breathed out a breath of precious air. A silvery streak of bubbles shot in front of his face and rushed upward. He was on his back looking up toward the surface. I'm too heavy with this jacket on, he thought. It's pulling me under. I'm going to drown. This river is bigger than Shenango River. It's more powerful. His last reserve of air, he had been keeping in his lungs, escaped with a silent scream. He sucked in a little water and managed to swallow it. He kicked for the surface. If I'm going to drown, at least I have enough brains to put my feet down. Or do I? He quit kicking and put his feet down.

Suddenly, like a life preserver thrown just in the nick of time, his feet touched bottom. He stood there in four feet of water, coughing and catching his breath. I must be as dumb as a bag of stones, he thought. Screwball should play that stupid Cuckoo! tune, and right now.

Looking to see if anyone had seen how he had panicked and almost drown in four feet of water, he took a few embarrassed steps. The river widened and the water became a wide and shallow stretch of one-foot-deep riffles. They all stood up and sloshed to shore. Breed looked at Hog's lips. They were bluish purple, and his jaws shivered uncontrollability. "Ain't cold, huh, Hog?"

Hog wouldn't admit he was wrong. "It wasn't cold when we got in," he said and rubbed his arms. "This river must get colder downstream."

Breed knew Hog was only putting on a tough front, but he was, too. He would never admit that this river was bigger, faster, and stronger than the familiar Shenango River, where they knew the location of every hidden rock, broken acid jug, drop-off, and whirlpool. This blue river was a powerful king, and they couldn't control it. Breed knew he would have to fight it every inch of the way. This was not the make-believe Land of Oz. There was no man behind the curtain controlling this river. This river was its own god.

As Screwball walked along the bank, a small thicket of brush blocked his way. He lifted his foot to kick it out of the way but stepped around it. "Why are we so tired?" he asked and walked around the brush.

"We're not tired," Breed said and kicked the brush out of his path. "We just haven't had enough to eat. We're just weak from no food."

Flick joined the excuse. "That's gotta be it. We can't be as strong as we are when we have something in our bellies."

Breed knew this could be a lie. None of them ever had enough to eat, even when they were home. This river was just too powerful, but no one was going to admit it. No one wanted to be a candy ass. He looked at both shorelines. Only small stick-like trees lined the banks. "We got to build a raft," he said and sloshed on down the river.

"Maybe we can find something that can float," Flick said, falling behind Breed. And the others followed.

One hundred yards downriver, waist-high water was stained red and blue. An old shed, as big as an outhouse, stood twenty feet from the shore. Old and broken boards, and rusty fifty-five-gallon drums littered the bank. Beyond that, a single-strand wire fence encircled what looked like an old dump. Between two wooden fence posts, a wild wind kicked dirt and papers across a battered road that trailed off into a lifeless brown field of dead grass.

"Hey," Screwball said, "we could follow that old road and get back on the main road and hitchhike home."

"We could," Flick agreed. "But who's gonna pick us up?"

Breed didn't hesitate. "The cops?"

Hog nodded. "We've come too far to have those half-wits pick us up now."

Suddenly, Breed felt like he had been standing in the middle of the railroad tracks, and the front end of a fast-moving freight train had just plowed into his mind. He whirled around and looked to Flick. "If we ever get home, won't the cops be there to arrest us?"

With sudden realization, Flick's eyebrows shot up. "That's right. We could be trying to get home just to get thrown in jail."

Screwball looked skeptical. "I never thought of that, but if Eddie didn't squeal on us, the cops won't even know we were with him."

"You guys are worrin' about nothin'," Hog said and glanced at the empty road.

Breed turned toward the road and toward Hog. "What are you talking about?"

Hog's face went tight. "Don't exaggerate things and get them all out of shape. That gas station where Eddie got caught isn't in Shitsplat. Those cops only have a vague idea of what we look like, and they don't know our names."

"Oh yeah! Screwball grinned sheepishly. "Then why don't we just go up on the road and hitchhike?"

Hog looked to Screwball, groaned inwardly, and adamantly said, "Our adversaries have drastically reduced in numbers, but they are still quite formidable."

Screwball tilted his head in a questioning slant. "What?"

Chuckling at Screwballs look of puzzlement, Hog replied, "In other words, we're probably far enough away from the gas station that the cops around here don't know us. But that constable you used for a shis kebad may be close. Even if he has found out we didn't kill that bum, we can't push our luck."

"No use getting arrested for acting stupid in public." Breed tipped his head toward the road. "There might be bullet rain over there. Let's build a raft and keep goin' downriver."

Relieved, they all nodded in agreement and sloshed ashore.

Breed's gaze swept the area and rested on the hood of an old truck. It looked like the front of a boat. "That would make a good boat if we had another one just like it."

"No way," Hog said and waved his hand down. "It's too heavy. It'll sink."

Flick kicked a fifty-five-gallon barrel. "If these things were empty, they would float."

Breed lifted his foot and rested it on a barrel. "We could use them to make a raft and float downriver."

Hog leaned on one of the barrels. "It would be easier than spending the rest of our lives walking on those tracks."

Screwball lifted his foot high and kicked a barrel over. "All we gotta do is empty the damn things."

The screw cap at the top of the barrel stopped whatever was in the barrel from coming out. "We ain't got a wrench to get these caps off," Hog said.

Breed reached into his pocket and took out that piece of metal. "This will work just like a wrench." He held the metal and tapped the screw top until it came loose and then he twisted it off. Black sludge oozed out like poison gravy.

"After we put the caps back on," Flick said. "What are we going to tie them together with?"

Breed looked around the perimeter of the dump. "We can hook them together with those wires on those old fence posts."

Flick walked to a fence post and wiggled it until it was loose. Then he put his shoulder to the top of the post and pushed it to one side. It broke off even with the ground. The sudden break cause Flick to tumble toward the ground. He broke his fall with his hands. As if he had fallen on purpose, without missing a beat, he looked up. "This will work and the wire's already nailed on."

Hog and Screwball wiggled and kicked fence post out of the ground or broke them off until they had enough to make a loose floor on the drums. Breed and Flick unscrewed more drums, pushed them over and let the black slop ooze onto the ground.

After the drums had drained, Breed screwed the caps back on and pounded them tight. Then they each took a barrel and rolled it to the water. As if they were cattle, Breed corralled the barrels into the shallow water. While he held them in position, Flick and the others laid the fence posts across the tops, wrapped the wires around the barrels, and bent the wires secure. Using stones for hammers, they pounded them tight.

As they worked, brown rust seemed to jump off the drums and smear onto their clothes. Screwball pointed at Breed's butt. "Looks like some giant wiped his ass on us."

Breed wiggled his butt in the water. "The water will take it off."

Flick picked up an old baldheaded tire mounted on a rusty rim that still had air in it. "This will make a good life preserver," he said and threw the tire into the water. Breed tied it on with one of the loose fence post wires and let it trail behind.

When Flick jumped on the raft, his feet fell through the wide-spaced fence posts. "We need something to fill in these gaps."

Breed went to the shed and pulled on the broken door. It screeched off its rusted hinges. Then Hog pried two long boards from the side of the shed and held them over his head. We can use these for paddles. Flick jumped off the raft, scrambled up the shore, and they all dragged the door into the water and onto the raft.

When Screwball jumped on the door, his weight made the structure bob on its drums. Trying to get the rust off his hands, Flick bent over, put his hands in the water, and brushed them together. "That was a lotta work. Let's take a rest."

The sound of a heavy truck motor groaned in the distance. Flick looked back over his shoulder.

Breed shrank back and looked, too. A cloud of dust puffed around the spinning wheels of a truck coming down the road.

Screwball threw his hands into the air. "I hope you enjoyed your rest." He jerked his thumb toward the oncoming truck.

With Screwball standing on the raft, they pushed the raft into the current. As it gently jerked and increased speed, they pulled themselves onboard. Although Breed stood on the front like a sea captain on a great ship, the current's power made him feel small. "This river is big."

Flick gazed at the wide expanse of the river. "She runs big and she runs strong." He pointed forward. "The promised land is that-a-way."

Breed sat down on the raft, and like a big powerful friend, the river pulled the raft like his own Shenango River had done when it had rescued them from the flats gang. Once again, they were cradled in a water-god's big hand. Breed prayed the mighty river would carry them downriver, swift and safe.

While Flick let the hair bug on his makeshift fishing pole trail behind with hopes of catching a fish, along the shore, a muskrat flitted silently through the underbrush until it came to a clump of reeds where it slipped under the water.

Just the sight of it caused Breed's thoughts to turned to food. "Hey, Flick, are muskrats any good to eat."

"I don't know, but if we catch one, we'll find out."

When the raft drifted onto a quiet stretch, Breed sank slowly to the raft, stretched out, and leaned on one elbow. Relaxing, he thought about the steel rat traps he had hidden in the cellarway of his parent's shack. If he had the rat traps now, he was sure he could catch that muskrat. It would be different than when he had used them to catch rats in the old woodpiles behind his shack. Then every day after school, he was King Rat. Someone would always say, "Hey, Breed, let's check your rat traps."

And when a rat was caught alive, hanging on by one bloody foot, the kids that would usually jump or run from the sight of it. But after a while some become brave. They gathered around, yelled at the rat, threw stones, jabbed it with sharp sticks, and kicked at it until it was dead.

Breed looked up at Flick. "I wonder if muskrats are like rats."

"I doubt it," Flick said. "Rats can crawl through holes smaller than their body because their bones are like rubber." He paused and looked along the shore. "But muskrats are probably like any wild animal. Corner them and don't give them a way out, and they'll go for your throat."

"Rats are really tough little buggers," Screwball said with a trace of genuine seriousness. "But they're no match for cats. Even if a cat doesn't catch a rat it's chasing, it steals the rat's life."

431

Hog, who had been lying back peacefully, suddenly sat up. "Pardon this humble man's blind perception, but if you believe that, you're crazy."

"Oh yeah," Screwball came back laughing. "How do you think cats get nine lives?"

Hog tried to tighten a crooked little grin. It didn't work. He let out a little laugh, waved his hand down at Screwball, lay back down, and muttered, "Please forgive me for the intelligence of my remark."

Around a bend, where the water clarity began to fade, a grove of black dead trees stood on a stretch grassless land.

"I'll be damned," Flick said. "That hobo wasn't lying. There's the peach trees but something killed them."

Thinking about how good the peaches would have tasted, Breed stared at the horrible sight until it passed by.

A long way downriver, snuggled on the end of an island, the outline of a cabin popped up ahead of them and stuck out like a thousand-dollar bill on the sidewalk.

"Hey look," Breed said, and his voice raised its pitch like he had just picked up that thousand-dollar bill. "That old hobo was right again. That cabin's right there!"

When Breed turned to his right the fragment of paradise changed. In the distant sky, beyond the tall trees, smoke from some kind of a steel mill spewed gunmetal smoke into the sky. Searching for a source of pollution that would surely be coming from the steel mill, he scanned down the trees and stopped the edge of the water. A four-foot wide discharge pipe jutted out of the riverbank. Next to the pipe, chemicals had eaten the life-supporting roots sideways, causing the stunted trees to grow lopsided. Oil and thick yellow-brown water gushed out of the pipe like a torrent of terror. Breed breathed in. A rotten egg odor broadcasted into the river air and deposited a taste of death on his lips.

"I don't think we'll be doing any fishing here, "he said, and held his breath until they drifted past the pipe.

Screwball pointed toward the cabin. "Whoever lived there put up a sign."

The raft loomed close. Breed read the weathered sign out loud. "When you're here, you're still nowhere."

Flick stuck a board in the water and pushed. "Let's guide this raft so we can get on that island." He pushed again. "Maybe we can stay the night."

Breed grabbed a board, stuck it in the water and pulled. "Maybe we can sleep inside next to a warm fire that crackles in the stove."

"If it's as nice as your buddy the hobo said it was," Hog added, "we can live there."

Using the board for a rudder, Flick steered the raft toward the island. "Just to see how it feels, I want to sit on that porch."

Breed stood up on the front of the raft and leaned toward the island. The oil and thick brown water from the discharge pipe only ran on one side of the island. The other side looked calm, quiet, and clean. "I can feel the fish biting already."

The raft crept onto the end of the island. The steel drums below the raft clunked and scraped on the sand and stones of the shallow water next to the shore and stopped. Breed jumped off. The others stepped to the back of the raft. The front lifted into the air. Breed dragged it onto the shore. Flick threw the life preserver tire on the island for an anchor and walked toward the cabin.

Breed and the others followed.

The weathered boards on the sides of the cabin looked like they had fought off many a winter, and green moss and climbing vines were invading the lose cracks in the boards. Some of the boards had fallen off and stuck in the ground below. Behind a window that glass had fallen out and smashed on the ground, a dilapidated burlap bag that had been used for a curtain blocked the view of the inside. Even with a neglected single shutter hanging off-kilter, on one rusting hinge, the cabin seemed like it had once been a friendly place, filled with people, but for some reason, probably the discharge pipe, it had been abandoned.

Flick stepped up onto the porch. Breed stepped behind him. His foot broke through the rotten wood floor and sunk into black oily ooze. "Damn," he bitched. "I just got rid of that rotten gut car smell, and now I gotta smell this."

While Screwball told Breed, "Enjoy it while you can," Flick turned the rusted handle of the splintered door. The door fell off its disintegrated hinges and dropped to the inside floor of the cabin. Expecting to see at a few things the hobo said were in the cabin, Breed shook the filth from his foot and poked his head inside the frame. As musty air of the old cabin blasted into his face, he could see there was no pot-bellied stove, no chairs, no table, nothing but black crud-covered walls veined with dark-green mold. He realized he was not in another world of another time. Nodding weakly, he turned to Hog. "There goes that dream."

Hog's face clouded with distress. "It figures," he said. "This cabin's just one dream on a big list of shit that's not going to happen. It's a constant in life. Dreams are good, and they are a necessary part of life, but ultimately most dreams are just bullshit."

Flick placed his foot on a crumpled pile of stones that used to be the chimney. "I guess we ain't stayin' here tonight."

Screwball pointed to an old, rusted frying pan half stuck in the dirt. "I thought you guys wanted to sit on the porch and catch fish." He stretched out his foot and tapped the handle of the pan. "You could fry them in this pan."

"You can, if you want," Flick said and turned toward Breed and the others. "Before the whole place caves in on our heads, we better get out of here."

They all jumped off the porch ahead of Breed. In a hurry to catch up, Breed took one step to jump. Crack! His foot broke through the porch floor and sloshed into the black oily muck, again.

Screwball turned and stared at Breed's shiny oily shoes. "They look new."

As if he were trying to scrape off dog shit, Breed dragged his once new-shoed feet sideways across the sand until he was in front of the raft.

Then he swished his feet in the water until the filth was almost gone and jumped on the raft with the others. As they continued downriver, Breed sat on the back of the raft and watched the little, broken-down cabin grow small until it disappeared like a broken promise.

Like a man with x-ray vision seeing something beneath the surface, Flick stared down into the oily water. A tear formed in the corner of his eye. "Must have been a paradise in its time," he said, and hiding his face, he looked forward.

Breed continued to look back toward the cabin. At one time it had been a green and lovely island with fish leaping out of the clean water and wild game everywhere. In the crisp autumn air, the sunlight would have been dancing on the water, and the rustling leaves on the trees would be twinkling with golden movement. But just like the steel mills had ruined the Shenango River, the island and the cabin had been ruined, too. But in the distance, it looked inviting and promising. "If they wouldn't have dumped that shit into the water," he said and sighed, "we could have been on permanent vacation for the rest of our lives."

In a dismayed gesture, Hog turned his palms up. "Now it's just a broken-down piece of shit."

With his back to the others, Screwball lowered his head and gazed into the water. "We really didn't miss anything." Keeping his shoulders forward, he bent his head at the neck and cast a sideways grin in Breed's direction. "If we would have moved into that cabin, it would have become our home. Then if we wanted to go on vacation, we

436

would have to get away from that cabin to go on vacation. There is no such thing as a permanent vacation." He turned, put the penny whistle to his lips and played a soft, Cuck-oo!

Hog stared at Screwball's back. "And there ain't no such thing as you sayin' anything that makes sense."

Screwball didn't turn around, but his shoulders shook with restrained laughter.

"Makes sense to me," Breed said, paused, and said, "I think."

The river slowed and widened. Breed tilted his head all the way back and looked up. Towering to his right, trees lined the riverbank and ended where even taller stone cliffs reached for the sky. As they drifted between the shadows of the tall stone cliffs, water cascaded down the faces of mighty jagged rocks and sprayed white horsetail streaks into the air. When they drifted further downriver, it was like some magnificent movie had just ended. The big green river turned yellow-brown. The beauty of the cliffs fell behind, replaced with dark shadows of ugly man-made cliffs of slag from steel mills.

Breed never thought he would be happy to smell toxic water and see the ugly, blue-mouthed ceramic sewer tiles jutting into a dead river, pumping out turds that slid into the mill-poisoned water like fat brown snakes. The disgusting sights and smells were like sickening salutations from Shitsplat. Listening to the busy scratching of river rats scuttling along the barrels on the underside of the raft, he knew he was getting close to home, and even though the smells were enough to kill anyone's appetite, he was still hungry. But in this water, there were no fish for that hair bug to catch. But civilization was close.

The river turned darker brown, connected with another river, and grew wider and slower. Just before a railroad trestle, the raft slowed to a crawl.

Flick stood up on the raft and pointed toward the trestle. "Hey, let's get back on the railroad."

Hog leaned back on one elbow. "You're crazy," he said and spit into the water. "I ain't trampin' around those bends. They don't go nowhere."

Screwball stood up, took a long step, stood in place, and swung his arms like the fast walking hobo on the tracks. "Don't you want to go to Canady? There's peaches just around the bend."

As if contemplating going back on the railroad, Hog looked up at the railroad tracks of the trestle and then turned toward Screwball. "Ahh, blow it out your ass."

"Hey!" Screwball said with immediate urgency. "There's an Irish Setter up on the trestle."

In the distance, the sound of a diesel locomotive sounded.

All eyes turned toward the dog.

Another blare of the diesel's horn sounded, but now it was close. The train was moving fast.

"That Irish Setter better get off that trestle," Hog said.

Everybody started calling the dog, trying to coax it off the trestle.

But it only sat and stared in the opposite direction.

One more blast of the fast-moving locomotive and, Clunk! The front of the locomotive hit the dog. With a puff of its brown fur accented by red splotches, the dog flew through the ties of the railroad tracks and dropped into the water. Apparently with no air in its lungs, the dog immediately sunk to the bottom.

Hog got ready to dive in after it. "Maybe we can save it."

"See if it comes up."

The dog never came up.

"Ah shit! That was a nice dog," Hog said with a heavy heart. "I guess the trains go too fast here, too."

"I guess we could drift some more," Flick said turning away from where the dog had gone under. And as if in a slow-moving funeral procession, the raft drifted toward shore. Under the trestle, it clunked on something hard and stopped solid. The sudden stop caused Breed and the others to slide a short distance across the top of the raft.

Breed stood up and wiggled the end of the raft. "Ahh, man," he complained, "the bottom's snagged on something under the water." Disappointed and fatigued, he sat back down.

Flick stepped from side to side. The raft rocked. "We should be able to rock it off," he said, and they all paddled and rocked. The raft would not move.

Flick jumped off the raft and onto the rocky shore beneath the trestle. "Looks like this is where we get off."

Screwball leaned back and put his hands behind his head. "I think I'll just stay on this raft the rest of my life. It'll be better than gettin' back on that stinkin' railroad."

Hog crossed his legs and leaned back on his elbows. "Me too."

"It won't be that bad," Breed said and pointed upward at the trestle. "One of those trains got to be going slow enough to grab onto."

"Yeah," Flick said, "we ain't in the wide-open spaces anymore. Just in case you're too dumb to smell it, we're close to a steel mill."

Screwball lifted his foot and waggled it in the air. "Yeah, almost smells like Breed stepped in another pile of guts."

Breed shuddered at the thought of another gut-foot smell, but pondered the predicament that had been heaped on them.

Announcing itself with its diesel horn buzzing, the sound of a train with metallic screeching and the familiar dull thumping of couplings from individual cars shifting back and forth, filled the air.

As Breed thought about how the many trains they had tried to catch, but couldn't because they had been traveling much too fast, he didn't get excited. But when the familiar stuttering sound of air pressure going to the brake lines signaled that a slow train was beginning to pick up speed, he sprang to his feet. "Let's get up on that trestle," he cried. "The train that hit the dog must have been a passenger train. There's another train up there just starting off."

440

With great haste, Flick wigwagged his way up the big stones of the steep bank and motioned to the others with his arm. "Come on, you guys. We can catch this one."

Screwball lackadaisically placed his hands behind his head. "That's an interesting observation."

In no mood for Screwball's antics, Breed gave him a questioning stare.

With realization and his smile fading, Screwball sat up, got to his feet, and stepped behind Breed.

Breed stepped big and hopped up the rocky riverbank. At the top, he paused to catch his breath and gave a thankful farewell wave to the raft that had made going down the river so much easier than walking the tracks. Hog and Screwball ran past him, and the slow train was before him. He looked up at the top of an empty gondola car. His cut eye felt like it was going shut. He forced it open and watched. Flick and the others had already grabbed on, climbed up the ladder, rolled over the sides, and disappeared down into the car. Breed grabbed onto one of the round steel ladder rungs on the side of the car and swung himself off the ground. And he couldn't believe it. Right in front of his face, a faded yellow chalk mark, read ON Shop. This car was going to Ferrona yard for repairs. He climbed up and dropped somewhat wearily down into his new ride home.

Screwball looked at Breed's bad eye. "Too bad you didn't step in another pile of guts," he said. "We could call you one-eyed shit-foot."

Breed waved off Screwball's remark and sat on the wooden floor. It didn't matter what Screwball said now. Breed felt good. He was finally riding again. The clackety clack of the wheels beneath him was music. The hobo under the bridge flashed in his mind. Maybe I'm getting train crazy, he thought. I hope I don't turn into a hobo. Maybe I'm hooked. As the train lumbered slowly into a greater speed, the wheels began to rumble, playing a hobo lullaby. Maybe that hobo was right. Maybe those wheels will bring me back again and again.

As the train hurried though the sedimentary heat of the settling day, Breed tried to tighten his belt around his stomach. All the notches had been used up. He felt like a skinny dog begging for scraps when there weren't any. The thought of those endless tracks and the empty feeling he had felt when he had walked down those dry, life-ending tracks made him sad. I'm not train crazy, he thought. Not at this rate, not my hungry ass, no way, man. I'll be home by morning. There will be food. There will be a warm place to sleep, and a bath in the sink, a warm bath, not the cold water. I'll probably get my ass beat for being gone, but that will pass. It'll be worth it. I'll heal up just like before. That hobo lullaby is playing all right. It's playing music I want to hear. It's telling me, I'm going home. I'm not going to spend the rest of my life riding around in the dark going train crazy. I'm going where there will be light. His eye throbbed shut and he felt pain in his chest. I won't be sick in no light at all. I won't have to worry about railroad

bulls in black leather jackets with their flashlights
and clubs. I'm going home.

443

CHAPTER 25

Riding toward home, Breed leaned his back against the cold steel wall on the inside of the gondola. To his right, in just about the same place as one had been in the other gondola, a gigantic gash ran down the steel wall of the car. He lifted his hand and gestured toward the gash. "How come this car's ripped in the same place as that other car?"

Sitting with his elbows on his knees, Screwball stared at the gash. "Maybe it's the same car."

"I don't care if it is the same car," Flick said. "Just as long as it gets us home."

A curved piece of scrap sheet metal, about four-foot-wide and six feet long, screeched against the wall of the car. The irritating screeching sent pain into Breed's teeth. To get away from the sound, he turned toward Hog.

Hog's face soured. He lifted his foot and kicked at the bothersome sheet metal. "We should throw that thing over the side."

The metal screeched again. Hog stood up and pulled on the metal. "This thing's going over the side." He tried to lift the metal. It bowed and its heavy end remained on the car's floor. He quit trying to lift it and pulled it away from the wall.

It quit screeching.

He sat back down.

With a teasing glint came into his eyes, Screwball pointed to the sheet metal. "I thought you were going to throw that thing over the side."

Hog gestured to the sheet metal. "I don't want to hog all the fun. Be my guest."

Screwball opened his mouth to reply, but up ahead the train's horn buzzed. He turned toward the sound. The train slowed to a crawl, and the night air became moist, and felt like trapped tropical heat.

When the odor of dirty steam penetrated Breed's nostrils, he looked up. Edges of the black sky were bathed in an orange glow, and snakes of yellow smoke twirled toward him. They were near some kind of outlets coming from a steel mill, probably a crick or big pipe pumping out hot Sulfur-smelling water. As the gondola continued on down the tracks, lights from an enormous gantry crane passed over their heads. Looking through the tear in the wall of the gondola, Breed watched men with grease-spattered faces driving smoke-spewing forklifts along filthy redbrick paths. After that sight flashed past, the orange night became light. The train slowed, more. As if they had come from an insect farm, mosquitoes, hordes of little black gnats, and just about every kind of insect Breed had ever seen, descended down into the car like starving refugees who had just gained free admission to an all-you-can-eat smorgasbord.

Breed covered his face with the front of his T-shirt, but the bugs crawled into his hair and fluttered around his neck. He waved his hands and tried to shoo them away. But his waving encouraged them. Their numbers increased.

Flick pulled the back of his jacket over his head and looked out the opened zipper. Above his head, insects swarmed in a dense cloud. "It's too late in

445

the year for these many bugs." He slapped at a black band of gnats. "What's going on?"

Screwball laughed through the front of his shirt. "They found fresh meat."

A mosquito sent a high-pitched threat into Breed's ear. He slapped at it and stood up. "Let's get out of here."

Flick pointed outside the car. "We can't."

Barely visible through the steamy mist, countless stinging insects filled the air. All around the car, tall, galvanized buildings and wobbly containers, stacked like steel building-blocks, left just enough room on both sides for the train to get through.

Breed looked for a place to jump off.

The train lurched and pulled up a grade.

The glow from the lights of the gantry crane faded.

The sky turned black.

The bugs and insects dissipated.

The air returned to its seasonal coolness.

Screwball pulled his shirt away from his face. "Hey, Breed, you can jump off now."

Breed waved off Screwball's remark, breathed a bug-less sigh of relief, and sat back down. As the train picked up speed, with his good eye, Breed watched through the gash in the railroad car's steel wall. The night sailed past. Lights in the distance grew brighter and the train slowed.

Flick jumped up and looked over the side of the car. "We're going to stop."

Bright lights turned night to day. They were in the center of a town. The horn on the great diesel

446

train sounded, sending out two long blasts, a short blast, and another long blast. A railroad crossing appeared, and the train decelerated. Rapidly closing couplings clunked on down the string of cars, and the train came to a stop. The smell of railroad dust wafted into the car, and intermixed with an evasive rotten smell that had come and gone as the train was moving.

Breed stared through the gash in the gondola's wall. People in Chevys and Fords peered over long shiny hoods and watched the suddenly silent train. After a while, several horns beeped in anger.

On many of his swimming days Breed and Screwball had sat on top of the Clark Street Bridge and watched people in cars wait for trains. It seemed like a long time ago, but it was still clear in his mind. Most of the people did not know what the letters on the railroad cars stood for, but he did. NYC meant New York Central. EL meant Erie Lackawanna. PC was Penn Central. B&O was Baltimore and Ohio. N&W was Norfolk and Western. Breed knew them all. He wondered why people waiting on trains didn't care if they knew the real names of the railroad cars that passed before their very eyes.

Up ahead, the air horn on the locomotive buzzed two shorts.

Flick's eyes widened. "Whatever it was they stopped for must be fixed. The engineer just whistled off. He's going ahead."

As if the possibility had just occurred to him, Screwball blinked. "Should we jump off while it's going slow?"

447

Breed flashed him a self-satisfied smile. "This car was marked ON. It'll take us right to the Clark Street Bridge." He shrugged. "No use walkin' any more than we have to."

Screwball nodded weakly.

The train lurched forward.

The string of cars jerked on down the line and took up the slack that had happened when the train had clunked to a stop.

With his legs shaking from the jerking movements, Breed reached up and grabbed the top of the end of the gondola. He pulled himself up and peeked over the edge. When the train's horn blared out two longs, a short, and another long, it seemed to be playing "Here Comes the Bride". Up ahead, another railroad crossing came into view. From above, long white crossing gates dropped down and blocked the crossing. Red flashing lights blinked into the thick black of the secret night and reflected in the tiny rain puddles along the road. Strong headlights from the stopped cars shone on the wet moving railroad cars and made them look new and shiny. As if they had just been interrupted on their way to some magic destination or they were in a hurry to get home, the faces of the people in the cars looked madly twisted. Breed figured they looked that way because they were not seeing the same things or thinking the same thoughts or being force fed from the addictive blue glow of a black and white television screen. And the experience caused their minds to be lost in an unfamiliar place. But it didn't matter how mad or twisted their faces became, it was impossible for them to drive through

448

the long steel string of slowly advancing railroad cars. They would have to wait. If the noise from the train made it impossible to listen to their car radios, for a short time, they would be forced to watch something real and think for themselves.

Just as the sound of the mighty steel wheels rolling over the rails was about to build up, the train jerked in succession and stopped again. Breed looked up. An old, dilapidated house just like the Jones's house that had collapsed with a single tap of the wrecking ball, sat next to the tracks. He wondered if other Jones-type people lived in that house. He hoped his plan to never work in a smoky steel mill would never bring him that far down the ladder of poverty.

After the line of railroad cars had gone through their sequence of clunking couplers and started to move again, Breed let go of the top of the car, slid down the side, and put the thought of the Jones' house out of his mind.

Outside, the sounds of gondolas, reefers, hoppers, piggybacks, tank cars, flat cars, and coil gondolas chattered over the shiny steel tracks.

Flick sat on the floor with his head leaned back against the wall of the gondola. He lifted it and looked toward Breed. "See anything familiar?"

"No, but I know what those people waitin' for this train are saying.

Hog jerked his head in a cocky manner. "Oh yeah, great mind reader. What are they saying?"

Breed looked to Screwball. "Me and Screwball heard it a thousand times."

"Those people didn't even know we were sittiin' on the bridge right above them, looking down," Screwball pointed out with a self-important air.

Breed pulled his knees up to his chest. "That's right."

As if he were one of the people complaining, Screwball rapidly worked his jaws. "They just sat there, bitched, and said, 'There ought a be a law.'" He shook his fist. "'Those trains shouldn't be allowed to take so long.'"

"The only thing they cared about," Breed added, "was how much longer they had to wait on the train."

"Talk about stupid," Screwball said in a flat pessimistic voice, "how about the time that train jumped the crossing and stopped all those cars. Those people blew their car horns over and over."

Looking like he was sick of the conversation, Hog made a sour face. "So who gives a shit? People wait on trains all the time."

Breed leaned his head toward Hog without looking at him and talked in a low voice. "The yard crew got the train back on the tracks, but that train sat and sat."

Screwball lifted his hands, grabbed an imaginary steering wheel, looked back over his shoulder, and pretended he was backing up a car. "A couple people backed up their cars." He pumped his foot on the floor of the gondola. "Some just sat there honked their horns and raced their engines."

450

Hog shook his head at Screwball's antics. "Simple things come from simple minds."

Breed acted like he hadn't heard Hog's remarks. "Later we found out that some really smart cop went into the yardmaster's office. He told the yardmaster that if that train wasn't off the crossing in ten minutes, he was going to take him to jail. Because the train was off the tracks, it sat for another fifteen minutes. The dumb ass cop arrested the Yardmaster."

"So what," Hog snapped with insulting delight. "He doesn't drive the train."

"Don't be simple minded," Breed said. "Without the yardmaster telling people what to do, nobody is authorized to do anything."

Screwball moved his finger around in a circle close to his ear. "It was two hours before the cops brought the yardmaster back. Yep! Yep! That cop really sped things up."

A sickening aroma wafted around the car. Flick waved his hand in front of his face. "That cop must have had his head up his ass."

"Yeah," Flick chimed in. "It's a good thing Screwball didn't have his stick close."

Breed laughed and it became quiet.

After a while Breed looked down at his hands. From grabbing and climbing up the steel ladder and holding on to the sides of the car, they were dirty black. He realized his hands were the hands of someone who didn't use his mind, and they made him feel like he had been sucked into living the sameness lives the Shitsplat people lived. When his friends and he had tricked the flats gang into

451

fighting each other, he had felt he had beaten the ignorance of physically fighting his way out of situations instead of thinking his way out. He dropped his hands in disgust. Now he was going right down a trail that every other kid in Shitsplat had traveled and would travel. The steel mill mentality of sameness was creeping into his mind. He was afraid of it. He hated the wasted minds of those people worrying about nothing more important than what turn they were working or where they were going to drink their next beer. Eventually their minds would be like the Jones's house. With enough neglect, one little tap of knowledge would cause their precious high-paying jobs to change. It would cause their phony futures to collapse into a great dust cloud and become rubble. Although big money could be made in steel mills, spending one's life there would be a contagious wasting of the mind.

As the train rumbled out of the town, the crossing and the city lights faded in the distance, Breed pictured the crossing gates in his mind. They rose up like the arms of a great black and white god. The friendly, red, flashing warning lights quit flashing and turned to black and matched the color of the black iron bell that stopped clanging, and the red caboose swayed and clacked down the tracks with a steady beat. Even before the crossing gates lifted, people restarted their car engines, and all the bitching and moaning about waiting on the train would be forgotten until the next train crossed their path. But Breed didn't care about what they thought or did. He was on his way home.

He put the thoughts of the crossing behind him and relaxed to the music of the familiar sounds of riding in an open gondola. It reminded him of the camping trips to Shell Island and the slow-moving freight trains he had hopped just for the fun of it. He rubbed his eye. It felt soft and was swollen shut. Using his fingers, he forced open a tiny slit. He could see but it hurt. Now his whole body ached, and his neck was difficult to hold up. His jaw hurt when he talked, and his chest felt like it had a rock in it. The sky opened up, and a cold rain covered him in sheets. Each time the wheels on the gondola hit a rough spot in the rails, his rear end pounded on the hard-wooden floor. But the homeward feeling rose within him and he felt better.

Flick dragged the bothersome piece of scrap sheet metal over to the corner of the gondola and leaned it at a forty-five-degree angle against the wall. It was a tight fit, but they all managed to huddle under it. The rain pounded on the thin metal, and the movement of the car caused it to rub against the rusted steel wall. Like the agitating sound of a long stick of white chalk being pulled over a dry blackboard, it squeaked and squealed.

Breed looked to Screwball. His shirt had been soiled by dust and grease. Traces of chaff still sprinkled his fair hair. In one grimy hand he held the penny whistle. He lifted it to his lips but didn't blow. The rusted steel screeched again, louder. As if he had just sucked on a lemon, Screwball's face twisted grotesquely. "That sounds like a dentist drill." He looked to Breed. "Ain't that hurtin' your teeth?"

453

"I wouldn't know," Breed said. "I have never gone to a dentist."

As if he were ashamed that he had actually been fortunate enough to go to a dentist, Screwball peeped one note on the penny whistle, lowered his head, and looked away.

The sound of the rain roared in Breed's ears. The moving sheet metal squeaked, and its high pitch penetrated his head. He put his hands over his ears to make it stop. It helped, but then his stomach growled. Thoughts of food, any food, entered his mind. He thought of all the apple cores he had not eaten, and he wished he had one now. He thought about all the ends from the millions of loaves of bread that rich people always threw out in their manicured green lawns for to the birds to eat. It would be nice if just one piece of that bread could be thrown his way. He thought about the kernels of un-popped popcorn in the bottoms of all the bags of popcorn that were thrown away. He could chew on them for a long time. He thought about all the little catfish he had thrown back into the river and wondered if he could rig up some kind of fishing line and catch some now. He could build a little fire and cook them. It would be warm, and he would have something to eat. But he didn't have any bait, and he was in a gondola car. Every idea that entered his mind was shot down. The thoughts of food and how to get it haunted him. He ran his fingers through his wet hair, shivered, scrunched up next to Flick, and tried to get warm. When he looked at Screwball, he flashed him a stupid grin. It reminded Breed of that stupid baseball cap

454

Screwball had gotten from the toolbox of Mercury. If Breed had it now, it would keep his head dry. And he wondered how warm he could be wearing those dirty, greasy coveralls they had made the dummy out of, and that cabbage they used for the head. He could eat it raw.

The rain slowed and Flick spoke up. "Figuring the time it took Eddie to drive us to Buffalo, and if we're going the right way, we'll should be at the Clark Street Bridge before morning."

"Hey," Screwball said with a voice filled with sarcasm. "I thought you guys weren't ever going back home."

A wolfish grin spread across Hog's face. "Hey, that's right." As if he were collecting money, he held out his hand. "Are you guys going to pay rent to live at home?"

For a moment, in an uncomprehending daze, Flick stared at Hog. Then he moaned. "Ahh, man. I forgot about that."

Breed sat up, opened his good eye and talked with a raspy voice. "It might be better than sittin' in this cold rain and havin' a wood floor poundin' on our asses."

In a defeated tone, Hog talked out the side of his mouth. "It might be better than running around the country with nothing to eat and fightin' those drunken bums at the hobo camps."

Flick gave a sigh of resignation. "I guess we could manage to give our parents a little money and keep the lion's share for ourselves."

The car buffed toward one side. Screwball tilted, thrust out his hand, and stopped himself from falling. "That sounds too easy."

"What the hell?" Breed reluctantly said. "We must have gotten so greedy we couldn't even think to do a simple thing like that." He tried to clear his sore throat and continued with a raspy voice. "And anyway, that movie money my mother took off me should cover the rent for a little while."

Screwball twisted his head to one side and contorted the side of his face. "If money makes you stupid," he said in a tone of amusement, "I wonder if slugs do, too. If it does, and I had to pay rent, I'd wait until my parents got drunk and give them a bunch of slugs."

"I don't know if money makes you ignorant," Hog said and smiled. "But I'll take all the stupidity I can get."

"Talking about stupidity," Screwball brought up, "I wonder what happened to Eddie."

"He can't sit still for long," Breed said, his voice beginning to be entangled in phlegm. "I think he does all those crazy things just to be doing something."

Eddie's gonna be all right," Flick assured everybody. "Guys like him always survive."

Screwball leaned back and crossed his arms. "He's probably sittin' at his house watchin' television drinking a big bottle of Coke."

"Probably is," Hog said and blew a breath of fog into the cold rainy air. "And he probably stole it, too."

456

As if he had just taken a big drag off a cigarette, Screwball inhaled and blew out a long stream of fog air. "Hey, if it weren't for the cold and the rain, it would be a nice night."

Hog batted his hand down and growled. "Yeah, right."

Breed stared through the gash in the gondola's wall. The black trees morphed to gray and then to dark green. Light from civilization temporarily lit the night. It shone on Flick. He looked at his hands. They were filthy. He tried to wipe them clean on his pants. "After this sorry ass trip," he said and stared at his dirty hands. "I might even consider working in the mill."

Breed grimaced at the thought, but he didn't say anything. He couldn't. Flick's statement was a shock. After all the talk about going insane and not conforming to the pressures of working in the mill, Flick was changing his mind. He was leaning toward doing just was expected of a kid from Shitsplat. He was going to waste his life in a steel mill. He was going to join those end-of-the-line people.

Breed had been counting on Flick to be one of the first in the neighborhood to change the repetitious cycle of working in the mill. From the first encounter with the flats gang, Flick had been the one who had held them all together. He had been the leader. He had inspired others to go beyond their limitations and perform the impossible, but now, after a few hardships of the real world, he was giving up.

As if he were trying to convince himself, Hog said, "Those mill workers make a lot of money."

Screwball's usual smile was replaced with a determined smirk that bordered on cocky. "When they're not on strike, they never go hungry, and they don't have to jump trains to get anywhere."

Hog nodded in agreement. "I'll probably work in the mill. Anything has to be better than this."

Breed realized that his own desire to be something better than a common mill worker was stronger than his friends. What they had said or had done in the past didn't matter. They would be working in a mill that they would never own, and without owning big property there is no real power. At any time, the owner can tell you to get out, but no one in Shitsplat really wanted the mill life to end. For them, it an easy life. For Breed, it was a waste of life.

As he thought about the chaotic shack he was going back to, the train traveled over a stretch of uneven tracks and thumped slow and steady. It was the same beat Hank Williams had used when he sang railroad songs with his real dad. When Breed was just a little kid, his house in Stoneboro wasn't so bad. When Hank came, his dad and Hank sang and drank all night long, but there were never any arguments or fights.

The gondola hit a hard spot in the rail and pounded against Breed's rear end. It reminded him of when he had sat on Hank William's bony knees and looked up at that big white hat Hank had always worn. And he remembered that to keep his back from hurting, Hank held his shoulders back against the chair.

His mother wasn't so bad back then either. She used to smile and say, "Hey, Hank, sing 'Take a Message to My Mother.'"

Hank always had matchbooks he scribbled songs ideas onto. That had been a better time. Maybe when Breed got home, better times would come again.

The sad thought of failing to get out of Shitsplat still tugged at his mind, and he argued with himself. So what if I didn't make it on my own. The others didn't either. And they want to go back home, too. A lot of kids in Shitsplat got it wrong and never will get it right. He shuddered from the cold and tried to conserve warmth by pulling his thin jacket up over his neck. The bottom rode up and exposed the small of his back to the cold coming off the gondola's steel wall. I don't even have a decent jacket. If I would have used my brains, I would have at least left with a warm jacket. I feel like a soldier in a war without a rifle or a uniform. I can't go out in the real world without decent clothes and nothing to fight with. I'll get out of Shitsplat, but I'm going to think my way out. Paying a little bit of rent ain't gonna be no big deal. The soreness of his throat burned. But compared to the cold and wet, his throat was no big deal, either.

The thought of going home, the gentle rocking, and the clacking of the train relaxed his mind.

They all huddled together for warmth. The squeaking metal quit. The gentle to and fro of the traveling car and the warmth lulled them to sleep.

The long train traveled on. Breed awoke for a moment and off to the right, in the soft moonlight, he caught a glimpse of the old cement remnants of the Erie Extension Canal. Like old sentinels guarding a closed museum, the aged, hand-mixed brown cement of the slanted locks zipped past his tired eyes, but he noticed that there was no flash of dark water near the locks. The canal's shallow brackish water had been gone for years. It was just as well. It kept the misquotes down.

Flick coughed.

Hog and Screwball woke up, grumbled unintelligent remarks, rolled over, and went back to sleep.

Flick opened one eye. "Did we pass the canals yet?"

"Yeah," Breed said, "we just passed one."

"I wonder when they were built."

"Fourth of July, 1825."

Flick put his elbow on the floor of the car and propped his head up with his fist. "What are you a smart ass? How do you know that?"

"The canals are on the river, and anything to do with the river just sticks in my mind."

"You got something there," Flick said. "It must be the same way with me. I like cars and anything about them is easy to remember."

"I can remember things about the river that I would usually flunk on a history test."

"Like what?"

"Like the Fourth of July was the day they dug up the first spade full of dirt to start the thing, and that was in Newark, Ohio."

460

"That canal's really big and that's a lot of dirt to move with a shovel. If you know so much about it, then where did they get all those people to work on that thing?"

"They shipped in workers from Ireland, Germany, Norway, and Italy. They called them immigrant workers. They could really dig."

Hog opened his eyes. "Why don't you guys work on shuttin' up and go to sleep?"

Screwball mumbled, "If you wanna work on a canal, you gotta dig it."

Breed smiled at Screwball and moved his arms like some sort of music conductor on a roll of high notes. "They dug it all right. The canal ditch was forty feet wide but only deep enough to float canal boats."

"Some kind an animal must have floated down your throat," Hog said. "You sound like an old bullfrog."

"I wonder why they closed the canals," Flick asked.

"I wonder why you guys don't shut your mouths," Hog snapped.

Breed swallowed to clear his sore throat. It hurt, more. "The railroads were faster," he croaked. "The canals were just too slow."

Screwball mumbled in his semi-conscious sleep, "Yeah, so slow they had to speed up to stop."

"It's a good thing," Flick said. "If we were traveling on a canal boat, we'd starve to death before we got home."

"I guess you're right about that," Breed said, held his throat and closed his eyes. He thought about the canal and the workers that had toiled many years to build them. Now they were all gone. It seemed such a waste. All that work for a few years of use. Now the canals just sat there, abandoned and waterless, standing like monuments to times past. They had served their purpose, and their time had expired. Now they existed only because they were. No one thought about the significance of the canals or made plans to resurrect the man-made towers of history. Back when being President of the United States had meant something, people would glance at the canals once in a while and say, "Yep, that's the canal locks. President Garfield worked on them. Too bad he got shot in office only a year after he was elected," and be on their merry way.

Curled on their sides and pillowing their heads on their arms as best as they could, Breed and the others drifted off to sleep, slept soundly, and didn't wake up when the train rocketed past Shell Island. Breed dreamed a dirty old yellow carp jumped in the backwater. No one was camped out on the island to fish for it. The fish jumped again, anyway.

The leading locomotive slowed and sounded its horn for the crossing below Ferrona Yard. The old crossing watchman came out of his outhouse-shaped shanty, held the stop sign, and swung the red glass-globed kerosene lantern. Traffic stopped, and the train they were riding, slowly clacked right on past Ferrona Yard. The Clark Street Bridge, Breed could have walked across and gone home, was there. The spring water he could drink, was there. The watercress he could fill his empty stomach

462

with, was there. And his warm bed, had been just a short walk away. But he didn't wake up. It was just a semi-dream that was part of the fleeting scenery that vanished into the night.

The train traveled on.

When the sun arced up out of the horizon, a sudden drop in speed awoke Breed from a deep sleep. As he tried to adjust his eyes to the new morning, the train had stopped. While they had been sleeping in the haze of morning, the railroad yard crew had already started switching out the train.

"Throw this one down number nine track," a voice outside the car said and the rusted screech of a railroad car's coupler being opened pierced Breed's ears.

Then a voice commanded, "And don't be lollygagging around. I wanna get out of this rain."

By the swift rolling of the wheels, Breed knew the crew had sent the car down the track much too fast. When the speeding car coupled up, hard and solid, to the cars already on the track. Bang! Clunk! Squeal! pounded in Breed's ears. The sheet metal screeched away from him and the others, and it made his teeth hurt. The others jolted wide-awake. The wet misty dampness of the dark and cloudy day greeted their sleepy eyes. They had slept all night and well into the morning.

Flick stretched his arms out and yawned. "We must be in Feronna Yard."

Breed painfully pulled himself to a sitting position, and was amazed how his strength had been drained by the poor food, lack of rest, and the beating. He looked through the gash in the gondola's side. In the distance, as a flock of blackbirds winged irregular flight across the gray sky, the locomotive engine that had brought them, pulled away and headed for the main track. Flick pulled himself up over the edge of the car and poked his wet dirty face over the top.

Breed stood up and pulled himself up beside him. They both peered into the miserable day. Nothing looked familiar. When he realized the Clark Street Bridge could not to be seen and heavy traffic clogged the railroad crossing, dread washed through him. This was not Feronna Yard."

Almost crying, Breed asked, "Where are we?"

"I don't know," Flick said. "It ain't Feronna Yard."

Screwball put the whistle to his lips.

Flick, Breed, and Hog glared at him.

"Opps!" He lowered the whistle and slowly slipped it into his pocket.

CHAPTER 26

Peeking over the side of the car and seeing nothing familiar, Flick's voice strained to the point of crying. "Where in the hell are we?"

Breed's voice was hoarse, and when he talked, his throat painfully burned. "That chalk mark was supposed to make them take this car to Ferrona Yard," he croaked out.

"Well, we ain't there. Maybe that hobo's full a shit."

"I wouldn't doubt it," Breed said resigning that they may not have been on their way home. "With our luck we're probably in Buffalo." With his face streaked with sweat, he dropped back down into the car, sat on the wet floor, and although he felt like he had stuck his head under a faucet running with hot water, he was freezing. He reached up. With the sleeve of his shirt, he wiped his forehead. When he dropped his hand, his teeth chattered, and his whole body burned with fever.

Hog wearily sat on the floor, put his elbows on his knees, and held up his head. "It's the shit happens phenomenon. You know, Murphy's Law. If we're not in Ferrona Yard, we're gonna have to start walking again."

True to form, Screwball took the stimulating opportunity to say, "That's an interesting observation."

Before anybody could reply, a familiar sound traveled through the air. Breed wiped the sweat from his forehead, quit breathing, and listened. Gravel crunched under heavy footsteps.

Breed jerked on Flick's pant leg and whispered, "Someone's coming. Get down."

Flick dropped back down into the gondola and whispered, "Maybe it's one of those railroad bulls the hobo told us about. He could knock us in the head and leave us to die."

Breed stood up, and glued his back to wall of the gondola. With his good eye, he watched through the gash the wall.

The footsteps crunched closer.

He breathed slow and silent.

Everyone in the car was still.

They listened.

The gravel-crunching footsteps crunched up to the car and stopped.

While two men talked on the other side of the car wall, a sick feeling raged in Breed's chest. He couldn't hold his breath any longer. Trying to be quiet, he breathed shallow and hoped the men would go away.

"All these shop cars go over to NK Yard," an older voice said.

"I don't have any bills for these cars," a younger voice said. "What are they doing here?"

"Must be that drunken crew again."

"They can't even get cars into the right yard."

"I'll tell you one thing," the older man said and crisply snapped his words out. "This is the B&O not the Erie. We ain't getting per-diem on broken-down foreign cars."

Breed watched out a small hole in the car's wall. For a moment the man with the young voice came into view. When he jotted something on a stack of dog-eared manila cards he held in his hand, Breed knew he was a clerk. "We'll get them out just as soon as that switch engine gets clearance to cross over the main."

The other man laughed. "Not today. The other end of number nine's all tore up. Engine went on the ground last night."

The young clerk took a step. The gravel crunched once. He was out of Breed's sight, but Breed could hear him ask, "What about the per-diem?"

"We ain't got no bills," the older man replied. "So we won't be getting any money. That drunken crew probably doesn't even know these cars are here."

"So?" the clerk questioned. "What should I mark on the car?"

"Go ahead, back up—"

Before the older man could finish, the clerk, shot back, "Don't be pullin' that go ahead, back up shit on me, again."

The older man chuckled. "Take it easy young fellow. Just to teach them a lesson, I'm gonna send these cars back to Buffalo. Go ahead, back up and mark the car."

Breed's heart stopped. If they stayed in the car, they would end up back in Buffalo. He bent his head closer to the gash in the car wall. The crunching gravel sounded, again. He caught a glimpse of the railroad clerk just outside the wall.

He jerked back.

The older man and the clerk stopped.

The clerk chalked the car to go to Buffalo and took a few steps.

Breed bent to the gash and watched.

Walking, the clerk and the older man studied lines of penciled car numbers on stacks of manila switching cards they held in their hands.

The clerk stopped, looked at the numbers on the card at the top of the stack, and made a few marks with his stubby yellow pencil. "I don't know why they made two yards so close together," he said and erased something on the card. "The city of Youngstown has enough room for two railroads. Why do they have to jam them together and cause all these mix ups?"

The older man laughed and replied, "Don't worry about it, young fellow." He patted him on the back. "That's what I get the big money for."

The clerk shook his head, put the cards in his back pocket, and walked up the tracks. "May I ask how am I supposed to get broke in if you guys don't tell me anything?"

The older man laughed. "Yes, you may," he replied and simply walked away.

To keep from laughing out loud, Screwball put his hand over his mouth. The sound of gravel crunching under the clerks' feet grew faint.

"Youngstown!" Flick whispered. "Hot dam, the old hobo was almost right. We're only about sixteen miles away. If we get home before dark, we might be able to pull off some sort of bullshit story about hopping a freight and getting lost."

468

Grinning, Screwball bobbed his head. "Yeah, we could say we just spent sixteen miles on the Erie Canal."

Flick ignored Screwball's attempted humor. "After those clerks get out of sight, we can get out of this car and find one that's going to Ferrona. We could still be back in time to go to school in the morning."

"Yeah," Hog said, "that's if the cops ain't already waiting for us when we get there."

"The cops don't know nothin' about Buffalo," Breed said to make Hog feel better, but he didn't know if it were true.

"Just how do you know that? And what about the guy that got stabbed with a stick?" Hog wanted to know.

"Buffalo's too far away. And that drunken guy only got stabbed in the stomach. He should be okay," Breed reasoned, "and Eddie has some kind of oath with his family that he will never tell the cops anything."

"Just as long as we don't tell anybody anything about being near Buffalo," Flick said, "they won't tie us in with Eddie and the stolen Merc."

Hog crossed his arms and leaned against the car wall. "I wonder if Eddie's in jail."

"Heck no," Breed said. "His old man bought the cops off just like he did with those gambling tickets."

"That's right," Flick said, "guys like Eddie always come out on top."

As if he were holding a bottle of pop, Screwball curled his hand. "He's probably out in his garage

469

holding a Coke in his good hand and thinking about working on some kind of monster go-kart after his other hand gets better."

"We're almost home"," Flick's said and his face brightened. "Before the day's over, we'll be eatin' and drinkin', too."

As if he were checking the time on a wristwatch, Screwball lifted his arm and looked at his bare wrist. Then with a taunting grin plastered on his face, he said, "We got a lotta time. You guys wanna stay here and wait for them to switch this car and go back to Buffalo?"

"You should go back," Hog said. "I think you left your brain there."

Now that Breed knew where they were, he felt a little better. But that sick feeling was still in his chest, making it difficult to breathe. The thought that they were finally going home and the cops wouldn't be waiting for them, made him believe everything was going to be all right.

A flock of pigeons flew down and landed on the edge of the gondola.

"Hey, Breed," Flick whispered. "My stomach feels like it's touching my backbone. Maybe we can catch one of those pigeons and eat it."

The sick feeling in Breed's chest subsided. "Mine too," he said and breathed easier. "Maybe we could eat it raw or something."

The pigeons didn't move. They just sat on the edge of the car wall above Breed's and Flick's heads. Then one pigeon dropped fresh crap onto the wet wooden floor in front of Breed's feet. Then another pigeon took flight and crapped just above

Flick. The fresh crap landed on Flick's foot. Breed looked at him. He shook his head and said out loud, "If I ain't steppin' in dog shit, it's pigeon shit from the air. What am I, a shit magnet?"

Breed tried to smile. This would have been a good time to say, "Hant," or "That's an interesting observation," but he couldn't manage it.

Screwball flicked the end of his foot into the air. "That's an interesting observation."

Scowling, Flick tried to wipe his shoe on the wet side of the car. The white pigeon crap didn't come off. He looked up at the remaining pigeons. "I won't be eating those birds."

Breed's stomach growled with hunger, and the sight of that pigeon crap didn't help. He looked away from the pigeons. "Me neither."

In warm friendship of being together in misfortune, Flick put his arm around Breed's shoulder. "Hey, Breed, cheer up. When we get to Ferrona we can get a good drink of that spring water at the end of the yard. We know where the watercress is. On the way home, we could munch on it."

"That sounds good, but first, we have to find the right car to get there."

"Maybe we can find one that doesn't stink so bad," Hog said.

"Yeah," Screwball said and wrinkled his nose, "this one smells like something died and is floating around our noses while it rots away. Maybe it's an invisible ghost of shit."

471

"We're probably sittin' on top of a pile of guts from a gut car," Flick said, poked his head over the car, and scanned the area.

Breed sat on the wet, wooden floor and looked up. "Do you see anything?"

Flick looked back and talked down. "The clerks are gone," he said. "But I can't see any marks from here. There's more cars across the way."

Trying to get rid of the obnoxious gut car odor, Screwball waved his hand in front of his face. "Let's get away from this ghost of shit."

Hog reached up and put his hand on the top of the gondola wall. "Let's get out go over where those cars are lined up on the other track. If we get closer, we might be able to see chalk marks."

Flick looked toward the yard office. The door opened. A gang of men with picks, shovels, and bars came out and paraded toward a section of ripped up track. "There's a track gang workin' on the tracks. They might see us."

Breed stood up. "That won't matter. We'll just walk slow like they do."

"Right!" Screwball said. "Then we can hide in plain sight."

Frustrated at Screwballs remark, Flick smacked his hand against the side of the car. "What?"

Imitating a tired railroad worker, Screwball drooped his shoulders. "If we hunch over and walk slow, like we're getting paid by the hour, they'll think we work here."

Flick grinned at Screwball. "That's so stupid, it just might work."

472

Screwball looked at Breed's swollen eye. "I don't know, Breed, if they see your eye, they might think you're a pirate."

Breed playfully pushed Screwball toward the wall of the gondola. "Just get your ass up over that wall."

They climbed out of the gondola, kept quiet, hunched, and walking as each step was their last, they slowly walked over the rails.

As few track gang workers watched them make their way across the tracks, Breed realized that his friends' and his ragged clothes weren't the type of clothes railroad workers wore. Breed's and his friends' clothes looked like kid's clothes. They were kid's clothes. Kids were wearing them. There was no way Screwball's plan was going to work.

But the track gang wasn't paying any attention to them. Just when Breed figured they had fooled the track gang, Hog turned and shouted at one of the track gang members that had a long nose. "Hey, Hook Nose, I'll bet you can smoke a king-size cigarette in the rain without getting it wet."

Hook Nose stopped digging around a switch stand, looked up, and leaned on his shovel. With a sweat-drenched expression of triumph, he said, "That looks like the kids that came down off the hill and stole our gas yesterday."

Flick kept looking forward. "Goddamn it, Hog, what did you have to do that for?"

"They're too slow to catch us. We need a little excitement."

473

Shaking his head, Flick said, "Keep it slow and easy. If we look like we're not in a hurry, maybe we can get away."

Not to be outdone by Hog, Screwball jumped into a puddle of water, and splashed Hog.

"Thanks a lot, Turd," Hog snapped.

Screwball smiled big. "Grin and try to look happy." Then he placed the penny whistle to his lips, pointed it at Hook Nose, and blew. "Cuck-oo! Cuck-oo! Cuck-oo!"

A worker threw his shovel down into the creosote soaked lifeless dirt. "I ain't fillin' my tank up for them to steal. Let's get those thievin', smart ass bastards and kick their asses."

A bent over worker straightened up and growled. "Those lazy ass cops won't do a damn thing to stop those slum kids," he vehemently bitched. "They're over there fuckin' around blowin' a goddamn whistle while we're sweating our asses off. Let's get 'em."

Screwball pointed the whistle at the complaining man and blew a string of Cuck-oos.

"Yeah!" Another worker said and thrust his fist toward Screwball. "Let's shove that whistle up his ass."

Hook Nose snapped his head sideways, sucked air into his snot-running, hooked nose, and threw his shovel onto the steel pile of rails. It clanked once and then pinged metallic sounds into the air. "We can put an end to that shit right now," he said as if it would be the end of all their problems.

474

A worker, holding a crowbar, shook it in the air and yelled across the yard. "Hey, you cock suckers, come back here!"

Screwball turned around and yelled back, "But we're tryin' to quit." Cuck-oo!

For a moment Hook Nose stared in wonder at the stupidity of Screwball's remark. "Tryin' to quit, my ass," he said and started after Breed and the others. "I'll take the price of my gas out of their asses."

The crowbar-holding worker ran behind him.

When Flick turned and looked, Hook Nose was coming at them and fast.

Flick shouted at him, "We didn't do nothin'."

Hook Nose kept on coming and yelled, "Stop right there!"

"I'm sick of assholes blaming us for shit we didn't do," Hog said and yelled back, "Hey dip shit. Fuck off!"

Not to be left out, Screwball chimed in, "You know what you can do?"

After Hook Nose's face filled with confusion, Hog shouted to him, "Go fuck yourself."

Cuck-oo!

An eerie feeling crawled up Breed's back. He looked to Flick. "Now what?"

"Whatever they were bitchin' about, it's worse now. I ain't stickin' around." He took off running over the many tracks that ran across the huge switching yard, and Breed and the others took off right behind him. Breed tried to keep up but lagged behind. After a few quick steps, he grabbed his painful chest and slowed even more. The workers were close. A departing train's big diesel engines panted like some kind of gigantic dog, and the long string of cars behind it, gained speed. Breed didn't know where the moving train was going, and it was blocking their escape.

"Jump on," Flick said. "It doesn't matter where it's going."

Flick slowed down. Hog and Screwball ran toward the car. Breed caught up to Flick. "Come on, Breed," Flick huffed, "don't let those assholes get you. We can catch it."

Breed ran faster and the string of cars picked up more speed. Strong diesel engines sucked fuel into bad injectors and made the upstroke on the combustion cycle blow black smoke out the stacks. The powerful wheels spun and lost traction. The engineer hit the sanding lever. In front of the massive steel wheels of the engine, dry sand blew onto the tracks. Now the wheels bit against the fresh sanded rails and gained traction. The long train was pulling out of the yard.

Breed and the others sprinted after it. The whole track gang was directly behind them.

The train was leaving.

They hadn't caught it.

Gasping for breath, Breed talked out loud. "Those guys, huff—, look really pissed off, huff—, huff—. What did we do?"

Flick inhaled deep. "I don't know, huff—, huff—, and I don't care."

"They ain't gonna catch me," Screwball said, dashed to the open door of a boxcar, and drove in.

"Me neither," Hog said, put his arm on the floor of the boxcar, and swung inside."

Flick's adrenaline must have kicked in. He increased speed and gained on the fleeing train. Breed tried to force his aching legs to move faster.

They wouldn't.

He fell behind.

The stampeding workers were too slow to catch Flick, but Breed didn't know how close they were to him. He forced his swollen eye open and looked back. If they were close behind, they were screened by heavy brush. He couldn't see them. Just as he slowed, Hook Nose was behind him sucking snot. Air from the man's hand grasp at Breed's back. Breed's heart pounded painfully, and his throat was on fire. Flick dove into the boxcar, rolled once, and sat in the doorway. Cold mists of oxygen-depleted air, blasted from Breed's mouth.

"Come back here, you black-headed bastard!" Hook Nose screamed.

Breed forced himself to go faster. He got close to the open door and wanted to quit. He looked on the side of the car. In fresh yellow chalk on the car's damaged side was marked, SHOP, FERRONA YARD. Something was finally going right. If he could pull himself into the car, he would be going home.

Flick stood in the doorway. His hand was stretched out for Breed to catch onto. "Come on, Breed. You're almost here."

Breed reached down into his soul and forced one final burst of energy into his legs. He caught up to the moving car and swiped at Flick's outstretched hand. It would have been a solid catch, but Hook Nose ran up behind Breed and grabbed the back of his shirt and pulled. The slowing effect caused Breed to miss. But he kept on running. And Hook Nose kept on hanging on to the back of Breed's shirt.

From deep in his throat, Flick forced up a hawker and spit it into his own hand. Then he raised his hawker-filled hand and cocked it back. "Here's a treat for your trick or treat face." With one flicking motion, Flick flicked the hawker with marksman accuracy. It flew off the ends of his fingers, sailed through the air, and splat on that hooked nose.

Surprised, Hook Nose released his grip on Breed's shirt and grabbed at his hawkered nose.

Breed's heart pounded in his ears. With each thump, it sent pain throughout his body, but he forced the pain out of his entire being. Flick was hanging onto the side of the box car with one hand and leaning out with his other hand stretched to the limit, waiting. Breed slapped Flick's palm and grasp his thumb in a tight grip. Flick held on. With his legs making great strides, Breed loped alongside of the moving boxcar.

Flick gripped his hand tighter. "Jump on," he screamed.

Breed added his strength to Flick's and sucked in a determined breath of much-needed air. He leaped and pulled. Flick pulled, too. Breed landed on the edge of the open boxcar floor. With his feet hanging over the edge, he stopped for just a second, and reached up and held onto his throbbing chest.

He was safe, and it looked like the workers had given up.

Now he could rest.

But wait!

Hook Nose regained his footing, reached into the car, and just missed Breed's pant leg. If he got it on his next try, Breed would be pulled out onto the hard ballast stones. He might even get sucked under the moving wheels of the train. He tried to move away from the hand. For some reason his arms and legs were useless. Nothing worked.

He tried to crawl into the boxcar and get away from Hook Nose's swiping hands. But he still couldn't move. He wondered why the hooked nose bastard wouldn't give up. If Hook Nose got close enough, he would jump into the boxcar and pull him out.

What's the use? Breed thought. I can't even see. I'm caught. Then out the corner of his good eye, something came up fast. It was a switch stand. The very thing the hobo had said would rip a man's legs right off. Hook Nose grabbed Breed's leg, and pulled it out of the car. He placed his arm on the edge of the car and still running alongside the car, he was trying to keep a hand on Breed's leg and pull. But his running legs were right in line with the switch stand. The green and red metal arrow, on top of the switch stand, waited like a mad butcher's meat cleaver. Breed tensed and waited for Hook Nose's leg to be sliced off.

But Hook Nose didn't see a scrap railroad car brake shoe that was right in his path. The toe of his work-boot caught it. He let loose of Breed's leg and tried to catch his balance. But it was too late. Just before the switch stand, he fell to the wet ground, cussing. His hands skidded and scraped across the black oil-soaked gravel until he stopped in a push-up position with his head up watching Breed ride away.

Breed swung his foot away from the switch stand. The train increased speed, and Flick, Hog, and Screwball pulled Breed into the boxcar.

Hook Nose stood up. With his eyes crossed and looking over his hawkered hook nose, he examined his hands. They were scraped and bloody. "Goddamn it!"

"Hant!" Hog taunted and Screwball blew, Cuck-oo! Cuck-oo! Cuck-oo!

"Cuck-oo, my ass," Hook Nose said and yelled back to the other workers, "Call the yard office! Tell them to radio that train to stop!"

"Let them go," the track gang leader said and laughed. "Maybe that'll teach the little bastards a lesson when they have to walk all the way back home from Ferrona Yard. And by the way, Hook, wasn't you supposed to pick up that scrap brake shoe last week?"

Hook Nose wiped his nose and started to speak. The leader cut him off. "Goddamn it! I told you somebody might trip over it."

Off Breed and his friends rode. Beneath them an eerie flap and clack of the steel wheels rolling over the shiny rails, filled the car like the applause of old hobo ghosts.

No one talked. They were transported across the city of Youngstown and then clicked past the

480

rotten egg smell of a foundry, then on down the line, swaying and bumping through the stainless-steel world of the production steel mills and over the railroad trestle that crossed the smoky Mahoney River, a lifeless strip of liquid polluted by heavy black oil that would catch fire and burn. Then they lumbered around the bend and passed a steel finishing building just in time to breath in the harsh abrasive grinding yard particles that filled the boxcar. When they continued on into the suburban air that hovered above the poisoned river, where fish couldn't live, they picked up more speed and the rocking car became smooth. The boxcar's wheels clacked past a stamping plant, where heavy blows from metal, being forged into one-piece shapes, thumped at the car's walls. After the train burst through the stink, smoke, fumes, and fine mist, fresh, green country air filled the car.

Breed inhaled, tilted his head back, and watched out the open boxcar door. Like moving fingers in front of a television screen, trees fluttered past. With the to and fro easy rolling rhythm of the advancing train, he breathed slow and deep. That awful smell from his dream wafted into his nose. He picked up his right leg and sniffed it. It smelled bad, rotten bad.

Screwball looked at Breed and held his nose. "Goddamn gut car."

"That hobo warned us about those invisible stinkin' guts," Breed said. "That rotten smell was on my foot when we left Buffalo, and now it's there again."

"Maybe it likes you," Screwball teased.

Breed waved his hand over his leg and tried to fan the smell away. "I thought I had it washed off when we went into the water, but I must've stepped in some more."

"What are you bitchin' about?" Hog asked, arching an eyebrow as if surprised. "You're getting' a free ride."

"That's an interesting observation," Screwball added. "Hant! Enjoy it while you can."

"Hey, Screwball," Flick said, "that stink should be on your foot, too. When you run, you look like you're trying to shake dog shit off your foot."

Sounding like he was tired of the conversation, Hog growled, "Why don't you guys just blow it out your ass."

Screwball contorted his face and wrinkled his nose. "It smells like Breed already did."

Making a face, Flick moved away from Breed. "That stuff's really bad. It's stinkin' up the whole car"

"What pisses me off," Breed said, "is you can't see it."

A flash of amusement flashed across Screwball's face. "If you could see it, it wouldn't smell bad at all."

"What the hell's the matter with you," Hog snapped. "It doesn't matter if you can see it or not, it still stinks worse than shit."

Screwball raised his hand and shook it in a negative wave. "No, no, no. It only smells that way for the benefit of the people who can't see it."

As if dumbfounded, Hog and Screwball exchanged glances, but didn't say anything.

As the train continued on down the line, Screwball and Hog backed away from the odor.

Hog looked to Flick. "You know what?"

"What?" Flick answered with agitation in his voice.

Waving his hand in front of his face, Hog, said, "You wanna know what I did to that usher that kicked me in the ribs?"

"Remind me about. Later," Flick answered as if he no longer wanted to know.

The gut smell reminds me of how I shit in a box, wrapped it up, and sent it to the usher's house."

Flick's face wrinkled with puzzlement. "You can't send shit in the mail."

"I did, and I hid in the bushes and watched. After he opened it, I yelled, 'Hant!'" He snorted. "The kid thought he was really getting something good. You should've seen his face." He let out a big horse laugh and let it trail off. "Teach that asshole to kick me in the ribs."

Breed could picture the look on the kid's face, but it no longer seemed important or funny. He smiled a faint smile, and held his stinking foot as far away from his body as he could. His arms ached like a toothache, and his legs had gone limp. He swallowed painfully and surrendered to sleep.

A loud heavy, Bang! cracked the afternoon's silence and rumbled throughout the switching yard. Flick was knocked across the boxcar floor. His thumb bent back and the joint popped. Holding the ailing thumb, he stood up and pushed the protruding bone of the joint. It popped back into place with a dull cartilage clunk. He grimaced. "Damn that hurts." Shaking his hand, he walked to the open door.

Every move Breed made was impaired with pain. If they weren't home, he didn't want to waste energy and go through the pain of getting up, grabbing the edge of the car, and looking out only to be surprised with the continuing irritation of not being home. He breathed in deep breaths, lay on the floor, and looked up. "Hey, Flick, where are we this time?"

"It looks familiar," Flick said with enthusiasm. "I think we made it."

Breed sat up, and through his red-rimmed eye, he looked out the door. The old railroad phone Flick had used last summer to agitate the old grouchy yardmaster was right outside the boxcar door. In the distance, the top of the Clark Street Bridge stood like a tall "Welcome Home" monument.

Breed breathed deeply. Although the air stank of diesel fumes, he was glad to be alive.

They were home.

Looking drawn and exhausted, they jumped out of the boxcar, and like zombies, they slowly walked across the familiar switching yard. But they didn't do what they had said they would do. They didn't stop for the drink of spring water, and they didn't stop and get watercress to munch on the way home.

After the excitement of finally being home began to wear off, Breed was down to a hobble, weakening by the minute. With each agonizing step he took, his chest and legs felt like they were on fire. Just before he got to the path that led to the bridge, he tripped over an old brake shoe and fell. He caught his fall with his hands. They were torn by the gravel, but he got up and kept walking. At the beginning of the bridge, he stopped and leaned against the slanted I-beam. With the rotten gut car smell wafting up from his foot, he looked toward home. Screwball ran ahead and stopped in the middle of the catwalk. Making his simpleton face, he put the penny whistle to his lips and blew a long string of Cuck-oos!

Flick and Hog looked at each other. "At least we won't have to put up with his crumby jokes every day," Hog said. Then they caught up to Screwball, ran across the bridge, and kept on going.

Although Breed knew for his own good, he had to go home, he wasn't too keen on the idea. He lowered his body, crouched to rest, and decide what else he could do.

But his decision was interrupted. The Wart-faced kid, that drove the pink Ford, walked onto the bridge and stopped in front of Breed. Breed knew a person's wind was better on an empty stomach. Being that his stomach was as empty as it was going to get, he figured if the kid started something, the empty stomach might be an advantage. Staying crouched low, he looked up. Again, the ugly grin stretched across the beady-eyed kid's face. Then he clenched his fists and blasting his bad breath, he yelled, "Hey, you one-eyed freak."

Breed didn't answer. To avoid the kid's bad breath that was worse than the gut car odor, he lowered his head and looked at his cut and blood-streaked hands. The uncut, unscratched parts were caked with the black powdery dirt from the grab irons of the gondola. And then he noticed his clothes. They were torn, spotted, and striped with railroad dirt and grease.

"Hey!" the kid said in a menacing tone. "I'm talkin' to you!"

With his eyes burning from lack of sleep, Breed looked up.

The kid looked right into Breed's face. "What's your filthy ass doing on *my* bridge?"

The kid's words struck Breed's heart like a sharp knife. He was in worse shape than he had been after his mother had beaten him, and he wanted to slink away just like he had done the last time.

But then he wondered how he would ever adjust to being forced off the bridge he had come to know quite well over the years. Suddenly the kid wanting to make changes that would keep Breed off the bridge became an encroachment upon something private and familiar. The old bridge become very dear. He realized how far into the terrible depths of despair he had allowed himself to be plunged. He had been weak and wrong. There was something that had guided him back to the bridge. He needed to teach himself he could be a man of strength. He knew he should be afraid. But when he thought about what he'd just been through, he no longer felt fear. Not only did his body feel like an iron-hard frame, an exhilaration, like an athlete entering the fray, filled his entire being. This wart-faced kid became a bothersome fly that needed to be swatted away.

The kid backed up and stood, shaking his clenched fists in anticipation. "This time, your wise ass friends ain't here. Come and get it."

Breed never liked leaving something unfinished. Now, his vision of a lost opportunity had come back. He hadn't sought a victory before, and he wasn't going to wait for this opportunity to pass. He did not hesitate. He jerked away from the I-beam, came up out of his crouch, and so he could get inside of the kid's punching range, he took a long stride forward, and came up face-to-face with the kid. In spite of his sore throat and swollen eye, he blasted the words right into the kid's face. "Hey! You penis-breathed cock sucker. If you don't fuck off, I'll beat that ugly ass wart off your shit face!"

The kid smiled a cocky smile, "Is that a threat?"

"That's fact," Breed spat out, and before the kid could react, Breed reached up with both hands and grabbed the kid by the front of the shirt. With sizzling speed, he viciously slammed the kid back against the bridge I-beam.

Klunk! The kid's head slammed against the solid steel.

He let out a high-pitched yelp, lifted his hand to his head, and held it there. As the kid stared in surprise, Breed's new speed and strength surprised himself even more. When he looked at his hands, they were bleeding. The force of grabbing the kid's shirt had opened the cuts, but he felt pity for the defenseless kid. As if they were dangerous weapons, he lowered his bloody hands. And the

487

front of the kid's shirt was marked with blood from Breed's hands.

Then Breed turned his head, until, with his good eye, he could look into the kid's face. His facial expression had changed from bully to whipped pup. The way Breed saw it, it was over. He turned and started walking away, but the kid looked at the blood on his shirt and got over his feeling of being whipped.

Apparently believing Breed's cut hands would make him an easy target, the kid bucked up, and started toward him. For a moment Breed thought about running. He knew his throat was raw and burning, but he no longer felt it. His mind became focused on the kid. A new confidence and maturity surged throughout his body. He had seen other kids change when they had come back from basic training in the army or an overseas tour of duty. He felt he had changed, too.

The wart-faced kid called after him. "Where do you think you're going?"

Breed kept walking. This kid was a foot taller than Breed but Breed felt big. He remembered how the kid had waited for him to turn, punched him in the back, and laughed about it. Breed stopped, walked back to the kid, stood a few feet from him, and just stared.

Compared to the freedom Breed had had, and the places he'd been, the kid looked inferior. He was nothin'. He hadn't change one bit. Breed wondered how anyone could not change. The kid would be doing the same thing until he was buried in some Shitsplat cemetery. Breed could find no reason why he should be afraid of someone like this kid.

The kid's anger intensified. "I asked you a question."

Breed didn't answer. Stepping toward the kid, the bottom of Breed's burnt shoe scraped on the steel grating of the bridge. He looked down at his ruined shoes and thought, This is the rotten kid that pushed me over the edge. He's the one that made me mad enough to take off with Eddie. If it weren't for his smart mouth, my new shoes wouldn't be burnt and ruined. Maybe it's my fault, too. I went right along with the others and came back here just like some candy-ass baby who couldn't make it on his own. This wart-faced kid makes no sense. Why was I so afraid of him? The kid's trapped in an artificial world. He's never been anywhere. He never needed to get tough.

Rolling his shoulders and arms like a prizefighter loosening up, the kid stood as if he were a big star in a movie. Then with a face filled with hate, he cocked his arm to throw a punch. "You better start runnin'."

Breed knew the kid, like so many others, had made the mistake of judging others by comparing them to himself. The kid was afraid to face Breed and fight. Just like before, he wanted Breed to run so he could hit him in the back.

Breed didn't move. All of a sudden, he knew he didn't have to run from anything. Running away was no longer a necessary habit of existence. He didn't have to walk on those railroad tracks forever looking for a better place to live. Shitsplat people were the same as people living any place. It didn't matter how good a person was or if a person could sing like Buddy Holly, there were evil people everywhere. If someone didn't show them they couldn't get away with it, they would kill the good of the earth. Breed felt a new power. He felt above it all. Now he knew he could change anything that needed to be changed. And he was going to start right now.

He cocked his head and felt his forehead wrinkle. Pain shot into his swollen-shut eye. With his good eye, he continued to search the kid's face.

Although serious distress filled his face, the kid didn't flinch. He drew his fist back to throw a punch and held it. "I'm warning you."

Breed didn't wait to be hit. He planted his feet. In a blur of speed, his fists lashed out. The viciousness of multiple punches caused the kid to lose his balance and stutter-step to the side. The kid managed to rear back and swing. Breed ducked under it, and angling up to come in right under the kid's ribs, he punched him hard. In immediate agony, the kid doubled up and leaned forward. Before he fell, Breed used his gondola grime-covered hand to reach over and hold the kid by the front of the shirt. His grip was so strong that the kid's shirt ripped and buttons flew off. Breed looked at the big black wart on the side of the kid's bleeding face.

The kid dropped his threatening fist. "Get off me," he cried and tried to shake free.

Breed tightened the grip on the kid's shirt. Usually he would have yelled right back. But now

490

he felt different. Now his words weren't the winy words of a child, he would have uttered before he had left. Now his words were filled with the calm confidence of someone who was absolutely sure he could do what he says. They were overpowering. He was a new man. "I should throw you in the river." He glanced to the water below, and slammed the kid against the catwalk railing. "Throw you in, let a big carp suck that third eye off your ugly face."

The kid looked sideways at the water and cringed.

Breed released his grip.

The kid straightened up, lifted his hand, and touched the wart on his face that Breed had called a third eye.

Breed held his cold-eyed stare.

The kid opened his mouth to say something but turned and reached for a rock that had been placed on the catwalk of the bridge. Before he could pick it up, Breed dropped down, grabbed the kid's ankles, and at the same time he rammed his shoulders into the fronts of the kid's knees and jerked the ankles back.

The kid flew backwards.

Crack! The back of his head slammed on the steel railing catwalk of the bridge. Almost falling over, he shook his head, then crouched low, and slowly reached for the rock.

Before he could touch it, Breed wound up plowed his fist into the kids nose.

The kid slumped until he was sitting on the bridge. With blood flowing from his broken nose, he grabbed the rock, again. "When I get up, you're a dead man."

Breed's good eye flared up with fiery disdain. "Go ahead," he encouraged. "You'll get more than a broken nose."

The kid's nostrils flared. His breath came in short huffs, and his face paled with resignation. He slowly withdrew his hand from the rock and struggled to his feet. He began to lift his hand to strike, but his shoulders abruptly sagged, and he let his hand fall to his side. With tears flowing from his eyes and a nasal sound to his voice, he whined, "You don't play fair." Then he placed his hand on his bloody nose, got to his feet, turned, and whimpered away.

Breed sat down on the cold steel catwalk of the bridge and held his head in his hands. The gut car odor from his shoe rose up and invaded the good air in front of his face. When he turned to get a breath of fresh river air, somewhere down the street, a loud motor backfired and whacked its exhaust noise into the air. Breed raised his head and listened. The familiar sound grew louder. He wondered if Eddie had escaped or his old man had bought the cops off. Maybe he was driving some new contraption he had built.

The roar of the loud motor approached the bridge. A car with a blown-out muffler blatted across the steel grating of the bridge and disappeared.

As he sat there, Breed felt a slight vibration, signaling someone was walking on the bridge. Figuring the kid had come back, Breed heaved himself to his feet, looked in the direction the kid had gone, and shifted his stance to face him full on.

When Breed didn't see the kid, he turned to his right. The odor of gut car guts wafted into his face. Flick had come back, and he had stepped into a pile of guts, too.

Relieved, Breed sank down and sat back down. Even though the gut car odor was overwhelming, Flick knelt on one knee in front of him. To Breed's surprise, a couple of unmistakable tear tracks were running down Flick's cheeks. He sleeved them away and placed his hand on Breed's shoulder. "Did that punk try to start something?"

"Yeah, but I wasn't in the mood."

"You don't look so good."

"I feel pretty bad."

Flick grabbed Breed around the waist, and they hobbled to the end of the bridge. Breed felt like he was going to die. "Let me take a rest."

They stopped and Breed sat on the familiar railing.

Concerned, Flick stood beside him. "Don't die on me, Breed. We made it this far. We can make it home."

Breed caught his breath and looked into the river of liquid understanding. It seemed to say, "Welcome Back." And it made him feel a little better, but every joint and muscle in his body hurt, and it was hard to move anything without extreme pain. He wanted to sit on the railing longer, but he could be home in a few minutes, and he knew Flick was just as hungry and tired as he was. He didn't want to be a crybaby and make Flick wait for him.

Ignoring the pain, he stood up. His words came out between wheezes of agony. "We ain't even got a mile to go. Let's get movin'." He put his arm around Flick's shoulder, and together they hobbled off the bridge.

"At least the cops didn't catch us," Flick said with joyful relief.

A hollow whirl echoed across the broad reach of the river and came up behind them. Breed and Flick spun around. A cop car with its red lights spinning and its siren whirring, passed them, pulled to the side of the road, and stopped right in front of them. It was the cop that had chased Eddie and the go-kart, and after Eddie had sailed into the river, the cop had pointed at Eddie and said, "Dumb shit."

As if he were about to cry, Flick trembled and lowered his head. "I think they got us."

Breed stared at Flick. He hadn't noticed it before, but white crusts had formed in the corners of his eyes. Now, his eyes that had always been bright green were dim. Black railroad gondola filth that would never come out, spotted his clothes. Breed looked down. Flick's shoes were worn past the color, and the raw leather seemed thin and useless. Resting on the tops of his gut car-stinking shoes, the bottoms of his pants legs were frayed and ripped up one side. When Flick turned his hands over, the gripping surfaces of his fingers seemed to be a permanent rusty color. These were the same fingers that had helped Eddie steal the Mercury, the same fingers that had made it all the way to Buffalo, the same fingers he had had when he had dodged the cops, ducked bullets, hopped gondolas, walked for miles, and drifted down streams and rivers. It all seemed like a cruel joke. To make matters worse, the cop was going to throw them into a stinking Shitsplat jail.

Shaking with cold and exhaustion, Breed whispered to Flick, "I don't really know if I want to go home. I feel like I ain't got no place to go. I'll stay here. Take off. I'll pretend I'm sick. It'll keep the cop busy."

Flick flexed to run but relaxed. "You don't have to pretend."

The siren whirred down to silence. Like a vulture, the cop hunched over the steering wheel. He looked in Breed's direction, dropped his hands, opened the door, and placed one foot on the pavement. "Come here, son," he said in a non-threatening voice.

Breed couldn't believe it. One of the unwritten rules of status conduct is that when confronting someone inferior to you, you do not talk or answer any questions or show concern. You just turn, walk away, or ignore them. But this cop was actually showing concern. Moving with the shuffling gait of an old man, Breed turned and walked to the door. "Yes, Officer?"

The officer arched his eyebrows in surprise and slowly shook his head. "Where the hell have you boys been?"

Flick hesitated, but spoke. "Ahh, sir, we got lost and hopped a train."

The cop got out, opened the back door, and looking at Breed, he stood still and held onto the door. "Did you get thrown off the train?"

Breed managed a weak smile. "Almost."

Shaking his head, the cop lifted his arm and gestured to the inside of the car. "Get in. I'll give you boys a ride home."

Breed hobbled to the back of the car and slumped down into the seat. Flick shuffled around the other side and hopped in. The cop drove away from the bridge, but he kept a wary eye on them through the rearview mirror. "In your travels, did you boys happen to see a customized red Mercury?"

Not only was Breed's throat swollen and dry, it was constricted and felt like someone was choking him. Not wanting to painfully speak, he looked toward Flick.

"We didn't see too much of anything, officer. We were on the railroad most of the time."

A suspicious look came across the cop's face. "That's not what I heard," he said, and then the gut car smell engulfed the car. The officer's face grimaced, and he breathed in shallow breaths.

The interrogation stopped.

He rolled down the window.

When he stopped in front of Breed's shack and set the cruiser's emergency brake, the dirty-white picket fence was still there. The shack was still there. But the whole setting looked smaller, unimportant. It no longer lurked like a monster of sadness. Now it seemed tame. Breed had come to realize that life was all about his own stupidity. Any problem it could muster up against him would be trivial. His throat was on fire, and his joints reeked with pain, but he felt strong inside. There was nothing he couldn't conquer.

The cop looked back over the seat. "I'm not saying you had anything to do with that the red Mercury or a lot of other illegal things, but because of the little adventure you have been through, I'll make you a deal."

Breed squirmed in the seat. "What?"

The cop grinned at them with scornful satisfaction. "You can join the army or go to jail."

Breed figured joining the army wouldn't be nothing compared to what he they had already been through. The only problem was that even though they both looked old enough to join, they weren't. Nodding in fake amazement, Breed and Flick accepted the deal they couldn't keep.

The cop looked to Breed. "Okay, son, get out. I'll take your friend home."

Breed knew it was an old cop trick. Separate the two suspects then they'll mix up the stories. Say the other one has already told the truth. He didn't want the cop to get Flick alone. Trying to convince the cop that he was sicker than he was, he coughed and held his hands over his face.

Flick leaned forward. "He's pretty sick, Officer. I'll get out here and help him into the house."

A look of pity came over the cop's face. "You sure you can make it?"

Breed bucked up and put on a cheery face. "Yes, Officer, it must have been somethin' I ate." But he thought, Something I didn't eat.

Flick jumped out, ran around the cruiser, opened the door, and helped Breed out.

Now that the car wasn't moving, the gut car smell hovered in the car. The cop held his breath, reached over, and keyed his microphone. With his head out the window, he reached down and took the emergency brake off. Between huffing the bad taste out of his lungs, he quickly said, "Shut that door. And make damn sure you get to the army recruiter."

Flick slammed the door. Then, scarcely loud enough to hear, the cop laughed gloatingly. "Dumb invincible shits."

The cop car blew away in a gust of speed. Breed figured Eddie's father had paid the cop off, or just like when Eddie had been stupid enough to fly into the river on his go-kart, the cop figured they had learned their lesson.

Flick helped Breed across the road. They hobbled to the front of the shack and sat on the ground. They were in front of the dirty-white picket fence, where it had all started, but this time they knew they could stop the looks of not being wanted and not being welcome because they were different. All they had to do was make money."

As the unbelievable details of the adventure, Flick and he had just survived, plunged into Breed's mind, his spirt rose and he knew Flick also felt the spontaneous exultation over the miracle of surviving the worst nightmare of their lives.

It hurt Breed's jaws to talk, but he managed to say, "California here we come!"

Flick looked at Breed and joked, "We ain't old enough to join the army. You want to go see if Eddie's home so we can take off again?"

498

Breed answered as if he really meant it. "I was going to the army recruiter and lie about my age. Then I could get out of Shitsplat and make some big money. But if you have other plans, I'm ready. Let's grab something to eat and blow this pop stand."

Flick's brow puckered with uncertainty. "You're serious ain't you?"

Breed stood up, walked a few steps, paused, and with a mischievous grin that could match Screwball's, he looked back over his shoulder and said, "That's an interesting observation."

Although Screwball lived out of hearing range, Breed was sure he heard a taunting Cuck-oo!

THE END

DOUBLE DRAGON NOVELS BY
RONALD K. MYERS

Action/Adventure/Mystery
DILLINGER'S DECEPTION
IMPOSSIBLE GOLD

Military Espionage/Action Adventure/Thriller.
ALMOST FREE

Humorous/Historical Fiction/Action Adventure
I'M GONNA CUT YOUR EARS OFF
FREE RIDE

Futuristic
STAY ON THE BLUE GRASS
THE ORANGE TURN
PYGMY WARS